Praise for *As Waters Gone By*

"A tattered life finds rebirth in Cynthia Ruchti's latest gem. Skillfully crafted, the characters step off the page as they struggle with questions of faith and forgiveness, ultimately discovering God's plan for a new and beautiful future."
—**Lisa Wingate**, national best-selling author of *The Prayer Box* and *The Story Keeper*

"This story is like one of the recipes served up at the Wild Iris Café—delicious, nourishing, and not to be missed. From the food to the setting, the winsome characters, and the beautiful wordsmithing, readers will escape to a remote island only to return nourished with the truths and healing found inside the pages. More than just a delightful and satisfying read, this story will give you hope."
—**Susan May Warren**, RITA & Christy Award-winning, best-selling author of the Christiansen Family series

"Ruchti is one of the most beautiful writers in the market. Her newest novel, *As Waters Gone By*, is a mesmerizing and lovely tale of second chances and love that survives in spite of trials. Highly recommended!"
—**Colleen Coble**, author of Seagrass Pier and the Hope Beach series

"I just read the last page and closed the book with a deep, contented sigh. Emmalyn's tender story transported me like no other story has in a very long time. I've read everything Cynthia Ruchti has written and declare this novel her best ever."
—**Deborah Raney**, author of *The Face of the Earth* and the Chicory Inn Novels series

"Cynthia is adept at crafting tender stories of quiet hope. She includes just enough jagged-edged characters to make us see ourselves between the pages and opt for courage in our own lives. Her stories will stir your emotions and settle your heart by the time you turn the last page."
—**Robin Jones Gunn**, best-selling novelist and author of *Victim of Grace*

"Ruchti has a way of wrapping the reader with her words . . . like a cozy blanket. *As Waters Gone By* is a touching, tender novel exploring the hard question of 'How do you love when life doesn't go your way?' With a look at injustice, Ruchti brings her characters full circle into love and healing. She'll take you there too. Excellent read."

—**Rachel Hauck**, award-winning, best-selling author of *The Wedding Dress* and *How to Catch a Prince*

"Know how you keep a highlighter in your hand for underlining 'jewels within the pages' in your favorite nonfiction book? You'll need one for Cynthia Ruchti's latest work of fiction. You may even need two; *As Waters Gone By* is filled with them! Mine started with 'Isn't that what the homeless do? Wander?' in chapter one and ended with 'Daddy!' in the final chapter."

—**Eva Marie Everson**, author of *The Road to Testament*

"Cynthia Ruchti puts her readers in a ferry boat and takes us over waters of hope and forgiveness to new shores. With skill, she introduces us to unique characters that are relatable and loveable. Her prose warms the heart. The relationships falter between husband and wife, step-mother and child, daughter and mother and friends . . . and they change, just the way relationships do. *As Waters Gone By* is an authentic story told with grace. I loved this book!"

—**Jane Kirkpatrick**, best-selling author of *A Light in the Wilderness*

"With a cast of charmingly eccentric characters, Cynthia Ruchti once again brings a lyrically written story of trial-tested faith and hope that glimmers in the dark. *As Waters Gone By* is a stay-up-all-night story best read under a cozy quilt with a cup of hot chocolate and a large box of tissues."

—**Becky Melby**, author of *Tomorrow's Sun*, *Yesterday's Stardust*, and *Today's Shadows*

"A beautifully written story that will never let you go—a woman's sacrifice to find the joy of love."

—**DiAnn Mills**, Christy Award-winning author of *Firewall* and *Double Cross*

"With characters so real they jump off the page and into your life, *As Waters Gone By* is the newest don't-miss release from award-winning author Cynthia Ruchti. I laughed and cried along with the

main character throughout the true-to-life plot. Ruchti's got another winner on her hands. Highly recommend."
—**Robin Caroll**, author of *Hidden in the Stars*

"A feast for the soul. An exquisite blend of richly drawn characters, truth, and triumphant hope, *As Waters Gone By* is truly a book worth savoring."
—**Jocelyn Green**, award-winning author of the Heroines Behind the Lines Civil War series and co-author of *The 5 Love Languages Military Edition*

"Cynthia Ruchti weaves hope with each beautifully written word through a love story that captures your attention—and your heart. With each turn of the page, *As Waters Gone By* captures God's power to heal a heart, fan the flame of love, and connect distant hearts."
—**Pam Farrel**, author of 40 books, including best-selling *Men Are Like Waffles, Women Are Like Spaghetti*; *Red Hot Monogamy*; and *10 Best Decisions a Couple Can Make*

"Please. Read this book. It is deeply moving and profoundly important, especially in these days when our collective understanding of justice has gone awry. As the mother of an incarcerated son, I wept, laughed, and nodded vigorously as I related to both Emmalyn and Cora with their evolving and complicated thoughts and feelings. Ruchti writes, 'How many humiliations had he known behind bars? And where did the line lie between "You deserve this" and "Designed to break you"?' The humiliations and brokenness are experienced not only by the incarcerated person but everyone who cares about him. And yet, when justice, grace, and mercy roll down like waters, every heart can be healed. This book is one candle lighting that path."
—**Sue Badeau**, author of *Are We There Yet: The Ultimate Road Trip Adopting & Raising 22 Kids*, speaker and board member of Justice for Families

Other Novels by Cynthia Ruchti

They Almost Always Come Home
When the Morning Glory Blooms
All My Belongings

as waters gone by

CYNTHIA RUCHTI

Abingdon Press
Nashville

As Waters Gone By

Copyright © 2015 by Cynthia Ruchti

ISBN-13: 978-1-4267-8727-0

Published by Abingdon Press, P.O. Box 801, Nashville, TN 37202

www.abingdonpress.com

The persons and events portrayed in this work of fiction
are the creations of the author, and any resemblance
to persons living or dead is purely coincidental.

Macro Editor: Jamie Chavez

Published in association with the Books & Such Literary Agency

Library of Congress Cataloging-in-Publication Data has been
requested.

Printed in the United States of America

1 2 3 4 5 6 7 8 9 10 / 20 19 18 17 16 15

To the ones from whose heartache
this story is drawn
And the One from whose heart
hope is born.

Acknowledgments

Many of the same people influence, inspire, or otherwise deserve acknowledgment for every book I write. I could start anywhere on the map of where this book has been and find key people who talked me through, prayed me through, or prodded me though each landmark.

Thank you to my husband, Bill, for first showing me that enchanting island a ferry ride away from Bayfield, and for being willing to stop at that elbow in the road because I fell in love with a yellow-leafed tree and the water over its shoulder.

Special thanks to Kelli Illick from Second Wind Country Inn for accompanying me back there on a blustery day to see if it still held the enchantment it once had. It did.

I'm indebted—as always—to the team at Abingdon Press for their tender care of the stories I write, their attention to detail, their refusal to settle for less than the absolute best cover for each story, and their waves of endless encouragement. Ramona Richards, Cat Hoort, Katie Johnston, the marketing team and sales team, and all who serve as conduits of hope through story, thank you.

Freelance editor Jamie Clarke Chavez held my feet to the flames, but in such a gracious way that I thought it was to warm my toes. Which it did. Jamie, your excitement about these characters lingers in my heart.

I can't imagine walking this writing journey without my agent, Wendy Lawton of Books & Such Literary Management. We live too many miles apart, but Wendy, I feel your influence on me and the impact of your wisdom as I write.

Mike, thank you for helping me craft certain scenes with accuracy they couldn't have had without your input.

Jeannie, thank you for not holding back when I needed details about what it's like to sustain a marriage that far away from the one you love. Bryan, thank you for loving her well. May your own story of boundless grace and dauntless hope reach far.

My writing friends at ACFW, AWSA, CAN, and other associations are a much treasured source of encouragement. Those who've devoted themselves to walk the path with me—Becky, Michelle, Jackie, and my faithful readers—keep me from sliding into ditches.

Family—nuclear and extended—you mean so much to me. Everything I write somehow traces back to my love for you and for the One from whose heart hope is born. May that hope anchor you, my incomparable family, and you, my cherished readers, no matter how severely the wind howls.

You will surely forget your trouble,
recalling it only as waters gone by.

Job 11:16 NIV

1

Too far to swim.

The moat-like stretch of Lake Superior glinted in the October sun as if the waves were rows of razor wire.

Once her feet hit the island in the near distance, the floating drawbridge ferry drawn up for the night, the shore of Madeline Island would form the walls of her existence.

Max talked about the concrete walls of his prison as if the confines protected him from the outside world. Was it too much to hope sand and rocks and deep water would do the same for her?

Did I do the right thing, Max?

One last ferry for the day. She'd missed the next to the last. Three minutes late. Only three minutes. The sluggish gas pump could be blamed. Or her failure to check the website for the ferry's off-season hours. Emmalyn Ross had one more chance before dark, or she'd be forced to stay in Bayfield overnight, forced to talk to people, risk having to explain what she was doing there and why she was alone.

Five years ago, she'd been three minutes late getting to Max's desperate voice mail message. "Emi, I'm in trouble. Can you come get me?" His smudged words stuck like indelible mascara smears. She hadn't noticed the message until he'd already left the restaurant-slash-tavern, until he'd already pushed the accelerator toward their incomprehensible future.

11

A ferry attendant tapped on the car window. Emmalyn fumbled for the button to lower it. The rear window responded. Wrong button. She raised the rear window and lowered the driver's.

"Missed this one." The attendant, a middle-aged woman with a portable credit card reader in hand, gave Emmalyn the impression she was a retired teacher in a second career.

"I see that." Emmalyn looked past the attendant at the maze of orange cones—any empty maze now—where vehicles must have waited for the ferry she was supposed to have taken.

"There's another." The attendant pointed to the schedule in her hand. "Last one of the day. Wanna pay now? You can do that."

Why would Emmalyn hesitate?

"Unless," the attendant added, "you think you might change your mind."

"I can't."

The attendant's eyebrows registered surprise at the velocity of those two words.

Emmalyn smiled a third-grade-picture-day smile that seemed normal at the start but stretched her lips too taut. "Yes, thank you. I'll purchase my ticket now." She had forty-five minutes or more to kill. Paying ahead would use up—

Three of them.

Across the water lay a room at—she checked the computer printout on the passenger seat—The Wild Iris Inn. When the attendant swiped her credit card, Emmalyn felt the now familiar reflex. The swipe sounded like the slash of a knife. It sliced a deeper gash in resources that at the peak of her career, before The Unraveling, could have borne a thousand swipes without a conscious thought.

The house in Lexington—people always assumed Kentucky, not Minnesota—emptied quickly once she'd crunched numbers to a fine dust. Losing Max's income, then losing hers when the economy decided chefs in high-end restaurants were expendable, and the slow demise of her catering venture . . .

"Thank you." She slid her credit card and the receipt into her purse and followed the attendant's gestures for exiting the parking lot.

Some towns chart well on graph paper. Nice, even streets. Identically sized blocks of buildings. Every street running either parallel to or perpendicular to the others. Not Bayfield, Wisconsin. It had more curiosity going for it than just its location on the northernmost point of the state, along the largest body of freshwater in the world, within sight of the geographic and geologic curiosity of the Apostle Islands.

Some streets wandered. A handful of them played by the rules. The rest curved and sauntered and climbed at steep angles—posing threats to weak clutches and tires on ice—or meandered until they ended abruptly at the water's edge. The marina. The city park. The ferry line.

Emmalyn resisted the lure of an organic coffee shop and the gift shops along Rittenhouse Avenue. She chose a wandering street. Seemed fitting. Isn't that what the homeless do? Wander?

At the elbow of the backstreet she'd chosen, she pulled her Prius to the curb beside a junkyard. No, a park. Both.

Several decrepit boats sat at odd angles, paint worn away to its gray roots, boards missing, jagged holes in the hull, decks unsafe for their intended purposes. Shipwrecks. Emmalyn followed the path that wove among them. Hand-carved benches invited her to stop and take in the history of ships dragged from—or retired from—the waters a few feet away, and the well-landscaped garden tucked around the unseaworthy vessels.

The deeper into the park she walked, the tighter her jaw tensed. "You don't make gardens out of life's shipwrecks."

A tenacious late-blooming rose—an intense fuchsia color—nodded toward her. She ignored it, driving her hands deep into the pockets of her jacket.

"Not from shipwrecks. I ought to know."

Emmalyn retraced her steps to the car. It held no appeal. She'd sat in the driver's seat for six hours getting this far north, this far away from The Town That Knew Too Much. Half a block away, a massive boat—would it qualify as a yacht?—was being cinched onto a trailer hooked to a heavy-duty pickup. The boat dwarfed the truck so profoundly, it reminded Emmalyn of the tugboat pulling a cruise ship in a children's book among those she'd collected. The lower two-thirds of the hull dripped water, like a fish held aloft by a proud fisherman.

The book, buried now under other useless stuff in the storage unit, had probably seen its last peek at daylight. House. Life. Career. Hope of children. Gone. Marriage? Yet to be determined. What *hadn't* she and Max messed up?

The yacht, following obediently behind the truck, headed for winter quarters. A season of inactivity. A season. Not a lifetime.

A ripple of irony's laughter coursed through her. She was jealous of a boat's hopes for the future.

Gravel crunched beneath her feet as she crossed to a grassy area near the marina. She noted the gazebo first, then the playground beyond it. Of course. A playground. Pink noise—sweeter than white noise—lured her to the water's edge. Waves against rocks. Startlingly clear water, burbling in pockets between the bowling ball–sized boulders lining this portion of the shoreline. Round and oval pebbles a hundred yards closer to the center of town. Sand beach somewhere. Rugged cliffs only a mile away. Such a changeable shoreline.

Madeline Island stretched long and low in the distance. A twenty-minute ferry ride, if she remembered correctly. Against the expanse of green forest fancied up with the yellows, reds, and oranges of a north woods autumn, a spackling of white marked the landing spot in the village of LaPointe, the island's only civilization center. A room waited for her not far from the landing. The real adventure wouldn't begin until morning when it was light enough to survey the mess Max had gotten her into.

Her wedding ring felt tight on her finger. The pretzels. Too much salt. In her thirties, salt hadn't bothered her like this. When she hit forty . . .

The day was grayer than she'd hoped. They all were. Scudding clouds made the marine blue shrink-wrap on the dry-docked boats all the brighter. Like a shower cap for watercraft, the plastic hugged the forms, protecting them from the winter too quickly approaching. Within a couple of months, the ferry would be retired, too, thwarted by ice several feet thick, she'd heard.

A shiver wiggled its way north from her toes.

She knew cold. She knew cold and lonely. Now she'd know cold, lonely, and stranded.

She wandered past the gazebo, stirred by a sound stronger than waves. Laughter. Children's laughter.

Two boys, maybe four and five, chased each other down the spiral slide, giggling when they landed on top of one another at the slide's end. A woman tough enough to be their mother warned them to leave space between them—one at a time—or someone would get hurt.

The mother stood at an odd angle, like a runway model thrusting her hip to the side. She wore a pink and purple little one on that hip and a striped shirt stretched over the baby Emmalyn guessed to be no more than two months away from making its appearance.

Bayfield was not the place to come.

Too much laughter.

She returned the young mom's wave but angled herself toward the water again, focusing on the lapping water, the ceiling of dryer lint clouds, the curve of the harbor to her left. Motionless masts hid her view of the ferry dock.

How much time did she have left to kill?

According to Max's sentencing, another eight months.

Five years, Max?

Emmalyn remembered chanting the question so often after he went to prison, it wore a divot in her vocal cords.

"My lawyer warned me it could be worse." Max's voice—emotionless—had used *my* and *me* as if the sentence affected only him.

"What am *I* supposed to do?"

"What do you mean?" He'd barely paused. Barely paused. "Go on with your life."

Who had he turned into? This wasn't the Max she'd lain next to every night, his fingers tracing the curve of her arm until she fell asleep, the Max who made other women jealous for how good Emmalyn had it. The Max who could have taught seminars on how to treat a woman . . . before.

The phone connection from prison had crackled in her ear while she tried to cobble together an answer to his, "What do you mean? Go on with your life."

Go on? Incredulity was invented for moments like those.

She'd try. Contrary to her mother's opinion, she was no wimp. But Max had to know how ridiculous his words sounded. This isn't how life was supposed to turn out.

When the "go on" conversation faded—unresolved and hollow—Emmalyn told herself, for the first time ever, that she was grateful not to be pregnant. Going on alone would be hard enough.

More than one doctor informed her the sensations she'd felt were emotional, not physical. Women can't feel a womb shrinking. Emmalyn swore she could. It shrank by half the night Max told her to go on with her life.

A grocery store's produce mister rained harder than the light drizzle that started. But Emmalyn left the water's edge and headed back to her car. The ferry ticket lady suggested she get her vehicle in line a good ten minutes before departure. That still left a vacuum of an additional ten minutes.

The young mom from the playground herded her littles into a rust-bucket minivan parked a half block in front of the Prius.

A man exited the driver's side, his neck hunched against the drizzle, and loaded the stroller into the back. He'd been there all along? Sitting in the van rather than engaging with the kids' play? Missing the laughter?

His mother didn't raise him right.

Not catching the next-to-the-last ferry made her regret having stopped at the orchard for a small bag of apples before finding her way to the landing earlier. She forgave herself for that when her stomach complained it hadn't been fed for hours, as insistent as a terrier nudging his stainless steel bowl across the kitchen floor in a not-so-subtle hint.

She reached for a Cortland in the bag on the passenger seat, polished it on her jeans, and bit through the taut red skin. If she chewed slowly, she could fill the time gap without rousing a memory or a longing.

As if they ever napped.

She closed her eyes and groaned with brief pleasure. The apple's flesh was sweet yet tart, juicy. A good year for Cortlands. Max preferred Jonagolds. She'd bought only Cortlands since he left.

Left? Since he was taken away.

The orchard sales person must have thought it strange Emmalyn stood so long staring at the bin of Jonagolds. The teen had asked, "Want a sample?"

Emmalyn had shaken her head no.

"Would you like me to carry them to the checkout for you? Five pounds? Ten pounds?"

Another head shake.

"Jonagolds are more versatile than either the Jonathan or the Golden Delicious from which they're derived. Are you looking for an eating apple, pie apple, making applesauce . . . ?"

Smooth sales pitch. No to all of the above. "I'll take a bag of Cortlands," she'd said, pointing two bins to her right without losing her eye lock with the Jonagolds. "Five pounds. For now. I'm . . . I'm moving to the area."

"Welcome. You just missed Apple Festival. It gets a little crazy around here, but a lot of fun."

"Not much of a fun-seeker."

That sounded pathetic. True, but pathetic. One of these days, she'd fix that. As soon as she figured out how.

She held the apple in her teeth and put the car into DRIVE. Twelve minutes early was better than three minutes late for the last ferry of the day.

Almost ten years ago, she would have tugged on Max's sleeve, coaxing him to let her weave among the fabric threads of this town. He'd accompany her through the first four or five specialty shops before she noticed that look in his eyes—pained patience—and suggest he wait for her at the coffee shop. Had he brought a book? He'd be fine if it took her another hour to see more, to ooh and aah over more artwork, more history, more children's books they didn't need yet.

And remarkably, he *would* be fine. Genuinely. A coffee shop armchair, a strong African brew, and uninterrupted time in a biography or legal thriller—ironic now—seemed a gift to him, not a concession to his wife's lack of shopping fatigue. One of the things she'd appreciated about Max. At her side, sharing the experience for a while, then content for them to be engaged in their own interests. Could they ever gain that back? So much distance between them, not to mention the razor wire.

She could almost see him standing at the counter in the coffee shop she passed on her way down Rittenhouse Avenue toward Front Street and the ferry landing. He'd gaze up at the chalkboard of choices as if they mattered. He always ordered the tallest and strongest they had.

She turned left at the L in the road that swung past the public pier, Apostle Islands excursion launch, and the lighthouse shop. Ahead to her right, in the spaces between harborside buildings, she could see glimpses of the lumbering ferry approaching with its load of vehicles returning from the island. Tourists done exploring the island for the day? Mainland residents finished with their workday on Madeline or Madeline residents heading toward their evening shifts on the mainland?

She'd paid for a single round-trip ticket. But at those prices, she'd have to soon check into a resident discount. Was that possible? She doubted the few stores on Madeline Island could provide the furnishings she'd need to change Max's hunting cottage into what would have to pass for a home. If she were frugal, she could survive on what the court costs and restitution hadn't taken, and the abysmal proceeds from the sale of the Lexington house. For a while longer, anyway. But the ferry fee for everything but the barest minimum of supplies—from what she'd heard—could be an uncomfortable drain.

Her cell phone rang. How bizarre would it be if Max's first call from prison in nearly four years came just as she left everything about their old life behind?

The phone slithered out of her hands and dropped between the seats before she could answer it. She fumbled for it, found it, and answered before the call could switch to voice mail.

"Hello?"

"Emmalyn Victoria Walker! Where are you?"

"It's Ross, Mother. You were there at the wedding." Emmalyn restarted the engine and turned on the air conditioning. October, but the car had grown stuffy in the last ten seconds.

"You didn't smart-mouth like that when you were younger."

Saved it all up, Mom. Saved it all up. "Did you want something?"

"Yes! I want to know where in the continental United States you are, since you're not at home. I checked."

"The house sold."

The gasp Emmalyn heard was likely accompanied by her mother's hand slapped to her chest to cover the stab wound. "You didn't tell me!"

"I didn't tell anyone else."

"Obviously. We've been talking about what to do with you."

"We?"

"Your sisters. Honestly, Emmalyn, you're making this so difficult for everyone."

Me. I'm making things difficult. For them. What does a person say to that?

"Emmalyn? Are you there?"

"Yes, Mom. I'm here."

"And where is that? I'll meet you. Where do you think you're going to stay until you find someplace new? Use some logic."

"I had to jettison the logic. It was weighing me down."

"What?"

Emmalyn held the phone at arm's length, breathed in through her nose and exhaled to the count of ten. Another breath in. "I already found someplace. Mom, I have to go. They're about to load the ferry."

"Tell me you didn't."

"But I did."

"Emmalyn! Not that rattle-trap cottage. You gave up that beautiful house in Lexington for an outhouse?"

She checked her rearview mirror. A truck pulled in behind her. "I didn't exactly give up the house, Mom. I was days away from it being taken from me if it hadn't sold. And the cottage does have indoor plumbing." She was pretty sure.

"You could have been working." The words held an untamped tension.

Sixty hours a week wasn't enough for her?

"At a job that gave you an actual income, I mean."

"It wasn't a job, Mom. It was my business."

"Still didn't pay the bills."

The apple she'd eaten churned in her stomach. "Mom, I love you," she squeezed out, "but I have to go now. I'm hanging up."

"This is not over. What is Max going to say about all this?"

"Hanging up now."

"Emmalyn!"

"Mother, he gave me power of attorney in case I had to sell while he was in prison. And I had to. End of story."

The ferry attendant tapped her window and motioned for her to put away her phone before pulling forward. Emmalyn would explain later why she hadn't had time to say a proper good-bye.

Hers was the third vehicle in the "outbound" line. The fourth had pulled tight behind her—a power company truck. Emmalyn wondered about the weight limit for the ferry now secured to the dock, letting down its heavy steel tailgate, emptying its contents into the "incoming" lane like a toddler dumping Matchbox cars from the coffee table onto the family room floor.

She watched them pass, wondered about their stories. Where on the island had they come from? Where were they headed? Did they have mothers like hers? What dream, expectation, or nightmare made them choose this spot on the planet—woods and rocks and water and little else?

This undeniably beautiful spot.

Step into the water.

It wasn't a "drive through a bridge guardrail" kind of impression. It seemed an invitation to an adventure a twenty-minute ferry ride away, an adventure she hadn't felt because it hadn't started yet.

"If it's all the same to you, I'll ride on top of the water instead."

No one answered. No one had spoken.

A bearded deckhand swung his arm to direct the line of cars to board the vessel. She followed obediently, riding the brake, certain the hand's encouragement to inch farther forward would end in a bumper tap. *Forward. Forward. Stop!* His raised clenched fist made that direction clear.

Emmalyn locked the transmission in PARK and turned off the engine. Twenty minutes, once they got underway. Twenty minutes to a new life. She balanced the apple core on the console, wondering for the hundredth time if moving to Madeline Island was an Eve-like bad decision. She'd never hear the end of it if it were.

2

Without fanfare, the Prius tires rolled onto island asphalt. Emmalyn glanced left and turned right onto the aptly named Main Street, signs pointing toward the marina and the Madeline Island Golf Club, neither of which was her destination. Her online search told her the room she'd reserved for the night lay no more than a few buildings from the landing. There. The Wild Iris Inn and Café. Interesting. Two stories, painted the violet-blue of wild irises. Shutters the vibrant green of iris leaves. Every other bright, wild color showed up somewhere in the window boxes, the patio tables and chairs, and in the fence separating the patio area from the sidewalk.

Even in the shadows of dusk, it made a statement.

Emmalyn parked on the far side of the building, grabbed her purse, and dodged the fading efforts of the drizzle on her way to the only obvious entrance—through the narrow path between the patio tables and across the apron of concrete to the—squinting didn't change it—melon-colored front door.

A small foyer held a demure lime green dresser that sat along the right wall, a staircase Emmalyn assumed led to the rooms, to her room, and a massive glass door leading into a darkened café. The Wild Iris Café.

"And the office would be . . . ?"

She shifted her purse strap on her shoulder and planted her hands on her hips, the international sign for frustration. Despite the CLOSED sign pressed against the café door glass, Emmalyn reached for the knob and twisted. Nothing. Among the brochures for local attractions, a violet-blue envelope with an inked iris running on the left side—hand-sketched?—and a single letter—M— leaned against the base of a lamp.

M.

Her? *Emmalyn?*

She picked up the envelope. The flap was tucked, not sealed. She slipped a finger under the flap. What's the worst that could happen? Embarrassment? She had a lock on that already.

The note inside, also addressed to M, said: *Broom's in the corner. Knock three times on the ceiling if you want me. Glad you're here. B*

Seriously? The ceiling?

She let her head drop back. A stenciled iris and the words "Yes, here," marked the spot high above her.

No.

Her head dropped forward. She found no clearer answer on the floor.

Emmalyn reached for the broom handle. Tap-tap-tap.

She replaced the broom in the corner and looked for a tiny red light. She'd been caught on a hidden camera. That had to be the—

Footsteps sounded overhead. No way. The doorbell really was on the ceiling.

"M? Is that you?"

Emmalyn leaned into the stairway. "It's . . . I think . . . I'm Emmalyn Ross."

"You either are or you aren't."

She took the three steps to the first landing. "I'm Emmalyn Ross. I wasn't sure if the M meant me."

"Come on up. Your room's ready. Did you eat? How was your trip? First time on the ferry? Quite a rush, isn't it? Welcome to Madeline Island. Oh, look at you! Aren't you cute!"

The look Emmalyn was going for was sophisticated. Crisp. Tailored. Classy. She'd managed to give the impression of *cute*.

The voice came from high above Emmalyn, straight up two landings, from a pixie-faced young woman whose lion-mane hair—same color, same style—bounced as she talked. The young woman brushed it out of her eyes with her forearm and repeated, "Come on up." Then added, "I'm Boozie."

Really? You had to announce it?

"Boozie Unfortunate," she said as Emmalyn reached the second landing.

Oh. It was her *name*. A stage name? An . . . unfortunate . . . name, at best.

The last ferry had sailed. Comfortable or not, Emmalyn and Boozy or Boozie or whatever were sleeping under the same roof tonight. She extended her hand. "Emmalyn Ross. Pleased to meet you."

"If you were staying more than one night, I'd make you put that thing away." Boozie nodded toward Emmalyn's outstretched hand. "In favor of a hug." She shook briefly. "Hugs are more my style. Pirate Joe says I can be too forward."

Not all sentences warrant a response.

"Room Thirty-Seven. Here you go."

Emmalyn felt her eyes widen like the aperture of a hand-crank camera. "The Wild Iris Inn has thirty-seven rooms?" It looked the size of a large family home from the outside.

"Goodness, no! Six rooms. Five, if you don't count mine. I picked random numbers for the rooms. Thir-ty sev-en. Very rhythmic, don't you think? Four-teen. Nine. Twen-ty-two. Fif-ty-eight, for obvious reasons. And my room." She gestured with arms wide. "Three. Beautiful number, isn't it?"

A headache poked at a dime-sized spot on the back of her neck. Thump. Thump-thump. Thump-thump-thump.

"Go on in," Boozie said, standing back from the open door. Random Number 37.

The room was as calm as Boozie was animated. As simple as she was complicated. A corner room. One of its windows overlooked the curve of the Village of LaPointe as it hugged the shoreline. The other looked out over the expanse of water between where she stood and where she'd come. The lights of Bayfield twinkled like a lit Christmas village at the Hallmark store.

A painted-white wrought-iron double bed dominated one of the windowless walls of the room. A white down comforter and white pillows served as a canvas for one of three spots of color in the room. Tucked into the corner between the two windows was a light teal-and-white toile wing chair and reading lamp. A reclaimed dresser in a darker shade of teal sat nearby. And one of the many pillows on the bed sported a pale teal ribbon belt and saucer-sized wood button with HOPE burned into its face as the belt closure.

"Serene," Emmalyn said.

"That's the idea." Boozie smiled. Her freckles danced with each other when she did.

"Bare isn't always serene." Ten minutes on Madeline Island, and she'd already said too much. She felt the pull of the hallway at her back, the pull of the stairs, the road. But it dead-ended at a silent ferry crossing. At least until morning.

Boozie laughed, the sound of unadulterated joy. She raised one hand above her head, tucked the other across her tiny waist, and twirled once, her tea-colored skirt—or was it an antique petticoat?—swirling like a petunia petal. The unlaced army boots detracted from the ballerina effect, but somewhere within the young woman was the heart of a dancer. Or insanity.

The hallway called.

"M, so much wisdom! So true. So true." She closed her eyes and spread her arms to the side, palms up, revealing a line of tattoos on the insides of both forearms. Words. Emmalyn would have to get closer to read what they said.

"'Bare isn't always serene.'" Boozie opened her eyes and nodded her head, as if contemplating. "I know just what to do with that."

She danced to the narrow closet and grabbed a collapsible luggage rack from its interior. "Here you go. A place to put your things for now. You haven't eaten, have you?"

She hadn't. Did she want to admit that? "I ate an apple on the ferry ride."

"Come on down to the kitchen. I'll fix you something. We close early on Mondays. But for you . . . " Her petticoat skirt flounced as she twirled toward the door. "Come."

The directive sounded like an aproned great-grandmother trying to get a *young'un* to eat. For whatever reason, Emmalyn pushed aside her misgivings and followed her to the main floor, through the glass doors of the darkened café lit only by light from the foyer, past vacant tables and chairs—a hodgepodge of furniture—to the café's kitchen.

A motion sensor lit the room.

"Impressive."

"Liability issues," Boozie said, snatching a handful of items from a stainless steel refrigerator. "It's not that we mind feeding hungry people on a midnight raid. We just don't want to be sued if they trip on something in the process. Solution? Motion sensor lights."

Emmalyn failed to suppress her smile. "I meant, the kitchen."

After depositing the food items on a stainless work surface, Boozie flipped two switches on an appliance that looked like a massive waffle iron. Two red lights on the temperature knobs responded. "You're impressed by a commercial kitchen?"

Emmalyn dragged her fingers along the smooth stainless worktable. "I am . . . I was a caterer. I did . . . I did catering. For a while." *Courage and truth will be your biggest allies, Emmalyn.* Her dad's voice. Did he have any idea how much courage it took to tell the truth? She'd give anything to be able to ask him.

Boozie pushed the ingredients closer to Emmalyn. "I should let you do this yourself, then."

"No, please. I'm intrigued to see what this is going to turn into."

"Nothing fancy."

Emmalyn watched carefully as the woman worked. With a name like Boozie Unfortunate, who knew what might be produced in her kitchen. "Do you have a large staff?"

"I'm usually out front. Two cooks this time of year. They rotate shifts. Pirate Joe buses. He's learning more tasks. Four part-time servers. Not a large staff. But as you saw when we came through, we can't seat more than twenty or twenty-five inside at one time. Another dozen in the courtyard during warm weather."

"Do you wish you had more space?"

Boozie laughed that water-over-rocks laugh. "The tourists do. We like it this way. When we're back down to three hundred residents from four or five thousand, this seems just right."

"LaPointe only has three hundred residents in the off season?"

"Not just LaPointe. The whole island. Are you staying long?" Boozie spread something dark and gooey onto the slices of rustic bread. "I should have asked first. Do you like onion jam?"

"I'm not sure."

"Vidalia."

"Oh, the jam? I'm sure I do. I'm not sure how long I'm staying. My husband and I own the—" Courage and truth. "I own a cottage where Big Bay Road turns into Schoolhouse Road."

Boozie laid down the butter knife and planted her palms on the stainless work surface. "You do not." The brightness in her eyes spoke of wonder, not denial. "You're the one? That L in the road with the big maple?"

"Is the maple tree still there? I hoped it would be."

"Glorious as ever. You own that?"

Emmalyn watched the young woman lay thin slices of pear on top of the onion jam, followed by turkey, some kind of pickle, and Swiss cheese. She topped the stack with another slice of the rustic bread and slid the concoction between the grill plates on the oversized waffle iron.

"Not the tree. That's part of the easement, I'm sure. I own the hunting cottage just beyond it."

"Right on the water?"

"A hundred feet from the shoreline, but last I knew, it had a clear line of sight to the water, yes."

The sandwich sizzled. Boozie grabbed a square turquoise plate from a rack of anything but matched tableware. "Tea, coffee, hot apple cider?"

"The apple cider sounds nice. If it isn't too much trouble."

Boozie headed back to the fridge. "M, would you adopt me?"

Something misfired in Emmalyn's heart. "What did you say?"

"I've been secretly envious of you since I was a kid. I didn't know it was you, of course." She poured two pottery mugs nearly full of cold cider and deposited them in a small microwave. Punched four touchpad buttons. The microwave stirred to life.

Envious of *me*? Boozie, if you only knew . . .

"I used to bike out there. Past Big Bay State Park and Big Bay Town Park. You might have caught the connection to Big Bay Road." She stabbed an index finger into the spot on her cheek where a dimple should be. "Every time I came to that corner, with the tree in front of me and the water to my right, I'd dream about what it would be like to live in that spot. Something about that tree, especially now with the leaves turned. If I can't own it, you'll just have to adopt me so we can keep the property in the family."

She didn't mean any harm by that. She couldn't know. Emmalyn drew in a breath. *Rub some dirt on it,* her father would have said if he were here . . . and alive . . . trying to lighten the tension. *Dirt. Yeah, Dad. That's a good way to get an infection.*

"Hey. Hey, I didn't mean for real."

Emmalyn looked at the young hand on her shoulder. It lay, soft and caring, like a toddler trying to comfort its mother. Her eyes drifted to the pale forearm attached to the comfort. And the tattoed word. HOPE. Like the pillow upstairs.

Boozie retracted her hand. "I didn't mean to make you cry. I thought it was funny . . . a woman your age adopting a woman my age."

"How old are you, Boozie?"

"Twenty-four. I know I look fourteen. I'll be grateful for that someday. That's what everyone tells me."

Old enough to be your mother. Technically.

Boozie lifted the handle of the electric grill pan. A perfectly browned Panini. She slipped a spatula under it and in one smooth motion planted it onto the turquoise plate. Three grape tomatoes joined it, held from sliding by a carrot/cucumber ribbon that encircled them. "Do you want to get this plate? I'll bring the cider."

"Where?"

"Let's sit by the fireplace."

Had Emmalyn seen a fireplace? Ah, there it was. Along the wall midway toward the front of the building. Two wing chairs angled away from it with a just-the-right-height antique table between.

Her appetite gone, Emmalyn sat from pure politeness. As delicious as the sandwich had looked moments ago, it didn't hold the attraction of the quiet, conversationless room waiting for her upstairs.

"Okay," Boozie said, setting a mug in front of each of them and offering Emmalyn an eggplant-colored napkin. "Concession and confession."

Conversation. Emma stifled a sigh.

Boozie flipped a switch under the mantel. Instant fire. "I had to allow this concession. I would much rather have a real fire, the smell of real wood smoke. The insurance company said I could have this or nothing, so . . . "

"It looks natural."

"It does, doesn't it? We looked long and hard for this kind of flame. Anyway, confession time."

"Shouldn't we turn on a light?" *And not talk?*

"If you don't mind eating by firelight, it would help. The locals get nosy if they see a light on. They assume they missed an email about the Wild Iris open on Monday nights now. Which it's not. Except for you."

As complicated as life had gotten back in Lexington, Emmalyn's mind reeled with unanswered questions about life on Madeline Island, and within The Wild Iris Inn and Café, in particular.

"So, confession time." Boozie leaned across the table, her hands cradling her mug. "I don't know what I said to upset you, but I was obviously insensitive about something, and I apologize. You don't owe me an explanation, but I hope you'll forgive me." She sat back then, as if waiting for official word before progressing.

"There's nothing to forgive." *Not from you, anyway.* How long was the young woman going to wait?

"Alright then. Let's pray. Do you mind?"

Mind praying? Or mind if *she* prayed?

"Holy One, Father of all . . . "

Guess it didn't matter if she did mind.

". . . thank You for bringing M here to The Wild Iris. Thank You for making us practically drown in the depths of Your love. Thanks for inventing pears and onions and for filling our souls with Yourself, the Living Bread, Jesus. Amen."

How would Emmalyn swallow now? The crazy one with the bizarre name and a huge heart and a HOPE tattoo was crazy about Jesus. What was she supposed to do with that knowledge? Run?

Boozie stretched her arm toward the turquoise plate and shoved it closer to Emmalyn. "Eat."

"Yes, ma'am." Emmalyn picked up the prayed-over panini and had it halfway to her mouth before she read the word on Boozie's other forearm. HEALING.

Hope and healing.

What unusual packaging for that message.

3

Fake fires don't flicker low. They don't make embers that sputter and signal it's time to call it a night. Emmalyn would have to say it aloud. She was tired and wanted to go to her room. As soon as the conversation took a breath, she'd do just that.

Boozie chatted while Emmalyn ate every tantalizing crumb of The Wild Iris signature sandwich. Yes, the onion jam was homemade. The bread, too. One of four breads available daily. Emmalyn listened to the list then forgot most of the options as she worked to keep up with the pace of Boozie's island life, which seemed a much safer topic than Emmalyn's.

Mid-sentence about the historic roots of the building in which they sat, Boozie's eyes widened. "You were a caterer."

Emmalyn sipped the last of her cider. "I was."

"We could use help."

"I'm not looking for a job." Yet.

"More of a consulting role?"

"Really not interested right now. I think I'll have my hands full with the cottage."

Boozie nodded, knowingly. "With the roof and all."

"The roof?"

"You haven't been out there yet?"

Emmalyn folded her napkin and laid it on the table. "No. What about the roof?"

"Probably not as bad as they say." Boozie's head tilted at a sympathetic angle before she pressed her lips tight.

"'They' have been talking about my cottage?" A slither of distress wriggled in her chest.

Boozie drained her own mug. "I thought that's why you've come. To fix the place."

Truth be told, I've come to fix me. I think. "The roof's in rough shape?"

"It wasn't, until the storm. A big old pine tree decided it wanted to wait out the storm inside, from what I hear."

"Boozie! Shouldn't I have been called?"

"The town clerk's probably the only one who knew who owned your place. No one's been there for years. Right?"

It had been more than eight years since Max and his buddies had hunted here. Nine since Emmalyn and he had fallen in love with a stretch of beach beyond a sun-yellow maple.

"Some of the guys tarped it."

Emmalyn's facial expression must have asked the question before she could get it verbalized. Boozie hurried to explain.

"After a storm like that, the guys make the rounds, checking on people. What I heard was they got the limb lifted out of the way and nailed a tarp over the hole to keep any more rain from getting in."

Any *more* rain. In the space of a few words, the redecorating she faced before a hunting cottage could become a place for her to retreat turned into a major repair project. The hesitation she'd felt on the road fully matured. She couldn't do this. What was she thinking?

Max, this too. This too is all your fault. Somehow. It had to be.

"Pie." Boozie stood. "We need pie."

"I don't really—" Emmalyn would have finished the sentence with "eat pie," but Boozie had teleported into the kitchen already. For such an organic-looking young woman, she must not have a good grasp of the difference between good and bad carbs.

Introvert? Extrovert? Boozie fit under the Tidal Wave category. But with a gentle touch that made people forget they were being carried someplace other than where they were headed. Or maybe it was only Emmalyn who reacted that way. Maybe others had spines left in them. Hers had eroded over the course of the last five years. Ever since the night Max called to say he was in trouble, the SUV was totaled, and the fertility clinic was missing a front window and a pile of bricks.

And that the homeless man leaning against the foundation was in the hospital. Not expected to live.

But he did.

The man wasn't expected to walk again, though.

"Dutch apple pie. Fixes everything." Boozie placed a significant wedge of pie in front of Emmalyn. "With maple vanilla whipped cream." The woman smiled as if inching the corners of her mouth up a degree for every calorie represented on the plate, as if proud of herself for finding a way to fit even more into an already decadent dessert.

Emmalyn looked for evidence that the layers of Boozie's clothing hid reckless pie-eating, then stopped herself. Health-conscious was one thing. Shallow was another. She couldn't afford to be shallow, not with what lay beneath the top layer of who she was. "It looks delicious."

"Joe's work."

"Pirate Joe? I thought he bused tables."

"You've been paying attention." Boozie's eyes sparkled as she chewed.

"I . . . notice . . . details. *Obsessed* with details, some say." She dug her fork into the tower of physically unnecessary but emotionally critical calories. The fork vibrated with gratitude. Or was that her hand trembling? She didn't need pie. She needed to be alone. With time to think. And the number of a good roofer.

"So, a detail person. Exactly what we need."

"At The Wild Iris? As I said, I'm not looking for a job. I don't think." She mentally subtracted roof repair from her malnourished savings account.

"Anything you'd suggest for us?" Boozie swept both arms to the side, one after the other, as if encompassing the entire restaurant with her question. "Some people resist change. The Wild Iris thrives on it. We have our nonnegotiables, like our signature panini and our root soups. It was one of the server's ideas to present a trio of root soups in hollowed out baby pumpkins for the fall. That's been a big hit."

Big hit. Hollowed. Baby. Baby. Baby.

"You'll have to stop in for a taste of that sometime while we still have baby pumpkins available. Such a short season. M? Are you allergic to celery root or something?" Boozie leaned in. "You don't have a super-expressive face. More like a model for high fashion. But when a muscle twitches, it shows."

Emmalyn took a bite of pie and motioned, "Chewing."

"If that doesn't appeal to you," Boozie said, "we have other choices. And that might be where you could help us fine-tune a little. Right now the menu is a little overwhelming for our kitchen crew. You know what I mean?"

Such a short season.

"M?"

"I guess the trip wore me out more than I realized. I'd better call it a night. Thank you for the great meal. Can you put it on my room tab?"

"Will do. Pie's on the house. Do you want to take the leftovers to your room? A little hot tea to go along with that? Sure you do. I'll be back in a sec. You go on ahead. I'll leave it on a tray outside your door."

Emmalyn picked her way carefully through the shadowed café, aiming for the lamp-lit foyer and the stairs that would take her to a pocket of numb serenity in Random Room 37.

Every bed looked lopsided since Max left. Optical illusion. Even this one he'd never seen seemed to tilt her direction when Emmalyn sat on it, a teeter-totter with no one on the other seat. She moved to the chair instead. Only room for one. Good thing that's all she needed. Room for one.

She tucked her feet underneath her and wrapped the chair's chenille throw around herself, to the chin, amazed at how cool she could feel in a room that seemed overly toasty when she'd arrived. A thermostat hung at eye level near the door. She chose instead to sink deeper into the chair and fling the throw tighter around her shoulders.

Moonlight skittered across the surface of the water. That barren moon. Lifeless, yet still illuminating the scene. *What's your secret?*

Three light taps jarred Emmalyn from her thoughts. She tossed the covering aside and crossed to the door. The *thank you* died on Emmalyn's lips when she saw only the tray in the hallway. No hostess. For all her exuberance, Boozie sensed when a guest needed privacy. Curious woman.

Emmalyn set the tray on the nearly bare dresser top, nudging a book—it looked as if it were created from handmade paper—out of the way with her elbow. She poured a cup of tea from the carafe. Lavender Earl Grey, she judged from the aroma. Nice. Decaf? What did it matter? She rarely slept a full night anyway.

The book lay open, intended to be read by others.

From the dates and the varieties of penmanship, she discerned it was a guest journal. She thumbed through a few pages, catching a line or two, landing for a few moments on some of the entries longer than, "Great night's stay. Thank you!" or "Warm chocolate chip cookies outside our door? We'll definitely be repeat customers."

35

"Thanks for getting our marriage back on the right track, Wild Iris. This is more than just an inn. We came in broken. We left healed. Many blessings."

Emmalyn came in broken. Still broken. 'Til-death-do-us-part broken.

She opened her small carry-on bag and dug out her Pima pajamas, her cosmetic case, and Journal #5 in her *Because You're Gone* journey. She settled into the chair/throw combo again, sipped lavender tea, and opened to the day's date. The spot stayed blank a long heartbeat before she wrote:

> Another night without you, Max. And I'm not even
> sure you miss me. It would help if you missed me.
> Not because I think I can't live without you. Because
> I think I can. And that scares me. It scares me that
> I might be wrong. It scares me that I might be right.

A few miles away, within sight of a majestic maple and sound of a majestic sea, a cottage with a broken roof waited for its broken owner to step in and fix things. That ferry, too, sailed a long time ago.

Emmalyn intended to skip breakfast to help compensate for the fact she'd finished the slice of apple pie the night before as an accompaniment to the tea. So the tea wouldn't be lonely. But the café's breakfast offering rose as a sweet fragrance to the second floor and snuck under the door to her room.

She'd slept with the windows uncovered, the moon her nightlight, fascinated that every time she woke, the moon was in a different position in the sky, but still there. Changing, but unchanged. Its blue light soothed her soul with its faithfulness.

If Boozie had a free moment this morning, Emmalyn would ask her about the brand of sheets on the bed. Soft as but even smoother than peach skin. She dressed in a fresher version of yesterday's outfit, black jeans and a v-neck sweater, traditional stack bracelets and her anniversary earrings—something about her had to sparkle—and stepped into heeled black and caramel boots that had more than outlived their price tag.

The smell of coffee lured her to the door. In the hall at her feet was another small tray like the one from the night before. This one held a large pottery mug, a stainless steel carafe, and a note. *Table by the fireplace reserved for you. Whenever. Morel quiche needs your critique. B*

After two cups and too many minutes trying to hide her lack of sleep with an obviously inferior concealer product, she bunched her favorite scarf around her neck, snatched up her cell phone, and descended to the café. The café's clock, its numbers painted on the paprika-colored wall to the right of the fireplace, said it was almost nine. She'd intended to get an earlier start.

A tented card with a calligraphed "M" marked the fireplace table reserved for her. Two older women sat near the window. Books in their hands held the kind of fascination Emmalyn had seen from restaurant patrons ignoring each other in favor of their cell phone screens. Somehow, the books seemed less offensive, more companionable. Three men occupied another table. Suits. Tablets. Business. Emmalyn lowered herself into "her" chair and scanned the room for sign of Boozie.

Moments later, a thin, scruffy man with rings in both ears and a slender, graying braid poured her a glass of water. She couldn't help it. Her gaze drifted to his fingernails. Not just clean. Exceptionally clean.

"Welcome to The Wild Iris. You must be Ms. Ross."

"Joe?"

"Yes. I mean, yes, ma'am. How . . . may . . . I . . . help . . . you . . . today?" The sentence sounded rehearsed with every intention of being genuine.

"Is Boozie here?"

"She'll be by later. She said you'd want the quiche? Better snatch it if you do. Only two servings left."

"Morel quiche?"

"Fancy mushroom."

"I'm familiar with morels. What else is in it?"

"You got your scallions, your light dusting of nutmeg, and your GROO-yer." He leaned closer. "Nothing but Swiss with its nose in the air, if you ask me."

Gruyere. Boozie had exceptional taste. "That sounds great." She'd eat the top and leave the crust. She couldn't afford to go from too-thin to hefty in one day.

"Juice? We got your basic orange, fresh squeezed, cranberry, and apple cider."

"Cranberry."

Pirate Joe held out a finger on each hand, as if using his digits to remember what she'd ordered. "And fruit or grainy sticks-and-twigs toast?"

Emmalyn unfolded her napkin and laid it across her lap. "Is that the rustic bread I had last night?"

"Yes, ma'am. It's all we have today. Usually have more bread options. If you want cinnamon rolls, you'll have to wait here until tomorrow."

"I'll have toast, please. One slice." How could she not enjoy his demeanor? It was the jam sitting in the antique jam jar in front of her that convinced her toast was the better of the two options. It looked like black raspberry.

Joe retreated to the kitchen. When had he had time to pour her coffee? Third cup of the morning. With a tarp over the roof of the place she was supposed to stay tonight, it would be more than a three-cup day, no doubt.

A stack of books sat near the far edge of the round table. She picked up the top one. It held a dozen or more ribbon bookmarks with a button on the end of each ribbon. The buttons were marked with names. Apparently, James was on page 12, Carmen on 134, Leane, Ranella, and Darby all had marked page 177, and Joyce had only three pages to go until the end. What emergency kept Joyce from another cup of coffee so she could finish the book? Maybe finishing wasn't as strong a goal as the process of reading.

Emmalyn thumbed back to the first chapter. A handful of pages into the story, her quiche arrived. Only something that delicious could have drawn her attention away from the book's captivating beginning. She took a buttoned ribbon and permanent marker from the bowl near the stack of books and wrote her name on the button—just the letter M—before thinking about how infrequently she might be back to this spot. She had a home of her own. A cottage on the water. It waited for her. Empty. Vacant. Full of—she sighed—potential.

Real butter on the toast? Of course. Wisconsin. She slathered it with a spoonful of the jam. Not black raspberry. Better. Black currant. A little more tang. This could be dangerous. Food had lost its appeal shortly after Max started eating his from a plastic tray. Apparently, her appetite was back.

The quiche arrived crustless. Ahh. It all evened out. Crustless and swoon-worthy. The Wild Iris had a good thing going here. She hadn't seen a menu yet to note the prices. But it rated high in her book on ambiance and food quality. The chef in her wanted out to play.

She hadn't really thought that. Had she?

When Pirate Joe approached with the coffee, Emmalyn laid her hand over her mug. "No thanks. I think I'd better switch to tea. But could I get that in a disposable cup? To go?"

"I'll bring you tea," he said. "But we don't do disposable."

"Just skip it, then," she said. "I really need it to go." How many hours of work lay ahead of her? And what were the odds she'd have someone hired to repair the roof before nightfall? Maybe she should consider another night in Random Room 37.

"Oh, I'll bring it to go." Joe turned, his scraggly braid dancing mid-back. "We just don't do disposable."

Huh?

Emmalyn finished the last bite of toast and wiped her mouth with her napkin, then laid it beside her plate. The two older women leaned toward each other. Sharing secrets? No, the taller one pointed to a spot in the book she read. Both sat back, hands over their hearts. What words, what scene evoked that kind of response from them? Did Madeline Island have a book club? Or was this it? The Wild Iris and random reading? Random passage-sharing?

"Here you go." Joe handed her a tall, narrow-bottomed marigold mug and offered a treasure chest of tea choices. "Just bring the mug back the next time you're in."

"Joe?" Boozie's voice sounded less animated than it had last night, but held its same mothering tone. "Joe," she repeated, more emphatically. "The lid?"

Joe cursed, then stopped where he stood, face pointed at the ceiling. He reached into his pocket and withdrew a dollar bill, walked to the hostess counter, lifted the cover of a pottery cookie jar and tucked the dollar inside. From the sound of rustling, it appeared the jar wasn't empty. He nodded to Boozie, curtsied, and returned to the kitchen.

Boozie took the chair beside Emmalyn. "Sleep well?"

"I slept. What was—?"

"The Jesus Jar? Joe has a mouth like a . . . "

"Pirate?"

"Sometimes. He's trying to break the habit. So every time he swears, he has to put a dollar in the Jesus Jar. The man is close to single-handedly funding a well for clean water in Congo."

Joe, poorer but wiser, returned to the table with a smooth wooden disk that fit atop the mug. "Ingenious, isn't it? Vocab word of the day—in-ge-ni-ous." He demonstrated that the glass bead glued to the center of the disk made for easy removal without scalded fingers. "It . . . has . . . been . . . a . . . pleasure . . . to . . . serve . . . you. Have a blessed day."

When he was out of earshot, Emmalyn angled toward Boozie. "A well in Congo, huh?"

Boozie leaned in. "We don't do disposable. Not in cups, plates, silverware . . . or people." She rubbed her knee through a skirt that looked remarkably like a tattered prom dress. Intentionally tattered. Paisley leggings and a Fair Isle sweater.

This is the same woman who created a minimalist retreat room upstairs. Speaking of that . . .

"Boozie, I know it's last minute, but I may need a place to stay tonight, too. I haven't seen the cottage yet, but a hole in the roof is a lot more serious than the sweeping and window-washing I thought it would take to make the place inhabitable."

"Do you want me to put a hold on your room?"

My room. Words like that fell so easily off Boozie's tongue. They got stuck on the way out of Emmalyn's mouth. "It's not booked already?"

Boozie laughed. "You've chosen the perfect week to arrive. Apple Festival week was insanely busy. But a Tuesday night in the non-tourist season? No problem."

Maybe it was the coffee. Maybe it was the warmth of the fireplace. Maybe it was the "no disposables" policy. Maybe it was having someone who cared. Emma didn't want to leave.

"Let's make it a solid reservation. I'm feeling more strongly that I need to secure a place here tonight. I might have been overly optimistic about the shape the cottage will be in."

"It's been a long time since it was lived in."

"Years."

Boozie shook her head side to side. "It's cheaper by the week."

"The cottage?"

"Your room at The Wild Iris." Her face brightened as she responded to a voice at the door. "Well, look who's here."

"Who?" Emmalyn turned to follow Boozie's line of sight.

"Your roofer."

Emmalyn kept her comment low. "No offense, but the roofer looks like a librarian."

Boozie stood to greet the newcomer. "She is. Emmalyn Ross, I'd like you to meet Cora Burman. Cora, Emmalyn." Boozie folded her arms across her chest as if she'd accomplished a global-impact diplomatic introduction.

Emmalyn shook hands with the four-foot-eleven woman with twice as many extra pounds as Emmalyn had lost during the crisis, 1950s cat-eye glasses, and the smell of old books. "Pleasure to meet you. You're . . . a . . . roofer?" She couldn't stop the squeak at the end of the question. No do-overs.

"Among other things." Cora's voice had to be a transplant. Its operatic richness didn't fit the rest of her. Or was it the rest of her that didn't fit her voice? "I volunteer at the library as often as I can. I'm a volunteer EMT. Teach organic underground gardening online. That's for pay. I'm licensed as a masseuse, but my massage table's out of commission until the ferry brings me a replacement part. Chair massages only, for now."

Emmalyn fought to form a response. "Organic underground gardening."

"That's my passion."

"Underground, as in . . . beyond the . . . limits of . . . the law?"

"Good one." Cora punched Emmalyn in the arm. "Underground as in under-the-ground. Below-ground greenhouses. Ideal for climates like ours, where the growing season is short."

Boozie stepped closer. "I get all my micro-greens from Cora."

The librarian/masseuse/EMT/gardener/roofer interjected, "I've got some skinny beans almost ready for harvest. Another day or two."

"Skinny beans?" Emmalyn needed to know about roofing costs, but the current conversation intrigued her.

"*Haricot verts.* When I use the real name around here, everyone except Boozie thinks I'm growing hairy Corvairs. Thought I'd avoid the razzing this once."

Boozie chuckled. "M would understand. She's a caterer."

"Was. I was a caterer."

"Well, you can take your pick of new careers around here. You can have two or three of mine, if you want." Cora smiled broadly.

"I'll be happy to get rid of the roofer label for more than one reason."

Did Emmalyn want a roofer who wasn't fond of the job? "I can call someone from the mainland, if you'd rather not—"

"Gravy, no! I'll help you out. I'm just looking forward to turning the nail gun back over to Wayne when he gets out."

When he gets out. Emmalyn knew that phrase. "I'm so sorry. Prison?" The word scraped her throat as much as it ever had.

"Might as well be. Fourth deployment."

Not the same thing. Not at all. "When will he be home?"

The woman pulled her phone from her Vera Bradley purse. "I learned not to keep a countdown calendar. It never moves as fast as I want. I'll get through this day. Then I'll get through the next one. Address?"

"Excuse me?"

"I want to program your cottage address into my GPS."

Boozie laid a hand on Cora's shoulder. "You won't need that. It's at the elbow where Schoolhouse and Big Bay join up."

Cora's eyes widened. "Oh. Nice spot. Right near Amnicon Point. Can I get my truck in there from the side road that runs parallel to the shore? Is that Chippewa Trail? Yes."

"I don't know. I think so." Emmalyn should have gotten up earlier. She should have been out there already, assessed what kind of shape the cottage was in. Braced herself. "I arrived too late last night to take a look at the place." Too late. Too exhausted. Too uncertain.

"When's the last time you were up here on Madeline Island?"

Her throat narrowed. Tighter. Tighter. She'd better speak while she still could. "The day we bought it. Nine years ago. My husband used it a couple of times for hunting until he—"

The two-person book club near the window leaned as if paying attention to the conversation.

Emmalyn changed direction. "It's been a long time. I'm heading out there now."

Cora returned her phone to her purse. "I have a chair massage at 10:30. How about if I join you out there after that?"

"How much for the estimate?"

"I won't know until I see what kind of hole we're talking about, whether the trusses are damaged or not, what kind of shingles you have on there . . . "

"I mean, how much do you charge to come out to give an estimate?"

Cora repositioned her glasses. "Have you seen the size of this island? It's no big deal. I won't burn much gas or time either. You've got bigger things to worry about. See you somewhere around 11:30."

"Thank you. I appreciate it."

Cora nodded to the book club. "Keep up the good work, girls." And she was out the door.

The sound of silverware clanking on floor tiles jangled from the kitchen, and a few moments later, the clunk of the cookie jar lid.

4

Detail people notice things like the burned-down bar—still open for business—on the road that teed with the main route through town. Tom's Burned Down Bar, the sign said. An unimpeded sun lit the tarps that served as a roof over part of the skeleton'd building. At first glance, it was a happy junkyard. At second glance, a mind-boggling curiosity. Emmalyn wondered what the locals thought of a decidedly untouristy-looking, opposite-of-classy establishment.

Ramps paved with old license plates and slabs of metal that looked like discarded submarine parts. Walls—open to the sky in places—draped with plastic leis and plastered with posters and quips.

She glanced at the charred bar in her rearview mirror as she continued on Middle Road, angling east for a few miles out of LaPointe before turning north to the spot where Black Shanty Road meets with Big Bay Road. She passed the entrance to Big Bay State Park and Big Bay Town Park after it.

How long would it be before these woods and meadows, the marshes and glimpses of water felt like home? Would they? How long would she be here? Cora might not be keeping a countdown clock for her husband, but Emmalyn knew exactly how many months were left until Max's release. What she didn't know was if he'd come back to her when the prison doors opened. She'd carried on a one-sided marriage for too long. How could they pick up where they'd left off before his incarceration? Not even six months into his time, he'd made it clear he wanted her to file for divorce.

That's what he said.

He couldn't have meant it. Not after all they'd been through.

Nothing looked familiar in her surroundings. She'd observed the scenery but not studied it when they'd vacationed on Madeline Island. And they'd been riding bikes when they took this route. A slower pace. Laughter. Observing blades of grass and wildflowers in the ditches. Nothing seemed iconically identifiable to her until . . .

Until the curve in the road ahead of her now. And there it was. Their tree. It registered none of the upheaval of the years since she'd seen it last. Just like it had then, the sunlight set the tree on color-fire, each leaf a yellow flame. Sunlight filtered through sweet-corn maple leaves lost no candlepower. If anything, the light was intensified after passing through the tree's fingers. A handful of yellow escaped the tree's gnarled grasp and floated to the ground, destined to improve the soil if no longer the scenery. A siren of light calling to a faint reflecting beacon deep in her soul ended in waves playing the beach stones with a maraca sound and a flirt of foam. Lake Superior. That close. The maple's noisy but artsy next-door neighbor.

Emmalyn could almost see their rented bikes propped up against the tree's trunk those years ago as she and Max explored the widened shoulder where footprints in the velvet sand told them other visitors like them had stopped to take in the view. Miles of north woods forest around them, then an opening where passersby could see Lake Superior splashing pebbles that eventually became sand. Intoxicating.

"I want to live here someday," she'd said, more whim than wish.

"It's a sign," Max had answered.

"Of what?"

He'd tilted his head and smiled that crooked, charming smile. "It's . . . a . . . sign. A *For Sale* sign."

He'd been leaning against it, blocking what it said, but stepped away to reveal a weathered *For Sale* sign with a phone number inked across the bottom.

They'd picnicked on the sandiest and driest part of the shore that day, taking turns imagining what they'd do if they could own a scene like that. Max brought up the issue of taxes several times. "Lakefront property? Babe, impossible."

"I know. I wasn't really serious."

In the end, they'd called the number of the realtor. Just to talk. Ask a few questions. The realtor drove out and showed them the property, including the small cottage somewhere in the trees beyond where Emmalyn parked the Prius. Right around this curve of shoreline. Right up this embankment—a science classroom's dream example of erosion.

She crested the embankment now, as they had then. What romantic notions had clouded their thinking that day? The sight that greeted her nearly stopped her heart, and in a wholly unromantic way.

If she counted only the sweet waves tickling the shore, or the bleached late-season sea grass responding to the breeze, the birches and pines and maple tapestry, she would have been charmed. But the cottage that had seemed adorable so few years ago had grown as pale as Emmalyn felt, as disappointed by life.

Windows shuttered, it looked comatose. She stepped tentatively onto the front porch, patting the wooden banister as if to say, "You poor thing." Emmalyn needed time to absorb the challenge ahead of her before Cora the Roofer arrived. She extracted her phone from her shoulder bag and opened the notes app. She wondered how many more days the temps would linger above fifty degrees so she could do exterior painting. It wasn't bad, really. All things considered. Mostly the trim work. Noted.

When had the cottage been built? The 40s? When she and Max first saw it, they were taken with its quaint concept. It was a word they'd turned to each other and said as if mirroring each other's thoughts. How long had it been since their thoughts were in the same library, much less on the same page?

But Max wasn't the issue today. Making a new home for herself, for them, loomed as the crisis *du jour*. And what she had to work with was the vacant quaintness with the wide many-paned windows on either side of double many-paned doors . . . shuttered to keep light from getting in or out.

She slid the key into the lock and braced herself for what she'd find inside.

"Why didn't I bring a flashlight?"

"I have two."

The rich voice from high above jammed her heart into overdrive. Her heel caught on the raised threshold in her retreat, but she caught herself. "Cora?"

"It's me. Up here."

As Emmalyn's eyes adjusted to the dusty half-light, she could see Cora's shadow through the eerie blue tarp where the kitchen ceiling should be at the rear of the cottage.

"My massage canceled on me. Just getting a feel for what we've got structurally up here. It doesn't look that bad. You didn't happen to call to have the electricity hooked up, did you?"

By the glow from her phone, Emmalyn made another note. "Didn't think of it."

"I won't be able to use any power tools until we get that taken care of. Or, I could bring my generator."

"I'll call right away. You said you had an extra flashlight?"

"In my truck. Wayne's truck. Out back."

Emmalyn Googled Madeline Island Electric Company on her way around the exterior of the cottage. No search matches. Bayfield County Electric Company. Ashland County Electric Company. A squirrel dashed through the crisp leaves at her feet. Time to pay attention to where she was walking.

"In" the truck could mean anything. The back of the overgrown pickup held a wide array of ladders, sawhorses, a massive toolbox, ropes, looped extension cords. Emmalyn wondered if the truck was this tidy when Wayne used it. After perusing the bed of the vehicle, she skirted around to the passenger side of the cab. A massive flashlight suitable for search and rescue or dark crawl spaces lay on the seat. She clicked it on and off to check its power. Strong enough to light the whole cottage. At least the first floor.

The flashlight was almost unnecessary by the time Emmalyn reentered the building. The blue haze was gone, the tarp removed. A jagged edged, branch-shaped open skylight let in the sun at the back of the cottage. She clicked on the flashlight anyway and set it on its heavy base on a table near the door with its beam aimed up to reflect off the lower ceiling in the living area. The two small bedrooms upstairs stood between Emmalyn and the rest of the roof.

"What do you know!" Cora called from her rooftop perch.

"What is it?"

"The clock in the kitchen is still keeping time." She stuck an arm down through the hole in the roof and pointed east. "Oh, wait a minute. I don't see the second hand moving. Must have stopped years ago at just this spot. Kind of freaky, huh?"

Emmalyn dodged shadowed furniture, most of which she catalogued as unsalvageable on her way toward the back of the cottage.

"Don't get too close," Cora warned. "I'm on a solid spot here, but I can't guarantee something isn't going to come crashing down."

"Is the damage confined to the kitchen?"

"The roof over the front half looks good."

"What do you suggest?"

"Skylight. If it were me, I'd take this opportunity to install a skylight. You'll never find shingles to match these. And I don't imagine you're willing to replace the whole roof at this point."

Emmalyn peered at the hole. "It isn't as bad as I imagined. But it went straight through the ceiling, too?" That explained the drifts of insulation on the floor of the kitchen.

"Good thing no one was cooking supper in there. Looks like the branch shot straight down. Too bad the guys removed it. Could have made a conversation piece."

She was kidding, wasn't she? Had to be.

"I like the skylight idea, Cora. How long do you think it would take me to get one out here?"

Cora stuck an arm down through the hole and pointed west. "If you like the one I have in the truck, we can make a deal. We got stuck with it when a previous client decided it was too large for her bathroom, but it was an 'as is.' No returns."

"Damaged?"

"Scratch and dent. Still in the box though."

Emmalyn remembered seeing a big box in the back of the truck. "Do I want a dented skylight?"

"Meet me out there and you can take a look. I'm pretty particular, and I'd put it in my own house if Wayne would let me. Would your husband have a problem with a skylight?"

Courage and truth. "He's been living in a prison cell for four years. He'd probably appreciate the extra light, providing we're still together when he's released. It's not . . . a given . . . from his side, anyway."

No response from the rooftop.

"Too much information?" Far more than she'd intended to share. Emmalyn's awkward chuckle landed somewhere near the pile of loose insulation.

"We have more in common than you'd think." Cora's voice had lost its business tone. "For one thing, we're both trying to figure out how to hold a marriage together when our men are missing in action."

"Nobody on the island knows about Max's incarceration."

"I won't be the one to tell them. That's up to you."

"Thank you." Emmalyn positioned herself to help slide the skylight box out of the truck.

"On the one hand, it's nobody's business." The woman used her knees to scoot the box toward the opened tailgate. A foot at a time.

"And on the other hand?"

"Keeping information like that to yourself means you're carrying"—another heave with her knee—"the whole load"—another final heave—"by yourself."

Emmalyn balanced the end of the box while Cora jumped down so they could lower the box to the ground together. Cora grabbed a box cutter from her tool belt and sliced the tape on one end.

The picture on the outside of the box had Emmalyn convinced this was far better than simply covering the hole in her roof, if it passed her own set of inspection standards. If Cora was "pretty particular," she might be shell-shocked by Emmalyn's level of particular.

Cora found a way to peel back the box sides so Emmalyn could get a good look.

"Here. This spot here on the edge."

"That's the dent?"

"That's it. I've gone over the whole unit. This is its flaw."

"Who would see that?"

"Angels and low-flying eagles."

Emmalyn rubbed her hand along the edge. "Wouldn't this part be facing the peak of the roof? Not visible from the ground?"

"True."

"Would it affect sealing it adequately? Would it leak?"

"I'd have to guarantee that for you. I'm confident it won't. But if it did, it would be on me to remove it and replace it. I'm not worried. If it were here"—she pointed—"that would be a different story. But this won't affect its structural or functional integrity."

Something that felt like a wave of excitement stirred. Excitement. "I like it. I really like the idea. How much for the whole project? Labor and everything?"

"Let me check inside on the second floor to make sure I didn't miss anything, no collateral water damage. Then we'll talk about price."

"Good thought."

"And you might want to consider having Joe work his exterminator magic. I'm sure you've noticed that mice have been leaving you little presents."

She had noticed. Mousetraps were already on her list. "Joe's an exterminator?"

"Not professionally. But he's got the touch. He's who we all call when the little critters decide they'd rather live inside than out. Now, there's a man with a story to tell. Funny how life does that to us. Drags us through something that turns into a story."

The two women took the narrow, twisting stairs from the living area to the slope-ceilinged second floor, flashlights well in hand. Talk of critters made Emmalyn see movement where there wasn't any.

When Max and friends used the cottage for hunting, they brought cots and sleeping bags. The larger of the bedrooms held a double bed. The smaller was empty. The master bedroom had a bed. The children's bedroom would never need one.

Never.

Max's sentence had seen to that. Not that there'd been more than a whiff of hope left.

"It's plenty warm up here," Cora said. "Considering the current natural air conditioning. This the bathroom? Petite. You planning on . . . ?"

"Replacing that toilet? Yes."

"Don't blame you. Might want to take pictures the day your new toilet comes riding across the lake on the ferry. Something to tell your grandkids."

That familiar hollowness settled in Emmalyn's middle. "No grandkids."

"Not yet. You're not old enough. Young people these days. Two extremes. Either they have their babies before they're out of high school or they wait until their 401Ks are healthy and their energy's gone." She backed out of the bathroom—one-way traffic—and shined her flashlight on the ceiling in the narrow hallway. "Are your kids in middle school yet? Now, there's a challenge."

This courage-and-truth thing was getting annoying. "Max and I don't have any children."

"Oh. Sorry. I mean, if that's your choice . . . "

"New subject, please."

Cora turned her flash-lit face toward Emmalyn. "Do you know what I'd do if I were you?"

Here it came. *Try what my nephew and his wife did. Seems odd, but it works. There's this new herbal supplement guaranteed to increase fertility. I know where I can get some cheap. Quit thinking about it. It always happens when you're not thinking about it. If you adopt, you're sure to get pregnant. Happened to a cousin of mine.* Which version of the above would Cora use on her? She sighed. "What would you do?"

"I'd have a painter spray-paint the entire place white, ceilings and walls. All this dark wood on the walls makes it like a tomb in here. And it's not as if it's high-quality wood. I realize we don't have the shutters off yet, but even with the windows letting in light, don't you think these dark walls will make it claustrophobic? Paint the whole thing white. Then you can tackle one room at a time with fancy colors, if you want. That's what I'd do."

She'd asked Cora to drop the subject and she had. Wonder of wonders.

"You don't want it to stay looking like a hunting cabin, do you?" Cora said.

"No. It needs to be a . . . a home."

"More like a beach cottage, since that's what it is." She drew a screwdriver from her tool belt and started removing the braces on the interior shutters in the smaller bedroom. "A little help, here?"

Emmalyn no longer cared if her sweater was cobwebbed and the hems of her jeans cockleburred. It was time to roll up her sleeves and let in some light. She held the bottom of the makeshift, removable shutter while Cora worked her screwdriver. Together they removed first one, then another of the shutter panels.

"And that's why you bought this place," Cora said.

"Dead flies on the windowsills?"

Cora frowned and stepped out of the way so Emmalyn could catch the full effect of the view. That endless expanse of freshwater. Waves like an ocean. Without the salt. A corner of the largest freshwater lake in the world lay right in front of her, sparkling in the sun as if dressed for a gala. She unlatched the window lock and opened it.

The breeze that blew in carried away bits of debris clinging to her soul. She closed her eyes and let the crisp October air reassure her she could have a future here, despite the hole in the roof, the mouse droppings, the bizarre collection of potential friends she'd met, the empty second bedroom, and the fact that her husband had changed their lives forever, not just for the five years of his sentence.

5

Before Cora headed out to round up a crew for the skylight installation, she and Emmalyn had removed all the shutters and stored them in the small, scruffy, unpainted shed behind the cottage. Emmalyn had gotten through to the electric company, who promised power would be reconnected "in a day or two." Cora would use her portable generator for power tools until then. But it would be a while before the cottage was habitable.

Emmalyn added to the list of cleaning supplies she'd need, kitchen supplies, the bare minimum furniture. Nothing in the storage unit back in Lexington seemed right for the cottage. Either too bulky, too much, or too memory-caked. She'd start fresh. That word again.

The trunk of the Prius contained boxes of kitchen essentials, a favorite lamp, and a small microwave in addition to her single-cup coffeemaker. She'd brought a quarter of one closet of clothes. It appeared the only ones she'd need for a while were painting togs and anything she didn't mind getting dirty.

When the interior pulled her into shadowed thoughts, she forced her attention to the view through the windows that faced the water. It never failed to calm her—a liquid version of the effect she'd found when she'd opened her Bible and soaked in it in her late teens. Before college, before Max, before marriage, her career, their frantic pursuit of a child.

She still carried her Bible around. It was in the backseat somewhere. It just didn't carry her anymore.

A dangerous thought. Time to take the stubby broom to the porch floorboards.

One thing. If she could get one thing about this place in order today . . .

One thing. Each stroke of the broom underscored how many broom strokes, brush strokes, how many near-strokes it would take for her to pull this place together.

But she wasn't alone. Her EMT/librarian/roofer/masseuse had committed to help her massage life into old wood, breathe air into the tired lungs of the cottage.

How had Max and his guy friends tolerated—? She knew the answer. They didn't care about the building. They had each other and a common goal. The island's whitetail deer.

Each other and a common goal.

Sweep. Sweep. Sweep.

That's what she thought she had with Max, too.

She leaned the broom against the railing of the porch and sat on the freshly swept steps. The sound of the waves had already become more music than nature. This part would be easy to get used to.

Whitewash the entire interior of the cottage? Not a bad idea.

Ho. Leee. Ho-leee. Ho-leee. Ho-leee. The wave sound was deeper, rounder, as it rushed ashore, higher pitched and thinner as it retreated, taking small pebbles and sand with it. HO-leee. HO-leee. HO-leee.

Holy. Holy. Holy.

Coincidence. Pure coincidence.

A beautiful distraction. The mesmerizing waves. Habit tried to steer her thoughts to her losses, as it always did when life got too quiet. But the rustle of waves kept interrupting, as if pulling the thoughts out to deeper water, leaving her mind damp but empty.

For months she'd been treading water with a flailing motion that made rescue impossible. Exhaustion served as her only reward. Now, here, she flipped onto her back and floated.

A beautiful delusion.

Emmalyn stood and shook herself as if dislodging a swarm of mosquitoes. Nothing had changed. Except her workload.

She'd hauled the unsalvageable furniture outside then realized it would have been smart to rent a Dumpster. Where did one dispose of the unwanted on Madeline Island? She pictured the comical scene—the back of Cora's truck piled high with the saggy plaid couch, the not-rustic-enough-to-be-cute end tables, the untouchable mattress from the bedroom, and the two spindle-less kitchen chairs riding the ferry to Bayfield for burial, *Beverly Hillbillies* style.

Maybe her first bonfire on the beach would smell like polyester, old varnish, and dense foam. Somehow, that seemed a sacrilegious thought. The beach deserved better than that.

Her skin prickled. She'd given up the tanning salon when the judge meted out Max's restitution fine, which like everything else was hers to pay, not his. Would the warm weather hold out long enough for her to tan naturally before the colorlessness of winter? She rolled her shirtsleeves over her shoulders.

She flipped the sofa onto its back and slid it, toboggan-like, along the lane to the end of the drive. Whoever she hired to remove it would probably appreciate that extra effort. On her second trip—this time with the scarred leg of an end table in each hand, she noted movement near the couch. A dark, curved back. A bear looking to pad his hibernation den? She stopped mid-lane. She could retrace her steps backward, slowly, and hope the animal hadn't noticed her approach.

It rose on its hind legs and stared at her. All six feet of him. A tuft of flannel peeked out between the sides of his open jacket. "You getting rid of this?"

Emmalyn felt her heart rate adjust from "BEAR!" to "Stranger Danger."

"Yes."

"Those too?" He nodded toward the bulky tables she gripped like dead chickens.

"I have more, if you're interested." She drew closer and laid the tables, legs to the sky, on the couch. "An old mattress, a couple of broken chairs . . . "

"What's your price?"

Price? He was willing to pay? Insane Stranger Danger. How could she quote him a price for what she'd been willing to pay to have removed?

"Want to make a trade?" His dark, bear-like eyes shone.

Cell phone. Front pocket. Speed dial 911. Someone could be here in . . . in time to shovel up the remains of her tortured body, attacked in the woods by a maniac with a penchant for plaid couches and broken women. She glanced at his booted feet. A monster chainsaw rested near his right ankle. So that was his method.

She slid one hand into her jeans pocket as slowly as she could while brushing the fabric of the sofa with the other. Magician trick. Distract the audience with action over here while the real action is taking place in your pocket.

"Trade?" he asked again, as if she hadn't heard. "Stack of firewood for all of it?"

She swallowed against the reality. He really and truly wanted the ratty sofa. And was willing to barter firewood for it. "That's more than fair, Mr . . . ?"

"Cranky. Cranzkolovski, but who can pronounce that?" He wiped his right hand—his chainsaw hand—on his camo pants and reached to shake a greeting.

Emmalyn resisted the urge to apologize for the filth on her own hand, the one she'd retrieved from digging for her cell phone. "Are we . . . neighbors?"

"That depends. Where do you live?"

His sixty-year-old eyebrows—apparently in a growth spurt since he was a toddler—wiggled when she indicated the cottage behind her.

"That so? Place's been vacant a long time."

"Thus . . . " she answered, pointing to the pile of furniture between them.

"I live in Washburn. South of Bayfield, but you probably knew that unless you arrived here by kayak." He smiled at his humor. "Come out once in a while to meditate," he said, nudging the chainsaw with his foot. "It's not quiet, but life doesn't always have to be quiet to be peaceful."

Such misguided logic turned his proverb into an old man's folly. She couldn't imagine finding any kind of peace with a chainsaw making its presence known.

"Cutting just down the road today. People still cleaning up after that last storm. Like you, I guess."

The blue tarp was back over the hole in the cottage roof. The ground was littered with storm evidence.

"Tell you what. I'll trade you the stack of firewood I have in the back of my truck plus clean up some of these fallen branches. That suit you? They'll make great kindling."

"That's more than kind of you."

"So it's a deal? I can't jaw long. Gotta get to The Wild Iris before Boozie runs out of that cream *broolee* she makes. When it's gone, it's gone."

"Yes, of course it's a deal. But I'm afraid I'm coming out way ahead on this bargain."

He paused and stroked his beard. "What means something to one person can't always be explained by another."

"One person's trash is another man's treasure?"

His upside-down-U mouth showed he was thinking on it. "If you want to say it that way. Tell me where you want the firewood and I'll unload it. The tree branches will have to wait until next time I'm out this direction, if you take my word for it."

With a roofing crew's anticipated arrival soon, Lord willing, Emmalyn calculated the most out-of-the-way place for a stack of firewood. "There?" she said, nodding to a long-abandoned, vine-covered pile of half-decomposed wood chunks laid like rolled cannoli between two standing pines.

"Good as anyplace." He picked up his chainsaw and started left down the side road—Chippewa Trail. She peered after him and noticed a larger-than-average and older-than-most truck parked near the intersection with Schoolhouse Road. "Back in a minute," he called over his shoulder.

By dumping more firewood than Emmalyn could imagine needing for the fireplace, assuming it could be restored to working order, Cranky had enough room in his truck for every stick of furniture she labeled unsalvageable. Before the day's end, the couch would wave its *Beverly Hillbillies* good-bye to Madeline Island from the deck of the ferry. Go figure.

<hr />

Cora's crew pulled in within minutes of Cranky's exit. While they scrambled up to and on top of the roof, Emmalyn took advantage of the last light of the day to sweep the main living area, taking care to stay out from under the workers. Her cardboard makeshift dustpan collected dust, sand, and the decomposed remains of candy wrappers, potato chip bags, and unidentifiable rodents. It would take some doing to turn the cottage into a place she felt comfortable inhabiting, much less calling home.

The flattened braided rug that covered most of the living area was a bear to remove, no offense to Mr. Cranky. Rolled like a burrito, it weighed far more than Emmalyn. She tried nudging the roll toward the door with her foot, but produced more groans than progress until two of Cora's crew members cut their water break short and assisted. Which means they asked her to step out of the way and shouldered the entire burden.

With the rug removed, she could see the potential for the hard-wood floor. Where protected by the rug, the floor's wide boards threatened to gleam when brushed by the broom.

Furniture moving had taken a toll on her back muscles. She was almost grateful—no, full-fledged grateful—when Cora called off her crew for the day.

"We'll need to work both inside and out tomorrow," Cora announced. "How early do you plan to be here?"

"How early do you want to start?" Emmalyn put both hands in the small of her back and stretched. How long would it take for her body to rebound? The enveloping white bed at The Wild Iris called to her as insistently as her hunger.

"Story Hour for the littles at the library at 9:30. Looks like we're talking close to 11:00 again. Hate to put it off until that late into the day."

The littles.

"Emmalyn? That okay with you?"

Kidlets. Littles. Babykins. Wonderlings.

"Emmalyn?"

Deep breath in. Exhale to the count of five. Relax your throat muscles on the exhale. "That sounds fine. I'll probably take the ferry into Bayfield and look for secondhand furniture and maybe pick up some paint before we meet up."

"You can say no if you want," Cora began tentatively, "but if you're comfortable leaving me with a key . . . "

"Oh. Sure. I should have thought of that."

"Nothing in much danger of getting stolen in here anymore, if you know what I'm saying."

Emmalyn tugged the spare key from the stainless steel ring. "Not that there ever was."

"Oh, I bet this place has some stories to tell," Cora said, patting the doorjamb. "They all do. And now"—she shrugged out of her tool belt—"you'll have your own chapters to write."

She dropped the key into Cora's outstretched hand. Who wants to read—or live—a story with every page blank?

The little stark room at The Wild Iris welcomed her with a lamp lit, a plate of cookies on the dresser, a carafé of something hot—smelled like apple cider—and a note from Boozie.

Overcalculated on the daily special. Leftovers in the fridge. Second shelf. Help yourself. I'll join you if I wade the rest of the way through this (what's the opposite of glorious?) paperwork. I almost said a word that would make the missions jar richer. Check out the new bath salts we're field testing for a friend of mine who makes them. Who needs a sleep aid with lavender bath salts? See you later. I hope. Hope floats, as they say. Hope springs eternal. Hope helps. It's all about hope. B

If hunger hadn't gnawed at her for the last several hours, she would have called cookies her supper and headed straight for the claw-foot tub. Instead, she washed her face and hands, slipped out of her work shoes and into cushioned sandals, and padded down the stairs and through the doors to the café. Boozie had a fire going in the fireplace and waited in her favorite wing chair.

"Beat you."

Emmalyn smiled. "I see that."

"Cora texted your progress. Slow going, huh?"

"Excruciatingly so." Emmalyn couldn't help staring at the plate in front of Boozie. A crust of what looked like banana bread and a wide-mouthed mug of a creamy soup. Boozie must have noted her interest.

"Chicken wild rice," she said.

"Sounds divine."

"The cooks and I still haven't adapted to the off-season crowds. Made a gallon too much. Froze some. But there's enough for seconds for both of us, if we want it."

A few minutes later, Emmalyn joined her at the small round table that had already become familiar, already a landmark of comfort.

"I'll wait," Boozie said, her spoon ready for another dive into the pool of cream, celery, wild rice, carrot bits, and other delectables.

"For . . . ?"

"I assume you have a lot to be thankful for besides something for your stomach, after seeing your new home for the first time."

Grace. She expected Emmalyn to say grace for the meal . . . and a few other things. She bowed her head. Nothing came. She waited in silence the length of time for a proper prayer of thanks, then raised her head and picked up her knife to butter her slice of banana bread.

As soon as she did, she realized banana bread, soup, a girl named Boozie, a lumberjack with only good intentions, and a librarian who repaired roofs would have made good thanks material. And that bed waiting for her at the top of the stairs.

The first bite of banana bread was satisfying enough to carry her until morning, but it begged for a second nibble, and another. She tested the soup while Boozie reported the LaPointe happenings. She detected a hint of nutmeg in the soup. Nice touch.

"Did you catch any of the sunset tonight? You're probably better positioned for sunrises there, aren't you? You'll have to spend some time at Sunset Bay, where North Shore and Big Bay Road intersect. It more than lives up to its name."

"I guess I will."

"Here." Boozie handed Emmalyn an electronic tablet. "Hit the arrow."

Emmalyn's finger hovered over the arrow as she studied the expression on Boozie's face.

"I didn't want you to miss it. The sunset."

Emmalyn watched the short video, then watched it again. By the final frame, she had to swipe at tears. "I . . . it . . . takes your breath away."

"Doesn't it? No matter what's going on in life, you get a sunset like that and you think, 'I guess I'll keep going another day or two.'"

Emmalyn drank in the afterglow of a newborn sunset, an hour old, that happened while she worked. Could she have seen glimpses of it if she'd walked to the end of the short pier in front of the cottage and looked back above the tree line behind it? Boozie had captured its image. Nothing could capture its essence. Emmalyn would have to be there for that.

"I have something for you," Boozie said, pulling a small packet from her skirt pocket. A three-layered blush-colored tulle skirt with apron-like pockets. It poofed around Boozie like an awkward bridesmaid gown. Is that what she did? Buy up vintage bridesmaid gowns and convert them into her version of fashion? A few years ago, Emmalyn might have mocked someone with that kind of fashion sense. A few days ago. But every bit of it fit Boozie's off-the-wall personality. The velveteen packet the woman had drawn from her pocket now lay near Emmalyn's plate.

"What is this?"

"You may need them tonight."

Emmalyn emptied the contents into her palm. "Ear plugs?"

"Church night."

Emmalyn stared at the purple foam mini-torpedos.

"What we call church, anyway. I think God does, too."

She fingered the squishy foam. The plugs had the feel of PlayDoh. "Here? Your church meets here? In the café?"

"You haven't seen Pirate Joe when he gets his worship on. Or tonight might be one of those nights when he tries to argue us under that table about a verse of Scripture that sits crossways in his throat." She sighed, but with that ever-present look of contentment. "One never knows."

"Church. Here."

"We tried calling it something else in the beginning. Life group. Bible Study. Turns out it was church." Boozie shrugged her shoulders, palms up. "You're invited to join us, if you want. We try not to go too late because my crew has to be back here early to make breakfast in the morning."

"Your employees all attend?"

"Sooner or later. I ask them to serve the coffee and tea a couple of times and then they're hooked. They come on their own." Every word out of her mouth seemed so matter-of-fact, as if Emmalyn would have no reason to wonder over what she was saying.

"I think I'm going to take your advice tonight and soak in a hot bath and get to bed early. So, thanks for the ear plugs."

"It's the least I can do."

"Would you like my help pushing the tables out of the way and rearranging the chairs?"

"For what?" Boozie asked, fluffing the mane of hair off her neck.

"Church."

She chuckled. "Oh, you really should come sometime. If you're thinking rows of chairs in a semi-circle and a pulpit and ushers and everything makes a church . . . "

She had. What was wrong with that? "Well, thank you so much for another great meal. Loved the soup. And I don't think I've ever had better banana bread." She pushed herself to standing, using her hands on the edge of the table for fear her legs couldn't do the job alone after her day's labors. "Want me to take the dishes to the sink?"

"No, I'll take care of them. You get a good rest."

It sounded like something Emmalyn should have said to the woman half her age. Something a mother would say.

Emmalyn ran her fingers over the velveteen pouch. "I'm heading to Bayfield on the first ferry tomorrow morning. I need a few things from town before I go back out to the cottage."

"Do you want me to pack your breakfast so you can get an early start?"

"Boozie, you're spoiling me."

"Sometimes caring feels like spoiling. Gratitude evens things out."

Emmalyn would have to start taking notes when Boozie spouted wisdom. "Thank you. Breakfast to go would be a . . . a blessing."

∞

The worship music drifting up the stairway and under the door of Room 37 surprised her. She recognized many of the songs. None reminded her of "Kumbaya." Somebody down there had a great bass voice. Faint as it was, Emmalyn thought she detected acoustic guitar and flute. And some other instrument that sounded a lot like ibuprofen rattling in a plastic medicine bottle.

Good reminder. She popped two gel-caps before turning on the swan's neck faucet on the antique tub. The music, the steamy water, the light scent of lavender massaged soul-deep aches. Twice, she reached to unplug the tub and let out a few gallons of tepid water so she could add more super-hot. Submerged to the neck, she let the water wash away what had accumulated—the dust of the cottage's past, the stiffness of the uninhabited.

She drew in a full breath and slid lower. Her hair, shorter now than Max liked it, floated around her head like stubby seaweed babies. She sat up and poured a dime-sized pool of almond shampoo into her palm. The pads of her fingers worked it through her wet hair. As the water and the day's remains swirled down the drain, she leaned her head under the arched faucet and rinsed out the shampoo, lingering with the hot water pummeling the back of her neck until the rest of her threatened to cool off too much.

Sooner or later she'd have to break down and do some laundry. For tonight, another clean tee and capri yoga pants felt like a gift. As did the buttery-smooth sheets.

Somewhere hundreds of miles south and a little east of this spot, Max lay on a thin mattress. He'd eaten a colorless, tasteless dinner and retired to a room with steel bars for a door. The sounds drifting up to him scorched his ears.

And he did it to himself.

To the two of them.

The soft sheets irritated her skin, as if woven with metallic threads. She reached for the ear plugs and turned off the bedside lamp.

Moonlight glared through the window. She'd forgotten to pull the shade. In the early days, when he was still writing to her, Max complained about the light always burning in his unit, throwing his circadian rhythms off kilter.

Emmalyn draped her forearm over her eyes. The moon shone on.

6

She'd neglected to pull the shade. And to set the alarm on her cell phone. An ooze of light woke her. She bolted upright and looked through the tall window at a cornflower sky and the back end of the ferry, halfway across the water to Bayfield.

It would be close to an hour before the next ferry. And that would make her too rushed to get back before the roofing crew arrived. Shouldn't the homeowner—maybe owner was a better word choice—be there while they worked? She would have kicked herself if her muscles hadn't been in the mood to complain this morning.

Now what? She guessed furniture hunting could safely wait another day or two. But paint? She needed to know what the island had to offer. A hardware store? The prices couldn't be cheap. But she might be able to get started on the outside trimwork.

She calculated more delays in moving from The Wild Iris to the cottage. "Cheaper by the week," Boozie had said. After yesterday's discoveries and today's negligence, that might prove more important than she realized.

Boozie Unfortunate. Someday she'd hear the story behind that most unfortunate of names.

Emmalyn dressed and finger-combed her hair, then thumbed a note into her phone to pick up—yes, she'd sunk that low—a baseball cap. Weren't there caps on the stepback cupboard of Madeline Island souvenirs near The Wild Iris cash register?

Outside the door of Random Room 37 sat a rectangular thermal lunch bag. Inside was a breakfast burrito. Tucked into the outside mesh side pocket, bottled water. How long had the bag been sitting there? Maybe she could borrow The Wild Iris microwave one more time.

When the plan you're rushing toward is abandoned, nothing else seems worth hurrying for. Sounded like Boozie, but it came from her own thoughts. Didn't it?

She and Max had rushed toward a goal for five years of their nine-year marriage. Every month for five years. Then Max took all the hurry out of it.

Armed with a hooded sweatshirt over her left arm and the straps of her purse and the thermal lunch bag in her right hand, she descended the stairs toward whatever the day would hold, into the yawning breach of uncertainty. First stop, the souvenir cupboard in the café.

Perfect. A Wild Iris cap—sedate gray with all the bright colors in the iris emblem. She flipped the tag of The Wild Iris bibbed apron, just to check, but decided to wait until the only things getting it dirty were her cooking escapades in her renovated kitchen.

One of the book club ladies manned the register, slow with the credit card machine, but rapid-fire with conversation.

"Is Boozie here?" Emmalyn asked. "She made me breakfast. I wonder if I could heat it up in the micro—"

"Island Time already grabbed you by the heart?" Boozie bounced into the dining room, a silver 1920s sheath skimming her thin form. A silk magnolia hair clip held back her lion mane. Black army boots grounded her. How could her steps be so light in those anchors?

Emmalyn stuck her credit card back into her way-too-fancy-for-this-life purse, never mind that she'd gotten it B.C.—Before Crisis. "I thought Island Time was a phrase used in Jamaica or Hawaii."

"An island is an island, *mon*," Boozie said, extending a plate toward her. "Wild raspberry scone?"

She shook her head, then acquiesced. "If I weren't putting in so much manual labor, I'd have to refuse the excess carbs, Boozie."

"Are you a beer drinker?"

What? "No."

"Think how many calories you're saving right there. Tea or coffee?" She nodded toward the window table, vacant since one of the book club ladies was behind the counter. You break up a set . . .

Emmalyn reined in her thoughts. "Coffee. Please."

Boozie reached behind the book club lady, grabbed a Wild Iris mug from the shelf, and inked something on the bottom. She handed it to Emmalyn.

M. That's all. She'd written M with a permanent marker. Permanent.

The Wild Iris manager/owner/cheerleader pointed toward the coffeemaker at the wait station. "Family. Help yourself."

Emmalyn dropped her purse and jacket in an empty chair at the window table and made her way to the coffee. "Oh, can I rewarm my—"

"As if you'd have to ask."

She scooted past the cook and Pirate Joe, who mumbled, "Life and death are in the power of the tongue. Life and death are in the power of the tongue" as he wrapped cloth napkins around real eating utensils. Unmatched. But real.

Less than a minute in the microwave and her meal steamed and stimulated Emmalyn's sense of smell. Sausage and sage? And Stilton? Interesting breakfast combination. She patted a free hand against her middle. "Enjoy being flat while you can."

Pirate Joe's eyebrows seemed to inch up his forehead. Usually a woman with her hand on her middle like that, uttering a phrase like that, meant something else entirely.

This was not the time to explain how wrong he was.

She grabbed a fork from the pile of clean cutlery on the counter in front of Pirate Joe. "Eating like this . . . " No, that was wrong. "The Wild Iris feeds its customers well. Too well." Ugh. That would have to do.

"Here," Pirate Joe said, tossing her an orange, which she caught against her chest. "Just got these in. Vitamins and fiber and all."

She exited the kitchen before she got entangled in a conversation about the importance of fiber.

"So," Boozie started, "I don't know if we mentioned that the ferry is spot-on punctual."

"I see that." Emmalyn peeled the orange, starting the first cut with her thumbnail. Max insisted on using the tip of a spoon, but Emmalyn loved the way the orange fragrance lingered on her hands.

"Are you going to make the next ferry?"

"Probably not."

"And you're okay with that? Weren't you going furniture shopping?"

"And paint." Emmalyn took her first bite of the inventive burrito. "This is a crepe!" What had looked like a fast food breakfast turned out to be delicate and beautifully balanced in taste and texture. She could feel a food-swoon coming on.

"Paint, we can help you with. Unless you're thinking exotic colors."

Emmalyn glanced at the décor. Orchid. Lime. Paprika. Cornflower blue. "White. I was thinking white. Lots of it."

"Eggshell finish?"

"Eggshell would be great."

"How many gallons?" Boozie's thumbs flew through a text to some unknown underground white paint supplier.

"Five?"

Boozie's thumbs paused. Her eyes widened. "Big cottage?"

"Small cottage. Big problems."

"Is your car locked?"

"What? Yes."

"Really?" Boozie scrunched her nose.

"Force of habit." Like always knowing where she was in her cycle. Like checking for bargains on pregnancy tests she'd never use now. Like keeping her mental file of clever but easy-to-spell baby names updated. Alphabetically and by gender.

Boozie focused on the text. "Done," she announced. "Five gallons of white interior eggshell paint will be sitting behind your car in The Wild Iris lot in ten minutes."

"How do you do that?"

"Find things people need?"

"Yeah."

"I listen." She giggled. "I know what you're thinking. I'm more proficient at talking than listening, right? All a ruse to cover my mad eavesdropping skills."

Emmalyn's smile burbled from deep inside. Nothing had seemed funny for so long. So very long.

"What else do you need?" Boozie asked.

She swallowed another bite of the savory crepe. "I need to start looking for furniture. It'll be a while before the cottage is ready for it, but sooner or later I'll have to find a bed, a small couch, some chairs, lamp tables, lamps, a couple of dressers . . . " She pulled the list from her pocket. "Oh, and some porch furniture."

"Was anything salvageable?"

Her wedding ring tightened like a steel band. The stone—still sparkling somehow—felt heavier than normal. Not larger, just heavier. *Yes,* she could have answered. *Our first three years of marriage. Maybe four. Even after we shifted gears and started pursuing having children, fighting for it, battling against medical realities. The first years' worth of memories are worth preserving.*

"The bed frame?" Boozie's voice sounded as if it originated across the lake, not right across the table.

No. After a while, even the bed had become a place of desperation.

"You'd need a new mattress, of course. I'd recommend Ashland or Duluth. I know good places in both towns. More selection in Duluth. That goes without saying."

"The cottage had a mattress on the floor."

"Ohhh." Boozie drew out the word as if imagining the laziest of vermin who wouldn't even have had to scale those pesky bed frame legs.

"I got rid of all the old furniture. Someone came by and traded me firewood for it."

Boozie leaned back, grinning, as if proud of her strange little community. "What a blessing."

"Yes." Another rusty word: blessing.

The morning crowd filtered in and out of The Wild Iris. Boozie acknowledged some with a nod, others with a hug. She directed traffic and answered managerial questions and shook her head as she acknowledged the clunk of the cookie jar lid twice in succession. Turning back to Emmalyn, she said, "Other than the bed, how new does this furniture need to be?"

"What are you thinking?"

Boozie leaned toward two older gentlemen trading barbs as they guzzled coffee and argued over the date of the first measurable accumulation of snow for the upcoming season. Emmalyn hoped they were both wrong.

"Stockton, did your mom ever sell off her trailer?"

Oh, Boozie. Please. A trailer?

"Still killin' the grass in my backyard. Mothers," he muttered.

In her mind, Emmalyn crossed the room, grabbed the gentleman by his earlobe, and insisted, "You take that back." The man looked to be in his late seventies or early eighties. His mother was still alive? And they still bickered?

Reminder. Her mother and sisters deserved a phone call. One of these days.

"Tell M what you have available for sale. Anything she could use at her cottage? Nice stuff, Stockton. Nothing with antlers.

Nothing mauve, either. Do you think your mom would part with some of it?"

"Might be. She's planting bulbs this morning."

Planting bulbs. At a hundred and thirty years old, give or take. Emmalyn's stiff, barely forty-year-old limbs mocked her.

"Let me know when you're done there," Stockton said. "You can follow me out."

Emmalyn turned to Boozie, who by this time had stood and began clearing their table, her sequined sheath catching the light streaming through the front window. "And the nearest Ikea is . . . ?"

"Farther than you want to drive," Boozie countered, "and more than you want to spend."

"Guess I'm going Dumpster diving, then." Emmalyn glanced up at Boozie. No reaction. The clatter of dishes had covered her comment. Good.

Stockton's mom spent her retirement years buying and selling antiques. Her trailer—an eighteen-wheeler kind of trailer—bulged with possibilities. For a brief moment in the trailer, picking through iron bedsteads and wicker rockers, Emmalyn felt a surge of anticipation long dormant. She could envision something—the cottage reborn. A comfortable place, worn enough around the edges to respect its history, with a story behind each nail, each warped floorboard, every piece of furniture.

If the island had a full newsstand, she would have picked up a copy of *Cottages* magazine on the way from the treasure hunt to her place. Her place. The one she saw in her mind's eye. Not the one with a hole in its roof and more mouse evidence than charm.

Dreaming, anticipating, planning.

As quickly as that wave hit the shoreline of her heart, it receded, carrying little bits of hope out to sea. Anticipating what? Creating a cute, cozy place in which to be miserable about how it had all turned out? Pretending hope still existed for Max to want what she wanted? And what was that? What dream did she dare entertain now, with Max's sentence almost over and no resolution to whether he'd put their marriage on hold or put it out of his mind? The dream of children? Too late for that.

Two small bedrooms upstairs. All that had happened, all that had turned from improbable to impossible, and her first thought on seeing the smaller of the bedrooms was where she could put the crib.

Or that the wicker dresser would make a sweet changing table, the dresser she'd told Stockton and his mom to add to her tab. It would be delivered along with the rest of the furniture she'd purchased as soon as she was ready for it.

So, good goal—start thinking clearly before the paint dries.

Out of habit, she checked her face in the rearview mirror before exiting the Prius that she'd parked in back of Cora's truck. Sun filtering through the pines and birch trees that hugged the backside of the cottage mottled her appearance. She hadn't aged that much in the past five years, had she? Emmalyn dug in her purse for her lip gloss before catching herself. She'd crammed a baseball cap on her head, was about to pull work gloves over her scuffed manicure. Lipstick wouldn't have its traditional impact.

She grabbed the Wild Iris pottery mug from the car's cup holder—"Just bring it back later," Boozie had said—and made her way to the front of the cottage. So few clouds marred the sky, she could have counted them. The great lake showed its aggressive side, flicking an occasional whitecapped wave to remind the world how tough it could be when riled.

"Breathe deep."

Emmalyn flinched. God didn't sound like that, did He? That sounded more like . . .

"Some people take shallow breaths when the wind's blowing," Cora added from her rooftop perch, one hand on the chimney while she gestured with the other as if a Lamaze coach. "But if you breathe deep when the winds are strong, your lungs fill even faster, I say."

Emmalyn turned to face the water again and hide her amusement at her roofer's homegrown philosophies. Breathe deep when the . . .

. . . when the winds are strong.

"Wait there," Cora said. "I'll be right down. We need to talk. Privately."

Emmalyn closed her eyes. If she focused, she could feel the skin of her face warming, pore by pore. Despite the brightness making her eyelids mere shades, she relaxed her facial muscles. The wind stirred the scent of water, rocks, fish, pine, sun-baked leaves. She drew a breath and forced her lungs to expand farther than she thought they could, then exhaled. Again. Autumn in the upper Midwest. Almost an apple tartness to the air.

A sharp sound like a baby's brief cry stirred her. It came from a long-legged bird skittering along the shoreline as if the sand and rocks were on fire. It dipped its beak into the spaces between rocks, then hurried on without giving away whether it had found what it was looking for or come up disappointed. It danced far down the shore by the time Cora joined her.

"Have you walked this beach yet?" Emmalyn asked her.

"Been kind of busy." She brushed sawdust from the knees of her jeans.

"Want to talk as we walk? Or do you need to show me something with the roof?"

"Let me tell my guys where I'll be. They're good to go for a while."

Emmalyn started toward the water, picking her path through the tufts of sea grass and down the small embankment of sand. Those used to living on the water probably had a name for that. Erosion had eaten away chunks of the sand bank in front of the cottage. As she looked farther down the shore, she saw the sand swallowed by rock cliffs with trees jutting over the water and pines playing "I can lean farther than you can without getting wet."

She waited for Cora's crunching footfalls to catch up to her.

"You're one blessed woman to have this for your wake-up view every morning."

Emmalyn considered Cora's assessment. *Blessed* kept showing up in conversation. One of these days, she'd have to take it seriously. "It's a captivating view. No doubt about that. Do you live in LaPointe itself or . . . ?"

"We've got an old farmstead. Inland. Although on an island only three miles wide, you're never far from a view."

They walked side by side at a pace that gave snails an advantage.

"What did you need to talk to me about, Cora?"

"I have a painter for you. He does real nice work. And I happen to know he could use the income right now. But he's . . . "

"What? Expensive?"

"On parole. He needs someone to give him a chance. I didn't think it would be right if you didn't know that much, so you can decide if you're his chance."

The wet sand turned to small stones. Emmalyn bent to pick one that startled her with how different it was from the rest.

"Let me see that," Cora said, holding out her palm. "Could be you have an agate there. Nice find."

"What did he do?"

"Nick's a brilliant young man. Sharp mind. If he gets his feet underneath him . . . "

"I'll be alone out here most of the time, Cora. Don't you think I should know the reason he's on probation?" The irony poked at her eardrum with a toothpick.

"Parole. A little different from probation. And it was what some call creative bookkeeping."

"Theft? Wait. Embezzling? How old is he?"

Cora's steps slowed further. "Nineteen. His uncle runs one of the kayak businesses for the Apostle Islands. Nick has kept the books for him since he was sixteen. Prepared his taxes. Smart kid."

Cora snagged a stone shaped like a fat L and underhand tossed it to Emmalyn. "I don't know if it was the risk that appealed to him or if he thought he wasn't getting paid enough. Never heard the whole story."

Who ever does hear the whole story? Emmalyn divided her focus between the waves and the stones at her feet.

"His uncle found out and turned him in to the authorities to teach him a lesson. The court took it more seriously than the uncle intended. But the bottom line is he paid his time and the fine and has forty-eight months of parole officer home visits now. The locals are a little skittish about hiring him. Some of them."

"And you thought I'd be more gullible? Because I'm new to the island?" Emmalyn hadn't meant for her words to sound haughty. Of all people. Good grief. Of all people.

Cora stopped walking and waited for Emmalyn to fully face her. "I hoped you'd be more forgiving." Her expression pinched. "Usually those who are practiced at forgiving are better at it."

The cords in Emmalyn's neck stiffened. Rankled. That was the word for how she felt. A substantial, no-wind's-going-to-blow-this-down word. "Did Boozie insinuate I'm practiced in forgiveness? Because I'm not."

"I made an assumption. Does Boozie even know your husband's in prison?"

"She's a good guesser, but we haven't talked about it."

"Even if she did know, she's no gossip. I can list you a few gifted in gossiping. But that would be gossiping. It's just my opinion, but I think what the courts did to your husband was extreme, considering he obviously hadn't intended on harming anyone. And the deal with the accelerator recall. Why didn't his lawyer lay more heavily on that tidbit?"

The woman knew more than Emmalyn had expressed to anyone. Ever.

"Librarians are a curious lot," Cora said, as if sensing Emmalyn's question. "And we have access to all kinds of online information, not that it takes a library anymore." She leaned closer. "But you did not hear me say that. We need libraries. They're vital to our community life. If it weren't for libraries—"

"Cora. How did you know those particular details about Max's case?"

"I looked him up. Indirectly. I looked you up on the Internet. I like to know who I'm doing business with. Read the news articles from back then. It wasn't hard finding more than the little you told me. I'm sorry if that felt like an invasion of privacy. I assumed you'd want to know Nick's background like I wanted to know more about yours."

✦

Two emotions battled for dominance. Was Emmalyn going to seethe or let it go, grateful someone—a woman who'd been a stranger a day ago—cared enough to talk candidly about it?

Cora pulled her shirt away from her neck. "You know what? You're right. A person's background shouldn't matter as much as their present and their future. If a person wants to tell their story, fine. If not . . . "

Emmalyn sank to the pebbled beach, not caring that her seat would likely get wet, crossed her legs, and stared into the endlessness of the water.

Cora lowered herself to sit beside her. "But were you expecting to keep it a secret from the island forever? He gets out in a few months. How were you going to explain his showing up one day?"

"I'm not sure he will."

Cora tossed a rock into the water. "Why wouldn't he?"

Emmalyn thought she'd have at least several weeks before she was required to have this kind of conversation. And she didn't expect it would be with the roofer/librarian/EMT/massage therapist. "We're not communicating anymore. I don't know what his plans are."

"Why aren't you communicating?"

Massage therapist/marriage counselor. "He asked me not to contact him." The long-legged bird scampered toward them, then seemed to notice the human intervention in progress and made an abrupt U-turn.

"And you complied?"

A late season mosquito made its presence known. She swatted it into submission. "Max made it clear he doesn't want to hear from me."

"Guaranteed he does."

"How would you know?" Emmalyn bent her torso forward and said, "I'm sorry. You didn't deserve that."

"Emmalyn, Nick is my son." Cora folded her hands in her lap with finality. "I know."

A son fresh out of jail. A brother or brother-in-law who sent him there. A husband on deployment. A business that would fall apart if she didn't climb roofs and massage other people's muscles. Okay, so maybe Cora knew a few things.

"But I understand if you don't want to hire Nick to paint for you. I get it. Kind of a long shot. He works a few hours a week for Boozie, but she can't take in *every* stray."

Why did unconditional grace come so easily for Boozie and Cora? Maybe Emmalyn needed a mentor more than she needed her cottage finished.

With a resigned grunt, Cora stood and tossed one last stone into the water. "Well, I'm in the middle of the project, so . . . "

"When could he start?" It didn't feel like a poor risk. Not yet, anyway.

"Are you sure about this?"

"I'd want someone to give Max a chance, despite what he's done." The words bounced back to her as if they were ricocheting bullets. *Ping, ping, ping.* She pressed a hand to her chest to stop the bleeding.

Emmalyn wondered what the record was for not thinking about an incarcerated loved one? A whole hour? She had yet to draw close to the record.

The wind lessened enough for Emmalyn to start scraping the outside trim without flecks flying up her nose. The skylight and roof repair crew finished, leaving the skylight itself as the only hint they'd been there. Every scrap of discarded material, every stray roofing nail was picked up before they left. Cora trained her team well.

The air cooled considerably when the sun ducked behind the tree line. She stopped scraping and listened to dusk settling in while she stretched the cramped muscles in her hands.

The rustle she heard—dry leaves—wasn't quick, like the movements of a squirrel. It was slow, deliberate, with the heft of a human. Emmalyn looked at the paint scraper now lying on a window ledge. Not her preferred weapon at a time like this.

Step. Step, step.

She should have left a half hour earlier when her hands first started to cramp from gripping the tool's handle—alternating right hand to left. She'd considered it.

Closer. Then quiet. Whoever it was had crossed from the leaf-strewn wooded area behind the cottage to the silencer grassy patch others might call a yard. If this was Nick's way of introducing himself, they definitely had a problem.

Something flicked just past the edge of the cottage, then retreated. Emmalyn kept her eyes on the spot and waited, scraper clutched in front of her like a medieval sword. A doe tiptoed into the open, so close to the side of the porch Emmalyn could count the animal's impossibly long eyelashes. The animal paused, flicked her ears, then resumed her stroll to the beach.

She dipped her head and drank from the now nearly still water. Freshwater. Did deer drink ocean saltwater? How remarkable to have an ocean-sized expanse of freshwater. If she could keep up the property taxes, Emmalyn would continue to own a spit of land that touched the edge of the remarkable.

And on the spit of land was a not-as-sorry-looking-as-yesterday cottage breathing fresh air for the first time in a long while.

Within a few moments, the deer flashed the white side of her tail and disappeared into the woods. "Wish you'd seen that, Max."

She was talking to him again. Good sign. If only he wanted to hear it.

7

"What's this?" Emmalyn settled into one of the vacant chairs by the fireplace in The Wild Iris with her M-labeled Wild Iris mug nearly full of strong but smooth coffee. A birch bark basket sat on the cold hearth at her side, tagged "M."

"Early housewarming gift," Boozie said, sliding a plate of eggs benedict onto the table in front of her. "I thought these things might come in handy even before you move in."

Her mother always told her anything that looks too good to be true not only is, but probably has a despicable downside. After his arrest, Emmalyn wondered if her mother meant Max. Boozie's despicableness hadn't shown its face yet. Mothers can be wrong.

Hand sanitizer. Good idea. Human-friendly mousetraps— triple pack. A coffee-table book. A bit premature, but a lovely thought. Oh. The book held stories and pictures of some of Madeline Island's unique or historic summer houses and cottages. She flipped through the first several pages as she sipped her coffee.

Boozie returned from wherever she'd flown. "I thought you might need some inspiration."

"It's a beautiful book."

"I haven't been out to your cottage yet, but I imagine it's a few days from being inspiring on its own."

"An understatement. Except for the view. You're welcome to see for yourself." Why hadn't she thought of inviting her before now? "And thank you for all of this. You've made the transition so much smoother than it would have been."

Boozie tugged on the hem of her brocade vest. It just topped the waistline of the skirt of the day—apricot with a chiffon overlay. Another recycled bridesmaid number? Her tights mimicked the brocade pattern of the vest.

"The transition from landlubber to islander?" Boozie asked.

More like from hope atheist to hope agnostic. "I don't think I qualify as an islander with so few days under my belt."

"Some stay for years and never qualify. You? There's hope for you."

Her insights could be irritating sometimes.

Boozie pointed to something nestled in the tissue paper at the bottom of the basket and pirouetted toward the kitchen.

Hope for me? Boozie sounds so sure. How does a person get that sure? Emmalyn's hands stumbled as she unwrapped the orchid tissue paper. An embossed leather journal. The invisible magnet latch give way when she opened it. A title page read:

Letters to Max
(Until You Come Home)

A slip of paper, stuck like a bookmark after the title page, held a message from Cora. "I'm keeping one of these for my husband. Small things that happen in my day. Things I wish I could tell him if he were here. An occasional rant. Sometimes just a date and the page dotted with tears. Thought you might want to keep a record like this too."

Emmalyn had journals. "Letters to Max . . . Because You're Not Here!" It wouldn't be right to throw this genuine leather journal— this gift from a new friend—in the garbage. She'd hold onto it. But the temptation to tear out the title page nearly overwhelmed her.

Emmalyn scribbled a "Thanks for the goodies" note on a scrap of the tissue paper and left it by her untouched eggs benedict. "Sorry. Not hungry this morning. But put it on my room tab. I owe you so much more than that." She scooted out the door before Boozie returned and read any more of her mind, before Cora happened by and psychoanalyzed what was wrong with Emmalyn's long-distance marriage.

Very little. Other than the fact that he'd wanted a divorce and she thought she might still be in love with a man who mourned he'd ruined everything. Every. Thing. Emmalyn hadn't argued to the contrary. She should have objected.

She'd made it to the driver's seat of the Prius before the first tear fell. It had friends.

A motorcycle—no, a dirt bike—leaned against the scruffy-looking shed near the back entrance of the cottage. Nick.

Emmalyn sighed. Now? She looked heavenward. "Very funny."

Where was Cora's son? Emmalyn had locked the cottage. Unless he'd learned the art of lock-picking while in jail, he couldn't have gotten inside.

Yet another thought she shouldn't have entertained.

She circled the cottage to the front porch and found him sitting on the low steps, bent over a small book.

"Good morning. You must be Nick."

He jerked to attention and slid the book into a back pocket of his cut-off jeans. Cut-offs. And there it was just above his paint-spattered athletic shoe—an ankle bracelet where most kids wore a tattoo.

"Mrs. Ross. Nice to meet you." He stood and shook her hand. "Thanks for taking a chance on me."

The look on his face held her attention in a way the ankle bracelet couldn't. The monitoring system wasn't what defined him. It was that sparkle of brilliance tempered with humility in his brown-black eyes. The tilt of his eyebrows—appreciative, not cocky. The set of his mouth, as if he had more to say but couldn't find the words.

She knew the feeling.

"Do you want to take a look inside and see if it's a job you're interested in?"

"I already know I'm interested."

She wondered if his mother told him how Emmalyn intended to change the cottage's interior. It was no small task. "After you see it, I'll need an estimate. Supplies and labor. I have five gallons of paint I hope you think will work. I'll do the outside trim. Oh."

"What?"

"I was going to get some exterior paint in case I finished scraping today. If I could find some on the island."

"We might have some left over from another project. I could have my mom drop it off when she brings my ladders." He studied the façade of the cottage. "You're going with white, I hope."

A young man with color preferences?

"I mean," he said, "it fits the place. Makes me crazy when people put up a beach cottage here that looks more like a Miami condo or the wing of a space station. That's not what this island is about."

She trolled for something to say in response.

"Sorry. I should watch my language around prospective employers. I didn't mean crazy as in *postal*."

She laughed aloud at that. "Nick, you don't have to worry about my thinking you're crazy. When you hear how I plan to transform the interior of the cottage . . . "

"Mom told me."

"Let's go check it out." Emmalyn unlocked the front door and led him into the cottage. She flipped the light switch, which turned on the overhead bulb but did little to illuminate the cottage more than the natural light from the beachside windows and the skylight in the kitchen.

"Kinda rough as is." Nick brushed a hand over an interior wall and pressed his thumb on the window casings.

"Yes. There's no denying that fact."

"The whole thing white, huh?"

"All the ceilings, all the walls, all the trim. I don't usually like to paint over original wood, but this isn't anything fancy. I want to salvage the hardwood floors though, if I can."

"Of course," he said, as if twenty years older and an expert in home restoration.

"Two smallish bedrooms and a bathroom upstairs," she said.

"Uh huh." He pulled out his phone and thumbed a message.

"Nick?"

"Yeah?"

"Are you listening?"

"Calculating, Mrs. Ross." He showed her the phone screen. "I have a square-foot-paint-use calculator app."

"Oh."

"This . . . is . . . going to take a boatload of paint."

"I was afraid of that."

"So, what's my deadline? When do you plan to move in?"

Plan to move in. She didn't have a plan. She had no more than wishful thinking. "How long do you think it will take you?"

"You'll want to let the paint harden in for a good two days—a week would be better—before you sand the floors. Or do the floors first, but then you run the risk of—" His thoughts trailed off as he peeked at the configuration of the stairwell.

It had seemed a much simpler idea before she crossed the ferry. *Spruce up the hunting cottage with a bucket of water and Lysol* had turned it into a renovation project for an HGTV episode.

"But I should be done with my part within a week," Nick said.

"This next week?"

"I work fast, but I'm good."

"That's what I hear."

"And"—he pointed to his monitoring device—"I don't have much else going on in my life at the moment."

"Does . . . ?"—Did she dare ask? She knew too little about how all this worked—"Does everyone who gets out of jail or prison have to wear one of those? That seems . . ."

"Harsh?" He tapped his opposite heel against the bracelet. "It depends. If you're talking prison . . ."

"Prison." She needed to sound more casual. "Hypothetically." Yeah, casual enough.

"Some go from prison to a halfway house, depending on the offense. Some are released free and clear. It depends. For me, this piece of jewelry came because of a violation of the terms of my parole."

"Oh?" *Cora, you didn't tell me everything.*

"Small violation. They're making sure I know my place. The jewelry comes off in two weeks."

She didn't want to know the difference between probation and parole. If she never saw the inside of another courtroom, she'd consider herself blessed. Max had been so tight-lipped about everything once he was moved from the county jail to the state prison after his sentencing. She knew less than a nineteen-year-old.

A nineteen-year-old who could set off alarms if he left the island. So, he was *not encumbered* by other jobs at the moment and could get right to work on Emmalyn's cottage.

It probably helped, for the renovation schedule, that Nick wouldn't have to be picky with the cutting-in process. White trim against white walls and white ceiling allowed for a more casual application of paint. Emmalyn had done enough of her own home renovations to know that much. She doubted Nick could finish that week, but she wasn't ready to sand floors, anyway.

"What's your estimate?"

"I'll need actual measurements, not just the virtual." Nick indicated his cell phone app. He pulled a carpenter's measuring tape from his waistband. "Okay if I get started?"

"I'll be outside if you need me."

She should have been scraping trim while Nick measured and figured and thought about ladder placement to reach the ceiling of the stairwell. Instead, she took the *Cottages* book to the spot where sea grass and sand met, dangled her legs over the drop-off, and dreamed about the details that could turn an empty, hollow, bleached-out shell into a home.

Light touches of color. Wildflowers in odd-shaped vases. Pillows for the sofa and chairs.

She'd seen an image on the Internet of a lit-from-behind shelving unit with colored glassware. It would be perfect for the narrow wall between the kitchen and the stairs. She'd remove the doors from the upper cabinets and leave open shelving.

The opposite of the home she'd shared with Max in Lexington. Sleek, shiny, metallic . . . What had seemed modern and polished then sounded cold and closed off now. What happened to her? To them? Derailed in every aspect of their lives, including their taste in habitat?

How could they have stayed the same when their dreams died in a pile of broken glass, crumbled bricks, and twisted metal with Max behind the wheel? With Max responsible? Or, as the courts deemed, "irresponsible."

If the homeless man had died, the sentence would have ratcheted to life. Life. Because the man survived—broken, incapacitated, but without family to demand restitution—Max's crime was logged as drunk driving causing bodily harm. With an eyewitness who claimed he'd fled the scene.

Max hadn't fled anything his entire life. Hadn't taken a drink since college. But the courts pointed to the unanswered questions. Where had he been for those twenty-four hours, after which a blood alcohol test was meaningless? He'd called Emmalyn from a bar. The eyewitness. What else could they conclude? He didn't remember stumbling from the wreckage, but that's what the traffic cam showed. He didn't remember anything, he said, until he woke up the next day under a bridge a mile away.

Emmalyn had followed the nationally publicized court proceedings of the woman who claimed she'd taken a sleep aid by mistake. A bizarre side effect explained away her reckless endangerment issue. She walked out of the courtroom a free woman. Max had been prescribed the same sleep aid months before the accident. Could that have been it?

Not that it mattered anymore. He was only months away from having paid his dues, no matter what the root of his mistake.

"Mrs. Ross?"

Emmalyn clambered to her feet and brushed sand and leaves from her backside. "Finished already?"

"Do you want me to paint those cupboards in the kitchen, too?"

"I thought I could do that."

"I'll throw them in free of charge."

"Done." Emmalyn had enough other projects to keep her occupied. "Those five gallons aren't going to be enough, are they?"

"Can I call you with what I estimate we'll need and what I figure for labor costs?"

"Good idea. I should have your number, too, in case I need to reach you."

"Mrs. Ross?"

Should she ask him to call her Emmalyn? M? Somehow the "Mrs." in *Mrs. Ross* grounded her to a concept that had escaped her grasp for too long. "What is it, Nick?"

His gaze fell to his feet. Or his ankle. "I know I messed up." He raised his head, eyes level with hers. "I'm not going to mess this up."

"I know you won't."

"That means a lot."

"It means a lot to me, too, Nick. More than you know."

He turned to leave, then turned back. He waited, staring into the space several feet to Emmalyn's left. "Your place looks pretty sad right now."

She sighed for both of them.

"I think once I get the painting done, you'll see it in a whole new light."

"Life? Or the cottage?"

His eyes met hers then. The sterling silver ring in his eyebrow bobbed when he smiled. "Maybe both. Times two," he said, pointing to his chest. He drew the small book from his back pocket. "This is part of the rules of my release."

"A Bible? Your parole officer can do that?"

"The other kind of probation. The one Boozie has me on."

That's the book that kept his attention when Emmalyn arrived. "Getting anything useful from it?"

"Whole new light." He slapped it shut and repocketed it. "Anyway, I'll go see what I have for trim paint and exterior back home, do some calculating, and give you a call."

"Sounds good, Nick. You take care."

"If you like the numbers," he called from the side of the cottage, "I can start later this afternoon, after my P.O. meeting."

"Boozie or court appointed?"

"Boozie."

The rngh-rngh-rngh-rngh of the dirt bike engine signaled his departure.

She'd finished scraping the main floor windows and doors facing the beach when the first drops of rain pelted her. The sky showed it meant business. Emmalyn's weather app told her the percentage of rain the rest of the day was high. What could she do inside? Remove the upper cupboard doors. Clean out the fireplace. Set a couple of mousetraps with the single-serving peanut butter she'd purchased at the convenience store on Middle Road on her way out. The list grew.

The skylight that had made a dramatic difference in the dark back half of the cottage was little help with the sun gone and thick pewter clouds overhead. Emmalyn stood watching and listening for leaks. Cora would be glad to know she found none, not even when the wind kicked up and drove the rain sideways.

She would set the mousetraps just before she left for the day. No sense subjecting herself to the horror of a snap and squeal. The hollow feel of the cottage was creepy enough. She wasn't sure she was ready—or could afford—to hire Pirate Joe to do a professional extermination job.

The ceiling light did little more than throw shadows. *That's* all she needed. More shadows.

Fireplace. If she could get it cleaned out and make sure the flue worked right, she could light a fire—her heart sank—with the firewood now exposed to the driving rain. She walked toward the fireplace. It had to be done sooner or later.

A crack of lightning snapped off the lights and her last nerve. Done. She was done for the day, if the rain kept up. The dusty wood walls turned suffocating in the damp air. She flipped the light switch to the off position, locked the front door, and made a mad dash for her car.

She could wait for Nick's call at The Wild Iris far more comfortably than she could in the cottage that wasn't yet home.

8

October rains can lean either way—short and refreshing or elongated, drizzly, chilling. This batch fit the chilling variety. How different the water looked pockmarked with slanting rain. Battleship gray. Flat in color but hammered in texture. The low ceiling of miffed clouds gave the illusion the world's walls were closing in like a shrinking room in a thriller.

Emmalyn watched a while from the safety of her car now parked at the elbow where the two roads joined, the wide spot where the trees parted enough to give an unobstructed view of the weather's distemper.

I chose the life here, on this spot, in a soon-to-be-charming cottage. I chose remote, solitary. I chose sun-drenched days and a quiet beach and endless water. And I got this thrown in, too.

A pencil-thick branch skittered across the windshield, punctuating her thoughts.

This too.

How often did Max check the sky? What would it be like to not know or care about the forecast for the following day? How long did it take him to convert from the weather-watcher he had been to weather-neutral?

That's the sort of thing Cora expected her to write in the "Letters to Max (until you come home)" journal. As if he would ever read it. As if he'd ever see it. As if it would matter.

Emmalyn cranked up the heat in the Prius for the first time since early last spring and let the warm air assault her and fog the windows, curtaining her view. She snatched the *Cottages* book from the passenger seat, grateful it had survived the raindrop dash under her shirt.

She noted an unusual treatment for a bathroom backsplash. Glass doorknobs on a piece of driftwood for hanging coats and hats near the back door. She liked that. A rustic basket on a low stool near the stairs for items on their way up.

She skimmed some of the articles accompanying the images. History of the cottages. History of the island. And the story of how it got its name.

All along, she'd pictured a three-year-old girl with pink cheeks and outrageous curls, the cherished daughter of a lumber baron, who succumbed to an exotic illness despite her parents' diligent efforts and the fortune spent on turn-of-the-century doctors. Madeline. Sweet Madeline . . . whose cry could still be heard on moonless nights.

The article rearranged her thoughts. The original Madeline was an Ojibwa princess who married a French explorer in the 1790s. Her Ojibwa name didn't suit him, apparently. Equaysayway. He called her Madeline.

Good idea.

Before The Crisis, she and Max spent hours toying with unpronounceable names for the children they'd have. Names with no vowels. Names with no consonants. They'd lie in bed late on Saturday mornings, curled around each other as if hope were a real thing, designing imaginary nurseries for imaginary children who kept escaping their grasp despite dozens of in vitro attempts.

In the early years, the name game sanded the edge off their disappointment. Equaysayway's name would have made him laugh. He would have rehearsed it until he could say it without hitching, then use it in those brief successful days after another attempt when he'd lay his warm palm on her flat stomach and ask, "How is our little Equaysayway this morning?" She could picture it.

Emmalyn would have giggled. And pressed his hand as tight against her abdomen as she could without disturbing any cells dividing in there. But they didn't divide. Not for long. Her womb was "a hostile environment" for children. One explanation. The fertility clinic offered a bevy of reasons and an ever-narrowing but ever-more-expensive list of treatment options.

Until Max had enough.

Until the day he lost interest in children. Or her. Or the process. She might never know what pushed him.

It couldn't have been her.

No.

‹———›

The rain settled into an arrhythmia no longer life-threatening. Emmalyn set the heater to defrost and waited until the windshield and side windows cleared, then swung the car toward LaPointe, the western way. She took Schoolhouse Road until it blended into North Shore Road and took its own sweet time winding back to the village, carrying her past Steamboat Point, Sunset Bay, the airport, and the spot in the road where the fire department sat on the right and the two-story turn-of-the-century home converted to an eclectic library perched on the left.

Bookshelves. She needed several well-placed bookshelves. She repeated the word, searing it into her memory, for lack of paper on which to write and for fear of a ticket for texting while driving.

Four or five more blocks. She could hold onto the thought that long.

Tires from passing cars—both of them—sang a high-pitched song on the wet pavement and threw sprays of water against the Prius.

When the phone rang, she pulled into a vacant spot along the street and turned off the engine. Nick.

He gave her an estimate that made her ask for clarification three times. He was selling himself short. If he was as good as

Cora said, that kind of labor was worth far more than he quoted. Her quickly dwindling savings from the sale of the Lexington house would appreciate it. But her heart clenched at the idea of a young man so desperate for work, he'd expect so little.

When they were still in the talking stage, Max told her he'd been given a promotion in his prison job in the laundry. From eleven cents an hour to fourteen. It would help him save for an extra pair of socks. How many humiliations had he known behind bars? And where did the line lie between "You deserve this" and "Designed to break you"?

Nick waited for her answer. She agreed to his terms, already calculating how she could arrange a merit increase if he only worked for her a week or two.

When she ended the call, it struck her that she showed a nineteen-year-old thief more grace than she showed her husband.

But Nick hadn't crippled anyone.

Not that Max intended it to happen.

She should get another key made, so Nick could paint even if she wasn't there. The building was gutted. There was nothing to steal.

She sucked in a breath. Maybe she hadn't grown any more noble after all.

⸺

The rain passed, leaving a gray ceiling of clouds that looked like a tent roof bulging downward with pools of unspent water. Emmalyn stopped at The Wild Iris long enough to pick up a thermos of the soup of the day, grateful Nick hadn't left yet so she could find out his preferences for a sandwich and beverage. He, Boozie, and two people Emmalyn hadn't met sat at the window table with their Bibles open in front of them.

"I don't want to interrupt . . . "

Boozie closed her Bible—a purple, go figure, number with a zebra duct tape binding. The others followed her lead. "We have to finish up and get ready for the noon crowd," she said. "What do you need?"

Emmalyn invited Nick to place his order and made her own selection. Sooner or later, she'd have to start cooking for herself again. Once she had a kitchen. Until then, whatever came out of Boozie's kitchen more than met the need.

"You'll want to get drinking water, won't you?"

She'd gotten by with bottled water purchased at the gas station until now.

Boozie retrieved a massive plastic handled jug from the back room. "Fill this from the artesian well at Big Bay Park."

"The park?"

"That's where most of us get our drinking water. Lots of sulphur in what comes out of the tap. I imagine that's what you've found at the cottage. Once you're hooked on the artesian spring water, you won't want ordinary."

Emmalyn pictured having to drive someplace for drinking water for the rest of her life. "It's okay to swipe water from the park?"

Boozie tilted her head, her tangle of curls following a split-second later. "It's for the community."

"There's an artesian spring under the lake," Nick said. "It's good water."

"Okay. I'll stop there on my way out."

"It's right by the main parking area. You can't miss the well."

Max and Emmalyn vacationed in Colorado two years into their marriage. She remembered filling buckets from a similar well along a creek right in the middle of a small town near Estes Park. What was the name of that curious little village? Hauling drinking water had been an adventure then. Everything had been an adventure. They'd lingered in the luxury of a couple in love, taken with one another alone, unplugged from their work responsibilities, following their five-year plan flawlessly. The lack of children, intentional the first three years. Intentional. The thought sent a shudder through her. They'd wanted children, of course. By their timetable.

God didn't get the memo.

Water. Yes. She needed water. And oxygen.

Nick took his dirt bike home to exchange it for his mom's truck. Or rather, his dad's truck his mom used to keep the roofing business going. Nick was fatherless for the foreseeable future. Why hadn't Emmalyn made that connection sooner? A young man in trouble. His dad unavailable.

Boozie helped carry the meal to Emmalyn's car. She'd included hot-out-of-the-oven apple crisp for each of them, too, despite Emmalyn's protests.

With the trunk and backseat still full of the only things Emmalyn felt worth rescuing from her previous life, the passenger seat provided the only hauling option. She tucked the plastic water jug on the floor where a passenger's feet would go.

"My one concession to plastic," Boozie said. "It's unfortunate, but unavoidable."

"How did your family get a name like 'Unfortunate,' Boozie? And what's the story behind 'Boozie'?"

Now free of the load she carried, she clasped her hands together. "I wondered how long it would take you to ask."

"I didn't want to be nosy."

"Somewhere many generations ago, a grump-a-saurus member of our family line decided *Fortunato* didn't fit his personality or his station in life."

"And no one changed it back?"

"Personally, I love the irony. I'm one of the most blessed people I know. I'm not my name."

Emmalyn swung the car keys, considering.

"And Boozie," she said, "is not my name at all. It's French. *Bougie*. B-o-u-g-i-e. Pronounced as if it has zhee for the last syllable. Nobody's gotten that right since I entered kindergarten. So I let them adulterate it to Boozie. Makes me an interesting character, don't you think?"

One of many things.

Boozie walked her to the driver's side and gave her a quick hug. "Enjoy this process—bringing light to that cottage. The transformation is likely to take your breath away."

"Sometimes all I can see is the work ahead of me. Thanks." She positioned herself behind the wheel, slid the key into the ignition, then opened her window and leaned out. "Hey, what does *Bougie* mean?"

Already halfway to the door of The Wild Iris, the young woman twirled to respond. "Candle." She courtsied.

Fitting.

"Or spark plug."

Bingo.

The car smelled of warm apples and cinnamon as she drove the seven miles from town to Big Bay State Park. Big Bay Town Park connected to it. Between them, the parks shared two miles of sandy beach, Nick had told her. One of the best-kept secrets of the Midwest, he said. Emmalyn quickly found the artesian well with its sign inviting any who needed to come and drink. Or fill a plastic jug.

She did both, surprised at how cold it was and at the faintly sweet flavor. How much would artesian spring water have cost her by the bottle back in Lexington?

One other car occupied a spot in the parking lot. A dark green SUV with two kayaks on the roof and two bicycles on a rack at the rear of the vehicle. She hoped they hadn't been out on the lake when the storm hit. And where were they now? There, under the shelter house, near the massive stone fireplace. An older couple—maybe in their sixties—sitting on the table part of two picnic tables with their feet on the seat part, facing each other. Talking. Couples are supposed to talk.

The woman tossed her head back, laughing. He grinned and nudged her knee.

Emmalyn couldn't watch anymore. She lugged the full jug of water to the car, snugging it into its resting place on the floor, and turned the car toward the park exit. A squirrel almost lost its life under her tires, acting like it owned the road.

Some other day, when the park wasn't full of reminders, she'd walk the boardwalk and the beach. Not today.

She pulled behind the nameless cottage—it needed a name—moments before Nick and the truck arrived. Good timing.

"I brought work lights," he said. "Kinda dark in there right now."

"I hadn't thought of that. Did you figure you could use the five gallons Bougie . . . Boozie found me the other day?"

He continued to unload gear from the truck. "I'll start with the main living area, so if we have to move to another paint option for the upstairs, no one will notice. But by my calculations, that should be enough, depending on how many coats this takes. I have the sealant primer. And both interior and exterior trim paint."

"Great. Mr. Efficiency."

He ducked his head as if unused to compliments from anyone but his mother.

"Is it a little damp yet for me to paint outside? That was quite the soaker."

"If it were me, I'd wait. Nothing worse than going through all that effort and not getting the results you want."

His words sounded like the fertility clinic complaint department, if they'd had one.

"I haven't gotten to it yet, but hoped to remove more of the upper cupboard doors."

"That would help," he said, maneuvering a pail of paint in one hand and a stepladder in the other.

She unlocked the back door with its key from the key ring. After Nick unburdened himself of the ladder and paint, she reached the key toward him. "Take it. I'll let myself in through the front door key if I'm here and you're not."

He stared at the key in her palm as if hesitant to take it. She nudged it closer to him.

"Thanks, Mrs. Ross. For trusting me with this."

"Do you intend to make a career out of the mistake you made?"

He leaned back. "No."

"I didn't think so." She turned toward the wall of windows and the double doors facing the lake. A weakness in the clouds let a single shaft of light through.

Max's mistake wasn't a career deal either. It was one misguided night. One horribly misguided night.

"Do you have kids, Mrs. Ross?"

Impeccable timing, Nick. "No." How could it take that much courage just to turn to face him? "Why do you ask?"

"You'd make a good mom."

Were there no safe subjects in the world anymore? No topics that wouldn't stir the sediment from the bottom of the well of the uncomfortable? "I left some things in the car. Be right back."

She moved past him and out the back door. Was it raining again or were the trees dripping? She swiped at her face. No, that was her.

9

Within two hours, the place had a new personality. Even the primer coat made a difference. Anywhere Nick's paintbrush or rollers had tracked looked alive for once.

"This is good news," he said, holding an outlet cover in his hands. "There's plenty of insulation in the walls. Probably installed decades ago for winter hunters."

She hadn't thought about insulation.

He seemed so pleased with his discovery. "That would have been disappointing for you to find out later if the place wasn't insulated well." His finger poised over his phone, he said, "Do you mind if I listen to music while I work? The cords on my earbuds get in the way, though."

She stacked another cupboard door against the wall. "Fine." Would she still think so after the cottage shook with whatever twisted band kids listen to these days?

He propped his smartphone on a windowsill and hit PLAY.

A few measures into the song, Emmalyn asked, "Do you mind turning it a little louder?"

"No problem. I wasn't sure you'd be okay with this."

"Very okay." She recognized the worship song as one Bougie's "church" had sung. She hadn't heard the words clearly that night. Ringing through her small cottage now, they made at least as much difference as the paint did. They dropped like warm oil on the bare back of her emotions. *Everlasting hope/shining in our darkness/prison chains won't chain us/hope has freed us/freed us/freed us . . .*

The wet slurping of the paint roller, the scrape of ladder legs, and the music created an odd mix. She didn't mind.

They ate their sandwiches and soup on the front porch, grateful the steps had dried enough by then. Emmalyn thought she might bring the porch furniture over from Stockton's before anything else.

"Have you thought about screening in the porch?" Nick asked between bites.

"I love the unobstructed view of the lake and the fresh air." Captivated by it. But that sounded extreme when talking to a young man so recently captured.

"You won't like the biting flies. Most people up here have at least one screened porch."

"I'll have to consider that." She took a long drink of the artesian water. "Do you plan to stick around, in this area, when you get out on your own?"

"Might. I had plans for college."

"Had?" The breeze brought a faint sour scent of another dead dream. "Don't give up on that idea. What were you intending to study?"

A pause miles wide spoke of pain or confusion or a hesitance to let his temporary employer into his thoughts. She couldn't blame him. For years, she'd used the same pauses as fillers in her conversations with those closest to her. She drew in a breath, hoping a safer question would come with it.

"I've been afraid or"—he clinked his spoon around the soup mug's empty interior—"curious about what I no longer qualify for."

Emmalyn waited.

"With my record."

Waited.

He stopped clinking. "Do they let ex-cons major in Economics, graduate with an MBA, get a business loan?"

Her stomach tightened. Her mind entertained questions like that in the middle of the night for Max. What would Max do when he'd paid his debt to society? "I don't know, Nick. You'd like to start your own business someday?"

He set his mug on the porch railing. "I used to think so."

"What kind of business?"

Forearms draped over his knees, hands hanging, he stared at his feet. "Something like what my uncle did. I'd run it differently, but, yeah. Kayak rentals. Guided tours. Ice cave hikes and cross-country skiing in the winter. The Apostle Islands are incredible." He shrugged.

Except for the complications of his jail time and his reputation, the dream didn't seem shrug-worthy. Under other circumstances, she would have encouraged him to go after it. Maybe she still should.

It had been a long time since Max would allow a conversation about the future. Early in his incarceration, when they were still talking, if she voiced the words, "When you're released . . . " or "When you get out . . . " he'd change the subject. Was he an older version of the young man sitting on her cottage porch with a rap sheet and a foggy future?

Nick stood. "Gotta get back to work. Thanks for lunch. I can bring my own from now on."

"I don't mind."

"I'll . . . bring my own."

So. He didn't like her prying either.

Prying, Max? You think my wanting to know what happened that night is prying? You're my husband! We're supposed to be a team. One flesh and all that.

She'd regretted her tone the minute she felt it scraping against her own eardrums. He hadn't answered. Not their finest hour as a married couple.

When was that? Their finest hour?

A rogue breeze stirred the sea grass between her and the water's edge. She thought she heard it say, "It's yet to come."

The post office in LaPointe closes for the day at 4:15, as reliably as the ferry. Emmalyn had missed its open hours three days in a row. With Nick entrenched in the painting project and very little she could do on the interior until that was finished, she drove into LaPointe expressly to see if the General Delivery slot held any mail for her, and to rent a post office box.

The small brass door on Box 57 swung open on her third attempt at the combination. It felt weightier in her hands than she expected. Real brass. With a permanence to it. She was a resident. Officially. Not just a property owner. Six-month box lease? She'd opted for a year.

Leap of faith.

In Lexington, she would have shuffled through the stack of mail while she walked, looking for any tidbit more interesting than a political ad or a coupon for cheap Internet. Anything. Not necessarily a letter from a man with an eight-digit number behind his name, but . . .

A post office the size of an ice cream truck didn't seem the place to shuffle through disappointment. She waited until she got back in the car. And there it was. Double-whammy. No note from Max, not that she expected it. But a letter from her mother. Another from her sister Tia. And—let's make it a full house—one from her sister Shawna. All three in one day? People seek counseling for lesser ills than that.

Her mother's Palmer Method of cursive—old school and pinched, despite its curves—fit her personality. Tia's inventive half-cursive/half-printing penmanship evoked a smile. Tia understood Emmalyn better than most, but Tia's alternating half-empty/half-full outlook exhausted her if they spent much time together. And Shawna. Even Mom called her a "piece of work." Code for "prepare to shake your head in disbelief at the way that woman thinks."

Three letters in one day? They could have called or texted if they'd wanted to reach her. She rifled through the small stack one more time. Nothing from Max. One of these days, she'd have to write and tell him she had to sell the house.

Eenie, meenie, miney . . . Mother. Emmalyn slid her finger under the scalloped flap of the envelope and extracted a precisely folded note.

We're coming and that's that. What were you thinking, taking off to the ends of the earth as if we don't matter? Well, we can talk about that when we get there. We're coming in November. On the eleventh.

Emmalyn held the note at arm's length, as if the action would change the contents. She read two more paragraphs of community trivia about which Emmalyn had little interest, followed by her mother's traditional "Much love, Mom" benediction.

We? The second letter explained. Her mother *and* both sisters.

The eleventh. She had three weeks to make the cottage habitable and patch together the parts of her that were still unhinged. The cottage would be the easier project.

Shawna's letter reminded Emmalyn she was allergic to dogs, so "keep that in mind, sweetie." Good reason to get a dog.

Tia's began, "What do you hear from Max these days?" She meant well.

They were coming. Madeline Island's first locust invasion.

And for that attitude, Bougie would have her scrubbing bathroom floors with a toothbrush, if Emmalyn wasn't careful. Conditions of probation: *Embrace the prickly and assume the best.* Emmalyn's family barely registered on the dysfunction scale, compared to others. But since Max's deep dive, their love felt smothering. Lovingly judgmental.

She composed a mental text to Max, one she couldn't send: *Mother and sisters coming. Pray for me.*

Before it all fell apart, he probably would have enfolded her from behind if she made a request for prayer. He would have known she was being facetious. Prayer hadn't been important to either of them. Not until they started trying to have a baby. At a time like this, Max would have read through her whining, burrowed his face in her neck and breathed, "It'll be okay. I'll protect you from them." His whisper would have melted her into his comfort. He'd meant words like that. Back then. She struggled to recapture what that felt like—to be protected, cherished, to have him understand her quirky family, her quirky reactions to them, and love her anyway.

Her skin shivered from the effort of trying to recall. She'd conditioned herself not to need his reassurance. Almost five touchless years now, plus the season before sentencing. Would she face a lifetime of touchless tomorrows?

She had to stop doing that, flattening her palm against her everlastingly flat belly, as if pressing her waif nose against the glass of a shop of expensive dolls she couldn't afford. A child would have made their family complete. Two is a couple waiting to become a family. A family = (1 + 1) + 1 or more.

Max believed that once, too. Then he started interjecting Ugly Math: A family = 1 + 1. If he meant it to comfort her after another failed attempt, he had to know it didn't.

He had to know.

But then again, *he* already had a child.

Nick finished the painting on time as promised, including the cupboard faces. The cottage interior transformed from dark gray-brown to soft white, except for the floors, which still needed attention. She'd have to cross the moat to the mainland and rent a power sander, pick up whatever kind of poly coat the refinishing guy recommended, and make a trip to Duluth or Ashland for mattresses and the essentials Mr. Stockton's mother's hidden treasures couldn't supply.

Emmalyn stood in the pool of light from the kitchen sky-light—best idea ever—and looked across the living area to the view through the lakeside windows and windowed double doors. Once the floors were done, the slate would be clean, as if the waves had swept through the cottage and dislodged any bits of staleness, darkness, and washed them out to sea.

A snap from behind shot through her. She whirled toward the sound, deep in the bowels of the lower cupboards. Another victim of her trap line. If it weren't for the whole litter box issue, she'd get a cat.

Apparently the waves hadn't swept everything away.

She backed toward the front entrance, choosing to wait until the rodent was "really, most sincerely dead" before emptying the trap and resetting it. Small as the cottage was—in comparison to every home she and Max shared in their nine minus five years together—her footsteps hurt her ears with their hollowness. Who wanted to listen to every footstep? The furniture, pillows, and area rug would help muffle empty echoes. Wouldn't they?

Emmalyn rested her hand on the doorknob. Something had been deposited on her front porch. Rather, it sat there. A small white dog so still, Emmalyn had to look closer to ensure it wasn't a stuffed animal.

"Friend or foe, buddy?" She opened the door a crack. "Where did you come from?"

One ear twitched.

She crouched to make herself less threatening. She must have read that tip online. "Who do you belong to?"

Long lashes blinked, dislodging some of the mop of hair that hung in front of the dog's dark eyes.

"You're not coming in, just so you know."

The mop opened its mouth in a canine version of a grin.

"Seriously." Emmalyn slipped onto the porch and shut the door behind her, not locking it in case she needed a quick escape from a ferocious five-pound puddle of fluff. She bent with the back of her hand extended toward the animal. "Hi, little one." She kept her voice medium pitched and light. "Can I see if you have a collar?"

Emmalyn scratched the dog behind its ears while she felt for a collar. Nothing. It remained motionless. Such soft fur. Cockashon? Part cocker spaniel, part bichon? Wasn't that the breed Tia drooled over? The patch of caramel brown on its face framed an expression an artist or photographer would have found enchanting. Emmalyn would have, too, if she'd wanted a dog. Which she didn't.

She scanned up and down the beach. No tourists. No islanders. No obvious owners. The dog didn't appear to be traumatized in any way. But neither did it move.

"What's your name?" Emmalyn asked. Weren't all questions directed to dogs rhetorical? Wasn't *that* question rhetorical, too? She sank to the steps and called, "Come." The dog trotted over on short legs and climbed into Emmalyn's lap, lifting its face as if to say, "I thought you'd never ask."

Emmalyn reached into the outside pocket of her canvas tote-bag and withdrew the paper-wrapped leftovers from her lunch. Until she got a garbage can with a lock-down lid, she wasn't leaving any food scraps at the cottage. Bears and raccoons didn't need any help being annoying. The dog sniffed at the crust of bread, then snatched it politely. A dainty eater?

When finished, the dog rearranged itself, crawling upward to lay its head on Emmalyn's shoulder. With a sigh, it settled into immobility again. Breathing in and out. Content to be there. With her.

"I need a cat, not a dog," she whispered, mildly concerned about offending the creature.

It nuzzled into her neck.

"You can't make me like you." She stroked the silky fluff of fur on its back, felt the warmth of its body under her hand and against her chest. "You have to go home. And I have a pathologically hard time saying good-bye to things I love. So . . . "

How many minutes did they sit like that, with the shadows deepening and the water gentling to its dusk pace?

The voice in her head said, "You, animal, are not what I need."

Contrary to popular opinion, dogs must not read minds. This one ignored Emmalyn's internal thoughts. It slept like a newborn, limp against her shoulder, dependent on Emmalyn to keep it from falling.

Didn't it realize her parenting history made it *more* likely it would fall?

I don't have time for this. Core-deep, a thick warmth spread through her. Karo-syrup thick. Maybe she had a little time.

A flock of seabirds too far from shore to identify circled, dipped, fluttered. They lifted from the surface of the water in a frenzy of sunset-flecked wings and caw-noise. Their flock formed an ever-changing shape against the backdrop of sky. Rising, dropping toward the water, morphing into another dance form and rising again. She watched until they leaped offstage, to waters beyond her view. Waters gone by.

She removed her dog shoulder pad and set it on the top step while she stood. It blinked awake and looked at her as if awaiting further instructions.

"Come on. Let's find out where you came from, so I can get back to . . . " To her monastery room at The Wild Iris. "Come on."

She led the way to the beach, eyeing the sand for paw prints. None. The animal must have taken a path through the woods. The leaf-strewn yard yielded no clues. "Dog, you have to go home." She pointed in a wide circle. "Wherever that is."

The dog followed when she walked and sat at her feet when she stopped.

"You didn't parachute out of the sky. You had to have come from somewhere. We all do."

That reminded her. Her mother and sisters were coming. Soon. Too soon. If the cottage wasn't ready, they'd be forced to stay in LaPointe. Or Bayfield. Tempting, but inhospitable of her. If the dog stayed, The Allergic would need a room in town. Time to shake the dog from her feet and move from onsite to offsite planning.

And a cup of strong tea.

She locked the cottage door, nodded goodnight to the beach as had become her habit, and told the dog to stay while she climbed behind the wheel of her car. She lowered the driver's side window and pointed at the fluff pile and its melted chocolate eyes with another firm, "Stay!"

It did.

That meant she was alone on the drive back to The Wild Iris. More alone than usual.

10

The day of inevitability had dawned. Endless cleanup and detail painting at the cottage took a hiatus for a few hours while Emmalyn Ross perched on a vinyl chair, listening for the coin-operated washing machines to signal they had finished their loads. Her loads.

Not a scene she envisioned witnessing much less living. Her clothes sloshed and thumped their way through the cycles while she breathed through the weighted smell of laundry detergent, fabric softeners of various ilks, and toasted dryer lint. She should have asked Bougie to loan her a book to read. Too many hands had pawed through the dog-eared magazines on the counter. The only book in Emmalyn's room was the obligatory Bible on the dresser, the room's guest log, and the "Letters to Max" journal Cora gave her. She'd brought the journal for the sloshing duration.

Dear Max,

I'm living a public laundry life.

The words stared back at her from the page. True on so many levels. The undies of their inability to have children together had hung on the lines of the neighborhood and eventually the local press. Different reason. Now she sat in a windowed room with institutional washing machines and commercial dryers tossing her bras and panties, her blouses and slacks, in front of their round glass doors. The cottage had no room for a washer and dryer. Even after she moved in, this scene would be part of her routine from now on.

At one time, she might have found it socially demeaning—right or wrong. Now, having a place to clean her clothes felt like a gift, despite the lack of ambiance. A—there was that word again—blessing.

The rhythm of the giant dryers hypnotizes me, Max. Why? Something I can count on, I guess. Around and around and around. I wonder if you ever got another promotion in the prison laundry, like you hoped. Wish I could ask you.

And she did. She couldn't deny that she wished she could ask him. Her heart bumped unevenly like a tennis shoe in an empty dryer drum. She didn't mind being alone as much as she minded being without him.

Dangerous thoughts. Time to focus on the task at hand—creating a list for her trip to the mainland on the weekend. Bougie said she should check out the coffee shop in Bayfield and take time to visit the artists' co-op gallery across the street. It would be fun to find local artwork for the walls of the cottage.

Fun. She tested the word again. She'd used it without thinking—a word she'd retired from her vocabulary so long ago it tasted dusty now.

The Great Lake air was getting to her. The freshwater sea—less than a block away from the smell of dryer sheets and . . . oh, too funny . . . Tide.

"Roasted beet salad?" Bougie's question substituted for, "Welcome home. How was your day?"

"Sounds great." Emmalyn's response floated on laughter. "Bougie, you've spoiled me so thoroughly, it's going to be a shock to my system when I have to go back to cooking for myself."

"Goat cheese. Lemon basil vinaigrette. Arugula."

"Stop! I'm sold already. I must say it's an unusual late-evening snack."

Bougie adjusted the heather scarf looped around her neck. "I tried it out on the church crowd tonight."

"How did that go over?"

"Too many meat eaters among them. Not enough root vegetable appreciators." She released the disappointment with a flick of her hand. "I have hope for you, though."

Emmalyn snatched the pottery mug with M on its base and headed for the fireplace table. "Because I'm an ex-caterer?"

Bougie planted her hands on the back of the opposite chair. "About that . . . " Eyebrows raised, a corner of her bottom lip caught between her teeth, head tilted to one side. Her expression said, "I might as well start with the apology part."

"What is it?"

"Let me get your salad. I had mine with a cup of our tomato bisque."

"Perfect."

"Then we'll talk."

"Let me help."

"Hold that thought." Bougie disappeared into the kitchen and left Emmalyn alone with the aqua canning jar of late-season wildflowers in the middle of the table, a small chalkboard leaning against its base. On the chalkboard, Bougie's flourished penmanship had written, "Hope lives here. Even here."

She could replicate that look on a greeting card—old school framed chalkboard—and mail the message to Max. Could. Should. Would. Even after all this time, he might not open mail from her. But she had to send it. He needed to hear it.

She needed to hear it.

Even here.

"Sleeping, praying, or contemplating?" Bougie placed a long, narrow, rectangular plate before her.

She didn't remember closing her eyes, or leaning her head against the wing of the chair. If prayer could take the form of a soul-deep sigh, then . . .

"Contemplating."

"This is one of my favorite spots for that activity," Bougie said. "When the day quiets. With the fire chasing the chill." Her face brightened. "I have the most decadent hot chocolate for later. It's as rich as pudding. Impossibly soothing."

Half woman/half sage. What a fascinating mix. A candle. A sparkplug. A new definition of *friend*?

A small white cup on the rectangular plate held the tomato bisque. The cup slid on the plate when Emmalyn touched it. "Have you tried using a square of nori under the soup cup? To keep it from scooting?"

"See?" Bougie directed her question to the ceiling. "I knew it!" She opened her arms, palms up. "Thank you."

Was Emmalyn supposed to say, "You're welcome"? Such a small tidbit of advice. Was Bougie even talking to her?

"That's exactly the kind of help I was hoping to get. Oh. You should have stopped me. Sorry."

"For what?"

"You know. That's a great idea. Save grace for after the meal. I do that sometimes, too. Adds a new depth of meaning. Nothing holy should ever be automatic. Dedication? Yes. Routine? No."

Emmalyn kept an eye on Bougie and dipped her spoon into the soup. How did the woman draw such depth of flavor from such simple ingredients? "Do you have roasted red peppers blended in this, too?"

"Shh," Bougie warned. "Some of my customers think they don't like red peppers. But they love the tomato bisque. A culinary secret isn't a sin, is it?"

Why would she ask Emmalyn? The young woman presumed a much deeper connection with issues of divine importance than Emmalyn could boast. She smiled. "Your secret's safe with me."

Bougie pushed up the sleeves of what looked like thermal underwear. The perfect accompaniment to her ecru crocheted peasant skirt. The fashion intricacies she pulled off . . .

"M, *your* secret would be safe with me, too."

"My tomato bisque seems amateurish compared to yours."

"I don't mean soup secrets."

The fire crackled as if the logs were real, the flames consuming them. Yet they remained unchanged—a dead giveaway of their insincerity. Their pretend status. Emmalyn turned her head and stared into the flames that tried so hard to make people think they were real.

"If I'm going to hire you," Bougie said, softer now, "I don't need to know your whole story. But I think I'm entitled to bits of it as your friend."

She'd used the word *friend*, too.

"What story?" Emmalyn poured her visual attention into the soup.

"You're *the* Emmalyn Ross. Here's the apology part. I *detectived* you."

"What?"

"That's what my little brother used to call it when he investigated something."

Emmalyn set aside the soup spoon. "You had me followed?"

"Well, that wouldn't take much on an island this small, would it? No, I used the Internet." Bougie smiled broadly and arched her back, as if relishing her accomplishment.

"And you discovered . . . ?"

"That you didn't just 'do a little catering.' Executive chef at Balow's? M, why didn't you say something?"

All the weariness of the day's labor, which included the ever-present stare of a small canine project foreman, gathered itself into a heap and hung like a dental X-ray drape on her chest. "That was a past life."

"I didn't have to look long to find plenty about your culinary exploits. And here, I've been serving you ordinary Wild Iris fare." Bougie pointed to the as yet unfinished soup.

"This is anything but ordinary, Bougie. You have a nice thing going. You've got a keen sense of taste, and an obvious talent for this."

Bougie clasped her hands together and wedged them between her knees. "I knew there was more to your story. And there still is."

Emmalyn waited. If she'd been online . . .

"I don't need to know your whole story," she repeated. "But I think you need to tell. Don't you? We're all broken. All of us. What does that look like for you?"

Emmalyn waited for the typical hardening in her stomach, the familiar tightening in her lungs and throat, for the suppressed growl alarm that signaled someone had gotten too close to her truth. She'd been known to abandon family bonds over less than what Bougie asked. She waited for the crisp, crackling words that would shut down the conversation to burst from her mouth. They too had taken the night off. She was left alone with the truth and a friend's listening ear.

"My husband's in prison."

Bougie leaned forward, not back, as expected. "What put him there?"

Emmalyn sipped her tea and breathed courage in its jasmine aroma. If Bougie were as thorough at *detectiving* as Cora, she had to know most of it. "A freak accident. The court couldn't prove Max intended to ram the fertility clinic with our SUV. There was an issue with the accelerator—massive recall just weeks after the accident. And the court assumed the homeless man leaning on the wall of the clinic that night wasn't a target but 'collateral damage' from Max's intoxication, although Max wasn't a drinker. But he was deemed responsible."

"Your Max believes it was his fault?"

"We all know it was his fault." Emmalyn would have retracted the flatline of her words, but they hung in the air like swamp fog.

"What a heavy load for him." Bougie rubbed her upper arms then tugged the sleeves of her thermal top to the wrists.

"For *him*?"

Bougie reached to smooth the tablecloth in front of her. "Guilt quadruples gravity's effect. It's not easy staying upright with that kind of pressure pushing against a person." She used her palms like a panini press. "How's he handling it?"

"I wouldn't know."

At that, Bougie leaned back in her chair, clutched her hands together and pressed her thumbnails against her lips. Eventually, she lowered her hands and whispered, "He got a prison divorce? Such a sadness that it's so easy for the incarcerated to divorce a spouse. A handful of dollars and it's done. What if our prisons invested in—?"

"Bougie! We're not divorced. He suggested it four years ago. I said no."

"He could have pushed it through anyway. With or without your consent."

For a split second, Emmalyn let the faint comfort linger. "How do you know so much about details like that?"

"I know too many things."

"And yet, you keep soaring."

Bougie's smile bloomed and spread, folding the skin near her eyes into starbursts. "Grace always outweighs gravity."

A sweet sentiment. Miles away from Emmalyn's reality. "He won't let me contact him."

"Like he has much say in that." Bougie's laughter effervesced the entire room.

"He asked me not to contact him."

"What made you agree to that ridiculous request?"

"You were supposed to say, 'Oh, that's too bad.'" Emmalyn stabbed a roasted beet from the plate of salad. She painted a deep red smear with it on the bright white surface of the plate.

"Part of the dichotomy. I empathize. But I empathize too much not to tell it straight. And part of your dichotomy is loving a man who tells you he doesn't want you to. And you believed him." She shook her head, the attendant *tsk-tsk* silent.

"I don't know how to sustain a marriage with this much . . . distance . . . between us."

"And neither does he, apparently." Bougie reached to rub Emmalyn's shoulder.

"What's that phrase? 'If you love it, let it go'?" Emmalyn affected nonchalance.

Bougie's mouth formed a shape a trombone player would envy. Her eyebrows showed her intent to speak before the words came out. "'If you love it, set it *free*.' Not the same thing."

Emmalyn stifled the wholly inappropriate grin over Bougie's facial expressions. "Sounds the same."

Trombone lips became trumpet lips. Then flute. "Not the same."

"There's more to the story." Emmalyn's neck itched with heat.

"I'd have been surprised if there weren't."

"Max is . . . " She paused. Why would her mouth not stop the hemorrhage of information? "Max is the reason we'll never have a child."

"The sole reason?"

Between the effects of the tea and the soup, her internal temperature rose several degrees. She should push away from the table, away from Bougie's prying questions, and retreat to her room. Her instincts told her to go . . . and told her to stay. How do you reconcile a war like that?

The sole reason? No. It was partly her. Partly him. Them. Their insanely busy schedules early in their marriage. Their dwindling resources from failed fertility attempts . . . their carefully orchestrated five-year-plan that turned into three years of trying plus a five-year prison sentence.

And the unspoken expense—the child support he—they—paid. An indiscretion and dissolved relationship shortly before he met Emmalyn netted Max a daughter he supported but rarely saw. A daughter who reminded Emmalyn daily that Max's ex-girlfriend gave him a child and Emmalyn never would. Capped by yet another complication her gynecologist suspected was pre-menopause that flirted with Emmalyn just as their fertility counselor started to form the question, "Do you think there's any point in our continuing this pursuit?"

The sole reason? No. "Hope was slim. Max's incarceration guaranteed even that wafer-thin chance was taken away."

"If only you didn't love him . . . " Bougie let the words hover, swirl in the air around them, show their true colors.

Her nose burned. Her vision blurred. Tears she'd repressed scalded her eyes on their way out. Rising tides propelled by a strong current break through human attempts to sandbag. Bougie left her, but returned with a peace offering—tissues. Plural. How did she know one wouldn't be enough?

Emmalyn spent a couple of years' worth of tears before her vision cleared. Bougie's small, caring hand must have rested on her forearm the whole time. It was still there, rubbing and patting in no particular rhythm. The young woman hadn't attempted to say anything while Emmalyn cried. Where had Bougie learned the gift of wordlessness at a time like this? What had she been through that trained her in the art of comfort?

Emmalyn sniffed, blew her nose, sniffed again. "There goes my reputation for refinement and sophistication."

"Good. Now you can be real."

Emmalyn lifted her head to look Bougie in the eyes. Tears glistened on her young friend's cheeks. Emmalyn meant the refinement statement as a joke. "I've thought about writing to him again."

"Because . . . ?"

If she hung a shingle, Bougie could get paid good money to drag people's emotions through her obstacle courses.

"Because it's the right thing to do. No matter what he says."

"And? Don't think about it. First thing that pops into your mind."

"And I miss him."

The look of satisfaction on Bougie's face forced a fit of laughter from a well within Emmalyn as deep as her repository of tears. She held the sides of her head and closed her eyes, letting the laughter exhaust itself. "I miss him. Which means I love him. Which means I'm a fool if I don't fight to get him back."

"And there you go." Bougie's exaggerated Greek accent started the laughter again. "Have you seen the sea caves, M?"

How could that question in any way relate to—? By now, Emmalyn knew that in Bougie's mind, they connected seamlessly. "When Max and I were in the area years ago. Early in our marriage. Impressive."

"Deep caverns carved into solid rock by this." She dipped a finger into her tea and let a drop of it fall back into the mug.

"Tea did that?" Emmalyn nodded a skeptical agreement.

"The water. Water cut wide pockets out of solid rock. Rooms full of wonder from the action of this"—she dipped her finger again—"on this." She tapped the fireplace rock behind them.

"And the moral of the story is . . . ?"

"You throw enough love up against a stony heart and it's bound to crumble, sooner or later."

"Not every kind of rocky shoreline has caves like that. Some rock doesn't . . . cave."

Bougie wiped her finger on her napkin. "If he's a good man, he will."

"He's a good man." No more imperfect than she was.

"What's the worst that can happen?"

Emmalyn could have told a cardiologist which specific arteries in her heart were blocked, judging by the stab of pain. "Rejection. Humiliation. Embarrassment."

"Oh, those," Bougie said, dismissing the thoughts with a wave of her hand. "Grace outweighs them, too."

"I don't know how to do this." Emmalyn sensed she was pulling her feet, one at a time, from wet concrete on a 320-mile highway that led to Max's prison cell. "And by morning, I may wonder why I should."

11

Bayfield shimmered in the early morning light when Emmalyn drove her car off the ferry, through the parking lot, around the corner, and up the hill on Rittenhouse Avenue. The coffee shop—as unassuming as they come—nodded a greeting that suggested she'd find fortification within its walls. She ordered the daily brew and a crustless, muffin-shaped quiche with roasted red peppers and joined a handful of other patrons in the adjoining eat-in area. It looked as if a hole had been punched between two narrow storefronts to double the size of the coffee shop. Pressed tin ceiling, coffee crate tables, plump leather couches and chairs, South American burlap coffee bag pillows, and a coffee-colored hardwood floor invited her to linger.

The day stretched long and full before her. But she accepted the invitation to soak in her surroundings for a few minutes. As she sipped, she thumbed through a Bayfield area attractions brochure and eavesdropped on local conversations. Emmalyn smiled. She almost missed the sound of a cookie jar lid.

A touristy newspaper listed a unique mix of advertisers, including a hardware store in Washburn, just to the south on Highway 13. She keyed the phone number into her cell phone contacts list. Time to get serious. She'd call after she exited the coffee shop rather than force the conversation onto people who really didn't care whether or not her cottage floors were a mess.

The sweet rhythm of life floated between the two rooms. An artist on her way to take her turn staffing the co-op gallery across the street. The bookstore manager, who'd apparently hung a "Closed for Coffee" sign on the door of her shop near the art gallery. Two men discussing politics. A young mom with a little one in a snuggle sling that hung only slightly higher than where the baby had floated in amniotic fluid weeks earlier. The mom soothed the child with a hand on the curve of its back while she propped a book on the table with the other hand. She used her elbow to hold the book open to her spot when she picked up her coffee cup and bent her head to the cup.

The woman caught Emmalyn staring. "He naps better here than he does at home in his cradle," she said.

Emmalyn's smile wasn't broad, but surprisingly heartfelt. A small victory. She was happy for someone else's blessing.

Yes, Max would have appreciated this place. Would appreciate it one day soon, she hoped. He'd make easy conversation with the men and find something kind to say to the proprietors. He'd notice details like the extra narrow restroom doors and find them as amusing as she did. He'd comment on the rich, dark flooring. Maybe she should rethink finishing the cottage floors in a light stain.

Fortified for the heavy decision-making the day promised, she exited the coffee shop and placed the first call.

"Yes. We rent floor sanders," the phone voice said. "By the half-day, day, or week. What's the square footage?"

Mid-discussion, a tap on her shoulder jarred her. Cora. Emmalyn held up one finger to signal she'd soon be done on the phone. Cora nodded and moved a few steps away to wait.

The estimate for the sander and polyurethane jostled her more than the shoulder tap. Even with all that work, all those hours—days, really—the floor would still be rustic at best. What other option did she have?

"Bad news?" Cora was at her elbow again.

If Emmalyn had filled out a friend-match application, she couldn't have imagined either Bougie or Cora would have popped up as likely options. But she'd already grown to treasure their companionship and counsel. Cora's question was rooted in genuine concern. Emmalyn could see it in her eyes. "Not bad, necessarily. Mildly disturbing."

"Want to get a cup of coffee and talk about it?"

"Just came from there. I was headed to Washburn to rent a floor sander for the cottage. Now, I'm not sure."

"Do you plan to cover the water damage in the kitchen area with a big old rug or something? It may not sand out to a color that blends well with the rest of the floor unless you sand deep, and that can hurt the look of the grain."

Crisp leaves danced around their feet on the wide sidewalk on Rittenhouse. The breeze held a hint of the winter months around life's corner. Emmalyn flipped up the collar on her jacket.

Cora waved her to follow. "I'm on my way to my favorite indulgence. It looks as if you could use some, too."

"I don't drink." Especially since the disastrous night after Max's attempts to drown his misery, if that's what it was. Why hadn't anyone seriously considered the effects of his sleep aid? Bizarre behavior like his—acting intoxicated, fleeing the scene, not remembering having done so, even the frantic call with no explanation—were all over the medical news.

Cora turned and called over her shoulder, "Drink? Who said anything about drinking?"

"What are you talking about, then?"

Cora didn't explain until they'd entered one of the gift shops, bypassed the main floor of the shop, and climbed the wide worn stairs to the second floor display area. The island's multitasker straightened her posture. Arms extended, she glowed as she said, "This! Yarn!"

"Yarn is your indulgence?"

"Have you *looked* at it?"

Emmalyn took in the sight—the entire second floor of the store devoted to yarn, wool, knitting needles, crochet hooks, cotton thread, patterns, instruction books. And the yarns were unlike any she was accustomed to. Alpaca, merino, blends in colors that looked like a Monet painting.

"You need a warm scarf," Cora said. "I don't mind making your first one for you. After that, you're on your own. Pick a color you like."

"One?"

Cora's laughter warmed the room. "Narrowing it down is the hardest part. Ooh! Look at these." She pulled a skein from a cubby along the wall.

"I could rent a floor sander for the price of a handknit sweater."

"Not nearly as much fun, though. Do you like this one? It's as soft as doeskin."

They worked their way halfway around the room before Emmalyn said, "I wouldn't have dreamed you'd have time to knit, Cora."

The woman's expression registered just shy of shock. "You don't knit because you have too much time on your hands. You knit to create."

Apparently the whole world knew that, except Emmalyn.

Within minutes, the idea captivated her. Colors, textures, possibilities. A long winter lay ahead.

"Does knitting help get you through January, February, March?"

Cora didn't lift her gaze from a set of circular bamboo needles. "And loss. And loneliness. And days like today when I'm ticked at my husband." She looked up then. "Is that so shocking? That the Semper Fi wife of a military man on deployment to one of the most dangerous places on earth would dare get angry with a guy giving his life for his country?"

Emmalyn searched the recesses of her mind for something to say in response. Nothing came.

"Frankly, today I'm ticked *because* he's giving his life for his country. How's that for sacrilegious, blasphemous, and unpatriotic all in one lump?"

"Well . . . " Still nothing.

"Oh, I'll get over it. I figure these four skeins of imported wool ought to do it." Cora hugged them to her chest and sighed. "Or not."

The two had more in common than Emmalyn realized. "How do you keep going?" She'd voiced it aloud. Emmalyn feigned interest in samples of outrageously patterned handknit socks and a soft-as-goosedown baby layette of sweater, cap, and booties. Cora didn't have to answer.

But she did. "Figuring that out as we go along. After this many deployments, you'd think we'd have it mastered, wouldn't you? Every day is a 'Jesus, Help Me' day."

"I can't imagine that kind of worry, always concerned about his being in harm's way."

"Oh. His safety. Yes, that too."

"What did you think I was talking about?" Emmalyn peeked around a display to catch Cora's gaze.

"Marriage."

The dead tissue surrounding Emmalyn's heart twitched. One spasm after another.

"You know better than most, I'm sure." Cora's voice dropped low, as if the empty room had other ears than theirs. "It's not easy keeping a marriage healthy with that much distance between you. How do I make him know he's a valuable part of this family when he has practically no influence over what goes on back here while he's gone? Sure, we have email and texting and video now, when he isn't *incommunicado*. But it is not the same. And not every military family gets a surprise reunion on national television, just so you know. Some of us slug it out to the end. It takes a lot of hard work to keep a marriage alive when everything's changed."

Emmalyn's thoughts darted in and out of the folds of her brain. "I can't get his opinion on what to do about the cottage floors."

"I can't get Wayne's opinion on whether or not to replace the transmission on the company truck or junk it and get a new one."

The collar Emmalyn had turned up constricted her oxygen supply. "I can't ask Max to scratch that spot in the middle of my back that I can't reach."

"I can't rub the knot out of Wayne's neck, the one he gets when he sleeps on a bad pillow."

"I can't ask him what he was thinking the night everything fell apart for us."

Cora pinched her lips together. The lines relaxed as she whispered, "I can't tell Wayne I'm still upset with him for re-enlisting when we'd decided he wouldn't."

"Oh, Cora."

"But I love him and we need each other and we're as committed as tea bags dunked in the same cup of hot water." Cora sobered. "I don't want us to have to start from scratch on our relationship when he gets home."

Emmalyn sought out the curved comfort of the repurposed church pew now used as a bench for weary shoppers.

Cora joined her, took what looked like a toes-deep breath and added, "Wayne and I can't afford to let resentment make our marriage a glow-in-the-dark target for destruction. Do you know what the statistics are for divorce among military families?"

"Do you know what the stats are for divorce among the incarcerated?"

From the base of the stairs came a voice that said, "If you ladies need any help up there, just ask."

The two women looked at each other as if the question were utterly ridiculous. *Any* help?

Their synchronized "Thank you" ended in suppressed laughter that snorted through their noses and *phlpt*-ed through their lips. Cora bent over her armful of wool, then reared back, rattling the bench. The two couldn't look at each other without another fit of hysteria.

"That's . . . " Cora gasped. "That's one way we get through it."

"Embracing insanity?"

Cora bumped her, shoulder to shoulder. "Finding humor to pad the pain."

"And knitting?"

"Knitting. Yes." Cora stroked the lanolin-rich fibers of one of the skeins in her lap. "Knitting. We can do this."

The adrenalin of laughter faded. Emmalyn lost her will to let her thought remain unspoken. "I don't think I can do this."

"Maybe I just have a stronger God than you do." Cora said it as if it weren't an offense but an observation.

"Same God," Emmalyn said, emphasizing the weight of each word.

"Oh. Then . . . "

The silence stretched, growing thinner and thinner until it could no longer sustain itself. A few weeks earlier, Emmalyn wouldn't have imagined she would be the one to break anyone's silence. "I like this color." She rose and reached for a robin's egg blue.

Cora swiped at the corner of one eye. "Beautiful. It'll look great with your dark hair. Long scarf or short?"

"Can you do *this*?" She pointed to a display with a bulky rectangular scarf, asymmetrically buttoned at the collarbone level with a jar-lid sized wooden button.

"Can I? Prepare to be amazed." Cora's hand flourish reminded Emmalyn of a flamenco dancer. It wouldn't have surprised her in the least to discover Cora moonlighted in that role.

They gathered their purchases and headed downstairs to the checkout counter. "Someday when I have more time, I need to explore this level of the shop."

"Ah," Cora said. "Your flooring problem remains."

Emmalyn watched the shop owner key in Cora's items. "Are you buying those bamboo knitting needles?"

Cora's smile was a combination of grace and mischief. "My gift to you and the health of your marriage."

"Bamboo."

"Renewable resource and all that."

No endless cycle of sanding, tack cloths, poly coat, sanding, tack cloths, poly coat . . . "I wonder how much it would cost to put bamboo flooring in the cottage."

"One of my favorites."

The shop owner agreed.

"And if that dog keeps hanging around . . . " Emmalyn let the sentence drop.

"What dog?" Cora took her bag of purchases and receipt. "I didn't know you had a dog."

"I didn't either. It keeps showing up."

"Fluffy little thing with the cutest white and brown face you've ever seen?"

"It's your dog, Cora?"

"No. Not mine. I think it's made the rounds of every residence on Madeline Island at one time or another. It stays for a while, then disappears to show up someplace else."

Emmalyn's heart hollowed again. She hadn't thought she wanted the dog to choose her cottage as its home. She must have been wrong.

"It's the weirdest thing. She seems to show up where she's most needed. A new widower's house. Someone with a prodigal son or daughter. A house with a woman battling cancer. A young teen who broke her leg in gymnastics and needed a companion content to sit beside her. Then, after a while, she'll take off to who knows where and show up someplace else. We just call her Dog."

"Who does she really belong to?"

"I think her original owner may have been a tourist two summers ago, or someone on the island for a day trip. It's too far to swim from Bayfield. We think of her as ours, collectively."

Cora and Emmalyn exited the store, braced against the breeze but turning their faces toward the autumn sun. "Were we talking about bamboo?" Cora asked.

"I thought it might hold up to dog traffic. But it's not that I have a dog."

"But you might."

"Temporarily."

Cora waved at a passing motorist. "Everything's temporary, Emmalyn. And everyone. We love them while we have them."

Cora's son Nick had experience laying flooring, too. Emmalyn entertained the fleeting thought that she might single-handedly pay for his college education with her cottage projects, if she could have afforded it.

She'd anticipated the initial expenses to ready the cottage. The bamboo flooring cut deeply into her budget.

A week and a half later, the end result took her breath away. Beachy and crisp and durable.

"Dog's here," Nick called as he removed the last of his tools from the flooring project.

"My dog?" Emmalyn asked without thinking.

"Dog," Nick answered.

"Oh. That one."

"Want me to send it packing?"

Sorry, Shawna. I . . . I have a dog. I made reservations for you at The Wild Iris. Scratch that. For Bougie's sake, she'd get them rooms at one of the Bayfield B&Bs. "No, I guess it can come in."

Emmalyn held the screen door open as Dog entered. She trotted in as if expecting to find a water and food dish waiting for her in the kitchen. Finding none, she clicked her way to the fireplace hearth, curled up in an empty flooring box, and laid her head on her crossed paws. *Home.*

If only it were that simple.

"Dog needs a name," Nick said, making one final pass with the Swiffer.

"I think so too. But wherever she lands next might not want to use that name."

"Pick a name just between you two, then. Hold this end, would you?" He extended the handle of the Swiffer toward Emmalyn and peeled off the felted fabric.

"A name between the two of us?"

"Didn't Boozie ever show you that verse at the end of the Bible, the one that talks about Jesus having a name picked out for us that only He knows? She usually includes that when people ask her about her name. Boozie Unfortunate." He shook his head. Could he have been envisioning trying to get through high school with a name like that?

"I'm not as familiar with the Bible as I probably should be."

Nick pulled his dog-eared version from his back pocket. "Me either." He thumbed through several pages at the end of the book. "Here. This is it. Revelation 2:17. 'I will give those who emerge victorious some of the hidden manna to eat. I will also give to each of them a white stone with a new name written on it, which no one knows except the one who receives it.'"

A nineteen-year-old with an ankle bracelet monitor was teaching her what the Bible had to say. She had some catching up to do.

Nick left. Dog stayed.

With the flooring done, Emmalyn could start moving things in. The one small appliance already unpacked and plugged in— the coffeemaker—produced another layer of fresh fragrances to the cottage when Emmalyn brewed her first cup of coffee in her still-empty cottage. She took her mug to the porch. Dog followed. The wicker rockers needed new cushions someday soon. Or in the spring. How many more days would the weather allow her to sit in what had become her favorite spot? An unseasonably warm fall, they'd called it.

From her jeans pocket, she pulled a letter she'd been working on for days.

Dear Max,

I was wrong to listen to you. I was wrong about a lot of things, but I shouldn't have listened to you when you asked me to stop writing and not visit. Because you didn't follow through with the divorce, I assume that means you've entertained at least a faint hope we can work this out. Mine hasn't been as strong as it should have been. And of all times for me to listen to you, I picked the worst. Or maybe the best. My pain did a lot of the talking in the early months of your incarceration.

She reread the description of the changes she'd made to the cottage, the people she'd met on the island, the sunrises and sunsets she'd witnessed, the smell of damp sand and sun-bleached sea grass, the baritone voice of the water coming in and soprano voice of it pulling back out to sea, its *rubato* rhythm . . .

Dog nuzzled under her left arm and found a suitable position on her lap.

I have a dog.

She scratched out the "I."

We have a dog. It needs a name. Do you remember when I catered the gala for that international adoption agency? The memory of the regal woman who served as the contact person for the agency stayed with me all this time. Remember how she dressed in those elegant African gowns and headdresses? The yellow and purple kente cloth? When I asked the story behind her beautiful name, she told me her mother had four miscarriages before she was born, and a stillborn son not long before becoming pregnant with her. Her mother named her 'Comfort,' because the child comforted her mother in a time of deep grief. I've never forgotten her. I thought our stories intersected at the miscarriages. Now I see it was a different place altogether. Longing. And comfort.

Our dog's name is Comfort. I hope that's okay with you.

"And you," she said, scratching behind Comfort's ears.

I know time has run out for us to consider trying again to have a child of our own. But I don't think it's any accident that I was introduced to a woman named Comfort through the gala for international adoption. Maybe we can talk about adopting or fostering when you come home. I know I was the one who stood my ground against those ideas. Vehemently, at times. I'm seeing things differently now . . . on many fronts. We have a lot to talk about.

She paused, considering her final words. Nothing fit except:

I miss you. I'm waiting here for you.

Love,

Emmalyn

Courage helped her slide the note into the waiting envelope. Courage licked the envelope and sealed it.

Courage was going to need a battalion of helpers to get Emmalyn to slip it through the "Outgoing Mail" slot at the post office.

"Time for me to make a couple of calls to get the furniture delivered, Comfort."

The dog tilted its head toward her, but didn't move. Emmalyn could almost hear a dog version of "Go ahead. You won't bother me."

The beds for the master bedroom and spare room would be delivered the next afternoon from the store in Duluth. If Mr. Stockton could barter for the use of his brother's retired UHaul, Emmalyn's purchases could arrive in the morning. The couch and chairs she'd ordered online were scheduled for Friday delivery as well. She could be moved in and sleeping under her own roof before the weekend was over.

Just in time to prep for the arrival of her mother and sisters.

12

How many inn guests drag their feet when it's time to say good-bye to the innkeeper? Especially when the move is to a spot a couple of miles up the road? Bougie volunteered Pirate Joe to assist Nick with the manual labor of the move, but Emmalyn and Bougie had to say their good-byes at the threshold of The Wild Iris.

"I owe you so much."

"It'll all even out once you start working here."

"Bougie, like I said, I'm not looking—"

"For a job. I know. But you will. And it'll be waiting for you."

Emmalyn cocked an eyebrow.

"Yeah," Bougie said, "I've completely conquered my feelings of inferiority over your talents, M. You'd be a welcome addition here."

"I'd like to give the online cooking classes a try first. I just have to find a way to earn a living from them."

Bougie clapped her fisted hands together. "You can use the Wild Iris kitchen if you need photos, too. You have to have photos."

"Instead,"—Emmalyn sliced her words evenly—"what would you think about classes called The Cottage Cook? Making meals with more creativity than kitchen space?"

"I love it," Bougie said, elongating the L. "Are you thinking of selling ad space? Oh!"

"What?"

"Listen to us! We can talk business some other time. Right now you need to get out to the cottage before the furniture starts arriving. I told the men to meet you out there at eight."

"Thank you. The words sound so terribly inadequate."

"I'll see if I can pull free to deliver lunch to your work crew myself. Otherwise, I'll send it out with someone headed that way."

Emmalyn's throat tightened at the overflow of Bougie's generosity. "See you . . . soon, then."

"Soon."

By seven o'clock that night, Emmalyn had a fire going in the fireplace. Of necessity. A cold front smacked an icy palm against the island. The south-facing cottage fared better than some others, no doubt. But the cold wind that wove its way through the pines and hardwoods at the cottage's backside did an efficient job of cooling things off after the flurry of moving in. Too efficient.

The finishing touches would need several rounds of rearranging. She'd allow herself a grace period. For now, it was enough to have a chair turned to offer her the warmth of the fire and a view of Lake Superior at the same time. Comfort twirled in circles before taking up her position near the hearth. With three small table lamps lit around the main living area, and the fire's light, Emmalyn surveyed the transformation in its most charming evening attire.

She sank deeper into the chair and grabbed a chenille throw from the arm of the couch to cocoon herself and her tired muscles. The beds needed linens. After coffee. And a moment of inactivity.

Every window on the main floor rattled with the wind gusts. The bedroom windows had been replaced a few years ago when the small deck outside the master bedroom had been added and the French doors installed. When she could afford it, she'd have to replace the windows on the first floor.

She'd resisted turning on the electric heat. Living in Wisconsin, though not this far north, had taught her the tenacity of winter. An affordable source of firewood—beyond what Cranky had left her—topped the new list she'd started.

Comfort's presence had all but eradicated the last of the squatter mice. It was pointless to think about keeping a free-spirited dog. Emmalyn vowed to be grateful however long the animal chose to stay. The dog food she put out wasn't a bribe. No, not at all.

"I'm glad you're here, Comfort."

The dog lifted her head, bright eyes all the brighter in the firelight. She already responded to her new name. Good sign. When Emmalyn didn't say more, Comfort tucked her muzzle under her furry shoulder and resettled.

Emmalyn hadn't used the word *love* often in the past five years. But she did love how the cottage had turned out. Simple. Clean. Cozy in its best meaning.

Robin's egg touches broke up the soft white, but with a gentle hand. The beadboard backsplash in the kitchen. The aqua canning jars on the shelf above the sink. The robin's egg satin ribbon circling the nubby muslin pillow on the cream couch. On the second floor, celery played the part of the robin's egg blue.

A designer's version of shabby chic could read feminine. She hoped she'd pulled off shabby chic in a way that wouldn't make Max uncomfortable when he—

She reined in her thoughts. She still hadn't heard from him. The temp of the coffee faded as fast as the dusk beyond the windows. Cloudy tonight. The skylight wouldn't offer a star show or trace the path of the moon. Would she see anything through those massive windows in the bedroom?

She envisioned Max attempting to ascend the narrow stairs while she descended. Someone would have to move. Someone would have to break rank and do the right thing. Yield to the other.

A log spit and collapsed into the embers underneath it. One of Comfort's ears twitched. Emmalyn debated between putting another log on the fire and warming up leftovers for supper before it got any later. The trunk serving as a coffee table and ottoman worked well as additional storage. But as she removed her feet from where they'd rested, she wondered if she'd need to pad the top. Her heels ached. An upholstered ottoman wouldn't fit in the space. The trunk would have to do double or triple duty. A removable cushion for the top would help.

The cottage's diminutive size forced a reduction of clutter. The reduction of clutter forced an air of serenity reminiscent of the way she felt when Bougie first opened the door to Random Room 37 at The Wild Iris Inn.

What was she missing? Nothing of significance. She wasn't sure a trip to the storage unit in Lexington was necessary. She had everything she needed.

Everything not human.

God, I never wanted to be alone.

<hr />

The rain started as Emmalyn picked up her Letters to Max journal and her favorite gel pen. The rain stopped before she'd written a word. What was there to say?

Lightning flashed. No, not lightning. Lights. Car lights illuminating the driveway side of the cottage. She crossed the room and peeked through the side window, but whoever it was had reached the back door already and was knocking.

Emmalyn's watchdog looked up as if to say, "You got this? Good. I'm not done with my nap."

"Big help you are." Cuteness covered a lot of faults in the dog world, she guessed.

"M? It's us."

Us? Multiples? Sounded like Bougie. Emmalyn took another glance around the room as she neared the back entrance. Ready for company? Ready for nonjudgmental friends? Definitely.

"Bougie. Cora. Come on in. Oh, don't worry about your shoes."

Bougie held up a pair of embroidered Thai slippers. "We come prepared. All you need is two wayfarers dragging in wet leaves and sand after all your hard—Oh!" She angled past Emmalyn into the kitchen. "Oh, I adore this! I've heard you talk about what you were doing, but I couldn't imagine how it would all turn out."

Cora followed close on her heels. "Nice. Love the flooring." She winked at Emmalyn.

"Nick did the painting?" Bougie asked.

"I did some of the trim work, but most of this is his doing."

Bougie surveyed the great room. "He does beautiful work."

Cora seemed almost embarrassingly proud of her son. For good reason. The ankle monitor did not represent who he really was as a person, the potential of who he was becoming.

Emmalyn's thoughts drifted many miles away to a prison cell echoing the same truth.

"Come, sit down. Can I get you a cup of coffee or tea?"

Bougie nodded toward Cora, who toted a massive covered basket. "We brought treats. Some for now. Some for later." Cora deposited the basket on the kitchen island and the two women unpacked it. "House christening apple cider. I recommend we have it hot tonight. Baked brie with apricot jam."

"Yum," Cora said.

"Fruit, because . . . " Bougie paused. "You know. Healthy and all that."

Joy germinated from a seed no bigger than a flake of pepper, then grew as the women—her friends—expounded on the merits of each item they'd brought. Cora's homemade caramel corn. Kitchen towels. Had Nick taken them a color swatch of the pale aqua-blue paint on the backsplash? How else would they have been able to match it that closely? A collection of Lake Superior rocks in a glass cylinder—each one inscribed with a wish for her: peace, serenity, joy, grace, hope, comfort.

A white stone with your new name written on it, Comfort. Fun.

She picked through the stones, reading the one-word messages, imagining the exercise becoming part of her morning routine in this new chapter of her life: delight, embrace, blessing, courage, endurance, renewal, breathe, ask, seek, knock, bow, kneel, rise, rejoice . . .

And a mottled gray stone some local stonecutter had engraved with Max's name. The letters blurred before her, smeared by the saltwater pooling in her eyes.

"We brought bacon, too, if that helps your mood."

Bougie shot Cora a withering look, then pressed her fingertips to her lips as if she'd been the one to mention bacon.

The moment christened the cottage with tears and a laughter chaser. "Smoked meat," Emmalyn said between gasps, "fixes everything."

"The food world's duct tape," Cora added.

Bougie planted her palms on her thighs, took several deep breaths, then stood upright with renewed decorum. Admirable. She dug into the basket and removed a cloth drawstring bag. "See what you think of these, M."

The bag was heavier than Emmalyn expected. She opened the drawstring, peeked in, then poured some of the contents in her hand. "Bougie! These are stunning." In her hand lay a half dozen pale celery-green glass drawer pulls. Antique or flawless reproductions.

"I have the same design in doorknob sets, too." She pulled another larger bag from the basket. "If you're interested."

"Perfect for upstairs. How did you—?" What was the point of asking? They'd found ways to discover what she needed, what would bless her. "Where did you get these?"

"Would you believe the Dollar Store?" Cora opened the container of caramel corn and offered it to the other two women.

Bougie's smile sparkled with the same reflections of light that danced in the heart of the glass doorknobs. "*Not* the Dollar Store. Welcome home, M."

Had Emmalyn put that much thought into her friendships over the years? She was . . . What word captured how she was feeling? Blessed.

Indebted.

"Hey, Dog!" Cora headed toward the fireplace. "I heard you moved in. How are you doing, little one?"

"Her name's Comfort," Emmalyn said.

"Well, little Miss Comfort is making it clear she needs to go out. I'll take her, if you want me to."

Emmalyn's shopping list grew as quickly as her tasks list. "I don't have a leash for her. Yet."

"Not a problem," Cora said, opening the lakeside door. "I don't think a leash makes much of a difference for this one anyway. Comes and goes as she pleases."

"I've heard that about her."

"We'll be back in a few."

Bougie had apple cider heating in a pot on the stove already.

"We need to settle my bill, Bougie. And there's something else. It's a good time to talk about these two things with Cora out of range."

Her presence filled Emmalyn's kitchen with a soft but intense light. Bougie said, "Let's start with the 'something else.'"

Emmalyn could stammer or she could come out with it. "What makes you so skilled at loving people you barely know?"

"Not what," she said, taking a deep breath over the pot of cider. "Who. Next question?"

A sound like a breeze through birch leaves made her wonder if that were heaven laughing. She wished . . .

She wished Bougie had been born to her.

"Next question?" Bougie repeated.

"How much do I actually owe you? Be honest. How much?"

"I'm always honest. Spoon?" Bougie pulled open one drawer after another.

"Here. In the island."

"I haven't been avoiding giving you your bill any more than you've avoided the topic of working for me. Two issues more closely related than you imagine."

Emmalyn leaned against the island. "You were serious?"

"When have I ever not been serious? Don't answer that. Yes, I'm serious. We have a good thing going at The Wild Iris."

"You do." Emmalyn sampled the caramel corn as she listened.

"I could use your help trimming our menu, making it fresher, more appealing. I don't know, maybe we need an off-season menu that looks appreciably different from our high-season menu. Return customers are getting bored with our—"

"Bougie." Emmalyn studied her friend's face. "More appealing? Are you kidding?"

"I'm not a chef, or a professional caterer, like you."

"Years ago."

"I'm looking for an assistant manager, someone with the knowledge to help make menu decisions, an eye for style, willing to pitch in wherever needed, and with a heart for . . . " She paused.

"With a heart for what?"

Bougie set the spoon aside and turned to face Emmalyn. She clasped her hands low in front of her. "For people the world writes off."

The Pirate Joes of the world? The Nicks? The people like Max? Her heart for them was grossly undersized. Bougie didn't know what she was asking. "I don't know . . . "

Bougie raised her clenched hands to a spot under her chin. "Someone like you. You'd be an answer to prayer."

There's a first for everything.

"You'll probably want to try it out for a while, see if it's a good fit for your talents. Six weeks, maybe? That would more than work off your bill for housing and meals."

Emmalyn chuckled. "It would not. Unless you expect me to work around the clock."

"Three days a week. Our busy days. We could figure that out. And you could still work on The Cottage Cook."

"You do know this is completely unfair to you. I probably owe you a couple thousand dollars."

Bougie stirred the cider again. Her shoulders lifted, then relaxed, her beautiful mane of unruly hair following along. "I know you've been busy until now with the remodeling."

"How would you explain this to your accountant?"

"He already knows I'm not normal."

Solitude was one thing. Day after endless day alone in the cottage with no project left except learning how to walk upright with a broken heart was another. Having her enormous bill wiped out by a short stint as part of The Wild Iris team? Dabbling in the food industry again without all the stressors? Where was the downside? "I'm open to the idea."

Bougie's famous pirouette inaugurated Emmalyn's kitchen as a place where joy was possible. "Great! You start right after your mom and sisters leave."

Joy had a challenge on its hands.

13

"Are you still sorting mail?"

The postmistress glanced over her shoulder from the work-table a dozen feet behind the customer window. "All done." She stacked her project and came closer to the window. "Were you waiting for something in particular?"

Emmalyn shook her head. "Not expecting anything." Longing, but not expecting. And waiting? Yes. Constantly. "Thanks. Have a great day."

"You, too."

She wanted to respond, "Not likely. My mother and sisters will be here in an hour." Ahk! She'd told herself she would presume the best, "make nice," and not let them get to her this time. She would own her decision to move to Madeline Island and prove that the island had already been good for her. Bougie had suggested she memorize a verse from the Bible. Romans 12:18—"If possible, to the best of your ability, live at peace with all people." Emmalyn had a feeling the "to the best of your ability" was the part that needed the most work.

When Bougie offered empty rooms at The Wild Iris to Emmalyn's family at half price, Emmalyn repented of her original idea of planting them in Bayfield—a moat of water away. She accepted Bougie's irrepressible generosity and ticked off another few days she'd work as a temporary assistant manager. When her family's ferry landed, Emmalyn would lead them to the Inn so they could check in, then show the way to the cottage for their first meal together. Shawna insisted her dog allergy wouldn't be a problem since she wasn't sleeping at the cottage, as long as Comfort kept her distance.

Emmalyn strapped herself into the drivers' seat, unable to suppress her smile. Comfort. Keeping her distance. Sure.

If her mom and sisters had come a month earlier, they would have seen the cottage at its worst and the island at its best. Now the cottage shone and the island looked a little ragged around the edges—trees bare-branched, seasonal shops closed, summer cottages abandoned in favor of points south. Even Tom's Burned Down Bar looked deserted—more deserted than it normally did.

She'd planned activities for each of the three days the women visited. Big Bay State Park—a must. And the Town Park. Devil's Cauldron. Sunset Bay. They'd drive past the Madeline Island Art Institute grounds. Emmalyn vowed to participate in one of their summer workshops someday. She'd take them to the library, an experience in itself with its wild mix of books, crazy quilt decorating sensibilities in the children's library, sweet view of the lake from the landing on the stairs to the upper floor reading area, and the yard. How many libraries have a hammock in the lawn, a conversation pit, wildflower garden, handcrafted stepping stones?

It could snow any day, according to the weather gossips. Was it wrong to pray for the snow to hold off long enough for her family to see why this was exactly where Emmalyn needed to be right now?

Their opinions mattered. But not enough to throw her off track. Deep breath. The pull of the island, of the water, couldn't be fully explained. The pull of the people—who could explain that?

Emmalyn hadn't come to Madeline Island to get lost, but to get found, apparently.

And the process wasn't yet complete. Bits of her kept floating off, drifting to a dream place where she bent over a crib and it wasn't empty. Days ago, when she made up the single bed in the second bedroom, she'd thought of it as a repurposed nursery. If—

When Max came home, they'd talk about adoption. Sun-bleached as it was from its original colors, the dream lingered, gasping but still alive.

After picking up butter and ibuprofen at the convenience store near the Burned Down Bar, Emmalyn drove close to the ferry landing to wait. She got out of the car and crossed the street to stand at the water's edge, watching and listening. Disturbingly clear water, slurping and gurgling as it had the first day she walked the shoreline in Bayfield before crossing to the island. The distinctive navy blue and white ferry crept across the expanse of water in what from her vantage point looked like a wide curve from hill-hugging Bayfield.

Not long ago, the hills glowed with autumn colors. Now brown and gray tucked among the evergreens mottled the scene. The ferry closed in, its familiar engine noise crescendoing. Seagulls dipped and squawked. Emmalyn drove her hands deeper into the pockets of her wool jacket. Here they came.

The ferry docked with a surprisingly small thunk for a vessel that size. Two men secured it with wrist-thick ropes before the gangplank was let down and the first vehicles were waved off. Three familiar women caught her attention from inside a black luxury sedan, her sister Tia at the wheel. The sedan followed a VW off the ferry like a barge follows a tug. Emmalyn waved Tia to keep going and turn right at the stop sign then pull over.

The ferry boarded again immediately. Emmalyn waited for the six Bayfield-bound vehicles to move far enough for her to cross to her family. They insisted on getting out of the car to hug her. Smothered her with hugs.

"Well," her mother said, stepping back a pace, "I was afraid I'd have to give you my 'you're getting too thin' lecture. Not so." She smiled.

The gall.

"Quit it, Mom," Tia said. "She looks great. You look great, Emmalyn."

Shawna added, "It's the coat. Bulky coats will do that."

Her mom put gloved hands on either side of Emmalyn's face. "A coat doesn't bulk up a person's cheeks, dear."

She'd been called emaciated the last time they'd seen one another. Bougie helped her get unemaciated.

"So, where's this Wild Turnip Inn?"

Shawna and Tia exchanged a look. It must have been a long trip.

"Wild Iris, Mom. Unique, but I think you'll like it."

"We could have stayed with you. One of the girls could have slept on the couch."

Tia came to the rescue. "Emmalyn bought a dog, Mom. My allergies?"

"Actually, I didn't buy the dog. It . . . it chose to move in with me." That sounded odd, even to her, even though she fully embraced Comfort's independent side. "No point in our standing around here. Let's get you settled in your rooms and then head out to the cottage."

Tia held back when Mom and Shawna climbed into the sedan. She gave a side-armed hug and spoke without moving her lips. "Hang in there. We'll be gone soon."

Emmalyn leaned into Tia's shoulder. "It's good to see you again."

"You, too."

<hr>

Emmalyn's mom's eyebrows stayed unnaturally high throughout the check-in process. Bougie was in exceptionally rare form, dressed in an ankle-length ballet skirt and fifties sweater set. And thick, furry boots. Their rooms were pronounced "adequate" (Mom) and "charming" (Tia and Shawna). Bougie hadn't given them Emmalyn's old room—Random 37. For some reason, that warmed her heart. She'd done so much soul-searching in that room, it would have seemed an invasion of privacy to have her mother or sisters pillowing their heads in there.

Shawna volunteered to ride with Emmalyn when they left The Wild Iris. Before they'd reached the edge of town, Shawna angled herself toward Emmalyn.

"We need to talk."

"We'll have lots of time in the next two and a half days." Was she counting down already?

"I need to tell you something."

"Okay." Emmalyn kept her eyes on the road with only quick glances at her sister.

"Tia is pregnant. She didn't want to tell you, because . . . well, you know. But I said you'd be more hurt if she didn't."

Blindsided. Again.

"She's not showing yet, so you'd never know. Except her eating habits are crazy. And she gets up to the bathroom a dozen times a night. That'll be fun, rooming with her."

"This is a pretty stretch of woods through here, isn't it?"

"Did you hear what I said, Emmalyn?"

"I heard."

"Are you going to be okay with it?"

"What's the alternative?"

"Oh, I don't know. Falling completely apart, like you usually do."

I have not fallen apart often enough for you to consider it my default option. Interlopers. Her mom and sisters were interlopers on the island, trampling on the peace she'd worked hard to unearth. *If possible, as much as lies within your abilities, make peace with . . . everyone. God, do you know what You're asking?*

She glanced in the rearview mirror. The black pseudo-limo trailed a few car lengths behind. At the wheel was a woman only two years younger, living Emmalyn's dream.

"Em, you would have wanted to know, wouldn't you?"

"Of course." She forced the pitch of her voice higher than she felt. "What a beautiful thing. I thought they'd decided three kids were enough for them."

"Total surprise. I mean, royally."

"That's how it happens sometimes."

The road wound through woods and emerged to follow the shoreline before disappearing back into the woods again.

"How far is this place?"

A small sob caught in Emmalyn's throat. She coughed to cover. "Not far. The island's only fourteen miles long, tip to tip. From the air, it looks like it's shaped like a skinny duck taking flight. We're headed for the soft spot under its chin."

"I'd go stir-crazy. I'd be hopping that ferry to civilization every day."

"I do have running water, Shawna. And indoor plumbing, too."

"You know what I mean."

"And I'm working on building a little addition called Contentment."

Emmalyn didn't dare glance Shawna's way. This courage stuff took concentration and focus.

A deer tiptoed onto the asphalt ahead a few hundred feet. Emmalyn slowed, watching both sides of the road for companions.

"Do you have to put up with that all the time?" Shawna said.

"All the time." Emmalyn kept a straight face, but spun a Bougie pirouette inside.

Once they got past the awkwardness of letting Tia know that Emmalyn knew what Tia didn't want her to know, plus the subsequent sibling chiding of the blabbermouth Shawna, the evening meal went fairly well. They'd swooned over the cottage and Emmalyn's before-and-after pictures. Despite her mom's comment—*This doesn't look like you*—and Emmalyn's response—*It's more me than I ever knew*—true appreciation colored their tour of the cottage. Comfort seemed standoffish to everyone but Emmalyn. It was hard not to love that dog.

Tia had second helpings of the split pea soup, thirds of the homemade bread and black raspberry jam. Toasted coconut cake—her mom's favorite—waited on the kitchen counter.

"Let's have dessert in the living room," Emmalyn said. "Coffee?"

Tia blurted, "Not for me!" and put a hand to her stomach. The apology on her face made Emmalyn's breath catch. Tia shouldn't have to temper her excitement about this pregnancy because of Emmalyn's history.

"I have some herbal tea," Emmalyn offered.

"Perfect. Thank you."

"Mom? Shawna? Coffee?"

The last of the clouds parted and afforded the women a spectacular view of the lake, its waters night-calm and dazzling. They all wanted to sit where they could see the lake, which made it clumsy for conversing.

"So, Claire's back in the picture, huh?" Her mother cut into her slice of coconut cake with her fork but held it while she waited for a response.

Of all the names in all the world, that one had to slither its way into their evening? "Back in the picture?" Emmalyn congratulated herself for asking without an edge to her voice.

"With Max."

Tia slid to the front of her chair. "Not 'with' Max, Mom. They're just talking."

Max. Talking to the mother of his pre-Emmalyn love child. "They're writing each other?"

"I'm sure he mentioned it to you. Didn't he?" Her mother snagged another forkful of cake. "I think it's admirable she's keeping him informed about their daughter again."

Emmalyn supposed years of child support warranted an occasional update. What had Claire done after the support stopped when Max entered the prison system?

Who wouldn't sympathize with a child in need? But the monthly child support deduction from Max and Emmalyn's income had been a land mine they'd skirted from before their wedding. Their dream honeymoon shrank to a *nice* honeymoon because of child support. Even after their jobs netted them healthier paychecks, fertility treatments reached a limit too soon—in Emmalyn's eyes—because of child support.

Max's integrity kept him faithful to the payments even after Claire moved to Montana, taking Hope Elizabeth far enough away to make visitation too costly and cumbersome to be practical. Two weeks in the summer—most of Max's vacation time. A few days every Christmas break, every other Thanksgiving. Hard on all of them when Hope was two, three, four. Emmalyn wondered if the little girl found it a relief when her dad was taken away when she was seven.

"Emmalyn?" Shawna's question cut into the dangerous territory her thoughts wandered.

Smile. Breathe. Ignore the elephant. What's bigger than an elephant? Ignore the blue whale. "Can I warm up anyone's coffee?"

The coconut cake cut more smoothly than efforts to slice the tension in the room. Cleaner edges too.

"She's turned into a darling pre-teen," Mom said, insistent as a gnat. "Have you seen the pictures?"

Tia stood. "We should get back to The Wild Onion. Driving unfamiliar roads in the dark won't be fun. We have all day tomorrow together to catch up some more."

Shawna hesitated, then followed suit. "I wouldn't mind getting to bed early tonight. What time will we see you in the morning, Emmalyn?"

If I spend an hour speed-reading the Bible and another hour in intense "God help me!" prayer . . . "How about ten? We can have brunch in the café, then explore the island. I'll have a late lunch for us here. Weather permitting, we can walk the beach."

Comfort scurried to her, signaling she wanted to be picked up. Emmalyn complied. The dog nuzzled her neck as if to say, "You're doing fine, M. Keep it up."

T minus ten minutes to collapse.

"Need directions back to The Wild *Iris*?" Emmalyn retrieved their coats from the iron hooks near the back door.

Tia said, "I programmed it into the car's navigation system. We're good."

"Call if you have trouble. It's hard to get lost with so few roads, though."

Shawna said, "Keep heading for the duck's tail, right?" and offered an arm to their mother, who rose stiffly from the couch.

"You're not going to have us hiking steep trails or anything tomorrow, are you?" the elder asked.

"Easy trails. A great boardwalk along the water. But dress warmly."

"You couldn't have run away to Arizona. Or Cancun. No, it had to be where winter looks just like it does at home." Mom chuckled. Did she think that was funny?

"Let's go, Mom," Tia said, rolling her eyes when their mother looked away to slide her arms into her coat sleeves.

"We should stay and help with dishes."

Emmalyn collected dessert plates. "Don't worry about the dishes. They won't take long."

They each hugged her before heading out, her mom's hug punctuated with a warm kiss on Emmalyn's cheek. She leaned into it, into memories of a time when their relationship wasn't defined by angst. Long, long ago. She still craved her mother's love and acceptance. It had probably affected the disappointments of the recent past more than she realized.

The cottage quieted to its former serenity. Even the clink and clank of dishes in soapy water soothed.

Her cell phone buzzed a half hour later. A text from Tia. "Sorry. Will make her behave tomorrow."

Emmalyn sighed. *You can try.*

14

This island isn't big enough for the four of us.

Three minutes into breakfast and Emmalyn had sighed twice already. If asked if she loved her sisters and mother, she'd answer with an emphatic yes. How could love get so twisted? Was it her? Was it them? Was it the combo platter?

A year ago, she might have insisted it was all their fault. They seemed totally inept at dealing with the brokenhearted, kept trying to tell her life wasn't that bad.

Maybe it wasn't all them. Life could be enormously disappointing and still be good.

Did that thought live in her own head?

The look on her mother's face when Pirate Joe refilled her coffee and stopped at the cookie jar on his way back to the kitchen was worth a little relational discomfort. Emmalyn stole glances at Tia and Shawna and found similar expressions.

"Such a great guy," Emmalyn said. "It will be fun working with him."

"Working with him?" The trio of voices sounded rehearsed. They were that in sync.

"I start here on Friday." She broke off a bite of lemon curd scone.

Her mother leaned across the table. With a sympathetic hand on Emmalyn's forearm, she surveyed the smattering of customers in the restaurant and whispered, "Oh, honey. Are things that bad financially?"

Pretty close.

"Why didn't you say something? We'll help you out until you find something more . . . suitable."

Shawna spoke up. "Don't lump me in with your charity plan, Mom. I have needs of my own. The twins are attending private school next year."

Bougie swept past the table. Emmalyn stifled the urge to grab her wing-like sleeve and beg her to sit with them until the meal was over. From the way the women were positioned, only Emmalyn could see when Bougie made the international hand signal for "praying for you."

"What do you *really* need, Emmalyn?"

"Thanks, Tia." She ran her finger over the smooth handle of the stoneware mug with her initial on its base. "I need to work here. For a while." Her answer had nothing to do with her room and board debt.

Tia nodded her head. "That's it, then. Go for it."

Their mother cut the beautiful brown crust off the bottom of her scone and set it to the side with two fingers. "But, Emmalyn, these people are"—she leaned in closer, her bosom smashing into the lemon curd and clotted cream on her plate—"*strange!*"

Tia started it—the laughter. When their mother sat back, aghast at her daughter's manners, Shawna joined in. Emmalyn pressed her lips together, determined not to give in to the moment. Her mother's navy cashmere sweater might never recover from the yellow and white accessories smeared across the front.

"Girls! Settle down. This may not be uptown, but you can con- duct yourself with— Oh, good glory!"

She'd found it. She held her cloth napkin across her chest and excused herself with a huff. "I'll be right back."

"No hurry." Emmalyn was the only one capable of talking. The other two had launched into teary guffaws.

When they'd regained control, Emmalyn took a breath of courage and said, "Tia, I really am happy for you with this baby."

"I know it has to be hard on you."

"Don't . . . don't let it come between us. I want you to feel you can share the joy of it with me." Where did that tear come from? She'd been doing so well.

"Oh, hon."

"It's okay. I'll be okay. A little rogue wave of the old me." She dabbed at the tear, grateful one dab took care of it. "Besides, I think Max and I are going to look into fostering or adoption after he's released."

Her sisters traded looks couched with furrowed brows.

"Not right away. We have to get . . . used to each other again. Build our own relationship." *Providing he comes home to me, not Claire.* "I know I've been set against adoption all along. That's one of the things about me that's changed."

Shawna opened her mouth, but Tia shook her head in warning.

"What is it? I'm in a much healthier place than I was even a few months ago. This is good news. Why the somber looks?"

"Emmalyn." Tia bit her lower lip, then expelled a full breath in a *whoo* before drawing another. "You two can't adopt. And you aren't candidates for foster parenting."

"Max is a felon, Em."

"I'm aware of that, Shawna." Blood pulsed in Emmalyn's temples.

"Felons can't adopt."

"You're using the word *felon* as if you don't know Max, as if you don't know what a good man he was. Is. A good man who made a . . . a horribly costly mistake."

Tia dug in her purse for a tissue and handed it to Emmalyn. "This isn't about our opinion. You know we love Max. It's the law, honey."

She'd finally found a thread of hope. One small thread. *God, don't take that away from me, too. They're wrong. They have to be wrong.*

But they weren't. Shawna punched in a search on her smartphone. The criminal background check would stop most applications. Exceptions? A few. Convincing an adoption agency or the foster care system to overlook Max's prison record loomed higher than the national debt.

Emmalyn couldn't fake joy for the rest of their stay. It's a good thing they didn't expect it. The mood hung fog-low despite the beauty of their surroundings, the history of the island, the lure of the November cold but still inspiring beach. The waves put on an impressive show, their white petticoats can-canning throughout the afternoon. None of the three wanted to brave the whitecaps to ride the ferry to Bayfield for what had promised to be an elegant evening meal at the Old Rittenhouse Inn. They made grilled cheese sandwiches and tomato soup and ate them in front of the fire.

Her mother's embarrassment from brunch at The Wild Iris kept her tongue corralled. Or maybe the girls had pulled her aside when Emmalyn wasn't looking and warned her to take it easy on Emmalyn. Whatever the reason, the tone of the remainder of their visit softened.

"We could watch TV," Shawna suggested when the conversation died out.

"I don't own one."

"I wonder what the reception's like up here," her mother said.

Emmalyn let it lie. What would they say if she told them she didn't intend to purchase one?

"Scrabble?" Tia looked around as if the game board would already be laid out somewhere in the room.

"Most of the games are still in storage. In Lexington."

"Oh."

"I guess I've gotten used to the quiet."

She was sure her mother didn't intend her to observe how she pursed her lips and shook her head two inches side to side.

"So, what time is your ferry tomorrow?" Emmalyn asked, praying for calm water.

The visitors exchanged glances. Shawna spoke. "We thought we'd get a fairly early start. It's a long way home."

"What's 'fairly early'?"

"We'll check out by, oh, nine," her mother said.

"That means breakfast by eight. That's okay. I need to get used to setting an alarm."

Her mother shifted in her chair. "Don't bother, dear. We can say our good-byes tonight. Sleep in. You look like you . . . need it." Her final words faded to an almost imperceptible level.

Emmalyn didn't cringe. Numbness spread through every cell. Numb doesn't flinch. But it also doesn't feel. She stared into the fire, aware how recently it had been that she'd started to feel again.

<hr>

They'd gone through the routine of good-bye. Shawna and Tia hugged her tighter than usual. Emmalyn's heart thunked noisily in her chest when she realized she stood inches away from a womb growing a baby like the one she'd never have.

The thought didn't devastate her as it once would have. It saddened her to a depth few people dare dive without air tanks.

Her lungs screamed at her by the time the black sedan with road dust on its sleek fenders pulled out of her driveway. She felt her soul kicking hard to shoot her back to the surface where she could breathe again. How far? How much farther?

Her first breath came in a wild gasp followed by a body-wide shudder that startled Comfort from her nest near the hearth. Emmalyn dropped onto the couch, face first. Moving only one arm, she reached for the throw and tossed it over her back. A five-pound weight told her Comfort had disobeyed the house rules and jumped onto the couch with her. The dog crawled over

Emmalyn and settled between her shoulder blades, a heating pad for her heart.

Emmalyn flipped the satin belted pillow to its plain side and pressed the side of her head into it. She didn't move until Comfort hopped off. The clock on the wall said she'd been prone for two hours. Her neck protested that it might have been longer.

Comfort danced at the door, eager to go out. Emmalyn obliged. Her breath caught in her throat as she watched Comfort's paw prints mark a trail through new fallen snow.

The wind's blowing through a mouthpiece of tall pines. It sounds like a cross between a whistle and a roar.

Emmalyn laid aside her pen and took another sip of an imported tea that had been part of the Bougie-Cora housewarming basket. She picked up her pen again.

> It's a haunting sound, Max, when the snow is flying.
> In warmer days, it seemed a white noise background
> to other activities. Today, it's taking center stage.

She tucked her feet underneath her and snuggled into the asymmetrical scarf Cora made from the wool they'd chosen together. She fingered the smooth wood of the handcrafted button—heart-shaped—that sat just above her own heart.

> I start work at The Wild Iris Friday morning. Five
> o'clock, if you can believe that. Not my favorite time
> of day. That's probably close to when you'll be start-
> ing your day. Wish we could have coffee together to
> start our tomorrows.

The curse of ink. As soon as the last sentence formed on the page, she regretted it. Too personal, too soon? He hadn't written back yet. He might never write back. Somehow, she'd have to live through that. If she crossed out the sentence, he'd know what she meant to say and had recanted. Too late now.

She reread what she'd written. "To start our tomorrows."

Cora had said, "I can't survive if my primary thought is that Wayne might not come home from his deployment. I know it's a truth. But I have to let a stronger truth override that one."

When Emmalyn asked what that stronger truth was, Cora said, "He is my husband until he's not."

No matter how far away. No matter the danger he's in. No matter what he's done or neglected to do. No matter how long it's been since I've heard from him . . .

She'd finish the letter later. Time to head upstairs and figure out what she would wear for her first day on the job before she called it a night. If only she had a prom dress she could cut up.

❈

The view from the master bedroom never failed to amaze her—the lakeside French doors offering her a nearly wall-wide view of beach, water, and sky. Mesmerizing any ordinary day. Captivating on a morning bright with new snow. She abandoned the resumption of her wardrobe search in favor of sea-gazing, watching the fat snowflakes melt on the water's tongue like a million communion wafers or flakes of manna.

Biblical references. Not her normal fare. A hand of resistance pushed against her softening soul. But that's the thing about a softened soul—it has the strength to push back.

In a bedroom she couldn't quite call *theirs* yet, with a too-wide bed a symbol of loss and distance, she surrendered to the unexpected peace. It filled the room like music. She watched the snow until it stopped. It looked like four inches or more. First snowfall of the season. Which bickering old man at the café had won the bet?

Not enough snow to thwart her mom's and sisters' escape from the island. They'd called earlier to let her know they were as far as Bayfield. Without knowing, she could have told them the moment the weight of them lifted from Madeline Island. The air had changed between snowflakes and the music resumed.

A rude sound from behind the house stopped the music again. What on earth? She could only view that part of the property from the bathroom window upstairs. When she looked out, she saw a pickup with a plow blade attached to the front, plowing the lane to her cottage. She hurried downstairs, grabbed her "chunky" coat and slipped her feet into the boots she'd purchased none too soon.

Beside the back door, leaning against the cottage, sat a snow shovel boasting a plate-sized red satin bow on its handle. Nick waved and smiled from the driver's seat. He turned the truck around and headed back the way he'd come, plowing a wider path. He pulled onto the side road, waving again, and disappeared.

"Thank you," Emmalyn said to the cold air. She turned to walk back into the cottage and noticed that her car had been cleared of snow, too. If it didn't snow overnight, her morning routine would be much easier now.

"Bless you, Nick."

Saint Nick.

Ankle bracelet and all.

"God, let somebody somewhere see beyond Max's chains, too." The prayer rose unbidden, like a tension-releasing sneeze.

Also unexpected was the inaudible response she heard: *You. You see beyond them.*

She had a feeling that meant more than writing an occasional note.

The warmth of the cottage beckoned, as did Comfort's incessant bark. Emmalyn opened the door and let the dog slide past her, then pulled on gloves and shoveled a path from the door to the driveway while Comfort answered nature's call.

Emmalyn ducked into the cottage for her camera. Max would appreciate how the departing clouds allowed the sunshine to dust the snow scene in diamonds and purple shadows. She pulled in close for a shot of light landing on the snowy roof of the small, forlorn shed, lending it an elegance it hadn't had before the storm.

A puff of snow fell from branches high overhead. Then another. The trees were already shrugging their shoulders, shaking off the crystalline dandruff.

Emmalyn stood in the middle of it all, enraptured by the silence and shadows, the flashes of brilliance as individual snowflakes had their moment in the spotlight and simple weeds became pedestals for frozen sculptures. If it hadn't been for Emmalyn's own call of nature, she would have stayed in the scene another hour.

"Comfort? Come here, girl." Small footprints in deep snow littered the unwooded part of the backyard. "Comfort?" Her belly must have been dragging in the deepest sections.

Emmalyn walked around the side of the cottage, calling. No response. She shuffled through the heavy snow to the edge where the sea grass ended and the beach began. "Comfort! Don't . . . leave me," she chided. The humor in her voice disappeared more quickly than the snow melting into the water.

"Now? You picked now to find a new home?" she asked the absent dog.

<hr />

It was harder than she thought it would be—letting the dog go. She knew it was coming. Everyone had warned her. But as she stood gazing the length of the damp, snow-spotted beach late that afternoon, she wished they hadn't been right.

Emmalyn lifted her face to the sky and drew the deepest breath the cold air would allow. She turned toward the cottage. Comfort sat on the front porch where Emmalyn first found her. Except for the patch of caramel brown on her sweet face, Comfort blended into her surroundings of white cottage and white snow.

"Come on, dog," Emmalyn said, slapping her thigh. "Let's get inside. Big day tomorrow."

"Can you work Thanksgiving?" Bougie asked midmorning of Emmalyn's first shift. "Say no if you'd rather not."

"Spending it here is better than brooding at home," Emmalyn said, wrapping cloth napkins around sets of silverware.

"You weren't going to visit Max that weekend?"

The question caught her by the throat. "I hadn't planned on it."

"Waiting for an invitation?" Bougie tilted and ducked her head to look Emmalyn in the eye.

"Something like that."

Bougie crossed her arms over her chest. "You are one patient woman, M."

"Far from it."

"You've been waiting for that invitation—what?—four plus years now? Still patiently waiting." She uncrossed her arms, held her palms up, and shrugged. "Is there another word for it?"

She turned and busied herself at the hostess desk, leaving Emmalyn to consider words like *foolish, stubborn, self-centered, pitiful* . . .

Emmalyn pushed the words out of the way and focused on the task at hand, which took way too little mental attention.

Bougie smoothed a page torn from a magazine and laid it on Emmalyn's work surface. "What do you think of this idea?" she said, her expression that of a child waiting for a turn on the water slide. *This is going to be so much fun!*

Emmalyn didn't have a hard time understanding Bougie's anticipation. The idea fit The Wild Iris perfectly. "I love it."

"You do? Good. You'll help me choose some fonts and which sayings will translate best into wall art?"

"Happy to do that." Emmalyn considered adding, "All we really need to do is pull lines from what comes out of your mouth every day, Bougie, and we'll have all the conversation starters the walls can hold." Instead, she pointed to a couple from the maga-zine image. "I love how they kept the quotes high on the wall and wrapped the text around the room, from one wall to another, if necessary."

"Me, too. Are you thinking cream paint?"

Emmalyn considered the color mix in the dining area. "Cream would work against all these colors. The continuity would make it more elegant, I think."

"Agreed." Bougie closed her eyes briefly. "You're what I've needed to build my courage."

"Me? To build *your* courage? That's bordering on the absurd, Bougie."

"Even for me?" She pointed out the outrageously oversized lace collar on her emerald green satin knee-length, sleeveless gown.

"That used to be a doily, didn't it?"

"Two of them." Bougie said.

"Nice."

"I'm going to have to break down and add the coral sweater, though. Why do they even sell sleeveless in Wisconsin, I wonder?"

Working at The Wild Iris would never get boring.

"However," Bougie said, "sleeveless allows me to do this." She stuck her tattooed arms straight out in front of her. "Hope and Healing," she said, and clapped her forearms together. "Boom!" She held her arms out, as if expecting Emmalyn to check if the words had switched arms.

What must Jesus think of His lovechild, Bougie Unfortunate? Emmalyn pictured her worshiping, arms raised, waving her inked banners of Hope and Healing for all the world to see.

Pirate Joe slid the cookie jar from its resting place. He carried it to the table by the window, lifted the lid, and waited while the mayor deposited a dollar bill.

No. Never boring.

On Monday afternoon, The Wild Iris shooed its last customer out in plenty of time for Emmalyn to stop at the post office. She hadn't conquered the combination on the box before the postmistress poked her head through the window a few feet away.

"Got a son in prison, huh?"

Emmalyn's neck cracked when she turned her head toward the window. "Excuse me?"

"The letter you were waiting for? There's one in there from a correctional facility. It's stamped with it."

First of all, I'm not old enough to have a son in prison. But she was. *Second, isn't there some kind of privacy deal people who work in the post office have to sign? Third, nobody told you yet?*

"Husband. I have a husband in prison. He'll be released early next summer."

"Oh. My mistake."

Actually, his mistake. Or mine. Ours. Her fingers fumbled with the combination. First try, fail. Second try, epic fail. Emmalyn shuffled to the window. "Would you mind pulling my mail out of the box? I'm having a hard time with the combo today."

"Want me to come out and try?"

"Just . . . just want my mail. Thanks."

The flutters in her stomach reminded her of junior high crushes. Multiplied by—what was the equivalent of a terabyte? Terabillion? *Tera* already meant billion, didn't it? Mail in hand, she thanked the postmistress again and focused on staying upright as she exited. The drive to the cottage would feel continent long. This wasn't the kind of mail she dared open in a parked car in the heart of town.

She thought breathing was supposed to be involuntary. Not today. Her lungs ached from subconsciously holding her breath. Eyes on the road, the gravel shoulders, the unknown future, she forced an even, calming breathing technique she'd read women used in the early stages of labor.

The message in the letter could go so many directions.

Sorry, Emmalyn. Claire reached out to me. It stirred something. I'm having my lawyer prepare divorce papers again.

Then what would she say?

Emmalyn, I'd asked you not to write me. It just makes it harder. When are you going to get the hint?

Now. I'll get the hint now.

Well, Emmalyn, this is awkward. I've gotten over you, but apparently you haven't gotten over me.

I don't think I was supposed to.

She neared the elbow in the road where it turned from Big Bay to Schoolhouse. The ancient maple stood sentry as it always did, this time each bare branch covered in quilt batting. A blaze of color in the fall. Naked before the snow. Beautiful again. And in a few months, fully alive once more.

She blinked back tears, made the turn, then another, one more, and pulled up to her sanctuary for what could well become an altar experience.

Comfort scooted out the door as soon as she opened it, nearly knocking her over. Emmalyn glanced around the first floor for evidence that the animal hadn't been able to hold it. "Good dog."

Turning up the heat could wait. Tea could wait. Taking off her coat could wait.

She slid her thumbnail under the flap of the envelope stamped brazenly "This letter was mailed from a correctional facility." In red. Subtle. The return address made her teeth ache. In the system, he was known by a number and who knows what kind of nickname. In the public restroom at The Wild Iris hung a rustic shutter with a stenciled quote: *People know your name but call you by your sin. God knows your sin but calls you by name* (Ricardo Sanchez, revised).

Did Max know that? Would she have a chance to tell him? Could she convince him? Her own hold on the truth still crackled with newness.

She pulled a piece of notebook paper from the envelope, blank on the backside facing out. It took fierce determination not to read ahead when she opened it, to clamor for the words at the end. She started with the first line.

I'm a broken man.

Emmalyn clutched the letter to her heart and slumped into the nearest chair. She rocked back and forth, eyes pinched shut, her soul experiencing his words as if they were her own. Comfort's yip jarred her. Too cold outside for a small dog. Too cold inside for a broken woman who loved a broken man.

She rushed through letting Comfort in, turning up the electric heat, hanging her coat, starting the tea water. "Jesus doesn't give you strength, M. He is your strength." Bougie had found a way to work the statement into almost every conversation. The woman had more than her share of creativity when it came to speaking wisdom.

Emmalyn settled properly into the chair this time and reopened the letter she'd kept in her hand.

> *I'm a broken man.*
> *Broken and mending.*

What did he mean by that?

> *I've been worthless for anything since your note came. I don't know what I expected after cutting you off. Stupidest thing I ever did. Yes, even more stupid than not shutting off the engine that night or steering another direction. Such a small decision with such unbearable consequences.*

Emmalyn breathed a body-shuddering sigh.

> *I didn't expect grace. Didn't expect you would still care after all I've taken from you. But Emmalyn, I'm not the man you married. This place has changed me. And I'm not sure you would have written if you knew how much. Frankly, I should have told you months ago. The fact that I waited so long is tearing me up inside. I'm afraid you'll say this is really and truly the end of the line for us.*

15

Emmalyn's stomach churned. Whitecapped waves had nothing over the violent sloshing. The end of the line? He hadn't communicated with her for four of the almost five years he'd been incarcerated and he thought *this* might be the end of the line?

Anxiety rippled through her. She'd mailed another note since the first one. A tender note. Vulnerable. He obviously hadn't received it yet when writing this one to her. What had she said? Her mind traced back through where her heart had been as she put the words on paper.

"No. No, no, no! Not now, Max. Not when I was starting to hope again. Don't you do this to me."

The dog twitched at her words, then settled back into a dream that had more chance of coming true than Emmalyn's.

His change of heart? It had to be Claire, the one who could make babies. Claire, the one who succeeded in becoming a mother. The one he'd been speaking to from prison.

What if Emmalyn hadn't given up after eight months of unanswered mail, of her begging him to call her so they could talk? What if she'd persisted back then rather than eventually giving up? What if she'd acted as if her heart was merely wounded, not shattered? Would it have made a difference?

Max claimed he and Claire were over before their record-short relationship began. Their workplace romance had started to curdle almost the moment they decided to date. Within two months, they were history. She left the financial management office and their relationship on the same day. Claire told him about the baby after the fact, insisting she didn't want his involvement in the child's life. That lasted until she moved in with a guy who had a hard time hanging on to jobs and her newborn daughter developed an aversion to all but the most expensive brand of formula.

Emmalyn laid her head against the back of the chair in her cottage for one. Max hadn't asked for a paternity test. Did that make him a fool or honorable? By the time Hope Elizabeth turned three, Emmalyn stopped wondering. The little girl's eyes, chin, lopsided dimples, and sweet temperament mimicked Max's.

"How did Claire do it, Max?" Emmalyn asked the empty chair across from hers. "How did she worm her way back into your life?"

She knew the answer. They shared a child between them. The glue missing from the bond between Emmalyn and Max.

"See, Max? I can do math."

If a fire had been lit in the fireplace, she would have charred the letter and eventually removed it with the rest of the ashes.

But she hadn't taken time to light a fire. Curiosity drove her to read the rest, if nothing else, to see how honest he intended to be.

Where had she left off?

> . . . *should have told you months ago . . . tearing me up inside . . . the end of the line for us. Claire's been in touch. She's going through a really rough time.*

"I understand, dear. My life is *peachy* at the moment." She hadn't voiced the words aloud, but they still hurt her throat.

> *I'm more worried than ever about Hope. If Claire doesn't get her act together, they'll both be in trouble.*

What?

> *I've been praying Claire will—*

Back up the truck. He'd been praying? He said it casually, as if it were a common occurrence. She skimmed the next part and got to his final paragraph:

> *A lot of prisoners have a "Come to Jesus" moment in places like this. For some, it's for no more solid a reason than that sitting in chapel is better than sitting in their cell. Or that it looks good on their parole applications. They can fake "Glory, hallelujah!" during the songs, or memorize Scripture that justifies the crime that sent them here. Before you make any decisions about what our future might hold, Emmalyn, it's only fair for you to know this is real for me. And whatever happens between us, I'm committed to seeking full custody of my daughter when I'm released.*

Emmalyn had watched incessant waves shove stones around the beach the way thoughts tumbled inside her. He wanted Hope more than he wanted his wife? He was willing to abandon Emmalyn if he had to in order to keep the daughter he'd rarely seen? And where did he expect to find the money for legal fees to fight Claire for custody? They'd exhausted most of their joint savings on—she would have laughed if it weren't so sad—fertility treatments and Max's defense. Plus renovating the cottage.

Wait. He'd gotten religion? The kind her mother supported on Christmas and Easter? Or Bougie's kind?

She'd heard nothing from him for so long. And now, this cryptic message. If she could have texted a response to him, it would have been in all caps.

Emmalyn cracked a small branch across her thigh, splitting the wood into roughly one-foot lengths. She picked up another and busted it into smaller pieces. She tented the smaller pieces—

teepee style—over a wad of dryer lint she'd scavenged from the automatic laundry in LaPointe on her last run. Someone—Cora?—told her dryer lint made great kindling. One match and the lint flamed up, lighting the shredded paper egg carton and eventually the twigs she'd tortured.

As soon as the fire took well enough to add wood thicker around than her thumb, she'd toss in the letter. She'd reread it enough times to reproduce it if asked. But holding onto it, letting it live under the same roof, the same skylight, seemed emotionally destructive, a penned roadside bomb that could detonate if she stumbled over it in the dark.

She fed the fire a small birch log and watched its curled bark flame. Another minute or two . . .

A tap at the door can elevate a person's heart rate faster than a double espresso, she discovered. She replaced the screen on the fireplace and followed Comfort to investigate.

"Bougie?"

"Surprise!"

"What are you doing here?" Emmalyn stepped back to allow Bougie in through the narrow back entrance.

"I forgot to have you sign a W-4." Bougie waved a manila envelope.

Driving out that far? At this time of night? "Couldn't it have waited until the next time I come in?"

Bougie shrugged out of her Red Riding Hood cape. "Could have. For some reason, it seemed like a better idea to bring it to you. That and the leftover double chocolate mousse."

Her nerve endings at war again, Emmalyn both wanted Bougie there and wanted to be alone. Chocolate mousse won the day. "Great idea. And"—she looked over her shoulder at Max's letter on the coffee table trunk—"in the nick of time."

She grabbed two small, square bowls and two spoons. Bougie scooped healthy portions for both of them from a large ramekin. They each claimed a chair near the fire.

"I expected the snow to melt by now. The first couple of snow-falls usually disappear pretty fast. Doesn't bode well for what kind of winter we may be facing."

Emmalyn ate her mousse in miniscule bites, both to prolong the enjoyment factor and to give herself time to think. How much did she want to divulge to Bougie? "It's warm."

"I should have brought whipped cream. Wouldn't that have just put it over the edge?"

For some reason, Bougie chose *edge* rather than *top*, as most would have when talking about pudding. Instead, she'd used a word that related to the place where Emmalyn's emotions clung. Over the edge.

"I heard from Max today." The fire spit its opinion of her flat statement.

Bougie pressed her eyes closed and took two deep breaths before responding. She put her dish and spoon on the coffee table, obviously avoiding the open letter with both the dish and her eyes. "I would be smiling, but you aren't."

A raw tooth too close to a metal fork. That's how Emmalyn could describe how she felt. "I'm not sure how to take it, but it appears he's telling me I don't matter anymore."

The younger woman opened her mouth twice to speak before anything came out. "Words translate poorly from prison."

How did she know these things? Or assume them?

"The distance," Bougie explained. "The lack of personal contact. The missing elements of facial expression, tone of voice, the ability to correct a misunderstanding instantly. The paper shortage."

"Paper shortage." A snort stopped just shy of escaping. "He could have called. He's allowed phone calls."

"How personal is the letter? Can I read it? Or do you want to read parts of it to me? Maybe I can help lend another perspective."

Emmalyn reached for the letter. Two options: the fire or her friend. "I'll have to tell you the latest about Claire first. And Max's daughter."

With a lap full of Comfort, Emmalyn started at the beginning, more details than she'd shared before. Bougie listened as she always did, an expression both serene and concerned. Only she could pull that off. It was as if she listened with her own lap full of comfort.

Emmalyn thought the ugly details would sting if voiced. And they might have, if it hadn't been Bougie on the receiving end.

When Emmalyn finished all she needed to tell, she handed her friend the letter. Naked in a snowbank. That's what it was like having a friend find out your husband's first love is someone other than you. And that she's back again.

Bougie's eyes glistened by the time she finished. Emmalyn didn't blame her. Sad and mad circled each other in Emmalyn's stomach like wrestlers waiting for a sign of weakness.

"Priceless."

"What?" Sarcasm wasn't Bougie's style. What did she mean?

"Isn't this priceless?" She laid the letter on the coffee table and placed her hands over it as if blessing it.

Emmalyn picked up the piece of paper. "Did you read the same letter I did?"

"He's seeing things differently."

"He's not the Max I married."

"No. Better."

Emmalyn narrowed her eyes. "What am I missing? He's reconnected with Claire. He's worried about her. And whether I like it or not, he's going after Hope Elizabeth when he's released."

Bougie pulled her stockinged feet underneath her. "M, he loves the God you're learning to love. He wants to be the dad he should have been all along. And he's invited you into the journey."

Invited her in?

"M, you're not Leah. You're the Rachel in this story. The loved one."

Whatever that meant.

Bougie laid her head on her shoulder, eyes closed again, her hand in Pledge of Allegiance position. "You'll appreciate its beauty more if you figure it out for yourself."

"I'll appreciate being able to sleep tonight if you just tell me."

Bougie stood, crossed to where Emmalyn sat, and bent to hug her. "Genesis, M. Genesis."

She closed the door behind her before Emmalyn could ask, "What about the W-4?"

The envelope remained on the kitchen island. She'd left the ramekin of chocolate mousse, too. Emmalyn tucked the dish into the fridge, washed their dishes and spoons, and banked the fire. The night promised endlessness. That's all it had to offer.

Well into her third cup of tea, she folded Max's letter and slid it into its envelope. Her Bible, part of the vignette of items on the table in front of the window, felt cool to her touch. The fire would fight drafts all winter, no doubt. She opened the Bible to Genesis, just a few pages in, and tucked the envelope there.

"Come on, Comfort. Time to go out." She held one hand on the doorknob until the dog reached her. "Don't waste time out there, okay? I want to go to bed."

She avoided using the word *sleep*. That was too much to expect.

16

Three a.m.

Her best and worst ideas came at three in the morning. Too much tea forced her out of bed and across the hall to the bathroom. The dog blocked Emmalyn's return to the bedroom. Comfort sat in the doorway, face lifted expectantly.

Emmalyn raised a knee high to step over the dog who then scooted across the hallway floor toward the top of the stairs. She ran down two, then up one. Down two.

"Please don't tell me you need to go out." Emmalyn leaned against the doorjamb, yawning, rubbing her arms for warmth. "I should build a doggie door."

She grabbed a sweater to throw over her pajamas, stuck her feet into flats, and followed Comfort down the stairs.

A sliver of moon on snow etched the room in blue-white shadow light. She didn't need to turn on a lamp to see well enough to let the dog out. But the silly animal kept her distance from the door. "Seriously? You either need to go or you don't. Make up your mind."

Comfort whined. She never whined.

"Are you hungry, girl?"

Whined again, but didn't head for her dish.

"Are you just being a dog, or is there something wrong with you? Because I can't afford to lose any more sleep and I sure can't afford a bill for pet therapy."

Comfort padded across the room and jumped into Emmalyn's favorite chair.

"Let's not start that. It's by invitation only, critter." Emmalyn picked up the dog, sank into the chair, and hugged the animal against her chest. The warmth of her little body felt good in the middle of the night. "Have I told you lately that I appreciate having you around?"

Comfort sighed and settled onto Emmalyn's lap.

"And that one of these days"—Emmalyn stroked along Comfort's spine, behind her ears, under her chin—"like it or not, you're going to need another bath?"

Emmalyn rested her head against the rounded back of the chair. Her eyes drifted shut, then popped open. She was up with a child in the middle of the night. Minus the child. She'd imagined the scene more times than she could count. But it was never like this. The thin slice of moon, the utter quiet, the warmth of the small body, the embraceable chair were the same. But in her dreams, it was an infant, not a dog. She hummed lullabies as she stroked a doe-skin forehead. And she had a husband-warmed bed to return to, not a husband on a thin mattress with a thin blanket in a cell block hundreds of miles away.

She clicked on the lamp at her side. It was darker than she thought. "You're the Rachel in this story," Bougie had said. What did that mean?

She opened the Bible to the beginning, removed Max's letter, and skimmed for the name Rachel. Creation . . . Cain and Abel . . . Noah . . . Abram . . . Isaac.

"Jacob marries Leah and Rachel," a heading said, twenty-eight pages into her search.

She propped her feet on the trunk and flipped back one thin page to get the background for the story. She'd heard about it in a sermon sometime in her distant past. Maybe in college when her roommate's boyfriend got all Jesus-y on them.

Jesus-y. What would Emmalyn call it now? And where did Max fall on that spectrum? Where did she?

Jacob needs a wife, she read. He travels east and starts up a conversation with some guys at a well. Rachel comes toward the well to water her father's flocks. Cue the music. Jacob's in love. She's beautiful, kind, hard-working . . . mostly beautiful.

"Bougie, I'm not seeing the connection."

Jacob works seven years not for money, but so he can marry Rachel.

Emmalyn stopped on a verse that read, "Jacob worked for Rachel for seven years, but it seemed like a few days because he loved her."

Max had been gone almost five years. It felt like twenty. In some ways, it felt like "together" had never happened.

At the end of the seven years, Rachel's father Laban tricks Jacob so he winds up with Leah instead. This part, she remembered.

Leah, whom he doesn't love, is his wife. He gets Rachel, too, but has to work another seven years for her, which seems like a cultural glitch someone should have resolved with an amendment to their constitution or something.

"When the Lord saw that Leah was unloved, he opened her womb; but Rachel was unable to have children." Emmalyn stopped reading. Breathless. Her own story in the crinkly, ages-old pages?

Leah has four sons, then five, then six, assuming each time that having a baby will endear her husband to her. She knew. She knew Rachel was the one her husband loved.

Into the pre-dawn air, Emmalyn whispered, "Leah did math like I do. Three or more is a true family. A child will bond us forever." The columns of words swam before her eyes. Leah was wrong.

Rachel is the one Jacob loved. Rachel made herself misera-ble while Leah made babies. Rachel grieved what she didn't have while Leah craved Jacob's love for Rachel, a depth of love she'd never know.

You're the Rachel in the story, Emmalyn. Not the Leah. Bougie's voice reverberated in the chambers of her mind, echoed in the middle of the night cottage sanctuary.

"I'm Rachel. The barren one."

She pressed the pages against the ache in her chest. A slow wave tilted her thoughts. It retreated, then pushed against her reasoning again until it moved. "I'm Rachel?"

The loved one?

⚯

The skin on her face resisted when she squinted against the light streaming into the cottage. A trail of tears had left a salty, taut reminder.

Grateful she had the day free, she eased into it. After a cold, clear night, the temps had already risen enough to add the drip-drip of melting snow to the ever-present sound of Lake Superior tickling the shoreline a few feet away. In her old life, she would have turned on the television in the kitchen of the house in Lexington, then the coffee maker, in that order, and caught up on current events and pop news before diving headfirst into the day. With no television in the cottage, she took her coffee to the French door entrance and watched the island wake up.

The numbers of sailboats and kayaks she'd seen earlier in the fall had dwindled to nothing. Cora said some winters the entire lake froze over, water captured in ice, mid-wave. What a spectacle that must be.

She needed a bird feeder, a doggie door, and . . .

A car built for cold weather and snow-covered roads. Hers had balked on city streets. How would it behave on the island? And how would her budget accommodate an upgrade? Things were tighter than they'd ever been. She had to tread carefully to make the proceeds from the sale of the Lexington house stretch until she found a job that paid in actual dollars. *No offense, Bougie. I'm grateful to whittle down my Wild Iris bill by inches.*

A doggie door. A permanent adjustment to the cottage. When Comfort decided to move on, would Emmalyn get another dog? She looked down at the mop of fur staring up at her. "I'd be hard pressed to find another like you."

But she was temporary.

Bird feeder. That, she could handle.

In a few days, she'd celebrate Thanksgiving as an employee of The Wild Iris. Much better than the turkey-for-one option. When her mother suggested Emmalyn drive down for Thanksgiving, she could truthfully tell her, "I'm working that day." One dysfunctional function avoided.

Her heart owed Max a letter. Not today. Tomorrow she had to work. Maybe Sunday.

She toasted an English muffin and smeared it with black raspberry jam. A fresh cup of coffee and her grocery list joined her for breakfast. On a whim, she retrieved the Bible from the living room and opened it to a place far, far from Genesis. A random spot. Like a Random Room 37.

Isaiah something. "Come, house of Jacob, let's walk by the Lord's light." The house of Jacob. Jacob and Rachel's story hadn't ended in Genesis. Her planned avoidance skidded to a halt.

She quickly flipped pages to something less awkward. Mark 10. "Jesus asked him, 'What do you want me to do for you?' The blind man said, 'Teacher, I want to see.'"

This Bible reading habit could get dangerous. She closed the book and addressed her grocery list. Bird feeder. *Teacher, I want to see.* Bird seed. *Teacher, I want to see.* Romaine, chicken breast, eggs, tissues. *Teacher, I want to see.*

She abandoned her breakfast and pulled her cleaning supplies from under the sink. Checked the mouse trap. Empty. Good. "Are you coming?" she called to Comfort from the base of the stairs as she headed up. The dog lifted her head, then lowered it. Emmalyn was on her own.

The room she bypassed every day—the spare room—stood blindingly bright in the morning sun, its all-white color scheme crisp, pure, glowing against the super-saturated blue of the sky and water scene through the wide windows. Everything looks better in sunlight.

"Everything looks dustier, too." Emmalyn watched dust motes slow-waltzing in the early light. The new windows on this floor meant fewer drafts. So the dust motes drifted lazily, no more sense of direction than . . .

Than Emmalyn had.

She dusted top to bottom, left to right, so she always knew where she'd been with the dust rag. So few items on the shelves in this room. Just enough to make it look finished. Not enough to make it looked lived in. Which it probably never would.

For months, Emmalyn had noodled ideas for her work-from-home job. Moving to the island upped the stakes. The job pool was larger than opportunity on Madeline Island, especially in the off season. She could turn the spare bedroom into an office if her Cottage Cook idea took off. And if she could convince one of her connections from pro-chef days to advertise . . . or . . . ?

Emmalyn lifted the chenille bunny from its perch on the shelf above the single bed. The one childhood toy she'd kept for her own baby. Its floppy ears and floppier arms and legs dipped with the dust motes while she ran her microfiber rag over its resting spot. Too late for cradles. Too late for cribs. Too soon for the wastebasket.

She replaced it on the shelf, plumped the pillows on the bed, straightened the comforter, and moved on to the next room, one with an equal set of lost dreams.

Working away from home had its advantages.

17

Prep for the Thanksgiving meal at The Wild Iris turned out to be anything but traditional. Emmalyn didn't catch the full significance until Thanksgiving Day.

"You're seriously expecting two hundred people today, Bougie?"

"Some years, we've had more than that."

"Are there that many residents on Madeline Island this time of year who don't have a place to go for Thanksgiving?"

"Most of them have a place to go. They come from the mainland, too. A couple hundred wouldn't be unusual."

"In here?" Emmalyn's eyes scanned The Wild Iris interior. It hadn't grown wings or appendages. Where would they put that many customers? They'd prepped for half of the Midwest to show up, and rearranged the floor plan, but Emmalyn expected Bougie's plans stretched out farther than this meal.

"They eat in shifts. Like any big family." Bougie looped her hair into a rough bun and stuck chopsticks cross-wise to hold it. She squirted hand sanitizer on her hands, offered some to Emmalyn, and said, "Here we go. Just unlock the door and move out of their way."

The directives weren't far from reality. The restaurant filled within minutes, each patron drawing a number from the upside-down pilgrim hat at the entrance and finding a place among the scattered tables. None voiced a complaint, even those seated at the tables with only a bowl of rice and weak tea.

What a sight. A table marked "Third World Banquet" with rice and tea. A table marked "Single Parent Family" with mac-and-cheese and hot dogs. A table marked "Homeless in America" with an odd mix that looked like it came from a mildly successful Dumpster-dive. "Homeless Anywhere Else" marked the table with a bowl of well-aged bread crusts. A "Winter before Thanksgiving" table, decorated with Indian corn and pilgrim hats, held bowls of wrinkled turnips, watery venison soup, and flakes of smoked fish. The table marked "Prisoners" held the kinds of compart-mentalized trays Emmalyn remembered from watching docu-mentaries of a 1950s cafeteria. On the trays were pools of runny mashed potatoes, gray-green peas, and a mystery meat that only the cooks knew wasn't made from roofing tiles. Max had com-plained about prison food in their early communications. Then he stopped talking about anything.

The final table boasted everything expected of a Thanksgiving meal—turkey, gravy, cranberry sauce, stuffing, mounds of mashed potatoes, sweet potatoes, green bean casserole with bright beans and homemade onion strings Emmalyn attended to herself, pumpkin pie, Bougie's pecan custard pie . . .

Wave after wave of patrons filed in, ate whatever meal was assigned them, the atmosphere far more sober than Emmalyn had ever seen it, and filed out to allow those waiting in line outside in the cold to come in. No one left without dropping a contribution into one or more of the canning jars in the middle of each table.

Pirate Joe got the nod from Bougie as what looked like the final guests prepared to leave. He took off his apron and settled himself at the "Prisoners" table. Alone. He sat with head bowed for more than a few moments, then picked up a dulled fork and tasted everything.

Emmalyn finished clearing the "Single Parent" and "Homeless Anywhere Else" tables and stood near Pirate Joe's chair. "May I get you fresh coffee?"

He looked up, intense emotion written across his face. Then a smile spread. "I'd be grateful. But it'll have to be stale coffee today. Extra weak. Remembering." He motioned toward the "Prisoners" sign.

She obliged, hard as it was to give him less than he deserved. She poured herself a cup from the carafé specifically marked for that table and joined him.

"You don't have to eat here," he said.

"I think I do."

He let the confession go unanswered.

The two ate in silence. And wonder. Freedom had a taste and texture not represented on their trays. It had choices they weren't allowed this day. They ate in honor of a conquered past, a hopeful future, and those still behind bars.

How did you spend Thanksgiving, Emmalyn? I shared an exceptional meal with an ex-prisoner named Pirate Joe. Best Thanksgiving ever.

The leftovers of the traditional meal were boxed for delivery to the mainland. Emmalyn helped a volunteer load her van for the trip to Ashland to a shelter for battered women. An unadvertised shelter. Joe told Emmalyn that Bougie knew its location. All too well. One day, it would be Bougie's turn to tell her story.

The sting of Max's letter got lost in Emmalyn's efforts to serve the community. It dissolved in a pile of runny mashed potatoes. She finished returning the restaurant to its original layout, set the tables for normal service the next day, and found Bougie to ask her if there was anything else she could do.

Bougie screwed a zinc lid onto the jar from the "Prisoners" table. "Yes, there is." She pressed the jar into Emmalyn's hands. "Go see your husband."

"It's not that I can't afford the trip." So close to a lie. She could afford a couple tanks of gas. Could she afford the emotional expense?

"Ah, but now you have greater incentive—not disappointing all those who gave so you could go."

An ache started low in her back and crept up her spine, spreading to matching spots under her shoulder blades. "I'm not even sure when visitation is allowed."

"Find out," Bougie called over her shoulder as she disappeared into the walk-in cooler.

⸻

That beautiful elbow in the road—road and woods to the left, a wide stretch of sand and water to the right—told Emmalyn she was within a few feet of her own door. Most of the snow had melted, so the lane was a little slushy. She tiptoed around the worst of it, stomped her feet on the porch, and reached to slip the key in the lock as her cell phone rang.

She stumbled into the cottage as Comfort raced out, threw her purse and tote bag on the kitchen island, and answered her cell phone while scooping purse contents from where they'd scooted across the granite. "Hello?"

A mechanical click almost moved her to end the call, but she heard a stilted voice say, "Will you accept a collect call from the state prison system?"

Her heart raced faster than Comfort's attempt to get outside. *Yes, of course, but . . .*

"Yes. I will."

Another click. A pause. "Emmalyn?"

"Max? Max, I can't believe it. It's so good to hear your voice." An icicle in blinding sun, her heart hurried to melt.

A deeper pause. "Em . . . I . . . they don't give us much time. Fifteen minutes. We'll be cut off in the middle of a sentence."

"It's okay. It's just so good to— I haven't written back yet. I wasn't sure what to say."

"Em, I'm losing hope!" His voice collapsed in a heart-wrenching groan.

She blinked back tears. She hadn't heard him this low since the night of the accident. He hadn't reacted this strongly even when the judge pronounced his sentence. "Max, honey, you're only a few months from getting out. Hang in there." She was so rusty at encouragement. The word *honey* made her cringe with its clumsiness. *Hang in there?* How utterly inadequate.

"No. Not that. My daughter. I'm losing Hope."

She "heard" the capital letter H on Hope now. And the sound of a man's heart shattering.

"Don't do this. Don't do this. Don't *do* this!" she hollered at the phone when the screen told her "Signal lost." They hadn't had their full fifteen minutes. It couldn't have been more than seven or eight when the line went dead in the middle of Max's explanation.

She'd heard enough to know it was serious. Impossible.

And she'd heard the name *Claire* far too much in those seven minutes with Max. This time, her heart lurched with sympathy rather than jealousy.

Claire's "trouble"? She'd exchanged her latest boyfriend and an affinity for a once-needed prescription into a love affair with cocaine. Cocaine. Sick, and she knew it. She needed to check in to a resident rehab center, but without family or friends willing to take Hope . . .

If Hope disappeared into the foster care system, would Claire ever be healthy enough to get her out?

Claire's family had their own problems, some worse than Claire's, if that were possible. She hadn't called on Max for help. What could he do from behind bars? She'd contacted him to tell him she was sorry for what she'd put him through, what she'd put her daughter through, and why he might not hear from Hope again, at least for a long while.

What a nightmare! Claire told Max it was cocaine. Emmalyn wondered if it had morphed farther than that. From Max's description, she talked like a heroin addict.

Emmalyn had listened, the shattering of her heart in harmony with Max's, oddly enough.

Before they'd been cut off, Emmalyn had ventured, "Max, is it true you believe in . . . God's power to . . . create answers where there aren't any?"

The line had gone dead before his response.

And now she sat in suffocating silence hundreds of miles from him, with compassion she wore like stiff jeans and a jar full of donations a foot away from where she leaned.

"Call back. Can you call back?" She plugged the phone into its charger, taking no chances. She double-checked the volume. Full-blast. "Call back!"

That sweet little girl, the one Emmalyn had tried to ignore. What must Hope Elizabeth be going through? How fast had she had to grow up? Was she okay?

Emmalyn didn't remember letting Comfort back in, but there she was, wet paws and all, asking to be fed. Emmalyn dabbed her paws with a towel she'd hung near the back door for that purpose, filled her food dish and water bowl, and wished the dog a Happy Thanksgiving.

Thanksgiving. This was Max's Thanksgiving—a message from Claire that his daughter might be in danger, or lost to him forever. What kind of clout would he have when released, an ex-prisoner who'd only had minor visitation rights, according to the law? What if Claire never did get Hope back? What then?

Her heart caught in her throat. Max had called her, knowing she could do nothing. He'd called her because he hoped she'd share his pain. He needed to know she cared.

She was Rachel.

And she knew Leah's—Claire's—phone number.

Emmalyn fingered the notebook-sized whiteboard she held in front of her. HOPE. A suited limo driver waiting near her at the carousel asked, "Are you giving it or taking it?"

"What?"

"Hope." He pointed to the word. "You know, like, 'Repent. The end of the world is at hand.' Or 'Smile. Your face will appreciate it.'"

Emmalyn swallowed around the ever-present lump in her throat. This was the right thing to do, wasn't it? Claire had sounded relieved. And life-weary. "Both."

The man moved ever so slowly a step farther away.

Until two days earlier, Emmalyn didn't know Duluth had an airport, much less an international one. Its proximity to the Canadian border made that logical, when she thought about it. Now she waited at the airport's end of the line—Baggage Claim— for the world to change.

It wouldn't be hard to recognize a twelve-year-old girl travel-ing alone—a girl with Max's eyes, lopsided dimples, and chin. But would Hope recognize Emmalyn, if not for the sign? The girl was six or seven the last time they saw each other. And Emmalyn hadn't smiled enough back then.

She'd rehearsed what she'd say the entire U-shaped trip from Bayfield to Duluth. By the time she pulled into Superior on her way to the bridge that crossed from Wisconsin to Minnesota at Duluth, she'd discarded every point of discussion. What does one say to a little girl whose mom is headed for rehab, her dad's in prison, and now she's exiled to a youth-forsaken island to live with a woman who's always had a hard time looking her in the eye?

Swallowed by the sea of travelers, the girl eventually emerged into an area open enough for Emmalyn to see her. So delicately beautiful. Clear skin. A gentle dusting of freckles across the bridge of her nose. Dark, satiny hair that moved like angelfish fins as she walked.

"How was your flight?"

"Fine."

Good start. One-word answers.

"Have you flown before?"

"First time."

"Did you enjoy it?" Dumb question. She'd said good-bye to her mother for who knew how long.

Hope looked at her feet. "I found out what a barf bag is for."

"Oh, honey." Emmalyn put an arm around the thin shoulders, thin despite the winter coat. The shoulders shrugged her off.

"Not me." Irritation edged her voice. "The dude sitting next to me."

"Oh."

The baggage carousel shuddered to life. "What color is your bag?"

"The color of a paper bag."

That poor child. How embarrassing for her. Emmalyn trained her eyes on the carousel, watching for a—

Hope stepped forward and snatched a camel-colored suitcase from the carousel. By the time Emmalyn realized that's what she meant by paper bag, Hope had wrestled the luggage to the floor and unlatched its telescoping handle.

"Here, let me help with that." Something in Emmalyn's soul clenched. That one bag and the small carry-on were all she'd brought? Not your average pre-teen. Emmalyn tugged the larger piece into following and led the way to her parking spot.

"Have you been to this area before, Hope?"

Her plush boots shuffled against the pavement as they walked. "No."

Except for the shuffle, the girl walked like a dancer, head high, shoulders back. Defensive posture or good habit? Time would tell.

"Are you hungry? I thought we'd stop somewhere here in Duluth or Superior. It's quite a trip from here to the cottage, if you count the time for the ferry ride and its schedule."

"Okay."

"What kind of fast food do you like?" Emmalyn would tough out whatever she answered.

"Does it have to be fast food?"

"What? No. What were you thinking?"

"There's a place in Superior that was on a *Diners, Drive-Ins, and Dives* episode. Their burgers are cheap but really good, Guy Fieri said. I looked them up online. The Anchor."

Emmalyn glanced at Hope as the girl thumbed her cell phone screen. "I've never been there. Sounds good."

"I thought the olive and cream cheese burger might be an interesting taste sensation."

Taste sensation? Who was this child? "I'm game if you are."

"They have a BLT, if you don't want a burger. Listen to this," she said, reading from her phone. "Our BLT is not blueberries, liver, and truffles."

The tension in Emmalyn's shoulders relaxed a little. "A restaurant with a sense of humor. I like that."

Hope stole a quick glance at Emmalyn. "Me, too."

"Then you're going to love The Wild Iris."

"What's that?"

"Where I work. I can't wait to introduce you to Bougie and the rest of the crew." Too much too soon? Emmalyn busied herself unlocking the trunk and loading the luggage into her car.

It wasn't until they were both belted in and Emmalyn backed out of the parking spot that Hope spoke again. "Bougie? A French name, isn't it?"

"How did you know that?"

"I'm taking French online. My school doesn't . . . didn't . . . offer it."

School. Right. Still some major glitches to get worked out.

Hope shrugged out of her coat without removing her seatbelt. "It means 'candle.' Did you know that?"

"I did. And it suits her perfectly."

Emmalyn focused on negotiating Duluth traffic. Hope leaned forward as they crossed the bridge into Wisconsin, entranced by the grain elevators, the barges, the immense seagoing vessels that had navigated their way through the series of Great Lakes to the Duluth harbor. Emmalyn kept her eyes on the road.

The girl seemed fascinated, too, by the contrasts of flatter, calmer Superior. Her phone's guidance system directed them to The Anchor. The massive anchor in front of the establishment might have been enough.

"'Hope is an anchor,'" Hope said as the two approached the entrance.

Emmalyn shifted her purse handle on her shoulder. "I suppose it is."

"The verse. It's my life verse, so far. Hebrews 6:19—'Hope is an anchor.' There's more to it, but that's the core thought."

The core thought? Emmalyn pinched back the guilt of having ignored this intriguing little girl for so long.

Guilt won the round. She hadn't ignored her. She'd rejected her. Subtly, of course. Or maybe not.

Loud, noisy families and louder couples or groups of friends occupied the other tables in the compact Anchor eatery. Emmalyn and Hope fought through the noise to make conversation, so for that and a hundred other reasons, they said little.

Hope asked for water with her meal.

"Would you rather have a soda? Soft drink?"

"Mom won't let me drink that stuff."

Your mother is addicted to cocaine, Hope Elizabeth. But she must have done something right. "Good to know."

"You . . . you don't have to follow all her rules," Hope added, a shadow passing across her perfect face. "But, water's fine."

The burgers were as delicious as touted. They finished their meals quickly without the pauses for lengthy conversation, and exited to the quiet crispness of the late November air.

"Is The Wild Iris crazy like that?" Hope asked a mile or two down the road.

Emmalyn chuckled. "It's wild, but in other ways. Not that noisy. Pretty classy, actually."

Hope locked her gaze on the scene outside the passenger window. What must she be going through internally? She was smart enough to know her mom wasn't well, and probably knew why.

How long before she opened up about it? Would she ever?

And how would Max react when he heard what Emmalyn had done? Their relationship couldn't afford a blowout right now. But Hope couldn't afford to be homeless, either. And Emmalyn couldn't ignore the air hammer nudge telling her she could do something about it, despite what that child had always represented to her.

What if the biblical Rachel had said to Leah, "Here. Let me help you out with your kids"?

It wasn't as simple as that. So not simple. Not simple.

"What grade are you in, Hope?"

"Sixth."

"Oh. Okay."

"It's going to be hard. Isn't it." Hope landed her sentence on a low note.

"Hard?"

"I looked it up online."

Interesting.

Hope turned in her seat to face Emmalyn more directly. "Fifteen students at the school on Madeline Island? And it only goes through fifth grade?"

"That's what I've heard. I haven't had time to look into it."

"That means riding the ferry every single day? Twice?" Hope swiveled to face forward. Silence enveloped the car's interior again.

"Do you want me to turn on the radio?" Emmalyn reached for the button.

"No, thanks. How much farther?"

"We have a long way to go." *A very long way.*

18

Almost two months earlier, Emmalyn sat in line for the ferry from Bayfield to Madeline Island with an apple and her purse on the passenger seat. Dreamless. Resigned. With a trunkful of misdirected apprehension. This time, she had a passenger—a dreamless, resigned, apprehensive passenger, from all signs.

"How much longer?" Hope sounded as if she were trying not to ask, but couldn't help herself.

"See where the ferry is now? It'll take about fifteen more minutes for it to dock here. Then a bit for the current passengers to unload. We should be boarding in, oh, twenty minutes."

"But—"

Emmalyn checked her face in the rearview mirror. No real point reapplying lip gloss now. They were nearly home. But she looked almost as tired as she felt.

"But what, Hope?"

The girl picked at a cuticle. "Daddy's supposed to call in fifteen minutes."

"Cell phones have to be turned off while we're on the ferry."

———

She calls him Daddy.
He calls her.

192

"I'm sorry. It's a safety factor, I assume."

First tears. Emmalyn imagined them in Max's eyes, so similar to Hope's. The girl worked hard to keep them from spilling. Her lips showed the strain of trying to stop the trembling in her chin. "Okay."

Breathless. Resigned.

The prison system wasn't conducive to the outside world's "Can I call you back in a sec? In a jiffy?" A true unit of measure, according to Hope's bottomless bag of trivia. *Did you know that a jiffy is a thousandth of a second?* Hope had injected into the mostly silent trip. If she was getting her information from the Internet, they might have to have a talk.

Emmalyn clicked her seatbelt into place. "Are you buckled up?" She turned the key in the ignition and wiggled the Prius out of the queue of cars, across the parking lot, and into the empty side lot by the old cooperage next door. "When your dad calls, I'll go for a walk so you can have some privacy."

"But the ferry—"

"We'll catch the next one."

Emmalyn reached over the backseat for her camera, grabbed her handknit Cora scarf for her neck, and waited behind the still steering wheel for Hope's phone to ring.

It wasn't a ring. It was a ringtone: "Right Here Waiting for You." Emmalyn blew Hope a kiss and shut the car door behind her. *Blew her a kiss? Emmalyn, you have no clue how to do this, do you?*

The cooperage now housed a sporting goods and outfitter shop, vacant—or nearly so—this time of year. She walked the exterior of the property, close enough to keep an eye on the car but far enough for it to be obvious she was giving Hope space.

A fountain of bile inched up her esophagus. Emmalyn was bending over backward for this twelve-year-old when she'd been out of communication with her husband much longer, apparently. Emmalyn. The wife. On paper, anyway.

Emmalyn glanced through the windshield again, a diligent though untested caregiver. Hope covered her face with one hand, shoulders shaking. *Oh, child.* Emmalyn intentionally pointed her camera toward the now-docked ferry. It looked the part of a lumbering albatross but glided through the water in the bay more smoothly than Emmalyn imagined it could on all but the worst weather days. She checked the posted ferry schedule as the ferry unloaded and prepared for the return trip. They'd have to kill a good chunk of time in town before the next one. Story of her life.

Maybe Hope would be interested in the shipwreck park. As sharp as the young woman was, she might find it educational rather than a testimony to despair. Would Emmalyn see it in the same light she had months ago? Or would she find the concept of a shipwreck park stirring, somehow, now that she'd seen even limping souls can dance?

Emmalyn heard the car door open. Hope waved wildly. "He wants to talk to you. Hurry!"

She jogged back to the car and took the phone. Her inhale was as jagged as if it had climbed stairs in her lungs. "Hey, Max."

"Em, I don't know what to say."

She didn't either, especially with Hope right at her elbow. "We're all getting used to the idea."

"I can't believe you'd do that."

"Without consulting you first? I know. There wasn't much time to—"

"I can't believe you'd do it at all. I can only imagine what this is costing you . . . and I don't mean financially. Oh, Emmalyn . . . "

Neither spoke for several moments, which seemed a tragic waste of limited time. "I'll let you talk to Hope again," she said. "We'll have to discuss a few things."

"Can I . . . call you sometime soon?" His request sounded like the end of a first date. An undercurrent of strength in his voice kept it from a pathetic plea.

"I don't want to cheat you out of time for Hope."

Another ocean-deep pause. "I never meant for any of this to happen."

"You take care, too. Here's Hope."

She forced a smile as she handed the phone to the girl with Max's bright eyes and curious dimples. Then she turned her face toward the water. Hope didn't need to witness Emmalyn's breakdown.

"Is this Lake Superior or Chee-kwah-MEE-gan Bay?"

The ferry rumbled underneath them. Solid. Sure. Protective. Unconcerned about waves and water depth and the turmoil in the heart of a forgotten wife and an abandoned child.

"It's actually pronounced more like 'Sheh-WAH-meh-gun.' Crazy, huh? And the answer is both. Chequaumegon Bay is part of Lake Superior. You can just see a hint of some of the other Apostle Islands off to the left of us. There are twenty-two islands in the Apostle Islands National Lakeshore. But—"

"I know. Madeline Island isn't included. Probably because it's the only one inhabited."

The girl's brain must fire faster than others. How does she retain all these bits?

"Will it be a lot colder here than in Montana?"

"Every winter's different, I hear. But the island is often more temperate because of the hills behind Bayfield and the buffer of the water. We'll see how this winter treats us." How long did Hope expect she'd have to stay with Emmalyn? She'd need to watch how she worded things.

The ferry closed the distance between them and the Madeline Island/LaPointe dock.

"Mrs. Ross?"

They'd have to work on that, too. "Yes?"

"Can I keep my phone?"

"Of course. Oh." Emmalyn toyed with financial numbers in her head.

"Yeah. Not an easy question. I don't think Mom can . . . pay you back. And I know Dad can't." She ran her finger around the perimeter of her phone while she talked.

"Let's not worry about those minor details right now." Did Hope text a thousand friends a thousand times a day? Was it a *minor* detail?

The ferry eased into its slot like a vessel much smaller and easier to maneuver. Hope stretched to watch what she could see above the high sidewalls of the ferry.

"Before you ask," Emmalyn said coyly, waiting for the signal to start the ignition, "it's not far now."

That crooked smile on Hope's face was worth the risk.

※

The last time she chauffeured someone's first visit to Madeline Island, it was her sister, Shawna. The skeptic. The tattletale. The one who considered nature a rude inconvenience.

Her first-timer today drank in the details. Hope Elizabeth didn't converse much from the ferry landing on the duck's tail to the duck's chin hairs, but quick glances showed Emmalyn the girl caught the significance of the beauty through which they traveled.

"That was the whole town?" she'd said, one of her few communications.

"That was it. Someday I'll take you the South Shore route. You'll see more of the marina and the golf course—beautiful golf course."

"I'm not really into golf," Hope had said.

Yeah. Me neither.

Despite the town's inability to impress the twelve-year-old, the scenery between LaPointe and the cottage kept Hope's head turning to catch everything within view.

"This is it, Hope."

The girl glanced at the small shed with its narrow door and one high window. The cottage beyond it seemed to bloom before her eyes. They widened like time elapsed photography of a rose-bud opening. "It's a long ways out here."

"That's true." Emmalyn popped the button to open the trunk for the luggage.

"This isn't what I expected."

Trust me. It's not what I expected either. Any of this.

They'd barely had time to stomp snow from their feet on the entry rug when Hope said, "You have a dog?"

"Hold back, Hope. She can be particular." Emmalyn tried to step between them in the narrow entry of the cottage.

But the girl had already scooted past her and dropped to her knees on the kitchen floor, arms wide open. It looked more like a reunion for the girl and dog than it did their first encounter.

"What's its name?"

"Comfort. She's a female."

"I had no idea you had a dog."

That's all it took? And why would it seem surprising? Had Emmalyn been so singularly focused when Hope had visited when she was four, five, six, that it was unthinkable Emmalyn would have let an animal into her life?

Yes. The answer was yes.

"She's adorable!" Hope's voice squeaked an octave higher than normal.

Emmalyn shoved the luggage past the lovebirds further into the cottage interior. "She has an interesting personality." When she'd arrived, the island had given her a cottage with no person-ality and a dog with an excess of it.

"Everybody does," Hope said, clutching the animal to her chest.

And she has an uncanny connection to people in pain. That helped explain Comfort's obvious and instant affection for a twelve-year-old homeless girl.

"You can hang your coat there on the hooks," Emmalyn offered.

Hope nuzzled the dog's neck one last time, then stood and did as asked.

Emmalyn let the dog out. "Necessity, honey," she said to Hope's pout. "She'll be back." *And then someday she won't.* No need to break that news to Hope just yet. "Let's get you settled into your room."

Hope followed Emmalyn through the cottage at the pace of a glacier's movements. "Are you okay, Hope?"

The girl stopped in front of the French doors and pressed her palms against the wood on either side of one of the panels. "This is what you look at every day?" Her voice was no louder than the swish of waves on shore on a still evening.

"Every day."

"It's, like . . . perfect."

"I know." And she did. Exile could be a good thing. Breath-stealing scenes can help clear a person's lungs. "Come on. Upstairs. You should see the view from the second floor."

Halfway up the narrow stairs, Hope asked, "Did you grow up here?"

Emmalyn thought about her answer. "Yes. But not the way you'd think."

Hope didn't push for more. How much of Emmalyn's life story did Hope know? Oh, dear. She'd likely meet Emmalyn's mom and sisters someday. That would take careful planning and more ibuprofen than Emmalyn had on hand.

"Your room is mostly white right now. That might not appeal to you. We can paint, if you like." *Please, nothing purple.* She stepped past the doorway to let Hope enter first.

Her gasp made Emmalyn's heart soar. Hope ran her small hand over the bedspread, the headboard, the low rocker in the corner. She touched everything on the shelves. Her hand paused near the flop-eared chenille rabbit. "Can I . . . ?"

That was mine.

"Oh, look!" Hope said before Emmalyn could respond. "A perfect spot for my computer." She smoothed her hand over the converted sewing table. She twirled to face Emmalyn. "Do you have Internet?"

And the first real conflict. "I don't have a television." She waited for the fallout.

"Yeah, that's fine."

What? "But I do have an Internet connection. I want to start an online business someday. Maybe."

"Fun."

"But we should clear this up right at the start. I know a lot of young people your age are"—*not the word* addicted—"*into* gaming pretty heavily. And I don't want you to get so hung up on it that—"

"I'm not a gamer, Mrs. Ross. I need the Internet for my dad's blog."

"Your dad has a blog."

"It's his ministry thing. He talks about what it's like in prison and what it's like to be free even though you're in prison. He's funny sometimes, too. Dad doesn't have computer privileges other than restricted email, but he sends me his blog ideas and I post them for him."

"Your dad has a blog."

"I figured you didn't know or you would have said something."

Emmalyn reached for the rabbit and sat on Hope's bed with it propped in her lap, her arms draped around it. "A blog."

"I'm not a gamer, Mrs. Ross. You don't have to worry about that."

Emmalyn's heart pounded. She'd kept her distance from Max because she thought that's what he wanted. Or was it her resentment that made her justify her distance? Either way, she'd missed everything important.

"You don't have to call me Mrs. Ross." *Right now, the term rattles me.* "You can use Emmalyn, or some of my friends call me Emi. Bougie calls me M, like the letter M."

"I like that. M. Kind of like *Mom*, but not quite."

Right. Not quite.

⟨⟨⟨

Comfort split her time evenly between their laps. Hope preferred the couch. Her petite size—small for her age—and lithe legs could curl into all kinds of configurations Emmalyn could no longer manage. Emmalyn guessed Hope hadn't crossed the puberty bridge yet, but wasn't about to tackle that subject. Unless she had to.

"Will you be hungry for supper soon?" Emmalyn set aside the knitting needles and project Cora had talked her into. *You don't knit because you have too much time. You knit to create.* Emmalyn added, *Or to avoid discussion without seeming anti-social.*

"Can I cook?" Hope's face brightened.

"You like to cook?"

"I've pretty much done all the cooking at home. Lately." She dragged her teeth across her bottom lip.

"Mind if I help?"

"What do you have in the pantry?" Hope hopped off the couch and padded to the kitchen. She didn't drag her feet as she had in her boots.

"Lots of stuff. Except no pantry. You can check the fridge and the cupboard to the left of sink. And the lower cupboard on the far side of the island, opposite the stools."

Again, the girl didn't shuffle her feet like she had when wearing her boots. "Hope?"

"Yeah?" The girl answered with her head in the fridge.

"Are your boots the right size for your feet?"

She closed the refrigerator door and looked at it, not Emmalyn. "They're Mom's. She wasn't going to need them for a while."

"Are they hard to walk in? They seem like they might be a little bigger than you need."

"I don't mind."

God of all heaven and earth, what do I do now? I don't know how to do this. "If you're sure you don't mind, that's fine, then."

200

Anything else, Lord? "If you ever decide they're uncomfortable that way, just let me know."

The girl's shoulders gave away her sigh. "Thanks."

"So, did you find anything workable in the fridge?"

"Do you ever—?"

"What? Just say it, Hope. You don't have to tiptoe around me." A few months ago, maybe. Not as much anymore.

"Do you ever do, like, pancakes for supper?"

"No!" Emmalyn answered, her hand over her heart as if she'd been shot. "Not without bacon. You'll find it on the second shelf." She winked.

Hope's laughter floated through the cottage, lighting the shadowed corners. No matter what age, a child's laughter changes things.

⚬⚬⚬

"What do you think?" Emmalyn waited for Hope's response.

"How do you know this stuff? Candied bacon?" Hope said, sliding her fork under another bite of pancake. "It's *délicieux*."

"How do *you* know the French word for delicious?" Emmalyn chuckled. "Never mind. Online classes, right? I'm . . . I was a caterer. And . . . chef. Once."

"And clarified butter. Who knew?"

"Simple pleasures." Pleasure like finding a pre-teen who gets excited about clarified butter. Just wait until Emmalyn introduced Hope to Bougie's crème brulee.

"I don't supposed we can have candied bacon every morning?"

"Uh, no."

"But I bet this place will still smell great in the morning."

Emmalyn would wake in the morning to the smell of tonight's bacon and the warmth of the conversation still radiating through her chest. "Have you given any thought to what you'd like to do differently with your room?"

Hope tilted her head. "I don't want to change anything."

201

"Okay."

"I probably won't be here that long."

She said it so casually. Did she believe it? Emmalyn searched Hope's eyes for a clue. The girl focused her gaze on the dog at her feet.

What had that child been through? What kind of scenes had she witnessed? Abused? No visible scars. That didn't guarantee anything.

They cleaned up the dishes together. Emmalyn half-expected Hope to object, but she handled herself in the kitchen like a seasoned pro. Without complaint.

Hope poured herself a glass of artesian water and added a twist of lemon. Emmalyn did the same before the two retired to the living area again. Emmalyn bent to start a fire in the fireplace. When it was well established, she sank into her chair and picked up her knitting needles and wool.

"What are you knitting?" Hope asked.

"Stitches," Emmalyn said, then cleared her throat.

"I know that much."

"Just stitches. I'm learning."

"At your age? Sorry. I didn't mean it that way."

Emmalyn faked a scowl. "It's a wonder I have any brain cells or memory left, but yes. I'm learning something new. I think it's a scarf. Sometimes you don't know what it is until you see what it becomes."

Her marriage. A stitch at a time. What would it become?

"Did you know," Hope said, brandishing her phone, "that a group of geese on the ground is called a gaggle, but if they're in the air, they're called a skein? Like a skein of wool? Who makes this stuff up?"

"I'm sure that tidbit will come in useful in your educational career."

A cloud moved across Hope's flawless face. "About school. We should probably talk."

"We have a couple of days to figure that out. And Christmas break isn't all that far away."

"Exactly." Hope studied the ceiling. "Which is why I was thinking . . . "

Emmalyn could feel her eyebrows creep closer to her hairline. She worked to soften her expression. Was she ready for this conversation? "Thinking is good."

"I don't want to go to a new school right now. I don't want to ride the ferry every day." Her forehead creased. The dimples disappeared completely. But there wasn't a trace of a whine in her voice.

"You'd rather not go to school at all? I'm sure the State of Wisconsin won't have any problem with that." She smiled.

"No!" Hope sat up taller and gestured with her hands as if pleading for understanding. "I love school. I mean, I love *learning*."

"I resist it sometimes, Hope." Way too often. "But for the most part, I love learning, too." She held up her knitting project for emphasis.

"Can't I learn here?"

Emmalyn felt her heart muscle shift uncomfortably in her chest. "Hon, the LaPointe school only goes through fifth grade."

"I know. We talked about that." She tapped the floor with one stockinged foot. "Here. In the cottage. Did you ever homeschool anybody?"

Oh, good grief.

"It wouldn't be hard. I'm self-motivated."

"I imagine you are." *Probably more self-motivated than I've been for the last few years, until coming here.*

"I'm already ahead of where I should be, according to academic standards."

Good. Grief. "I have to work, Hope." Why was she even entering this debate? "I have a job." That's what she'd call working for Bougie part-time. A job.

"I could do a lot of it online. I can stay here by myself while you're at work."

"No."

"No to staying home alone? I've done it a zillion times."

Claire! Why do the people least equipped to raise children have so little trouble giving birth to them? A familiar ache—one absent for a few brief hours—returned.

"It's no big deal."

Hope would make a great Toastmaster speaking candidate. She punctuated her persuasive speech with hand gestures to drive her point home. For "no big deal," she waved her hands in opposite directions in front of her.

Emmalyn struggled to control the pace of her breathing. "It's a big deal, Hope."

"I'm mature for my age."

"I'm not."

Hope blinked. "What?"

"Maybe it shouldn't, but it would bother me. I told your mom I'd take care of you."

Hope's face contorted. Her lips twisted into an uneven line. A hitch in her breath, then, "Do you know who took care of *her*? Me." She pushed herself off the couch and crossed the room before Emmalyn got fully turned around.

"Hope!"

To her credit, Hope didn't pound up the stairs. And the door to Hope's bedroom wasn't slammed shut. The soft click seemed all the more heartbreaking.

Emmalyn grabbed thick handfuls of her hair and tugged. It didn't make her any smarter. She'd been pseudo-mom for less than twenty-four hours and already had blown it. This was never going to work.

It had to. Hope had no other options.

Is this what motherhood was like? Her heart a ping-pong ball slammed from joy to pain, the child's sanity and her own at stake? A small crisis, in the scheme of things. But it crushed her. Logic wouldn't give her an answer. Some questions have no answers.

She wasn't a homeschool mom, no matter how you define it. She wasn't even a mom.

She was a shelter.

Okay. Shelter. That, she could do.

A door opened above her. Another opened and closed. Emmalyn heard the water running. And running.

Choices. One after another. She'd commit to making one right choice after another. If only she'd had a flash of that kind of wisdom four years ago. Maybe farther back than that.

Emmalyn climbed the stairs and talked through the bathroom door. "There are some really nice bath salts in the cupboard by the window, Hope. You're welcome to use them. If you want. They smell like"—her volume disappeared off the charts—"baby powder."

She crept across the hall, through the open door, and pulled the floppy rabbit from the shelf above the bed. It looked comfortable propped on Hope's pillow.

19

Sullen Sunday.

Bougie texted mid-morning to ask how things were going. Emmalyn texted back, "I totally missed the notice that it's Sullen Sunday."

"Love neutralizes sullen," Bougie'd replied.

It took Emmalyn an hour of pondering that statement and another cup of coffee before she could answer. "If I didn't already know I wasn't cut out for this, I'd think I wasn't cut out for this."

"U R. Jst need more practice."

Hope refused breakfast and stayed in her room until almost ten. When she did come downstairs, it was for a glass of orange juice. It didn't help that the sky sported its own version of sullen. Gray, flat, low, and spitting.

At eleven, Emmalyn called up the stairs, "Hope, I'm going for a walk on the beach. Want to join me?"

A voice called back through the closed door. "It's ugly out there."

"It's ugly in here, too. Let's take it outside."

The door opened. "Can we bring Comfort?"

"Oh, I hope so. Yes. Ten minutes?"

"I'll be ready."

They traded time in the bathroom. Emmalyn could still smell remnants of the baby powder fragrance of the bath salts from the night before. She noted Hope's towel had been hung neatly on the rack. More surprises. Her toothbrush and toothpaste stuck out of the top of a small zippered bag. Hope didn't plan to stay long.

The young thing beat her down the stairs.

Did Emmalyn dare break the uneasy, three-minutes-past-the-Cold-War truce? She had to. "Do you have gloves or mittens?" she asked as Hope zipped her jacket.

Was that the smallest of smiles on her porcelain doll face? "I guess I'll have to learn how to knit."

Emmalyn breathed deeply of the fragile moment of peace. It smelled like spring. "That would be fun. I know I have a spare pair of gloves you can use. Comfort, are you ready to go for a walk?" The dog didn't need to be asked twice.

Where the small stones were deepest on shore, they wobbled as if walking in a roomful of flattened marbles. The crunch of their boots as they dug footprints in the stones blended with the swoosh of waves and wind through barenaked trees and stiff-branched pines. Conversation seemed unnecessary, until Hope threw an arm across Emmalyn to stop her forward progress.

Emmalyn looked to where the girl pointed a dozen yards down the beach. The yearling deer, or one of its cousins, stepped out of the woods and paused, head alert, ears twitching. Its eyes wide and curious, it dipped its head, then lifted it and assumed a statue's pose. Hope bent slowly and picked up the dog, which acted unaware of the scene's tension.

Poor deer, Emmalyn thought. It probably thinks Comfort is an ordinary dog, the kind that chases and barks.

When the yearling retreated into the safety of the woods, Hope said, "That . . . was . . . awesome!"

Excitement on a child's face—priceless.

"One day, the doe walked right up to the porch of the cottage. I've seen tracks since then, but haven't caught it in the act."

"I would love to see that." Hope's awe replaced her previous angst.

"Maybe you will. You never know."

Hope turned her attention to the water. "Can you swim here?"

"Sure. It stays pretty cold, even in the summer. If you don't mind shivering . . . That small little dock isn't stable, though. It's pretty rickety. So stay away from it, okay?"

The drizzle ended. The sun worked hard to bore through the gray clouds, without success. Hope and Emmalyn traded vocabulary words to describe the breeze.

"Bracing," Emmalyn said.

"Invigorating."

"Brain-freezing."

"That's two words."

Emmalyn picked up a stone. "Hyphenated counts. Is this an agate, Hope?"

"I've never seen an agate except in a book. Is an agate valuable?"

"It depends on how beautiful you think it is." Everything traced back to her marriage. Everything. Emmalyn didn't know if she should be annoyed or should listen better.

"I've been in serious contemplation," Hope said.

A twelve-year-old broods, she doesn't "contemplate," does she?

"And I realize I may have overreacted."

She had Emmalyn's attention. "I'm listening."

"You don't know me very well yet. That's why you're afraid."

"I'm not afraid. That's not it."

Hope's mouth angled to the right. Her eyebrows arched high over wide eyes. The tilt of her head said, "Really?" without the need for vocabulary. The look spoke of sympathy, not sass.

"Okay, so I'm afraid sometimes."

"That's a relief," Hope said. "I thought you were perfect and perfect can be annoying. I'm glad you're sometimes scared, like me."

"And I'm strong."

"Me, too."

"Off and on."

Hope picked up a stone and tossed it into the lake. "Me, too."

Emmalyn mirrored Hope's action, their rocks disappearing under the surface of the water. Tomorrow, the next day, a month from now, they'd reappear farther down the shoreline from the action of several hundred waves. "Off and on. We make an interesting pair."

"Are there wolves on Madeline Island?"

"I've heard there are. Haven't seen any. But yes. Cora talks about hearing them at night."

"Cora?"

"A friend of mine. Her son painted the cottage. Cora put the skylight in the kitchen."

Without warning, Hope bent at the waist and grabbed the toes of her boots with gloved hands.

"Are you okay?"

The girl stood upright. "Stretching. Don't you stretch?"

"Pretty much everything about my life is a stretch right now."

The two reversed direction, walking in and out of silence. "Wolves are a reason, I guess."

Emmalyn waited for an explanation.

"A reason for you to be afraid to leave me home alone."

"Oh."

They jumped a depression in the sand, the place where a creek from somewhere within the heart of the island meandered to that spot in order to join the lake. Emmalyn had often stopped to watch the steady flow of ever-new water rushing through that depression, heading to wherever water goes when it's tired.

The terrain grew easier to manage when they neared the wide stretch of packed sand in front of the cottage. They danced back from the edge of an overachieving wave before turning to angle up the slope of rustling sea grass. Hope stopped before they reached the porch. She pointed up. "That's my room, isn't it? The window on the left." Her voice didn't register excitement, but neither did it speak of disappointment.

Emmalyn noticed she'd left a light on. Should she mention it? Not this time. "Yes. For as long as you need it."

"It's beautiful from the outside, too."

"Just like you, Hope."

The girl dipped her head. "Off and on." A muffled *Right Here Waiting for You* sang in her pocket. She tore off her gloves with her teeth and grabbed her phone. Emmalyn watched as she listened, keyed a series of numbers, then waited again. "Daddy?"

Emmalyn motioned that she'd go inside and give Hope privacy. But Hope followed her into the cottage, shrugged out of her coat and boots, and curled into a corner of the couch as she talked.

Privacy? Her husband was on the phone and she wasn't clamoring to talk to him? What was wrong with her? She should be snatching the phone and demanding some explanations. Or apologizing for backing off when she should have leaned in. Or just listening to the timbre of his voice and letting it move her back in time to the day they said their vows.

"We went for a walk on the beach," Hope said, her voice animated with what the beach does to a person. "Very funny, Dad. No, I don't have a tan yet."

Emmalyn appreciated the easy relationship between Hope and Max. A barb of jealousy chased the appreciation from the room. An easy relationship. She hung her coat, changed from boots to flats, and dove into lunch preparation. She pulled a container of tomato bisque from the freezer compartment of the refrigerator. Plus grilled cheese?

Not exactly Sunday dinner at Grandma's house or the chef's special expounded by a white-shirted server, but it would do. Sunday. Should she try going to a traditional church on Sunday in addition to the anything-but-traditional worship services on Tuesday night at Bougie's? For Hope's sake?

The girl had been listening to her father a long time. Emmalyn pulled two mugs and two small plates from the open cupboard shelves.

"But, Dad . . . Okay." She turned to Emmalyn. "He wants to talk to you again."

Having to cut her conversation short must have felt like missing the class trip to Disneyworld.

"Max? Glad you called." And she was.

"I apologize that this was sprung on you so fast." He sighed. "That it was sprung on you at all."

"I volunteered. Remember?"

"It's just impossible for me to do anything from here. Make any arrangements."

"For what?" His voice revived a necrotic brain cell or two. His words weren't making sense, though.

"I don't know. Boarding school, maybe? I have no idea how we could pull that off for the rest of this school year."

Emmalyn didn't want to use the term *boarding school* with twelve-year-old ears listening. Measuring her words and tone, she said, "That's not necessary, even if it were possible."

"What do you mean? The disruption in your life must have added so much new stress."

Did he think she couldn't handle stress well? What would have given him *that* idea? "I'm not who I was before . . . before all this."

"I can make calls to my lawyer, but I can't do much research to find a place—"

"Hope has a place, Max. Here."

A sterile voice broke into their conversation. "Two minutes remaining."

She despised the finality of the recording. How did a prisoner get anything talked through? "Max, Hope has a place here. We're . . . we're talking about home schooling for the rest of the year. Some online work. I haven't looked into curriculum yet. She just got here. But—"

"I don't care for that idea."

What? "It's not like I wouldn't give her every social opportunity. Madeline Island isn't the end of the world." Although that was *her* first thought crossing the ferry a couple of months ago.

"Please don't do that."

Four brain cells died for every two that had been activated. She talked as softly as she could. "Max, I respect your right to help guide your daughter's future, but under the circumstances, don't you have to cut me a little slack here? Do you really get to choose?" Probably not a chapter she'd find in a relationship handbook.

"I'm thinking of you," he said. "I want to make it easier for you."

"Me? Since when have you—?" Tongue biting isn't always metaphorical. It can be physical, she discovered. "Low blow. I apologize. Max, let us have a chance to work some things out here, okay? If it doesn't turn out, we'll shift gears. Max?" She turned to speak to Hope. "I think we got cut off."

"I'm here," Max said. "But we'll get dropped any second now."

"Then use your last few seconds to tell your daughter you love her. Here she is."

Emmalyn turned back to the container of soup. Frozen. She grabbed it and pressed the container to the throbbing at the back of her neck.

20

Her leg had fallen asleep, her foot pinched underneath her too long while she sat staring into the darkness. Emmalyn shook it, rubbed it, tried to stomp it awake without disturbing the household.

She had a household. Temporarily. The girl in the spare room upstairs decided to spend the rest of the day alone.

The prickles in Emmalyn's leg remained, despite traditional remedies. The cottage interior didn't leave much space for walking it off, but she stepped around the trunk to start a loop to and from the kitchen. Her leg buckled. Emmalyn reached out to catch herself, taken aback by how little control she had over a numb leg.

She collapsed to the floor. Her leg wasn't the culprit. It was the memory of photos in the courtroom. A paralyzed man no one claimed. Because of Max, homelessness was no longer his primary concern. His legs hadn't worked well before the accident, he'd reported. They didn't work at all after.

Cullen. He had a name. A single name that served as first, last, and middle for him. The investigators conjectured the man had invented it to cover something unsavory in his past. Or an unspeakable regret.

In that respect, she and Cullen and Max were family.

He'd been loitering where he shouldn't have been. Camped out on the sidewalk the night Max made an unscheduled visit to the fertility clinic, using their SUV as a doorbell.

Skid marks showed Max had tried to stop. A last minute wave of conscience? Clarity? Sobriety? Emmalyn couldn't look at skid marks on a highway without reliving the mind-numbing stack of evidence and the equally mind-numbing alternate explanations offered by Max's lawyer. The faulty accelerator raised a few eyebrows in the courtroom, but eyebrows don't make decisions about a person's future.

A sisal rug is perfect for a beach cottage, but it's abrasive when a person kneels on it, attempting to rise, but pressed down by the weight of a mistake or series of unfortunate events with life- and love-altering consequences. Emmalyn could feel every rough thread, even through jeans. She turned her face toward the back of the couch and dug her elbows into the seat cushions to take pressure off her knees.

She couldn't look at Hope without seeing Max in her eyes. She could give a little girl a sanctuary while her mom was in rehab. Emmalyn didn't realize Hope's presence would bring her eyeball to eyeball with an icon of imprisonment. She couldn't shake the thought of him. Didn't want to shake the thought of him. But the shards of what they'd had were so small now. Infinitesimally small. Like slivers of fiberglass you can't see to remove.

Cullen could kneel on broken glass without noticing. If only he could kneel.

Emmalyn rested her forehead on the tent peak of her clasped hands. She would have taken advantage of the posture and prayed if she could have thought of anything to say. Even the hopeless can squeeze out a "God, help us!" or a "Make this go away!" She'd screamed the words until she'd grown hoarse, years ago. Laryngitis—and hollowness—had prevented her from answering any of the press's questions post-trial, including the strokes of journalism genius—"How does it make you feel to know your husband was responsible for crippling a man?" and "Do you think your husband's actions were rooted in resentment over your obsession with wanting to have children?" Genius.

As if she hadn't thought of that before. Did no one understand it wasn't a want, it was a need? And that it wasn't an obsession, it was—

The only word that fit. She'd taken a longing and reshaped it into an obsession. In its longing form, it made beautiful sense. Its obsession form drained it of beauty.

Did the reporters think she'd come up with a sound bite no grieving spouse had uttered? Something headline-worthy? "I'm so proud of my husband for sitting hunched over and silent through-out the trial, so blessed that he's only being sent away for five years, so grateful we both have this opportunity to step away from the scene and work through what was obviously a symbolic gesture of his latent disgust for me." Emmalyn's mother insisted sarcasm didn't look good on anyone, but Emmalyn insisted on trying it on.

Stretching her leg to the side to work out the pinpricks must have made her look like a hurdler with bad form. She'd trained long and hard for it.

Four days after the sentencing, a local plane crash made the national news and attention was diverted from an SUV/fertility clinic collision and its consequences to the virtual debris field, body count, and black box recordings. God help her, Emmalyn was grateful for the diversion.

No. God doesn't help people who think like that.

Not the God she knew then.

Maybe *knew* was too strong a word.

She stood, tested her leg again, and maintained contact with a piece of furniture all the way to the kitchen. If Hope hadn't been there, she might have bundled up and gone for a walk again. Hope inside. Wolves and other critters outside. When times get tough, the not-so-tough go to bed.

The bathroom lamp didn't respond when Emmalyn reached under the shade to turn it on. Since the day she moved in, she'd left a small lamp burning in the bathroom on the low antique dresser. Her version of a nightlight. She padded down the stairs to get another bulb, padded back up the stairs, installed the bulb and hit the switch again. Nothing.

She traced the cord to the outlet. Unplugged. No wonder. She never unplugged this lamp. But she no longer lived alone.

Hope's blow dryer plug occupied the spot normally reserved for the lamp. Emmalyn could gripe, or she could make a note to get an adapter so everything had a spot to call its own.

She unplugged the inactive blow dryer and let the lamp have the power it needed for the night. Morning was soon enough to talk to Hope. The girl had gone to bed much earlier than Emmalyn assumed she would. Or gone to her room. Not always the same thing.

Emmalyn brushed her teeth, avoiding her reflection in the mirror as much as possible. Ice-blue eyes caught her. A thought squirmed somewhere just behind those eyes. She'd been jealous of Claire's reappearance in Max's life, communicating with him behind bars in a way Emmalyn hadn't mastered. Hadn't even attempted for too long, she had to admit. Jealousy sizzled like sausage in a hot pan over Hope's easy conversations with Max. Emmalyn's stuttered along and ended poorly.

She glanced in the mirror again to see if she'd left any toothpaste reminders on her chin. *Yeah, well no wonder you look miserable. Total disconnect between how you should have talked to Max tonight and how you did. Total disconnect between what you dwell on about the accident—and a host of other losses—and the depth of grace's possibilities.*

Unplugged.

The depth of grace's possibilities? She had to have picked that up at The Wild Iris. Was it one of the quotes Bougie wanted stenciled on the walls?

Emmalyn had made things worse than they already were. And she couldn't pick up the phone to apologize to Max. Not an option. The spouses of the incarcerated don't get choices like that.

The chair in her room seemed more appealing than the bed. She'd read for a while, let the guilt crawl off into a corner. But it didn't. It stayed right there in front of her eyes, blocking her view of the page.

God, what am I supposed to do?

She'd resorted to honest to goodness praying. It must be bad.

Bougie often reminded her not to lose hold of what she knew for sure. When Emmalyn had asked, "What can I possibly know for sure?" Bougie hadn't answered, but had tapped her heart and her ever-present Bible.

"What my heart tells me? What God said in His Word?" Emmalyn had flinched. She could feel the remnants of the conversation's impact even now. "What if my heart isn't telling me the truth?"

Bougie had spread her arms and twirled so slowly Emmalyn wondered if the music in her head were moving at all. "If you're planting your feet in what God said in His Word," she said, "your heart *will* tell you the truth."

Her book abandoned, Emmalyn stared into the night through the windowed doors to the small deck. Stars now salted the sky over the freshwater sea. Stars governed by the One who, according to Bougie, is never stumped.

Seriously, God. What am I supposed to do? I don't know Max anymore. How am I supposed to co-parent with him? How will we ever come to a decision on anything when our time on the phone is so short and every minute I commandeer feels like an hour stolen from his child?

She rose from the chair to draw closer to the stars. They shone but offered no insight.

Her feet chilled first. She climbed into bed not because she thought she could sleep, but because it seemed like the place to go when you've exhausted all other options. She pushed a mound of pillows into a workable nest, then sat up and reached for the extra blanket at the foot of the bed. If Max were there . . .

He would have heard her bothering the sheets for a comfortable position. He would have felt the mattress jostle as she pulled the blanket from the end of the bed. Without her having to ask, he would have slid closer and wrapped his arms around her like a buffalo robe. He would have cupped his warm feet around hers. His even breathing would have lulled her to sleep, no matter the cares of the day. That's what she knew for sure.

She turned on her side, facing the windowed doors, imagining his warmth at her back. Her gaze fell on the leather-bound journal on the bedside table. Emmalyn reached for it, hugged it to her chest. "Letters to Max, until you come home." That's how Cora had labeled it. Emmalyn had asked what to write in it. How to communicate with someone so far distant, in more ways than one. Cora told her to write as if he were sitting in the same room.

"That might never happen for us."

Cora had pulled a picture of Wayne from her wallet. Dusty brown camo. Tan helmet. A weapon Emmalyn couldn't identify strapped across his chest. A tan, barren landscape in the background. "It might not happen for us, either. But I write because it might. And because the marriage will have no chance at all if we're not communicating somehow."

Emmalyn pulled the pen from where it was clipped to the last page on which she'd written. One more glance at the night sky, the same sky that hovered over a cement block pod in a razor-wire compound three hundred miles away, and the pen moved across the paper.

Dear Max,

I owe you an apology. Dozens by now. But specifically tonight, for letting the time constraints of your phone call this afternoon and my frustration over . . . everything . . . dictate my response to the current difference of opinion. No excuses from me this time. I'm just sorry.

It seemed as if she should write more. But everything beyond "I'm sorry" became a defense about why she felt the way she did, or digging to expose the root of what got them into this mess.

"That's the thing about messes," Bougie had told her as they shared a quiet moment before the lunch crowd descended one day. "It doesn't matter what caused the trouble. The answer's always the same. Call out to God. Watch His rescue. Then thank Him." Emmalyn doubted it was that simple. But she'd seen it at work on the island. Her exile. Her refuge.

"Psalm 107," Bougie pointed out. "Doesn't matter what caused the trouble. The answer's the same."

Emmalyn turned back to the journal. She let the apology stand, closed the book, and turned out the light. The excess of pillows choked her tonight as she thought about the man she'd married having no choice at all about what kind of pillow he used or where he laid his head. She threw most of them to the floor and reserved the one that felt as solid as Max's chest. But no matter how deeply she pressed her ear into it, she couldn't hear his heartbeat. Only her own.

⎯∞⎯

"Did you know it's impossible to lick your elbow?"

Emmalyn slid a mound of scrambled eggs onto Hope's plate. "That's your thought for the day?"

"See?" Hope grinned. "I knew you'd try it."

Emmalyn brushed at her elbow. "I had a disadvantage."

"What's that?"

"Tennis elbow. Old injury."

"Nice one." Hope dug into her eggs, sun from the skylight turning her hair to the glistening molasses image from a shampoo commercial. "My real thought for the day is . . . "

Emmalyn scraped the rest of the eggs onto her own plate. "Go on."

"It's kind of personal."

"Oh." Emmalyn thought back to herself as a twelve-year-old. What would she have dubbed "personal"? Fights with her sisters.

219

Pouting that her mother wouldn't let her get her ears pierced. Cringing through health class. Oh, dear.

"Dad thinks you're his tattoo."

"What?" Emmalyn coughed into her napkin. "I'm sorry. What did you say?"

"It's in his blog post for this week. You can read it if you want."

"I thought it was personal."

Hope played snowplow with her fork and the rest of her eggs. "Not the part about you. The part about me."

"If you'd rather I didn't read it . . . "

Hope sighed. "We're kind of in this together, you know?"

"I guess we are, aren't we?"

"You work today, right?"

Emmalyn checked the clock. "Bougie and I are working on next spring's menu and a few details for Christmas. I'm looking forward to your meeting her."

"So, maybe I'll show you the blog tonight. It's kind of fireplace and hot chocolate material."

Emmalyn rested her chin in her hand and used her closed fingers to cover the smile forming. She'd found a measure of serenity in the solitude of the cottage. It's as if the serenity had to come first before she was ready to share her home with someone else. But now, few things would be better than sitting with Hope in front of the fire, sipping hot chocolate and discovering what had happened to Max's heart. "That'll be great. It won't take all that long at The Wild Iris. Do you have something to work on? Books to read?"

"Is the library open?"

"It might be open today. I'm not sure. We'll take the long way in and drive past to check on the schedule."

"I'll try to be quick. But . . . "

"But what?"

"Books!" Hope gestured with arms extended and palms up. "Need I say more?"

Twelve years old. Who would have thought Emmalyn's kindred spirit would be twelve years old? With the language skills of someone much older.

"We don't have a strict timetable today. Libraries are for lingering, don't you think?" Emmalyn said.

Hope pushed her hair off her shoulders and folded her hands in her lap. "Mom says they make her nervous."

To press or not to press. That is the question. "Did she say why?"

The girl shrugged, as if it didn't matter. "Lots of things make her nervous."

A light lapping sound drew their attention. Both turned toward the noise. The dog slurped its water like a Columbian coffee tester. The dog that had started out as a delicate thing. It was enough to lighten the mood in the cottage. "Your turn to wipe the mess and her chin," Emmalyn said.

"According to my records"—Hope said—"it's your turn."

"You keep a written record?"

Hope tapped her temple. "It's all up here. But that's not a bad idea." She pulled her phone from her pocket and whipped through a sequence of keystrokes. Then she caught Emmalyn's gaze and winked. "I'll do it." She slid off the high stool and grabbed a doggie rag. "Comfort," she told the dog, "you're wonderful, but you can be messy."

Emmalyn watched as the girl worked and the words sank in.

"How much longer will you need before we can leave, Hope?"

"Gotta brush my teeth," she said, tossing the rag and giving Comfort one last snuggle. "Once a week, whether I need it or not." She didn't turn to check Emmalyn's reaction until she reached the foot of the stairs.

"Good one."

Within seconds, Emmalyn heard the water running in the bathroom sink. She couldn't wait for Hope to meet Bougie. She put their dishes in the kitchen sink and ran a slow stream of water over them while she reached for the dish soap. *And Pirate Joe. Could be an interesting morning.*

21

Technically, the library wasn't open, but Cora was on the premises, putting up Christmas decorations, so she let Emmalyn and Hope explore the rooms while she worked.

Emmalyn had kept the introductions short. "Cora, I'd like you to meet Hope Elizabeth. She's staying with me for a while."

"Welcome to Madeline Island," Cora had said, her hands busy untangling tiny Christmas lights for the miniature tree on the main desk.

"Thanks," Hope had said. "Nice to meet you." In the time it took to say "meet you," Hope had zeroed in on a rack of new arrivals on the far wall.

"Niece?" Cora asked when the two adults were relatively alone.

Emmalyn braced for the first of how many times she'd have to tell the story. "Max's daughter." With Cora, she could share more. "Her mom's in rehab for a few weeks, or months."

Cora handed Emmalyn the balled-up section of the string of lights. "Nick's dating someone I'm not sure I approve of. Gas went up five cents over the weekend. And I haven't heard from Wayne in weeks." She shook her head. "But you take the prize for complicated. Hands down."

"It's been . . . good."

"How long as she been with you?"

"Two days."

"Uh huh. Beautiful."

"A stunner, as they say. She's a smart little girl."

Cora glanced Emmalyn's way. "She lets you call her a little girl?"

"She wants it clear that she's more mature than she looks. And in many ways, she is." Emmalyn watched Hope slide one book after another from the shelves, deciding within seconds if it was a book worth opening.

"Max's daughter? I cannot imagine the gall it took him to ask you to—"

"He didn't ask. I volunteered." Emmalyn fed Cora another length of untangled lights.

"That doesn't sound like you."

"I know. Against Max's better judgment, too."

Cora looked at Emmalyn without turning her head. "How in the world—?"

"And . . . I may homeschool Hope. Also against Max's better judgment."

The end Cora held dropped to the floor. She reached to pick it up and positioned herself facing Emmalyn with her back to Hope, as if shielding Hope from stray bits of the discussion. "Can you do that?"

"She doesn't want to take the ferry into Bayfield every school day, come in right before the semester break, and then be gone again as soon as her mom's released. I don't blame her."

"I mean, do you have a legal right to do that?" Cora's eyes looked huge behind her glasses.

"Way to throw that little detail into the mix, Cora. I have no idea."

Cora fiddled with the string of lights. "And Max is against it?"

"I think he's concerned about what it will mean for me. I don't really know all that's behind his objections. We haven't had a full conversation."

"Emmalyn!" Cora turned to see if Hope had heard that last bit, whispered as it was. No change in the girl's intense connection with the shelves of books.

"We will," Emmalyn said. "We'll talk. It's not easy."

"Trust me. I know. But—"

"Not to worry. I've already repented a dozen times—on paper—for not respecting his wishes. But you have to admit that sometimes you have to do the right thing against the objections when your mate is out of contact range or doesn't have the whole story."

"Huh."

"Huh, what?"

Cora folded her arms. "Two things. You called Max your mate. And 'the whole story.' Yes, I have to make decisions without Wayne's input sometimes. It's never ideal."

"Well, no."

"But isn't it up to me to *give* Wayne the whole story, to the best of my ability, when we disagree on a plan of action?"

"You're going all logical and morally sound on me."

Cora chuckled. At that, Hope looked up and pressed one finger against her lips. She'd make a fine librarian someday.

Emmalyn nodded over Cora's shoulder and returned to the conversation. "I already know I have some backtracking to do. And some renovation on burned bridges. But I also have a trunkful of questions about how to do this. Nick was a minor when he served time."

"Tried as an adult," Cora reminded her.

"Still, it's different. What if Wayne weren't overseas but behind bars? What's the spouse's role then?"

Cora took the tangled mess of Christmas lights, a small percentage smooth and useful. "Honey, if you can figure that out, you can give seminars to a whole bunch of confused spouses."

Emmalyn let herself get tugged away from the conversation. What if Max had intentionally tried to hurt someone, or done more than "significant bodily injury"? What if he hadn't been repentant? What if he'd thumbed his nose at the law and *cursed* his way through prison rather than *finding* his way? How would Emmalyn relate to him then? Where would they be?

"You still with me?" Cora asked her, giving up on the lights and turning her attention to repositioning the artificial tree's branches.

"Still with you."

"I read something in a magazine the other day. Or maybe it was on social media. Could have been a talk show."

Emmalyn glanced at Hope, wondering how much time they had before she wandered over. How did women with kids ever finish a discussion? "What did you read? Or hear?"

"This couple decided they could solve a lot of the tension between them if they saved all their head-butting disagreements for a specific day of the week."

Joining the branch-straightening, Emmalyn looked at Cora, urging her on.

"So, for instance, if things got heated in a discussion about finances, they tabled it until, say, Wednesday. They kept a running list of tough subjects that needed to be addressed, or negative comments they wanted to make, and refused to give them voice until Wednesday."

"Let me guess. By the time Wednesday arrived—six days later, three days later, one day later—they could tackle the subject without anger. Because they'd given themselves some distance?"

Cora smiled. "Like you and I don't have enough 'distance' between us and our men the way it is. But I have a feeling most of the hot topics on their list weren't even simmering anymore. When you make a plan to discuss something, you're not firing from the hip. It's intentional. Laid out logically. Researched, even."

Hope approached, a stack of books in her arms with one open on top. "Did you know a polar bear's skin is actually black, to help absorb the sun's heat? Talk about dark roots."

Cora put a hand to the part in her hair. "I had my roots done last week," she fake-whined.

Hope looked at Emmalyn for a clue whether or not it was appropriate to laugh. Hope smiled. "Can I get a library card?" she asked the librarian/decorator.

"Sure, sweetie. Put those books here"—she cleared a spot by blending two piles into one—"and I'll get you the application."

"She can put her books on my card," Emmalyn said, instantly regretting the offer when she saw the look on Hope's face. "On second thought, everybody deserves their own library card."

Hope's expression brightened. "Thanks. Did you know there's a library in Indiana that sinks more than an inch every year because the guys who designed it didn't figure in the weight of the books?" Hope shook her head, grinning, her dimples dancing. "Didn't think about the weight of the books!"

"I did know that," Cora said, as if thrilled to find someone else in the world who considered it more than a little amusing.

"Let's see what books you chose." Emmalyn turned her head to read the spines.

"You'll approve," Hope said, a tinge of defensiveness in her voice.

"I have no doubt." Emmalyn checked the titles anyway. "This one looks like fun."

"I thought I should probably know something about the fur trading history of the island."

"Self-motivated student?" Cora asked.

In sync, Hope and Emmalyn answered, "Yes."

Cora lifted one book and turned its cover toward Emmalyn, but addressed Hope. "Honey, I don't know about this one. It might be a little . . . raw for you."

Emmalyn took the book from Cora. *Loving the Addict: When Love Isn't Enough.* Another fissure formed in her heart. "It'll be okay, Cora. We'll read it together." Emmalyn looked into Hope's misted eyes. "Won't we, Hope?"

Hope's breath was hinged in the middle, as if broken in two parts and patched together. "I guess."

"We need to get moving," Emmalyn said after the awkwardest of pauses. It occurred to her she'd told Hope earlier they had no timetable to keep. But getting off the subject of addicts and mothers seemed like reason enough for a deadline.

Cora finished checking out the books with Hope's new card and said, "I'll see you two around. A pleasure to meet you, Hope."

"You, too."

"Emmalyn, don't forget to cash in that gift certificate for a free shoulder and neck massage one of these days."

What gift certificate? Oh. The one Cora gave her that moment, silently, with the look in her eyes. The stress-reliever massage. The tension-busting neck massage. "I'll be sure to do that. Thanks."

They exited through the add-on entrance of the converted Victorian home. The entrance was filled with carts of used books for sale. A quarter apiece. The two looked at each other.

"Another day soon?" Emmalyn asked.

"Great idea."

As soon as Hope had her seatbelt buckled, she turned to Emmalyn. "M?"

"Yes?" *Lord, please let this be a question about something other than addiction, abandonment, neglect, or prison sentences.*

"Do you decorate? For Christmas, I mean."

"I used to do more than I have lately."

"You know, it can be very educational to make homemade decorations. Origami uses, like, geometry. How many lights does it take to sparkle a ten-foot tree . . . ?"

Emmalyn pulled out of the library parking lot. "We can't fit a ten-foot tree in the cottage."

"Hyperthetically speaking."

Maybe Hope hadn't made a mistake with her pronunciation. Maybe the idea really was *hyper*-thetical. An excess of theories. "We'll look into it. Living on a budget . . . "

"I get that. One year Mom and I decorated the whole tree with tissue paper roses. And we got the tissue paper from some lady's baby shower. I wish I had a picture of that tree. It was something."

The phrase "baby shower" only stuck out in a sentence for pregnant women, new moms, and those who would never have a baby shower. The effort of reining in her thoughts exhausted her. Would it always be like this? The wild swings between disabling not-a-mom thoughts and crippling can-he-love-me-again thoughts? Then settling again into a middle ground that almost felt like peace? "We'll see what we can come up with. Something in keeping with the cottage's décor."

"Can I do my room however I want?"

"Does your plan involve beavers or chain saws?"

Hope giggled. "No."

"Then, okay."

Hope pulled out her phone.

"Texting your friends about it?"

"Addicts' kids don't have many friends, M." As soon as the words escaped, Hope stiffened. Like a soldier who'd let her guard down, her body language showed she'd heightened her alertness because of the breach. Mouth pinched. Eyes darting, then still.

The last fissure hadn't completely healed over when a new one developed in the muscles of Emmalyn's heart. She grieved not having thought about the friends Hope left behind in her exile to the island. She grieved that there weren't any.

"I'm taking notes," Hope said, her voice lacking the animation of moments earlier. "Decorating notes."

Emmalyn parked in front of The Wild Iris before conversation deteriorated any further. "Grab your things, Hope. We'll be here a little while."

In high school orchestra, Emmalyn had been taught to pay attention even when the music didn't require her to play. She was taught to count through the rests, always on alert. Always engaged.

Parenting or pseudo-parenting had a lot in common with that counsel. As easy as Hope could sometimes be, living with her, caring about her, meant staying alert even during the pauses. Emmalyn needed to both relax and to watch her every tone of voice, every word, her casual action as if she were counting through the rests. So she didn't miss anything. So she didn't break anything.

The bright colors of the exterior of The Wild Iris—even through the last days of November's gray filter—reflected in Hope's wide eyes. Bougie stood inside the front window, on tiptoe, splayed like an intentional belly flop. Spray bottle of a clear liquid in one hand and rag in the other, she wiped as high and wide as she could reach. Her outfit *du jour* was one Emmalyn had seen before— fuchsia tights, knee-length princess dress in the palest blue, and a gray heathered ankle-length open cardigan.

"Is that the cleaning lady?" Hope asked under her breath.

"She's the owner," Emmalyn said, surprised her voice held a hint of pride. "She's going to love you." She nudged Hope forward with a hand to her back and held the door for her. A faint scent of vinegar greeted them.

"Ooh!" Bougie dropped her cleaning supplies and vaulted off the raised ledge under the window. Her skirts billowed around her like an open umbrella devoid of spokes. "You're here!" She skipped the introduction part and went straight to hugs. "Hope, you're as beautiful as M said!" Then a hug for Emmalyn. "You're so blessed."

"Hope, this is Bougie Unfortunate. My boss."

"And friend," Bougie said.

Friends. Not the safest topic at the moment, Bougie. "Can I show her around a little before clocking in?"

"Sure. I need to finish this window first before we can get started."

Within minutes, Hope was settled into one of the wing chairs by the fireplace, which Bougie lit just for her. Emmalyn thought back to the night she arrived on the island and Bougie's exceptional kindness at the start of her own Madeline Island journey. *God, make this the kind of haven for Hope that it's been for me.*

Bougie had made her decadent hot chocolate for the three of them. "Whipped cream, Hope?"

"Yes, please."

"A *please* will get you a double portion," Bougie said, squirting from a stainless steel whipped cream dispenser. She looked at Emmalyn.

"Please?"

The three celebrated the joy of a simple pleasure, then Bougie and Emmalyn took their mugs, file folders, and both of their electronic tablets to the front window where they could spread out their ideas.

Hope opened one of the library books and stuck ear buds in her ears, the long white cord attached to her phone.

"So, how's it going now?" Bougie asked, her voice barely above a whisper.

Emmalyn matched her tone. "Wonderful and terrible. It depends on the time of day, the phases of the moon, and whatever topic we happen to trip over. She's delightful and in pain, but bearing it more gracefully than I bear mine sometimes."

"Good to know. But I meant how's your relationship with Max?"

"You make it sound as if we had a blind date and you want to know if we'll go out again." Emmalyn opened her tablet and scrolled through to the menu spreadsheet she'd created.

"So, will you? You've been blind dating for most of these five years, but neither one of you has showed up."

Emmalyn crossed her arms and leaned back. The first pinch of a headache nagged at her temples.

Bougie's mouth formed a tall oval cavern. "I have no idea"—she said, pointing to the ceiling—"where that thought came from!" An "I love you but you know I'm telling the truth" look engulfed her face. Chin tilted down, she looked at Emmalyn like an elderly woman would peer over reading glasses.

Emmalyn turned in Hope's direction. The girl rehearsed dance steps with her feet while poring over the book before her on the table. It was either a book about odd nature trivia or how to survive as the child of an addict. Whatever the book choice, it held her captive.

"Max and I need to see each other face-to-face," Emmalyn said.

"Hence the Thanksgiving gift."

"But I can't go right now. I can't leave Hope so soon. And . . . this . . . first time, I can't take her with me if Max and I are going to have the kind of conversation that's long overdue."

Bougie shuffled some papers, pulled out the one she'd apparently been looking for, and slid it toward Emmalyn. A new graphic design for the Wild Iris logo. The set of Bougie's mouth told Emmalyn graphic design was not at the forefront of her mind.

"I'll go. I will," Emmalyn assured her. "I can't right now. We'll have to limp along the best we can until we have an uninterrupted conversation that lasts longer than five minutes." Emmalyn turned her attention to the mug of cocoa.

Bougie pulled out a calendar. "Let's set a date."

"For . . . ?"

"For your trip to visit Max. It'll give you both something to look forward to."

Emmalyn rubbed the sore spots at her temples. "I thought I might have to use that money for Hope's needs."

"You think God can provide only one or the other? He budgets a lot better than that." Bougie extended her pen and the calendar to Emmalyn. "Two dates. One for your visit. One for Hope's."

Emmalyn slowly flipped through to the months of the new year. February, March . . . Bougie took the pages and flipped them back to the month of December.

"Christmas will be a busy time at the prison." Even Emmalyn knew that sounded lame.

Bougie choked on her mouthful of cocoa. She swallowed, coughed, and dabbed at her lips with a tissue from her sweater pocket. "Even if that were true, all the more reason to book something sooner than the holiday weekend."

"I'm not sure Hope will be ready for me to leave her by then."

"Seriously? She strikes me as being more independent than you give her credit for."

A surge of anticipation rode a wave of apprehension through her nerve endings. She could see Max face-to-face. Soon. If it went poorly, it could mean the end of everything, including her connection with Hope.

22

Did you want to see Dad's blog?"

Hope stood halfway down the stairs, balancing her open laptop in her arms.

Emmalyn blew out the match she'd used to light the candle on the mantel. "I do." *I do? Let's not get sappy, Emmalyn. It's a blog about prison life, for Pete's sake.* "Yes, I'd like to see it. Want me to come upstairs?" She'd been waiting for this invitation for days. She could have—maybe should have—searched until she found it online. Private blog. Closed group, she assumed from what Hope hinted. A wave of shivers skittered down her arms. What if she didn't like what she saw in it? What if the discoveries she made in his blog sealed their futures in separate relational hemispheres?

"I'll come to you," Hope said, descending. "Nice music."

"It felt like a music kind of night. Is it going to be distracting?"

Hope settled onto the couch. "You're talking to a twelve-year-old, almost thirteen. Music is like wallpaper. It's not distracting unless it's loud and painful."

Emmalyn reached to turn it down a few decibels anyway before planting herself beside Hope on the couch. Comfort hopped up to join them. "What kinds of things does he write about?"

"A bunch of stuff. This one's not as funny as some of them."

How long had it been since she'd thought of Max as funny? The humor drained out of their marriage the day of Emmalyn's first miscarriage. Devastating as it was, she'd rebounded better than she had after the second and third.

"Here. I'll show you how you can find it on your own computer. I have to send an invitation, then approve you for the group."

"So, there's a limited audience?"

Hope flew through several keystrokes. "Oh, there you are. You're not on social media much, are you?"

"Does that make me prehistoric?"

"Technically, in one sense, nothing's truly prehistoric, since we have the biblical record. By strict definition, prehistoric means before recorded history. But—"

Emmalyn laid a hand on Hope's. "You hereby have an A in your ancient history assignment for today. I'm not prehistoric, apparently. I'm merely anti-social."

The girl's smile competed with the candle flame in brilliance. "You are officially invited to participate in the group," she announced.

"I can leave replies?"

"Sure. Dad won't see them. I do. But I can tell him about them when we email through the prison link."

Emmalyn looked over Hope's shoulder at the screen. "Could I email him, too?"

Hope said yes, then shook her head. "You two need counseling."

"No argument there."

"He has to send a special invitation through the correctional facility email-only system, and the recipient agrees to the terms and all that." Hope turned the screen so Emmalyn could follow better. "Then the prisoner has a certain amount of time he can spend emailing those people. I don't know how many are on Dad's list besides me and my mom. Probably his lawyer."

Her mom. Claire. It made sense. They had to discuss child-raising issues. That's what people with children between them do.

"Didn't you already get an invitation? Like, two years ago?" Hope's expression changed. "Hey, it might have gone into your spam folder. Things like that happen all the time." She returned her attention to the keyboard. "But I bet Dad wondered why you didn't accept. Here," Hope said, pointing to a line of print. "This is where the invitation would have come from. Do you remember getting one like that?"

"I don't think so." Two years? Max and Hope had been emailing for two years?

"I'll get on his case. He'll send you another one."

"Maybe he'd rather not communicate through that method with me."

"That's crazy talk." Hope pushed herself deeper into the couch and propped her feet on the coffee table. Her face scrunched. "No offense. You're either together or you're not. And if you are—committed, I mean—then one of you is going to have to start doing the hard thing. If you ask me. Not that you did. And I'll go mind my own business now."

Emmalyn bristled. Her porcupine quills lay flat when she considered the wisdom coming out of the mouth of the babe. "Why would I have to pay for a counselor when I have you?" She nudged Hope with her shoulder. "But just for the record, we do have to keep this on an adult/child basis."

"Got it." Hope nodded. The screen color changed. Dark gray. Light gray. And a beautiful, fresh, new leaf green. "He calls his blog 'Living Free Behind Bars.'"

"Irony."

"Actually, I think they're steel."

Had Hope been this adorable when she was four? Emmalyn had been looking at Max's child through waxed paper back then.

"You know what?" Hope said, handing the laptop to Emmalyn. "I need to run to the bathroom. I'll let you read it for yourself."

The sound of her footsteps paused after three beats. Emmalyn glanced her way. With her hand on the banister and one foot on the step above, Hope looked as if she wanted to say something, but didn't. She disappeared upstairs and left Emmalyn alone with her husband's thoughts.

Sometimes I wonder if I'm telling my story to an empty room. Maybe I'm the only one listening. Maybe that's how it's supposed to be.

Could she do this? Could she bear to read about what prison had done to him? How he'd changed? The Max she'd married, the one she committed to, amazed her every day with his kindness, his patience with her, his tender touch. She missed being cherished.

I walk on eggshells. My cellmate says it's like that for everyone who gets within a year of their release. They're afraid to sneeze too loud for fear of winding up in the shu on a noise violation. Six months in the shu a year after I got here brought me as close to insanity as I ever want to be.

It shamed her that Hope would know what a "shu" was in this context, even though Emmalyn didn't. A year after he was incarcerated? When his letters stopped. When he stopped replying to hers. Right before she gave up trying.

But I can't shake the peace, no matter what shakes me.

That sounded like Bougie. She reread the line. It said the same thing it had the first time.

"Did you get to the tattoo part yet?"

"Not yet." Emmalyn blinked to clear her vision. "Hope, what's the shu he's talking about?"

She sat on the couch again, moving slowly this time. She put a thin arm around Emmalyn's shoulders and said, "Hang on. It isn't pretty. Did you ever watch *Shawshank Redemption*? A shu is the Special Housing Unit. Like solitary confinement, but worse."

"Your mother let you watch that movie?" She'd promised herself she wouldn't bad-mouth Claire in front of her daughter. Her growl stayed too deep to hear.

"Parts of it. She thought it would be a good education about what Daddy was going through."

"The setting of *Shawshank* was a long time ago. In the 1940s, wasn't it? It's not like that in the prison systems anymore. Nothing like that."

Hope raised her eyebrows.

Tell me it's nothing like that. "Why did they put him in the shu? Six months?"

"He doesn't tell me everything. I was eight."

"Oh, yeah. I keep forgetting you're not older than I am." Emmalyn pressed out a smile.

"You'll have to talk to him about it. All I know is it was a small room, a tiny window, no contact."

"It sounds more like a concentration camp than a correctional facility." She cringed. What kind of childcare provider talks with a pre-teen about concentration camps? *No more slips, Emmalyn.*

"One thing we know."

"What's that, Hope?"

The girl sat on her hands, her neck disappearing into her shoulders. "He lived through it. There's a lot to be said for living through something." She turned her face away from Emmalyn.

The candle sputtered, then settled back into a steady flame. Emmalyn stared at its light, bright flame in the middle, a halo of softer light radiating from its center. Silence stretched wide and long. Deep and far beyond the walls of the cottage. Echoing off the islands miles to the north, more remote, uninhabited, the islands as dark as the night in which they slept.

"Do you think my mom will call me?" Hope's question hung too long in the air.

"I don't know much about rehab, Hope."

"She usually calls."

They'd been through it before. *Oh, child.* Emmalyn put both arms around the girl and rested her chin on the shiny chestnut hair. "I'm sure she will if she can."

A wolf call sounded beyond the windows. It would have made Emmalyn flinch, but a child depended on her to be strong. She tightened her hug. Hope let her.

Comfort found a way to squeeze between them.

Anyone can hold a baby. Emmalyn held a child.

Until it became disheartening three years into the process of trying, Emmalyn had begged to hold the babies. Anyone's baby. She believed every forehead she stroked, every infant she lullabied was a hint of the joy ahead for her. Other women in their Empty Arms support group couldn't do it. They couldn't bring themselves to feel the weight of a little one in their arms and have to give it up a few minutes or a long nap later. Emmalyn became one of those women.

She'd had a child in her home two weeks in the summer, every other Thanksgiving, a few days at Christmas since Hope was a toddler. But Emmalyn had stiff-armed that gift—stiff-armed the God who gave gifts—and held out for a baby.

That longing might never go away. But as she brushed stray hairs from Hope's twelve-year-old face, that beautiful face, she felt something tentative within her find its moorings. The baby stage had consumed her. Beyond it lay so much more.

Until a person is whole, she can't see clearly. She can't hear well. She can't love right.

Three weeks until the shortest day of the year. The longest night. That's what the calendar said. This year, it came three weeks early.

Hope had gone to bed hours ago. Emmalyn heard the floor squeak too often. The girl couldn't sleep either.

The blue light from Hope's aging laptop tugged at Emmalyn. She couldn't finish reading. Not yet. She'd gotten through a half dozen of the most recent blog posts—usually dated a week or two apart. She'd found the tattoo reference. Few in his cell block were tattoo-free. He'd taken flack for being "uninked." He silenced the ribbing by claiming he had two. Branded as property of his Creator, with his wife's name tattooed on his heart.

Both statements left her breathless. After all this, after her absence—her long, hollow absence—he would say such a thing? As if he'd forgiven her, and found forgiveness, but had forgotten to tell her.

If he'd gone from faith-neutral to faith-filled, as he hinted in one blog post after another, why hadn't he made the move to contact her? Isn't that what God would have wanted? When she was thinking more clearly, she'd search for an unopened invitation from the correctional system email program. She wouldn't have trashed it accidentally, would she?

He could have tried again.

She could have tried.

She'd changed, too. Far more recently than he had. She hardly admitted it to herself, much less announced it to Max or anyone else.

What was *her* excuse?

Maybe it was too late for them to consider their marriage anything more than a memory. From here on out, if they shared anything besides concern for Hope, they'd do so as two people with a common past, a history of mutual mistakes, and an unspoken gratitude for grace that kept them upright.

No.

Not enough. The daddy Hope knew was the husband she longed to know.

Whatever it took.

A light shone under Hope's door when Emmalyn finally climbed the stairs after midnight. She rapped on the wood and whispered, "Are you still awake?"

"You can come in. I'm reading." She lay on her side with her back to the wall, a book propped in her bent arm.

Emmalyn sat lightly on the edge of her bed. Hope kept reading. "It's a good thing we can sleep in tomorrow. Today."

"Uh huh. I'll stop reading soon."

Emmalyn scanned the room. Hope's touches were visible, but so minimal it seemed obvious she saw it as a temporary home. "I need to talk to you."

She closed the book and scooted to a sitting position, pulled her knees close to her chest, and hugged them.

"I need to go visit your father." Emmalyn waited for an objection that didn't come.

"When?"

"As soon as I can."

Hope chewed her lower lip. She nodded.

"You're okay with that?"

"How long will you be gone?"

Emmalyn watched the Hope version of Max's eyes pool with tears that hung on the fringes of her eyelashes. "Two days. I know it seems like I'm abandoning you. Maybe I shouldn't—"

"You have to go. You have to."

"I'll find someplace safe for you to stay for those two days. Would you feel comfortable with Bougie?"

"Yeah. She's ettcentric. In a good way."

Eccentric. "I wouldn't take off so soon after you got here if it weren't so important. And your dad and I need to talk about you, too." She tickled the foot tenting the comforter. "Think I can convince him satellite learning is the best option for you right now?"

"You've been researching?"

"A little. Need to do more. But I think we can pull this off."

"Me, too." The tears retreated. "What about Comfort? She can't stay alone out here."

"Cora's son Nick may be able to look in on her a couple of times a day. That would be helpful. I'll try to bring back some Christmas lights. Make a list of anything else you need."

"I'm glad you're going. It's a start, right?"

If Emmalyn looked as tired as Hope did, it was more than time to call it a night. "I'll start making arrangements in the morning."

"I know where you can find the rules about visitation. You won't believe how particular the prison system is."

Emmalyn hadn't thought through all the details. "Thank you. You're something else, Hope."

"You really have to go see him. He thinks he ruined your life. You never told him he didn't."

⁂

Emmalyn tried lying on her left side. No better. Pillow between her knees. Every cell in her body still ached.

What's the last thing she'd said to Max? Before the 400 years of silence. Four years, give or take. What had she said? Her anger morphed into pathetic begging. She remembered that much. He would have been in the hole, the shu, when she penned, "I don't know what else to do but give up on you." And the final message: "Contact me somehow if that's not what you want. Say something!"

Sounded like a song from her iTunes list.

She hadn't meant it to sound so final. Had she? Pain says bizarre things. She'd thought it would shake him. It shook her instead. And he didn't even know.

Emmalyn had spent too many moments since then alternately convincing herself she didn't need him or that he didn't need her, that their marriage had been a season—like autumn. Too short, but brilliant . . . except for the deaths.

Then the flash of a memory of him would drag her into a small, shadowed room where hope pretended they'd have a future if they could navigate the disappointments of their past and the

241

gravity of the present. He was paying for a crime for which he was determined culpable. Is it possible—? No. She wasn't like that, was she? She didn't . . . couldn't have wanted him to pay for robbing her of their final low-percentage opportunities, their last-gasp attempts at having a child, her last hopes of becoming a mother?

Before. That was before. Some people say faith makes you blind, or that it clouds reality. Emmalyn hadn't really seen at all until she stopped using her eyes as her only source of vision. So much was still blurry, but clearer every day.

He seemed content with what they'd once had. Needed nothing more. Resigned himself to seeing her as a tattoo—a reminder from another era. What would they have to say to one another when they sat in the same room?

She'd start with, "I'm sorry for what I put us through."

And the second sentence? "Even if you don't say something, I'm not giving up on us."

And then he'd say . . . And then she'd say . . .

She ran her fingers through her hair. Her head throbbed with the possibilities.

23

Your purse stays in your car."

Emmalyn turned to the woman walking past where Emmalyn had parked in the visitor's lot.

"Oh. Right. Hard habit to break."

"Your first time here?"

Emmalyn pulled her driver's license and lip gloss from her purse then tucked it under the seat and locked the car. "That obvious?"

"You'll get used to things." The woman—shorter than Emmalyn's five foot seven by a few inches—tottered on cork platform shoes that completely fit her 80s striped leggings and silver lamé puffy coat.

Emmalyn took a couple of quick steps to catch up to her. "I read through the unabridged dictionary of instructions, but . . . "

"Just watch the rest of us. That's how I learned. My mom got reamed out by a guard for putting her feet up on a table when she visited my brother. Bunions."

Her brother's name was Bunyons? Oh.

The woman looked at Emmalyn in a way that made her squirm. "You're not wearing an underwire, are you?"

"Excuse me?" Emmalyn tugged her coat shut.

"An underwire bra will get you kicked out faster than looking cross-eyed at a guard. I won't make either of those mistakes again. Hey, I'm Regina. Reggie."

"Emmalyn."

The two neared the first set of gates. "Visiting your husband? Boyfriend?"

"Husband."

"He just got here?"

Who wouldn't assume that? Emmalyn was a greenhorn on visitation rules. *No, he's been here more than four years. For the first year, he asked me not to come. Then we . . . left each other alone.* No point starting that story. Even Emmalyn didn't know how to justify the silence between them, from her side or his. "He's been here a while."

"My brother . . . "

Bunyon.

" . . . is a lifer."

Emmalyn's breath caught in her throat. Reggie had said the words so casually, as if having a brother in prison for life were no more axis-altering than missing out on the two-for-one sale on bunches of bananas. "I'm so sorry."

"How'd you know?"

"You just told me he was in for life."

"Oh. I thought you meant you were sorry because of the news I have to give him. But how could you know that?"

Did Emmalyn want to ask? "What news?" The first set of gates let them into a holding area. They took forms from the guards and started filling out the visitor registration paperwork.

"Mom's gone. He's gonna freak. But you can't be in prison for life and not expect your mom to die while you're in there, you know? Bummer about the fog yesterday."

Who would have thought fog would cancel all prison visits? Fog! She'd driven the 320 miles through it, slept fitfully in her motel room, then wakened to an even thicker fog and the news that all visitations were canceled until the fog lifted. People could get lost in fog, breach the fence in fog, escape in fog.

Nothing about this was easy. She'd gathered the courage to make the trip, but would have logged the miles and emotional toll for nothing if the fog hadn't lifted by this morning, the last opportunity of the weekend. "Does that happen often, Reggie?"

"Often enough to be irritating. Did you drive far?"

"Far enough."

Emmalyn followed Reggie to an area that looked as if it had been swiped from an airport security checkpoint. The women removed their shoes, coats, and pocket contents and sent them through the tabletop scanner while they stood in line waiting to be waved through the body scanner.

"You!"

Emmalyn turned. One of the guards signaled for her to remain on the near side of the body scanner. She watched Reggie—passing inspection without a hitch—move on into the gated holding area.

"Yes, sir? What is it?"

"These your things?" He pointed to one of the trays.

"It's a note from his daughter. And a picture."

"Let me see." Flat, stiff words. *She* hadn't been sentenced to anything. Did the guards have to treat *her* like pond scum? "She's beautiful," he said, not like a letch would say it. More like the grandfather he probably was. A degree of warmth?

"She is."

The guard held the picture to the side of Emmalyn's head. "I see the resemblance."

No you don't. And that's part of our problem.

Her lips stuck together. Dry air. Nerves.

"See this?"

Her lip gloss. He plucked it with two gloved fingers and dropped it into a wastebasket under the conveyer belt. "I'll hold the photo and note until you come out. You can mail them to him."

"But I'm here. Can't I just—?" Obviously not. She couldn't risk angering the people with the power to send her home.

He searched the folds of her infinity scarf. Emmalyn didn't want to think about what kind of contraband a visitor might smuggle in an infinity scarf. They patted her down, which she expected. The body scanner beeped like every airport scanner did because of the metal plate in her ankle from thinking she could ice skate when she was sixteen. The chunky necklace and locket she wore on top of the scarf drew suspicion. Satisfied the locket was empty, they let it pass inspection, but held her gaze when insisting it had better be empty when she exited the visitation room.

Why was it necessary to demean and intimidate visitors? She knew. Or could imagine what others might have tried to pull. Being lumped in with "others" frustrated her on two counts. She hadn't broken any laws. But she'd pictured herself in a different class than "those kinds of people," which Bougie would probably tell her was a violation of some ancient God-law.

She smoothed her black Shetland sweater over her still-flat waistline. She didn't need Bougie to tell her.

She rejoined Reggie in the holding area.

"What did I do?" she asked, her voice low.

Reggie sighed. "What did they take?"

"My lip gloss. And a picture of his daughter. A note from her, too."

Reggie glanced toward the steel doors leading to the visitation room—*"Oh, the irony,"* Hope would say—a few feet from where they stood. "You'll get the hang of this eventually. Some guards are a little more lenient than others. Some are lenient one day and tough as overcooked liver the next." She smiled at her own word picture. "Lip gloss. You rebel." She smiled again. "We visitors aren't supposed to talk to one another when we're in there, so I'll tell you quick. You get one kiss and hug when you greet each other and one when you say good-bye. You sure you want to worry about messing up your lipstick?"

The room, once desert dry and hot, grew Arctic cold. "I don't think that will be a problem for us."

Reggie's eyebrows lifted, then dropped back to neutral.

Emmalyn fought for a face-saving way to approach the moment when all the other spouses in the room would embrace.

Reggie waved a card. "Did you get your vending machine card loaded? That's all you two will be allowed to eat while you're in there. I never stay long enough to miss a meal, but if this is your first visit . . . "

"Yes. I put thirty dollars on it."

"See how far that goes. Might want to load that thing a little heavier next time."

For vending machine food? Oh. Lunch, supper, snacks. Two days worth of that on an ordinary visitation weekend and she'd be overdosed on Cheetos and Oreos and clamoring for an all-celery diet.

"Ready?" Reggie nodded toward an approaching guard.

No. "I think so."

"Keep your hands at your sides until we're in the room. No sudden moves. The visitation area is monitored, like you had to be told that. You'll see the surveillance cameras everywhere. Are you staying until three, when visiting hours are over?"

"I don't know. We have a lot to talk about. I . . . " The air smelled of old building, inexpressibly damp cement, and industrial cleaner. And steel. Lots of steel. The visitation room held a hundred or so institutional chairs and several dozen plastic tables. Reggie's brother stood when Reggie neared. Emmalyn was on her own. She scanned the room for the Max she once knew, then scanned again for a version almost five years older. Reggie subtly motioned for her to sit down and wait.

She walked past the guard desk and a library cart full of books, dog-eared decks of playing cards, Scrabble, and other board games no one bothered to tape at the corners anymore. She waited. Five minutes passed. Ten minutes. Fifteen. She tried to catch Reggie's attention and finally did. Reggie motioned, "Sit. Down."

So much for saving face when Max refused to kiss her. How would she save face if Max refused to show up?

The vending machine occupied an alcove on the opposite side of the guard desk. A small microwave sat just outside the room. It looked like a bad idea made worse by the reason it had landed a job in a correctional facility rather than a motel continental breakfast room. Her stomach churned at the thought. And other thoughts.

"Emmalyn?"

She turned at the sound of his voice. Nobody spoke her name like he did.

Her cheeks warmed at the tenderness in his eyes. Tenderness. Not disgust. Not resentment. Not the brokenness he talked about, however he defined it. He took a step closer, leaving only six feet between them. Now what? She stood. Took a step toward him.

"Emmalyn," he said again, as if testing the word on his tongue. "I can't believe you're here." He gestured with his arms out, palms up, shoulders shrugged, like Hope did.

She knew better than to think she'd find him in black and white horizontal stripes. She'd seen the other prisoners in the visitation room in drab gray shirts and darker gray pants. Gray looked surprisingly good on Max. His hair had been clipped shorter than she'd ever seen it. She resisted the urge to reach up and find out if it was soft or stubbly.

After a moment, he lowered his arms.

"We're allowed a kiss," she said. *It's true. We never really leave junior high*. They danced around what should have been natural for them. "That's what I heard."

He surveyed the roomful of prisoners and visitors. When he turned back, his eyes glistened.

She took another small step forward. "People in Italy and Greece kiss to say hello."

"And France," he said, stepping closer. "And the Middle East. And France."

"You said that already."

He brought his hands to her shoulders, then the sides of her face. From her viewpoint, his kiss felt like pent-up agony and bliss in the same too-brief moment. She didn't have to ask how it felt from his vantage point. His eyes told her.

She reached around his middle and pressed her head against his chest. The smell wasn't the same. Whatever the prison used for laundry soap, it wasn't the "mountain fresh" version she used at home. But the solid core of him felt bracingly familiar. More muscled. His arms around her chased away every chill she'd ever known.

"That's enough." The guard pronounced his verdict, but turned on his heel as if acknowledging they'd need the four extra seconds it would take for him to return to his station.

Max extended his hand toward the chair where he'd found her. He pulled one opposite so they sat knee-to-knee, but not touching. A good foot between them. No more touching. He seemed to study her face.

Her hand reached to her cheekbones. "It's amazing how much five years can age a person." She tried to laugh it off, but the chuckle aborted itself.

"That's not what I was thinking." He bent forward and rested his forearms on his thighs. "I like your hair, by the way." He didn't look up. "We have so much to talk about."

"That's why I'm here."

"Where do we start?"

Emmalyn pinched back tears. "Hope?"

He lifted his head without sitting up. "How is she?"

"I wasn't talking about your daughter."

24

Y ou have a scar. On your chin."

Max rubbed the spot with his knuckle. "Would you believe a football injury?"

"No." A scar he hadn't had before. Her imagination threatened to bolt.

The noise level in the stark, acoustically disadvantaged room made thought a challenge, much less conversation. They leaned toward each other to hear, but that heightened the discomfort of some topics.

"How did it happen?" She nodded toward his scar. "Is that what landed you in the shu?"

He stared at the floor again. "Some stories are going to take a while for me to be able to tell. It's pointless to say it wasn't my fault. I mean, it wasn't. But it's pointless to say it."

"Pointless. Fault is less important than where do we go from here."

He leaned back then. "It's a good principle to live by."

"Life-changing," she said.

"It makes no difference at all right now, but I had no intention of ramming the building that night, Em."

"I know. That's what you said."

He looked just to the right of her left shoulder. "It must have seemed that way. Are you going to ask me what I did intend to do?"

"Would it fix anything?"

He played thumb war with his own thumbs. "Probably not."

"Do you need to say it?"

"Probably."

She pawed through a dozen responses, discarding eleven of them. "It's safe with me, Max. You're safe with me."

He angled his head and looked at her. "You've changed."

"You have too."

"I was afraid I'd ruined your life."

"You didn't." *I told him, Hope. Pray he believes it.*

His face brightened by two degrees, like the television ads show the effects of tooth whitening products. "We should be worrying about the stability of our 401ks right now. Not this." He indicated their current surroundings. A humorless room with couples and families trying to maintain a fragile peace between them despite the painfully awkward structure, and the rules designed to keep them apart.

The microwave dinged. Emmalyn startled, a hand over her heart.

"Are you okay?" Max's brow furrowed. "If *that* noise gets to you, you would not survive one night on the unit."

He probably meant to lighten the tension. It didn't work. Maybe they could save talk of what he'd been through until after he was home. Home. Free.

"I'm stronger than I look, Max. I've had to be."

His expression sobered. "I wish I could have given you what you most needed."

"You weren't capable of that."

"I know. I relive that reality every day in here."

Emmalyn stopped herself short of laying her hand on his knee. "Max, you can't ever give me what I need *most*."

"Especially not now." His voice faded like final breath sounds.

"I need more." Her responses wrote themselves while she watched from somewhere offstage. "I finally see how true that is."

How long would it be before she'd find the right words to tell people—to tell her husband—what she was slowly discovering? That a husband isn't ever enough. That a child isn't the ultimate solution to a relentless soul ache.

"So, why did you take in Hope, then?"

She reconnected to their conversation. What did he mean? "Because she needed a place to stay. And because she belongs to you." Wasn't that obvious?

"With all you've been through—we've been through—I can't imagine how rough that is for you, emotionally."

"Impossible."

His eyes showed white all around the pupils.

"A couple of months ago, it would have been impossible. I'm afraid of very few things these days."

"Except rabid microwave oven timers," Max said, nodding over his shoulder.

"That," she said, rubbing her palms on her knees, "was a simple startle reflex."

"Of course it was." His eyes tracked the motion of her hands.

She laced her fingers together. "Max, I'm not saying this is easy . . . with Hope. But I know it's what I'm supposed to do right now. She needs you. But if she can't have you, I guess I'm the next best thing."

"That's not what I hear from her."

"We've had our differences of opinion. She is a pre-teen, after all. But I thought we were—"

Max lifted his arms as if to reach for her, but stopped himself, turning the arms-in-mid-air stance into an elaborate hand signal impossible to decode. He dropped his hands to his lap and said, "Our words aren't working well yet."

"No. They're a little rusty."

He pantomimed oiling the hinge of his jaw. "Hope says you're exactly what she needed. Disagreements notwithstanding."

"She told you that?" She crossed her ankles to keep her feet from dancing.

He tugged at the dark gray fabric at his knees, straightening the imaginary creases in his pant legs. "And, yes. She used the word *notwithstanding*."

Laughter bubbled out. Before it died down, one of the guards shouted something Emmalyn didn't understand. Max and the other inmates left where they'd been sitting and lined up against the wall. None of the other visitors panicked over the move. Reggie caught her eye. Nodded and mouthed, "It's okay."

One of the four armed guards called off a name. That prisoner answered with his assigned number. Another name, then another, until all of the prisoners were accounted for. Emmalyn's heart twisted when she heard Max calling out his identification number, as if that's who he was. Emmalyn knew better. She hoped Max did, too. His attitude during the first year of his incarceration smacked of depression. Understandable. She'd thought it coldness, abandonment, disinterest in her. Now she wondered if he hadn't become disinterested in life itself in those early days following his sentencing. And what had he wanted to confess to her?

She watched him return to their little corner of a room that buzzed with noise like a squadron of B-52s at treetop level. He walked with a slight limp. Another story? One he could stomach telling?

"Max, did you get the letters I sent when I didn't know you were in the Special Housing Unit?"

"I got them."

"You never answered."

His pause paced the room. "I couldn't."

Emmalyn held both ends of a tug of war. Would it have mattered if he was prevented from responding or if it was a choice? Would it change anything now? His kiss hadn't said, "I was ready to give up long ago." It said, "Where have you been?" That's what it meant, didn't it?

She tasted him still on her parched lips.

"We have a lot of muck to wade through, Emmalyn. For years, I've rehearsed where to start, if I ever saw you again."

Me, too.

"Now that you're here, I can't think." He rubbed his hand over his short hair as if scrubbing something from his palm. "You're more beautiful than ever."

I don't need flattery, Max. That's not why I came.

"So . . . "—he raised his hand as if to brush her cheek, but kept his prescribed distance—" . . . intensely beautiful."

"It can't be the lighting in here," she joked. "Fluorescents do nothing for skin tone."

"You look content." He stared at his feet, then off to the far corner of the ceiling behind her. "That's what I was afraid of."

"It's like new shoes," she said, leaning to the side to catch his attention. "I can't wear contentment too many hours each day. Building up my tolerance for it."

The comment was supposed to make him smile. Why was his jaw clenching like that? He was afraid of her conten—? A worm of worry bored its way into her soul. He was afraid she'd found contentment in a life without him.

"Max." She waited. His face showed evidence he couldn't win the battle for composure this time. "Max, please look at me."

Turning his eyes to focus on hers seemed to exact a monumental toll from him. Shoulders slumped, head loose on its hinges, eyebrows raised in the middle of his forehead and drooped at the sides.

She drew a deep breath. *God, calm me. I'm lost here.*

"Do that again," he said.

"What?"

"Breathe. I love to watch you breathe."

I'm your Rachel, aren't I, Max? The one Jacob loved.

"Visitation is over for today, folks." The guard's voice cut through the incessant cacophony of conversations. "Wrap it up. Let's go."

"What? No!"

"Emmalyn . . . "

"Sir? May I ask why we have to—?"

Max shook his head. "Em, don't."

Had he called her "Em" before? He used her full name, or Emi. She shook off his warning. "I'm just going to find out—"

"They don't need a reason." The resignation on his face spoke of four and a half years of uncomfortable, demeaning experiences.

"But I couldn't come yesterday because of the fog."

"I know." He stood.

She joined him. "I can't leave Hope very often to come back." Realization dawned. "We have to talk about Hope!"

He drew her to his chest for their sanctioned good-bye hug. "I'll call when I can. And email . . . when I can. I'll write."

"I'll write too."

"Lean against me."

"I am."

"Breathe against me."

"I'm trying."

He bent to kiss her. The first four years of their marriage, she hadn't thought to memorize his kiss. She would this time.

As she exited the building with the sea of other visitors, pushed by guards with an efficiency complex, she watched for Reggie, but couldn't find her through the blinding snow.

Max, you can't give me my heart's desire. You've become my heart's desire.

"Well, it looks as if the snow we predicted for later in the afternoon decided to show up a little early," the meteorologist said.

Emmalyn snapped off the car radio. She didn't need the Christmas tunes either, a reminder of who wouldn't be with them for Christmas.

Visibility issues kept her from enjoying the artistry of the fat flakes of snow kissing her windshield. She focused on the road ahead, which stretched long and barren ahead of her. If she could keep up the current pace, and reach Bayfield by six-thirty, and if she didn't stop to eat, she could make the last ferry to Madeline Island that night.

She could have spent another night in the motel. What would that have gained her? So far the snow melted on the roadways as it fell. If it started to accumulate, though, or drift . . .

"And miles to go before I sleep." So many miles.

Her brain muddled, like the spots where saltwater and freshwater meet. All they'd discussed rammed up against all they hadn't discussed.

Satellite learning for Hope. She had to have a decision on that soon. He'd objected initially. Was it for Hope's sake or Emmalyn's?

Did they have a future? That might have been the next thing on their list if visitation hadn't been cut short. A semi passed her, drowning her car in a white-out. She let up on the accelerator so she could drift farther back of the semi and see the highway again. Okay, so maybe a little snow did affect the ability of a tower guard to catch prisoner shenanigans.

They hadn't gotten to the heart of the transformation Max hinted at in his letter and his blog. He'd seemed restless and uneasy, though. Guilt-ridden or . . .

Uncertain of her love.

She couldn't blame him for that, considering their four-year code of silence. And maybe he hadn't noticed her cheeks warming every time he looked at her, the sweat that puddled in her palms, couldn't hear her heart thumping like the rabbit's hindfoot on the Bambi movie. Maybe he didn't notice.

But he caught her breathing.

She tore the scarf from around her neck and threw it onto the passenger seat. She turned the heat so low it began to blow cold air at her face.

He liked to watch her breathing.

25

She missed it by thirty-nine minutes. The last seventy miles felt like a slalom event at the Olympics, the snow underneath a threat to her ability to hug the road's curves. She missed the last ferry of the day.

Bougie hadn't expected her until Monday morning, so the phone call didn't hold the disappointment for her or Hope that it did for Emmalyn. Bougie gave her the address of a Bayfield friend who she said wouldn't mind an overnight drop-in visitor.

Emmalyn didn't want to make conversation with a stranger. Or anyone she knew, either. She wanted a hot bath, a hot meal, and . . . her husband.

She'd have to settle for two out of three.

Emmalyn knew her Sunday night options in early December weren't limitless in tourist-dependent Bayfield. The town didn't shrink as significantly as Madeline Island did when the temperatures dipped and the calendar images held more white than color. She pulled a time-worn gift certificate from her purse. One night's stay at the Old Rittenhouse Inn, courtesy of a drawing she hadn't remembered entering until the certificate came in the mail. Emmalyn hadn't planned to use it. But if the inn had a vacancy, it could be her answer for a night of anonymous solitude.

A hostess ushered her into a room that oozed opulence—a dramatic contrast in every way to the correctional facility. Every way. Ornate fireplace. Soft carpet. Comfortable chairs—matching. Inviting bed. View of Lake Superior from three windows. Warm ambient lighting. Richly textured wallpaper. High quality linens. It smelled of sweet applewood in the fireplace, pumpkin, and nutmeg, for some reason. Emmalyn asked the hostess about the divine smells. She said the cook was pulling a fresh batch of pumpkin cookies from the oven. Was she interested?

Emmalyn didn't know she still had the energy to smile. When the hostess left the room, she sat in one of the chairs facing the lake view. There, across the expanse of snow-dappled dark water—the few brave lights of Madeline Island. So close, but so far.

She hadn't moved yet when a knock at the door told her the cookies were ready. And a pot of fresh coffee. Dinner service was over, but the cook had prepared a snack tray for her. The hostess set it on the round marble-topped table by the window and wished Emmalyn a pleasant evening.

The opportunity to stay in an elegantly appointed mansion like this should have made her happy. The view should have made her happy. But her husband lay on a thin cot in a building that smelled like damp cement and the body odor of hundreds of inmates. The snack tray on the table would have seemed a decadent feast to him—a variety of cheeses and fresh fruit, a thick slice of homemade bread and pungent apple butter, pumpkin nutmeg cookies.

The rich colors in the room might shock Max's eyes after years of gray and off-white. How could she relax into what the room had to offer her when he stared at the underside of someone else's bunk?

She'd lost so much. And still she lived in an embarrassment of riches, by comparison. She considered stripping the quilt from the bed and curling up on the floor in honor of what Max was missing. But the soft rug and the sweet-smelling quilt would still be too much. Hungry, but for so much more than a cheese plate, she picked at the snacks and prayed for her husband.

Hope called to say good night.

Emmalyn climbed into the bed, propped herself among the bed pillows, and pulled a corner of the quilt over her body. "Talk to me, sweet child."

"Sorry. It's me. Hope," she said in her characteristic way-too-grown-up voice.

"You are the sweetest child, Hope." How had Hope escaped the bad decision gene of her mother? How had she developed wisdom her mother lacked? So, children can turn out great even if their parents have problems.

"Bougie wants to know if you found a place to stay."

Emmalyn looked around the room again. Through the small door near the fireplace was a smaller room with a huge soaking tub. "I did find a place. Remember when I drove you past the Old Rittenhouse Inn when I brought you through Bayfield?"

"No way!"

She told Hope about the gift certificate and the marble-topped table, the fireplace and soaking tub and antique wallpaper.

"You deserve it."

"No, honey. I don't. I don't even want to be here. I want to be there with you."

Hope's sigh traveled well across the water. Emmalyn pictured her with at least one hand on a hip. "Will it help anybody if you don't enjoy the gift?"

"Bougie's been talking to you about grace, hasn't she."

"How did you know that?"

"Sleep well, Hope. I'll see you tomorrow."

"Hey, did you know that cat urine glows under a blacklight?"

Emmalyn knew for sure she was close to home now. "That's why we have a dog instead. Good night, Hope."

"You sleep well, too, after your appointment with the soaking tub and bath salts. Do they have bath salts? And take pictures of the room, okay?"

"Okay. I'll grab the first ferry in the morning."

Hope hesitated. "Take the second one, will you? I'm sleeping in."

They ended the call. Emmalyn lay against the pillows another moment before throwing off the quilt and pouring herself a cup of coffee. She dunked half a pumpkin cookie in the dark brew and fought back a tear. It was going to be so hard to give that girl back to her real mom.

Bougie had enlisted Hope's help wrapping napkins around silverware sets. "Math class," Hope said as Emmalyn came close to give Hope a hug. The girl quickly added the stack of wrapped utensils. "Forty-two sets times three in each set. One hundred twenty-six." She brandished the answer like a fencing sword.

"No worries," Emmalyn said, shrugging her coat and winking at Bougie. Lime tutu. Nice. "Any amount of time spent with Bougie is an education. And what are you wearing, young lady?" She stepped back to take it all in.

"My mom's boots."

"I recognize that part of the outfit."

Bougie waltzed closer. "I took her shopping at my favorite vintage place Saturday. That's okay, isn't it?"

"That's vintage?"

"Straight out of the *Leave It to Beaver* archives," Bougie said.

Hope stood. "Do you like it?" She twirled.

"Do you have a crinoline under that skirt?"

"Yeah," Hope said. "That's not a fun part. It itches."

"You'll get used to it," Bougie said, turning back to her project. "Or you can do what I do. Wear another skirt underneath the crinoline."

"It's . . . cute. Really. Not very practical." Emmalyn measured her words.

"Do I have to be practical all the time?"

Bougie raised her eyebrows and pursed her lips, waiting for an answer.

"No" Emmalyn said. She relaxed her shoulders. "No. Not all the time. It's adorable. We should take a picture to send to your dad. And mom."

"Neither of them are emotionally ready for this," Hope said, flouncing her skirt and sinking back to her chair.

Emmalyn shook her head, laughter easing another layer of the tension of the past three days.

"Tell me about Dad," Hope said. "Except for all the 'Oh, he's so handsome' part."

"He is," Emmalyn said, crossing the backs of her hands under her chin and exhaling an exaggerated sigh.

Hope rolled her eyes and shook her head. "Anything *else*?"

"He"—Emmalyn hugged Hope's shoulders—"sends this. And this." Emmalyn kissed the top of Hope's head.

"I don't remember the last time he kissed or hugged me," Hope said, her words featherlight and aching.

I do. Emmalyn squeezed her eyes shut, reliving the moment.

"Soooo . . . " Bougie slapped her hands together. "Anyone interested in sour cream coffee cake? Hot out of the oven."

Emmalyn's phone rang. An unfamiliar number. Her policy was to ignore unknown numbers on her cell phone. Something nudged her to answer this one.

"Mrs. Ross?"

"Yes?"

"This is the number given us by Claire Bostik. You're a family member or acquaintance?"

Claire, what kind of trouble are you in now? Emmalyn sauntered toward the door and addressed the two in the room under her breath, "Need better reception. I'll be outside."

"Mrs. Ross?"

"I'm still here. What's up?"

"You have Claire's daughter, Hope?"

The cold blast of outside air had nothing over the icy fist pummeling Emmalyn's stomach. "I do. Yes. Claire asked me to take care of her while she's . . . " What word? What word? How much should she reveal? Claire hadn't attempted to keep it a secret. "While she's at rehab. Who is this?"

"I'm with Child Protective Services for the State of Wisconsin. Delane Drummond."

Another fist punch. The Old Rittenhouse Breakfast inched its way toward her throat, sour and stinging where it had been sweet and comforting an hour earlier.

"Things have changed, I'm afraid." The woman's voice didn't lack compassion. Curious. How could she sense how hard it would be for Hope to go back to her mother this soon, before either of them—any of the three of them—were ready for it?

"Claire isn't in rehab," the woman said.

What kind of program would release her that soon? Wasn't there a protocol for someone that severely addicted?

"Did she tell you she was entering rehab?" The woman sounded confused.

"Yes. That's where she was headed after she put Hope on the plane to come stay with me." Emmalyn kept her back to the plate glass window of the restaurant.

"She is in a hospital in Georgia."

"Georgia? What's she doing there?"

"Taking her last few breaths. I'm sorry, Mrs. Ross."

Emmalyn leaned against the building. "What on earth happened? Wait. Last few breaths?"

"I've been in contact with a nurse there who is serving as temporary liaison for us."

"What? I don't understand what you're talking about. Can you explain this?"

"She was in pretty bad shape when she was brought into the hospital. Overdose. I take it that possibility would not come as a huge shock to you."

Emmalyn couldn't afford to let her body language communicate what she was hearing. She glanced over her shoulder at Hope. The girl smiled and waved through the window. Emmalyn waved back and turned away. "Not a shock. But she's never taken it this far, has she?"

"From all appearances, Mrs. Ross, it looks like it was intentional. I can't give you details. Privacy Act issues. But we have to move quickly."

"What do you mean?"

"Claire's fighting to hold on until she hears that Hope can remain with you, at least until CPS can evaluate the situation."

"Of course. Yes, of course she can." Emmalyn's heart raced. She pressed her palm against it to keep it from exploding out of her chest. *Claire!*

The woman let out a breath. "Good. Thank you. We'll have to do a home visit, initially, to determine if it's a safe place for Hope's temporary housing. I'll need to talk to the girl, too. Is it your opinion that she'll be amenable to the plan?"

Amenable to the plan? Her mother is dying! How can any twelve-year-old girl be amenable to any plan other than her mother getting well? "She seems comfortable here with me."

"Good. That helps. I need to get back to our liaison. There are papers to sign before . . . before Ms. Bostik is . . . unable."

"What about Hope? What am I supposed to tell her? Can I bring her to see her mom? We could leave by plane later today and—" Emmalyn would drain every account she had to make that happen.

"Honestly, Mrs. Ross, I believe we're talking hours, not days. Perhaps minutes. Stay by your phone. I'll call as soon as I know where we stand. As I said, I need to talk to Hope myself. But right now, I'd like to give Claire a little peace of mind."

Time. Of the essence. If she'd missed the morning ferry, she wouldn't be here for Hope right now. If the phone call had come an hour earlier, Emmalyn would have clawed her way across the water to get to Hope, ferry or no ferry.

"We appreciate what you're willing to do temporarily here, Mrs. Ross. The foster care system is backlogged so badly, I can't even describe it to you. But we'll talk later. Soon."

Emmalyn could feel the cold wind more prominently now. Then a surprising warmth. Bougie draped Emmalyn's coat over her shoulders. Bougie turned to tiptoe back into the building. Emmalyn stopped her.

"I didn't want to disturb your phone conversation," Bougie whispered.

"It's over."

"Most people put their phones away when a call is finished." Bougie guided Emmalyn's hand away from her ear. "What's wrong?"

Emmalyn swallowed around the tightness in her throat. "Do you remember Max's first words to me when he reconnected with me by phone?"

"Didn't he say—?"

"He said, 'I'm losing Hope.'" Emmalyn looked at the now silent phone in her hand. "Now it's me. Now *I'm* losing Hope, Bougie. And Hope's losing her mother."

26

Hope stuck her head out the door. "Hey, there's a woman on the phone who wants to know if we cater. Do we?"

We. Emmalyn heard the resonance in that two-letter word. Small shards of her fell off like sheets of ice falling from tree branches after a storm. Dangerous for those standing near.

Bougie looked at Emmalyn. "Cater? It depends on the situation, Hope. We've catered a few events. I'll take the call."

"I'm coming in, too," Emmalyn said, finding her earth legs again.

"I was starting to worry about you," Hope said, joining the two women on the snowy sidewalk apron. "Did you know that frostbite can start in as few as two minutes if conditions are right? Look at that," Hope chided, an inborn motherly instinct propelling her words. "You're not even wearing gloves. Let me get you some hot chocolate."

How much of this kind of truth can a twelve-year-old handle? Not an ordinary pre-teen. Hope Elizabeth. Emmalyn wrapped one arm around the half child/half woman while they walked side by side into The Wild Iris. "We need to talk, Hope."

The words stopped Hope's progress. "Okay." She stomped snow from her boots. From Claire's boots. "Let me get the hot chocolate. It's time for my recess anyway, isn't it?" Her reserved smile told Emmalyn she knew something was up.

A haze thicker than Saturday's fog floated in Emmalyn's mind. What now? And how would she explain to Hope that her tenuous peace would likely be shredded before the day was over. Bougie stayed close. She also stayed silent.

"Life has never been fair to that girl," Emmalyn whispered.

Bougie moved her lips but said nothing audible.

"Bougie, help me!"

"I am. I'm praying for you."

Emmalyn pushed the sleeves of her sweater to her elbows. The bracelet Bougie'd given her for an early Christmas present before she'd left for the prison slid back down to her wrist. Vintage silverware curved into jewelry with a delicate cluster of small gems and a pearl. Emmalyn fingered the gems, watching them dance in the light that had neglected to notice rooms are supposed to be dark at times like this.

"Hope shouldn't have to go through this."

"But she is. And she's held. Yours aren't the only arms around her, M."

Bougie's eyes sparkled like the crystal beads in the bracelet. She didn't talk like that because she was unaware of the realities of pain, or waving off the gravity of the situation. She felt it all. Deeply. But a steel cable of trust ran deeper still.

"Did you know that the winter of 2013–14 was the first time in five years it had been cold enough for the Apostle Island ice caves to be open to the public?" Hope asked as she set a tray on the fireplace table. Three mugs. Steaming. And a whipped cream dispenser. "Imagine. Frozen waterfalls."

"I heard that." Emmalyn needed another minute or two.

Hope slid one of the mugs to Bougie. "The pictures I've seen are spectacular. We should take kayaks out there to the caves in the summer, then see if we can visit the same caves when they're iced up. People use ski poles to cross the frozen lake to get to them." Her words poured out with no check valve. "Did you know Nick is good at photography? He said he'd lend me one of his old digital cameras he's not using anymore. Do you think it will freeze hard enough to see the ice caves this winter?"

Emmalyn waited until she settled into her chair. "Hope—"

"She did it this time, didn't she." The last word was swallowed in the child's hitched breath.

"Your mom has been sick a long time."

"Tell me something I don't know." She used her thumb to wipe a spot of hot chocolate from the handle of her mug. "Sorry. That came out wrong. She—" That beautiful, flawless face pinched itself into a mask of resignation overlaid with pain. "She wasn't always like this. I think her . . . addiction . . . wouldn't let her make smart choices anymore."

Emmalyn's helplessness overwhelmed her. What do you say to a child who knows too much? Knows too much. Like Bougie. "Did you read that in the book you got from the library?"

Hope's expression said, *You don't know anything, do you.* She sighed, then responded. "No. I saw it. Front-row seat."

"I'm so sorry, Hope."

The young girl shrugged. "I survived. Some of us do."

"It . . . it doesn't look like your mother's going to make it this time."

They sat in silence a few moments. Emmalyn watched a single tear fall from the child's bent head and land on the plum-colored napkin beside her mug. It left a dark spot that spread and was joined by others. Not in a flood. Individual droplets with time between.

"Can I see her?" Hope didn't look up.

"She's in Georgia. In a hospital in Georgia."

"That's one way to make sure I won't be around when it happens. Way to go, Mom."

Sarcasm or gratitude? The tears made it impossible to tell.

Hope's phone rang, an ordinary ringtone, not the one reserved for her father. She looked at the number, then held the screen toward Emmalyn. Emmalyn nodded and stood to give Hope privacy. Hope grabbed her sleeve. Emmalyn sat, praying like she hadn't prayed before.

"Yes? Yes, that's me. She's right here. Yes." Hope turned to Emmalyn. "She wants to know I'm not alone, I think. Say something?" her eyes made it a question.

"Hello? Yes, Ms. Drummond."

"It's a safe place to talk?" the woman asked.

Emmalyn glanced at Bougie, eyes closed, head bowed, lips moving. "The safest. We're here together."

"It's over."

Courage, Emmalyn. There'll be time for a meltdown later. "I understand."

"She signed her portion of the papers so we need to move forward with the temporary placement without further legal involvement at this point."

"Of course." What could she say with Hope mere inches away?

"It's time I talked to her."

"Yes. Here's Hope." She handed the phone to the delicate hand of a delicate but fiercely brave child.

"Hello?"

Her voice sounded small and fragile, like glass wind chimes in a barely there breeze.

"Yes." More tears fell. Hope's face twisted like a newborn winding up for a wail that never came. "I'm still . . . here." She handed the phone back to Emmalyn. "I . . . can't . . . "

"It's okay, honey. I'll talk to her."

Bougie pulled a chair on the other side of Hope, surrounding her with people who cared. While Bougie handed Hope tissues and rubbed her back, Emmalyn addressed Delane Drummond. "It's difficult for Hope to talk details right now."

"Perfectly understandable. Can you handle dealing with this? Would you like us to send a counselor?"

No, I can't handle it. But I know a Counselor who can run rings around your programs.

She turned her head, not to sneeze, but to flinch. *Put a lid on it, Emmalyn. This isn't the CPS's fault. They're trying to help.* "We'll be okay, but I appreciate the offer. We'll hear from you soon, then, about the . . . arrangements?"

"Do you know who we should talk to about having the body transported back to Wisconsin for the funeral? Or Montana? That was her last known residence, it appears. She mentioned a boyfriend but made us promise we wouldn't get him involved. Her records list a half-sister. I'm sorry, I don't have her name here in front of me. She'd be the likeliest candidate for permanent placement for Hope, especially under the circumstances with Hope's birth father. Does Hope have any connection with her mom's sister? Her aunt?"

Oh, Claire! What a mess you've made! "I can talk to Hope about it. Later."

"You have my number there on your phone from our earlier phone call? We need to get information about what to do with the bod—"

"I'll get your number added to my contacts list right away."

"You're doing us and Claire a huge favor by letting Hope stay with you a little longer."

Emmalyn traced back through the few words she'd heard Hope say in response to Ms. Drummond. "She agreed to it?"

"Not enthusiastically. But I wouldn't expect enthusiasm at a time like this."

"No."

"You take care. I'll be in touch."

Emmalyn swiped at the dampness on her cheek. "Thank you. For everything."

"Not my favorite part of this job, as you can imagine."

I wish you hadn't had to get involved at all.

When the phone call ended, Hope switched from leaning against Bougie's shoulder to leaning against Emmalyn's. She wasn't a noisy crier. But her narrow frame shook.

Pirate Joe entered from the kitchen, surveyed the scene, and pivoted for an immediate retreat. He slipped back into the room long enough to deposit four heavy-sounding coins—must be quarters—in the Jesus Jar. *Plink. Plink. Plink. Plink.*

Hope stiffened at the sound but didn't open her eyes. "Is that Pirate"—*sniff*—"Joe?"

Emmalyn stroked Hope's silk hair. "Yes, honey."

"I promised I'd teach him how to start a blog."

"That's kind of you," Emmalyn said, brushing wisps from Hope's face.

"Today. I promised I'd teach him today. Oh, no!"

Emmalyn and Bougie pulled closer. "He'll understand, dear one," Bougie said.

"No. Not that." Hope pressed her palms to her forehead. "I have to be the one to tell Dad." She sniffed again and sat up straight in her chair. "I have to be the one."

"Why does it have to come from you, Hope?" Emmalyn took a tissue from Bougie and blew her nose while she waited for an answer.

"I'm his daughter."

Bougie nodded toward Emmalyn. "M can tell him. She's his wife."

"Not that she acts like it." Hope pressed her fingertips against her lips. Her eyes revealed a new level of pain.

Bougie pulled back like an archer ready to release an arrow. Emmalyn waved her off. "Hope, there's too much truth in what you said."

"I'm so sorry," the girl pressed out through a veil of new tears.

"We'll talk about that later. But it's true. I haven't treated him like my husband. I let my pain do the communicating. I let pain and loss dictate my life. Even before your father went to prison. And that kept me from thinking clearly, until now."

Hope's eyes glistened, chin trembled.

"It's *because* I haven't handled things the right way I can tell you what doesn't work," Emmalyn said. "Your father and I are still figuring things out. We have a long way to go. But I care about you so much. Let me help you with this."

Hope's beautiful eyes, puffy and red, kept leaking liquid Broken Heart. She pushed her chair back and stood. "You're not my mom. You're nobody's mom!"

She bolted for the restroom. The words stayed behind.

Emmalyn waited fifteen minutes, then tapped with her fingernails on the restroom door and said, "Let's go home, Hope. I'll be in the car."

Emmalyn had read stories of flying bullets stopped by a Bible in a soldier's pocket. She pulled hers from the passenger seat where it had ridden all weekend and held it to her chest. The onslaught thudded, but didn't penetrate as it might have. She was nobody's mother. But she was Max's wife. And she could love anyway.

Emmalyn opened her eyes when she heard the car door click. Hope slid into the seat, head down, still sniffling.

Nothing human could make the scene less tense or soften Hope's distress. Emmalyn put the car into drive and steered it toward the cottage. Christmas decorations outside businesses and homes mocked the reality of what they faced. No, that wasn't right. Plastic reindeer and shivering inflated Frosty the Snowmen mocked reality. Lights mirrored their need. Peace on earth. Joy to the World. Emmanuel—God with Us. Yes. Yes. And yes.

The strings of white Christmas lights Hope had asked for sat on the floor of the backseat along with most of the other crafty things on her list. What were the chances she'd want to use them this year of all years? You can't lose a mom . . . or a baby . . . this close to Christmas without it changing you forever. Emmalyn should know.

How were they going to maneuver through the minefield of the next few hours, much less the holiday? And a funeral? And the possibility that CPS would see the cottage as too remote, Emmalyn as too inexperienced, and the family dynamic too bizarre. Even for foster care. If that's what they called what Emmalyn offered. Hope had a dad. An incarcerated dad. And he was committed to raising his daughter.

He hadn't yet said he was committed to reclaiming their marriage.

⚶

Not unexpectedly, Hope headed for the stairs as soon as they got in the door.

"Before you . . . get involved . . . in something else, Hope, I have to ask you a question or two."

Hope stopped, mid-stride, but didn't turn around. None of this was going to be easy.

"The social worker said your mom has a sister. Do you know her name? Have you met her?"

"Delia. I think she was named after a soap opera character from the eighties. Her life's a soap opera. Why?" She turned then and caught her lower lip between her teeth.

"Would she be your mom's next of kin? Would she be the closest adult to . . . take care of legal things and make funeral arrangements?"

"Aunt Delia?" Her shoulders slumped even farther forward. "I guess so. She's got money."

Great. Another item for the "who should get Hope?" tally. Emmalyn didn't have a job that paid in dollars. And her husband made eleven—no, fourteen—cents an hour in the prison laundry. Score another one for Delia. Blood related. Employed, or at least well-off by some standards. "Nice house?"

"It's huge. I think she makes out good, taking in foster kids."

Emmalyn saw something shift in Hope's countenance. They must have been thinking the same thing. What more logical location for Hope to be placed than with a family already set up for fostering kids.

"Where does she live?" *Please say Antarctica.*

"Chicago. I think I have her phone number as an emergency contact." She sighed. "I'll get it in a minute." She took the stairs more slowly than Emmalyn had ever seen the girl move.

Emmalyn logged in to the corrections email system, managed the hurdles of the user name, password, and scrambled code, and wrote a short email to Max.

Sad news. Call as soon as you can.

No. If she received an email like that, it would send her into worry-mode instantly, her imagination concocting grotesque scenarios. She deleted and tried again.

Hard news. Call as soon as you can.

Almost as bad.

Sobering news. Please call Hope as soon as you can.

She hit *send* before she pestered the words to death. Death.

Emmalyn called up the stairs. "Hope, I emailed your dad to ask him to call you."

"So did I."

"Oh. Good." What was Emmalyn's role? What part was she supposed to play? She wasn't even officially a stepmother.

Wait. That's exactly what she was. Hope's stepmother. Even if Claire had lived, that would have been true. She'd never given herself the label—the honor—before. She could use that to her advantage, couldn't she? Ammunition for keeping Hope at the cottage, at least until Max won his freedom?

When Claire called before her supposed trip to rehab, she'd said she had nowhere else for Hope to go. Why hadn't Delia been the logical choice then? Hope might know.

Emmalyn's phone rang. First thing tomorrow, she'd search for a calming ringtone. The number showing on the screen made her teeth ache. If she let it go to voice mail, she'd have to deal with her later. Later held no promises of being better. "Hi, Mom."

"Emmalyn! Did you see the news? Well, our local news has it, anyway. Max's ex-wife? The druggie? She o-ver-dosed. Killed herself."

"I'm not sure she intended to kill herself, Mom."

"You knew? Why didn't you call?"

"We've been a little busy, as you can imagine."

"I thought I might hear from you sometime"—she drew the words to their full potency—"since Christmas is only a couple of weeks away and you haven't said when you'd be coming. We're having turd-uh-ken this year."

"I don't think that's how it's pronounced, Mom."

"Always correcting me. Can't stop yourself, can you." Her exhale could have blown out two birthday cakes full of candles.

Hope bounded down the stairs. "Is that Dad?"

"No, honey. He probably won't be able to call until tonight."

"Who are you talking to?" her mother asked. "Who's there with you? Did you finally decide to start dating? Well, good for you! Wait until I tell your sisters."

"Mom, this is a bad time to talk."

"I'm sure it is," she said, adding an inflection that made Emmalyn's skin crawl.

"I'll call you soon."

"No, you won't."

I probably won't. God, You and I will have to discuss this, won't we. "'Bye, Mom. Gotta go."

Hope let Comfort in, wiped her paws, and carried her upstairs.

"We need another dog," Emmalyn said to herself as she sank into her favorite chair and reached for the throw. She held her phone in her lap, willing it to ring.

Phones are shy, apparently. They don't perform when watched.

An hour later, Emmalyn got up to make a pot of tea, her phone in one hand. She climbed the stairs, rather than hollering this time, to see if Hope needed anything. Her door was open. She lay on her side, mouth open, sleep-breathing. Comfort lay tight against her chest. The flop-eared rabbit poked its head out from

Hope's armpit. She'd wound the Christmas lights around the back of her desk chair and plugged them in. The glow, oddly bunched as it was, seemed to soften the edges of the night. Hope's phone rested on the pillow next to her head.

I don't know what to do for you! I can't make this go away. I can't even make it a smidgen easier. It's as awful as it seems. And I have no words to make any difference.

From somewhere in the recesses of her brain—or maybe her soul—she heard, *Love her. Love is always enough for now.*

27

When her tea reached the color of Grade A maple syrup, Emmalyn climbed the stairs again and settled into the armchair near the French doors in her room. On the distant shore, Michigan prepared for nightfall. It still startled her to think that here on the western side of Wisconsin she could catch a glimpse of Michigan to the east because of the curvature of both the Upper Peninsula and the Apostle Islands.

Even at a time like this, the scene held beauty. A pocket of miserable surround by a sea of exquisite beauty. And those waves, endless waves. From behind the walls and windows, she imagined the sound they made, the feel of the mist they stirred, the scent of water. Relentlessly brushing the shore, wearing down the rough edges of the rocks, sweeping life's debris farther out to the freshwater depths.

She reached for the book on the nearby table. After four attempts at the same paragraph, she put it aside and picked up the verse Bougie had given her to memorize. It's what people of faith did at times like this, wasn't it? Psalm 68:6 NLT—"God places the lonely in families; he sets the prisoners free and gives them joy."

And sometimes Social Services and the criminal justice system change those dynamics.

"God places . . . " She read it again. "God places . . . "

The phone in the other room sang its "waiting for you" chorus. The criminal justice system was calling.

Hope answered before the song got to the word "here." From the silence, Emmalyn knew Hope likely raced through the sequences of numbers she had to punch. "Dad? Oh, Daddy!"

Emmalyn cried through the entire muffled conversation. Quiet tears. Like Hope's. The achy kind, not the stinging kind. After a few minutes, Emmalyn heard Hope move from her room to the top of the stairs and call out for her. Emmalyn opened her bedroom door. "I'm here."

"I thought you were downstairs."

"I wanted . . . to be close to you."

Hope pressed a fist against the side of her head. "Can you tell Dad the rest?"

"Sure."

Hope handed her the phone and beelined for the bathroom.

"Max?"

"Emmalyn. I'm stunned."

"We all are." She retreated to her bedroom but left the door open. "Did Hope mention the possibility of her being placed with Delia?"

"That can't happen. We can't let that happen."

Emmalyn cupped her hand over the microphone slot and lowered her voice. "Is she a bad person?"

"Hope would not thrive in that atmosphere."

Whispering now, "She somehow lived through being the daughter of an addict."

Max's end of the conversation halted. He cleared his throat. "The grace of God. That's the only explanation."

It seemed strange to carry on a conversation with this new man who used words like *grace* and *God* differently than he had before. Odd, but endearing.

"Hope's back. Do you want to talk to her again?"

Hope signaled "no" and reached for a tissue to blow her nose. She sat cross-legged on Emmalyn's bed. The dog jumped up and into her lap.

"I guess she'd rather the two of us talked out the rest of the information."

Hope nodded.

Max groaned. "They're going to cut us off soon. Can we pray together?"

Emmalyn mouthed, "He wants to pray."

Hope patted the spot on the bed next to her. Emmalyn joined her and held the phone between them so both could hear.

"Max, I'm putting you on speaker phone. It's the three of us in on this." Four, if you counted Comfort's upturned face and alert ears.

"Father God, we have nowhere else to turn but You. Hold Hope and Emmalyn close to Your heart tonight. And show us the next step, we pray." His amen came long after. Pinched. Tight-throated.

"Amen," Hope whispered.

"Amen."

The call disconnected with the final amen.

The two sat side by side on the bed as minutes ticked by.

"Did you know," Hope said, her face turned toward the lake, "that when the pyramids were being built, there were woolly mammoths living on an island in Siberia?"

"No, I didn't." Where does a conversation go from there? "What made you think of that fascinating fact?"

"Something to think about that wouldn't make me cry."

Emmalyn had to risk it. She reached her arm around Hope and gave her a gentle hug.

Hope's gaze remained fixed on the water. "Do you know what Anonymous said?"

"Who's Anonymous?"

"Nobody knows. Do you know what she said? I think she's a she. She said, 'One day someone is going to hug you so tight that all of your broken pieces will stick back together.'"

Emmalyn tightened her hug. "We need to stencil that onto pillows."

Hope didn't say anything. But she didn't disagree.

Delia refused to pay for the funeral. Emmalyn couldn't. Claire would be buried by the State of Georgia. Emmalyn told Hope she'd find a way to get her there if she wanted to be present. Hope said, in her words, she "kind of did the closure thing already." Everybody stayed home from the event except Claire.

The call they knew was coming interrupted their first attempt at decorating the cottage for a somber Christmas. Cora was the one who'd suggested they put their tree on the porch in front of the window, so it didn't take up floor space in the cottage. She rigged an extension cord from the back of the cottage around to the front. They tucked scroll-like pieces of birchbark, pine cones dusted with glitter-glue, and more than enough strings of mini-lights among the branches of the tree Nick had cut down for them. Ms. Drummond from Child Protective Services interrupted the "let there be light" moment.

"Mrs. Ross, we need to set up an appointment for a home visit in order to complete our paperwork for this temporary placement."

Could she stop using the word *temporary*?

"When would you like to do that?" Emmalyn asked, nudging Comfort away from the tower of empty boxes the lights had come in.

"I know it may seem awkward timing, but I have family in Superior. I'll be with them Christmas Eve and Christmas Day."

You have to be kidding.

"I could drive up a day early and take care of the evaluation."

"December twenty-third."

"Yes."

"Two days before Christmas."

"As I say, I realize it's a bit awkward. Would that interfere with your plans?"

Not at all. I just have to find a legitimate job, prove it, keep both Hope and me from spiraling out of control during the most emotional days of the year, and help Bougie prep Christmas dinner for half the safe houses in Bayfield and Ashland Counties. "We can make it work."

"I'll see you sometime early afternoon of the twenty-third."

"If you give me your email address, I can send you the ferry schedule."

"Have it already."

She'd done her homework. "We'll see you then."

Cora, Nick, Hope, and Comfort stomped into the cottage from the porch. "Watch this," Hope said as Nick flicked the light switch for the porch and the tree came to life. "Isn't it magnificent?"

"Truly magnificent."

Hope's excitement faded. "Let's not do anything more. Just the tree."

"If that's what you want."

"What about candles?" Cora said.

"And candles."

Nick nudged her. "You don't want a gingerbread house or some droopy pine bough things on the mantel? Stockings? Something all girlie and sparkly?"

"No. Just this." She seemed mesmerized by the way the lights from the tree lit the path to the beach and the interior of the cottage, too. It had that effect on Emmalyn, too.

"Fine with me," Emmalyn said.

"You would not be happy at my mom's place," Nick said. "We don't have an inch that's not red, green, gold, or silver right now."

Cora folded her arms over her chest.

"And I love living there," Nick added. He'd ditched the girl-friend who had kept his mother awake at night talking to God, and the young man seemed infinitely happier. His easy big-brother friendship with Hope filled some gaps.

Hope remained at the window when the other three headed for the kitchen to make popcorn. Emmalyn snapped a picture of Hope silhouetted against the window, the tree, the night.

"I heard that shutter click," she said.

Emmalyn smiled. "It's for your father."

Nick pulled out his own camera, never far away. "Let me get a shot of the both of you. He'd like that, I bet."

Hope turned. "Just take one of Emmalyn. I don't want any popcorn. I think I'll go upstairs."

Emmalyn leaned against the island. She slid her arms forward and laid her cheek against the cold stone surface.

"What did I do?" Nick asked.

Cora put her arm around her son. "Nothing. Come on. We can make popcorn at home . . . in our over-the-top Christmas village extravaganza."

Emmalyn didn't raise her head. "Thanks for the help, guys."

"You're welcome." They exited quietly, leaving Emmalyn in her stretched-out version of the fetal position, draped over the island.

She laid like that, feeling the coolness of the stone seep deeper into her skin layers. "Max, I have an itch in the middle of my back. Would you scratch it for me? Thanks. Oh, and your daughter can't decide if she hates me or likes me. Could you take care of that, too?"

28

"Did you know that all polar bears are left-handed?" Hope called into the kitchen from the dining area of The Wild Iris.

Emmalyn looked up from the crust she was pressing into muffin tins for mini-quiches. "No, I didn't, Hope. Biology homework?"

"Weird fact."

"I'm checking your biology homework in twenty minutes."

"It's done."

Not a bit surprised. "Can you help with this project, then? Wash your hands, please."

"Actually," Bougie said, "I need you for another purpose for a while, Emmalyn. Hope, do you have enough to keep you busy for a few minutes?"

"Not a problem." She pulled a library book from her backpack.

Bougie draped a flour-sack towel over the crust and pointed to the alcove at the back of the kitchen where Bougie did the bookwork. Emmalyn spent a few moments at the sink, washing the dough from her fingers, then joined her. "What's up?"

Bougie slid a piece of paper toward her. "I'd appreciate your signature on this."

"What is it?"

Tucking her skirts—multiples—to one side, Bougie sat on a corner of the desk. "I'd like to go back to school."

"That's great. Where?"

"UMD offers a business administration and management degree."

"Duluth? That's quite a commute. Ninety miles?"

Bougie held Emmalyn's gaze an awkward moment before speaking. "That's why I'd like to make you part owner of The Wild Iris."

"What?" Emmalyn felt as if she'd swallowed her gum, but she hadn't been chewing any.

"I need to know I have The Wild Iris to return to after I get my degree. I don't want to lose this place."

"Of course not. It's all you, Bougie."

Her face lit. "Then you'll help me out?" She slid the contract closer.

"I don't have any money to invest in a business." Emmalyn's thoughts swam circles around the island as the two talked.

Bougie clapped her hands together. "I thought of that. So I had my lawyer draw up the contract for a one dollar purchase price for forty percent ownership."

"Bougie!"

"I realize forty percent doesn't seem like much, but the profits during the tourist season should hold you most of the year, with careful budgeting."

"A dollar?"

"If that's a problem," she said, "I'm sure there's enough change in the Jesus Jar to cover a small loan."

Dumbstruck. Dumbfounded. Speechless.

"Are you interested, M? You're what The Wild Iris has needed. What I've needed."

Emmalyn would have laughed if it wouldn't have drawn attention from others in the kitchen. How could Bougie not realize how lopsided their relationship was in the "needed" category? "I don't know what to say. I love this place." The truth of her response spread over her like ganache.

Bougie tented her fingers, as if praying, but tapped the fingertips together. "That's a good start. I'd need your decision by today."

"Today?"

She handed Emmalyn a pen. "The CPS lady is coming tomorrow, right?"

"Uh, yes, Ms. Drummond. I'm part owner of The Wild Iris Inn and Café." Bougie's contract offered her gainful employment, in a way.

"Cleverly done, Ms. Unfortunate."

"Your catering and executive chef experience will serve you well in this position. Food ordering. Bookkeeping. You're already helping with menu selections and design."

"And mini-quiches."

"There you go." Bougie's face could be so convincing. She had a persuasive Voice coaching her. "My mother and I spent a few seasons in a women's shelter when I was younger."

Bougie's story. Finally.

"We walked away from several of her misguided infatuations with only what our arms could carry. Most of my high school years, I didn't have an address. I don't want to lose this place."

"You could make me temporary manager or something." Compassion threatened to choke her.

Bougie caught her gaze. "I severely dislike the word *temporary*."

"Me, too."

"I have to know today."

Two foreign but welcome thoughts coursed through Emmalyn's mind. She'd lived independently since Max's sentencing. Now her first thought was to consult her husband's wisdom on the decision. Her second was to pray about it.

"CPS may still place Hope with her aunt instead of me, Bougie." The idea made her lungs cramp.

"And if so, where would you want to be?"

Emmalyn considered the stark days of winter without Hope. "Here. I'd want to be here."

"Is that what you want to do, Emmalyn?" Max's voice flowed over her soul like a chocolate fountain submerges a strawberry, the same general feeling she'd had when she realized how attached she'd become to The Wild Iris and all it stood for.

"You're gifted for it," he said. "From the descriptions you've written about The Wild Iris in your emails and letters, it seems intriguing, but not what I would have called your style."

"It's the style I want to become when I grow up, Max." Saying it aloud felt like a puzzle piece sliding into place. She tapped it for good measure. The outside edges linked together.

"I have no doubt you're the one person who could pull this off successfully, even with Hope's off-site schooling."

"That's not a sure thing yet." Emmalyn wanted to cling to optimism about CPS's upcoming evaluation, but the parade of past disappointments looped back around.

"I thought the curriculm sounded ideal for Hope."

"You're not against the homeschooling idea anymore?"

Max's response came slowly. "I was never against homeschooling. I was opposed to your feeling forced into an uncomfortable position, to my mistakes costing you more than they already had."

The more they'd communicated, the more kinks they'd worked out of communicating. The distance shrank. Steel bars narrowed and thinned. His blog posts gave her insights about what she'd missed. They read like high-quality nonfiction, like a story he should tell someday in a larger arena.

"Em? The curriculm?"

Emmalyn rubbed the tense knot in her neck. "It's not the schooling that isn't a sure thing, directly, Max. It's Hope being placed here. Not a given."

He was quiet longer than Emmalyn wanted. "In my heart, it's already a done deal."

"So you think I should sign the contract?"

"You don't need my approval."

"I'd like to believe we're in this together."

Another long pause. "We are."

Emmalyn vowed to create a Jesus Jar for bad attitude for every time the corrections system interrupted their conversations and used too much time to remind them how little time they had left.

"Tell Hope I'll call her as soon as I can, and that I love her."

The familiar muscle cramp in her neck intensified. "I will."

"And you. Tell . . . you."

The phone's dial tone made it impossible to reply.

Max had said it again, earlier in their discussion, unlayering more of the past so she could remind him again he was forgiven. "If I'd been where I should have been that night . . . "

Emmalyn had replied with her well-rehearsed and truer-than-true, "If *we'd* been where we should have been . . . "

Inching their way back to where they should be.

Emmalyn had been sitting on the steps to the inn's second floor, away from the noise and bustle in the café and kitchen. She re-entered the hub of activity. Bougie wiped her hands on a towel tucked into a vintage apron on her way from the kitchen, eyes questioning. Was Emmalyn on board with the contract or not?

Emmalyn nodded her head. Neutral as she wanted to remain, she couldn't suppress her joy. Hope caught the exchange. Her expression gave away nothing.

Bougie gestured, "Come. Come!"

Papers signed, the food prep for the Christmas meal for the women's shelters resumed. Pirate Joe taught her to peel potatoes a new way—praying for the woman or child who would eat them. The added layer of activity helped Emmalyn keep her mind off the swirling uncertainties that remained.

"M?"

"Yes?" Emmalyn kept peeling.

"We have something for you."

She put down the peeler and turned toward Hope and Bougie. Each held a stoneware mug in her right hand. Bougie offered the one in her left to Emmalyn.

"What is it?" The liquid in the mug didn't look like coffee, tea, or cocoa. She sniffed it. "Cherry juice?"

Bougie tilted her head. "It's the closest I could get to champagne. To the beauty of partnerships!"

They clinked their mugs. Hope, too.

Then, why the tears?

"Tireder than tired" is how Hope expressed it when they finally reached the cottage that night. But they fortified themselves with a great artisan pizza then set about to get the cottage ready for the CPS appointment the next day.

Hope was as picky about tidiness and turning end table displays into "vignettes" as Emmalyn.

"I hope the sun's shining tomorrow," Hope said, sweeping around Comfort's dog dish. "It always looks stupendous in here when the sun's shining."

"Stupendous?"

"It earned me extra points in Boggle last night, if you remember."

Emmalyn remembered. She also remembered the moment the blocks spelled MOM in four directions. Game over. For both of them. The sweeping slowed. Emmalyn watched Hope's elegant dancer posture slump. Just a little. Just enough for a . . .

For a mom to notice.

"Let's say you're officially on Christmas break as of tonight. No classes until after the new year. How does that sound?" Emmalyn wiped a spot from the granite on the kitchen island.

"Whatever."

"Even lifelong learners need time off."

Hope looked incredulous. "From learning?"

Emmalyn cringed at the harshness in her delivery. "Hope. Hope, please look at me. I will listen to anything you have to say, to anything, even if it isn't something I want to hear, as long as you say it respectfully. Understand, hon?"

She leaned farther toward thirteen than twelve in her facial expression. "Yes, Mrs. Ross."

Emmalyn would have turned it into a teaching moment if the phone hadn't rung. Hope ran from the room to the phone-arms of her daddy.

Fifteen minutes later, precisely, Hope leaned down the stairs and said, 'I'm going to clean my room, if that's okay."

Asking permission to clean her room? The mood fluctuations could be so much worse. Emmalyn shook her head. Only Comfort paid any attention.

Max, while Hope cleaned her room tonight—which, by the way, is never messy—I sat in the opposite chair from the one I usually choose in this cottage that looks so different from when you last saw it. Nothing's really the same, is it? This chair, this second one, is an exact duplicate of the one I sit in. I guess I've always left this one for you.

Hope prefers the couch.

I realize that by the time you receive this, Hope may be gone. I can't predict how Child Protective Services will react. Or if Hope will be in her "this is the best place ever!" frame of mind or locked in grief mode. I was just starting to get comfortable with realizing no one walks into parenting—or step-parenting—fully grown, no matter how old the child. Then I'll say the wrong thing, or she will, and we slide down the hill in this long, slippery trek toward how-is-this-going-to-look-long-term?

I appreciate the father you've been to her more every day. Your gentle but firm ways with her are an inspiration. She respects you. And I can see why.

Brief time out. I'm listening to Elsa's Procession to the Cathedral while I write, and I had to stop for the part when the French horns come in toward the end. I can't listen to that section with my eyes open. Or my arms at my sides.

I fell in love with you in that section, Max. The concert under the stars. You let me lean on you through that song. When the French horns came in, you drew in a quick breath and I melted into the music and your tightening embrace.

Your prison chapel Christmas Eve service will be finished by the time you get this, too. I wish I were there to share the moment with you. Well, not there. Here. I wish all three of us could spend Christmas together here in this room. With the indoor-outdoor Christmas tree lighting a path to the lake and you in the spot I'm occupying now.

Elsa's Procession one more time. I suppose I should be listening to Christmas music. But I fell in love to this.

She closed her eyes, tireder than tired.

"Bougie, Hope's gone!" Emmalyn sank to the floor, her back against the island, the skylight screaming a brightness out of character with the heaviness in her heart.

"What do you mean?" Bougie's voice through the phone should have been calming. It was always calming. Not this morning.

"She took the dog for a walk after breakfast. I told her it was okay."

"That's not unusual, is it?" The serenity tone was back.

"They left an hour and a half ago. I'm frantic, Bougie! She's never been gone this long. Never wanders far alone. The woman from Child Protective Services will be here in a couple of hours." Emmalyn drew a deeper breath than the gasping through which she'd tried to tell the story.

"Where have you looked?"

"Everywhere. The beach . . . both directions. The woods right behind the house. I looked for their tracks in the snow but what's falling now is filling in the tracks too fast. Visibility isn't great out there. Oh, Bougie!"

"I'll call reinforcements. We'll get to the cottage as soon as we can. I'll send Cora and Nick the back way, if they're home, and we'll watch the roads. Maybe she needed time to think."

"In a snowstorm? She's smarter than that."

"She's also twelve. And grieving."

"Oh, Bougie!" Emmalyn's throat closed off. "I can't . . . lose . . . another . . . baby! Erase that. I can't lose *this* child."

***

Emmalyn ignored the melted snow on her bamboo floors. The people crammed into the cottage at the moment brought enough heart and genuine caring to cover any messes. Their hugs counted for a lot, but her pulse refused to slow.

"Map of the island," Nick said. "Here's us. There's Amnicon Point. Oh."

"What is it?" Emmalyn leaned over the map. The irregular blue spot in the interior of the island, not far from them. "Bog Lake. She wouldn't have gone there. It's wild and impossible to—"

Nick drew their attention to the less gruesome possibilities on the map. "A girl and a dog trudging through a couple of inches of snow can't move very fast."

"Unless she hitched a ride with someone on the road." Cora shrugged. "Could happen. We have to think of every possibility."

Emmalyn's lungs threatened to collapse. "What if . . . ? What if she somehow got all the way to the ferry? Oh, Lord God!" Hope was bright enough to think through fifty ways to leave the island if she wanted to. This time of year, every way funneled through the ferry.

Bougie pulled off her Scandinavian mittens. "I checked with the ferry line. No single travelers. No young girls."

She might have been afraid of the meeting with Ms. Drummond. Afraid she'd make Hope stay. Afraid she'd make her leave. The alternative—that she hadn't intended to leave but had gotten in trouble, gotten lost, hurt—made Emmalyn feel even more ill.

"We'll fan out," Nick said. "We can cover more ground that way. Let's check in with each other every ten minutes via cell phone."

"You sound as if you inherited your mother's search and rescue skills," Bougie said.

Nick's mouth curled at the ends. "I could do worse than turn out like my mom." He circled four search areas. "Is one of us staying here at the cottage? Someone should be here if she . . . when she comes home."

Emmalyn's sniffs turned to sobs.

Bougie stepped to Emmalyn's side. "Whatever voice you're listening to, it better be the one saying, 'I've got this. Trust Me.' If it's telling you you've failed that girl, it's lying."

The front door flew open. "Mom! I mean, M. Comfort's missing! She was there one minute and then . . . just . . . gone. I've looked all over!"

Emmalyn clutched the sides of her skull, grabbing handfuls of search-dampened hair. "Hope! Oh—!" Her words disintegrated in relief. She ran to the girl, parting the crowd like Moses to get to her. "Hope! I was so worried I'd lost you!"

"I wasn't lost. Comfort is." Her facial expression danced with worry and confusion.

Emmalyn removed Hope's gloves and wrapped her hands around the girl's icy fingers. She switched quickly to a bear hug that left Hope begging for air.

"We'll get you something warm to drink."

"Already started," Cora called from the kitchen.

"Nick, you'll help me find her, won't you?" Hope's was the only face still wracked with pain.

"Sure, little sister. I'll look. But . . . " Nick searched the women in the room for a fitting response.

Bougie came to the rescue. "Honey, Comfort's an interesting animal. She comes and goes, showing up wherever, staying an indeterminate amount of time. She doesn't stay long with any one family."

"M, why aren't you worried about her?"

Emmalyn sat on the couch and drew Hope down beside her. "You know how I feel about that dog. I miss her when she's gone a couple of minutes. Frankly, I didn't think we were done needing her. You can imagine how I feel about her not living here anymore, if that's how this turns out. I loved that little mop." She pulled the knit cap from Hope's head and stroked her now stringy hair. "But I love you more."

Bougie rounded up the troops, wiping snowmelt as they backed out of the cottage to let Hope and Emmalyn pull their thoughts together before the CPS representative arrived. The two stayed on the couch, breathing in sync. Was Emmalyn the only one of them wondering if by late afternoon the cottage's two remaining residents would be whittled down to one?

29

Delane Drummond from CPS turned out to be a fan of shabby chic—heavy on the chic, of quaint cottages, of snow globe snowstorms, and of mischievous little dogs like the one that slept off her morning adventure in her favorite spot in front of the fire. She'd barked at the door ten minutes before Delane pulled in. Hope and Emmalyn threw a party for the prodigal puppy.

"Not funny," Emmalyn scolded the animal. Then she wiped the dog dry and dug a treat out of the pantry. "But welcome back."

Hope and Emmalyn had scurried to blow-dry their hair and pick up the last reminders of the morning's trauma. The two had passed each other with looks that said, "We're going to need to talk about this, but not right now."

When Ms. Drummond arrived, she walked into a cozy scene with no reminders of what could have happened.

The woman requested private interviews with each of them, then a group discussion. When it got to the part about employment, Emmalyn held her chagrin to a manageable level when she answered, "I'm part owner of The Wild Iris Inn and Café in LaPointe. Not far from the ferry landing."

Delane's eyebrows rose. "Cute place. I'd hoped to stop there for a cup of coffee before driving out, but they were closed."

"Our crew is delivering Christmas meals to the Bayfield County and Ashland County women's shelters this afternoon. They"—she glanced at Hope—"got a later start than they hoped."

Emmalyn tried to gauge how Hope felt about her individual interview with Delane, but couldn't get a read.

"As I told Hope, I've spoken with her Aunt Delia at length."

Max, I hope you're praying right now!

"It appears adding another child to their household would not be in Hope's best interests at this point."

Emmalyn's pulse started up again. "What does that mean? Can she stay here?"

"There's another consideration." Delane scribbled something on her leather-bound legal pad. "Hope's father."

As if rehearsed, Emmalyn and Hope both clasped their hands together in their laps.

Hope spoke. "Prison doesn't mean he isn't a good dad."

Emmalyn laid a hand on Hope's knee, not to stop her, but to applaud her. "He's a remarkable man."

"I can see that. He's written to our office every day since Claire's death. I know more about the two of you than I do most of the cases I see. I wasn't made aware, however, of your ownership of The Wild Orchid."

"Iris. The Wild Iris. A relatively new development for me." Emmalyn sat up straighter, as if that would help. "I worked there part-time until recently."

"I see." She scribbled another few moments. Was she taking notes or playing tic-tac-toe?

"Hope, your wishes count for a lot in situations like this. I want you to know that. But we have to consider many factors in our decisions. Safety. Stability. Security. Schooling."

A defense for the kind of broad education Hope could get on the island in addition to the compulsory subjects clawed at the back of Emmalyn's teeth, but she stayed silent. "Did you know that all polar bears are left-handed?" she wanted to say. "Or that cat urine glows in the dark?" But she didn't.

"Your words, Hope, pushed me over the edge in my decision. The board will review my findings. We should have a final decision for you shortly after the holidays." She stuffed her papers into her briefcase and stood.

"Wait a minute. We won't know anything until after the holidays?" Emmalyn felt a small hand on her knee.

"My personal recommendation is rarely overturned," Ms. Drummond said. "I can't think of a better place for Hope. You're blessed to be loved by so many, young lady. And I agree with what you said upstairs."

What had Hope said? Would Emmalyn hear the story?

Emmalyn's voice held steady. "Thank you so much for coming all this way." *No, no! Not a "remoteness" reference.* "For coming right before Christmas."

"My pleasure. Nice to meet both of you. Hope"—she took the girl by her shoulders—"I know this is a tough, tough time for you. But you're surrounded by people who care. That's a gift."

"I know," she said, her small voice filling the cottage.

<hr />

Emmalyn felt like dancing. Hope remained subdued.

"Are you feeling okay? You were out in the cold a long time." Emmalyn stirred the tomato bisque that had become their favorite. Grilled cheese sandwiches—gryuere—sizzled on the griddle.

"I'm okay."

"Anything you want to talk about?"

"No."

"Anything you *need* to talk about?" Emmalyn tapped the wooden spoon on the edge of the pan and turned off the burner.

"Did you know that the word *typewriter* is the longest word in the English language that can be spelled using only the top row of letters on a keyboard?"

"Interesting." Emmalyn flipped their sandwiches. "Anything else?"

"I'm going to leave again, you know."

It might have been some other muscle, but Emmalyn thought it was her womb that tightened. "I'll find you."

"I don't mean run away, which for the record isn't what happened this morning."

"Felt like it."

"Sorry about that. But I am going to leave. When I'm, like, eighteen. Unless I accelerate my studies and can swing early admittance to college." She chewed on one fingernail, forehead scrunched.

Twelve and twenty in the same tiny package.

"I believe"—Emmalyn swallowed—"that will be a difficult moment for me—sending you off to college. But I think I'll live through it."

"I can spend the summers here with you and Dad, right?"

"Right." Emmalyn blinked back tears. She had hope that Max wanted them all together as much as she did.

Hope pulled her hair into a ponytail and secured it. "Did you agree to take me in because you thought you had to? I mean, I get it if you did. Because Dad asked you to."

"I didn't give him a chance to ask." Emmalyn slid the sandwiches onto robin's egg blue plates. "I volunteered."

"Because you always wanted a child?"

"Because God knew I didn't need just a child. I needed to make a home for you. You."

They ate their supper in the living area, by the lights from the Christmas tree on the porch.

"The Christmas Eve service at The Wild Iris should be something to see." Hope set her spoon in her empty bowl. "Something to see."

"Would you like to go, Hope?"

"Nice play on words, M."

"What?"

Her beautiful lopsided dimples deepened as she said, "Hope shows up at every Christmas Eve service. It's kind of the point."

Waiting for You made a timely appearance. Hope pulled out her phone. "It's Dad!" She took the stairs two at a time on her way to her room.

Emmalyn tried to imagine what Max had written to CPS about her. "Failed me miserably for four years, but she's doing okay now." "Don't know if we can reclaim our marriage, but I guess it's worth a try." "She breathes nice."

She smiled in spite of the unknown. They had so much time to make up. And neither of them were the same as when they'd pledged forever to each other. The beginning of a new forever was five months and eight days away.

Hope stayed in her room long after the phone call ended. Emmalyn eventually let Comfort out and watched her like a hawk until the dog came back in. She washed the supper dishes, fed the sourdough starter Bougie had given her, and turned out the lights. When she passed Hope's bedroom door on the way to her own, she paused. The chalkboard sign Emmalyn hung on the door a few days after Hope arrived had been doctored.

At one time it said *Hope's Room*.

Hope had asked for a piece of chalk shortly before the CPS representative arrived. Emmalyn guessed she now knew what it was for. The sign read: *Hope Lives Here. Even Here.*

The door swung open and the sign clattered against the wood. "Hey, you're here," Hope said.

Emmalyn feigned nonchalant, as if her world hadn't tilted in the last moments.

"Is it too early to exchange gifts? It is, isn't it." The eagerness etched on Hope's face would have made a great advertisement for the joy of Christmas.

"I wasn't sure if you'd—"

"Want to?"

"Be here. I wasn't sure you'd be here, Hope." How hollow this night would have been.

"The Lord giveth and the Lord taketh away," she said, digging something from under her pillow. "And sometimes He just giveth and giveth and you wind up with an almost teenager whether you want one or not."

"Oh, Hope!" Emmalyn sat at the foot of Hope's bed. "Isn't it a strange time? I feel like celebrating that you get to stay. But, your mother . . . "

Hope nodded. "I'm thinking of becoming a vegetarian."

"What?" Was this another version of "Did you know . . . ?" "Any particular reason?"

"Because for the last couple of years, my mom made mostly unhealthy choices. And I don't want to live like that."

"We're going to figure this out together, aren't we?"

"So, do you want your Christmas present or not?"

"Mine for you is downstairs." Emmalyn turned to get it.

"That's okay. I can wait for mine," Hope said.

Emmalyn smiled. "I should refrigerate it then, if you're waiting until Christmas Eve."

Hope's curious dimples deepened. "What is it?"

"I don't know if you'll want it anymore."

"M! What did you get me?"

"Bacon." Emmalyn slid farther onto the bed and rested her back against the wall.

"You did not!" Hope poked at her knee. "Did you? Because, that whole vegetarian thing? That was a metaphor."

"So you're still into bacon?"

Hope sat cross-legged at the head of her bed, her mouth twitching with a barely suppressed giggle. "Is it going to be like this forever?"

Emmalyn's pulse locked into a sweet, smooth rhythm. "I hope so."

"Did you know . . . ?" Hope stopped, lower lip caught between her teeth.

Oh, that opening could lead to so many conclusions. How many atoms can fit on the head of a pin. The greatest number of skips ever recorded in a rock-skipping contest. The square root of . . .

A single, sweet, solemn tear slipped down Hope's cheek. She smiled through it.

"Yes, Hope. I know."

Bacon played a key role in their Christmas Eve meal. Bacon-wrapped water chestnuts, a treat new to Hope. Bacon-wrapped, goat-cheese-stuffed Medjool dates, which Hope pronounced a waste of good bacon. And bacon-flavored roasted brussel sprouts, which Hope decided were close enough to the life of a vegetarian for her.

"You know that little shed in the back?" she said.

"Yes. What about it?"

Hope slid onto the stool by the island. "We need to paint it, don't you think? It looks kind of . . . forlorn."

"Forlorn? What have you been reading, Hope?"

"Lots of stuff." She snatched a chocolate-covered strawberry from the platter of dessert options. "I think if we painted it, and maybe fixed the windows, Dad could use it for a man cave when he comes home."

Emmalyn set a glass cup of hot cider in front of her. "You don't think he'll appreciate the all-white and robin's egg blue décor we have going here? Even the dog's white."

"With a brown face."

"Right."

"Do you think it would work?" Hope exercised her puppy-dog pleading face to the max.

"You know, your father has a lot of decisions to make. And one of them is where to live when he's released."

Hope leaned closer. "Yeah, but you two are getting along a lot better now, so . . . "

Emmalyn felt at her throat for the agate necklace Hope had given her.

"He gives you flowers." Hope reached for a petal of one of the white baby roses in the antique tea cup in the center of the island.

"Yes, and I'd like to know how he pulls that off from prison. Are you sure you have nothing to do with that?"

"I swear," she said. "Not in a Jesus Jar kind of way. You know what I mean."

"It must be Bougie, then."

Hope shook her head. "Not her either. Must be magic."

"It's not magic, but it is sweet. I'll find out."

"In five months and seven days?" Hope glanced at the count-down app on her phone.

"Lots of winter between now and then." Emmalyn finished putting away the leftovers and grabbed a chocolate-covered strawberry for herself.

"Did you know that the daylight hours are already getting longer? For, like, three whole days now?"

Emmalyn chuckled. "You've noticed the difference?"

"I'm sensitive that way," Hope said, craning her neck, nose in the air.

They agreed to take the platter and their cider into the living area to take full advantage of the lit tree, the fire in the fireplace, and Emmalyn's real gift to Hope—portable speakers for her phone. When Max called, they'd share the news about Ms. Drummond's decision together.

After the fire died down, the apple cider was drained, and the platter of desserts had been given more than enough attention, Emmalyn gave voice to reality. "Hon, it looks like he's not going to be able to get through tonight. Who knows why? One of the hard things about life in prison."

"It's Christmas Eve."

"I'm sorry. I have another present for you. Out in the back entry. A new pair of boots. Your size. When you're ready for them."

"Thanks."

Hope took her cup to the kitchen. She stayed at the sink with her back to Emmalyn for much longer than it would take to wash one cup.

Emmalyn nudged Comfort from her lap. "I'm on my way to read and then bed. You?"

"I'm going to work on Dad's blog. I'll send him an email to tell him about what happened yesterday with the CPS lady. Anything you want to say to him?"

Emmalyn's thoughts traveled the long highway of miles and a ferry crossing that separated them. "Tell him we'll be right here, waiting for him."

30

~And after every winter, a spring.~

The bike ride to the Town Park exhausted them even more than kayaking from the park's picturesque beach landing and lagoon. The mosquitos vacationed elsewhere this warm day late in May, allowing them an itch-free excursion on glassy water.

"Your nose got a little sun," Emmalyn said as they prepared for the ride home, donning helmets, shouldering their backpacks, and adjusting the straps.

"Yours, too. Smell that?"

"What?" Emmalyn looked around the area where they'd left their bikes.

Hope posed like Kate Winslet in *Titanic*. "How can air smell sweet, like honey?"

Emmalyn mimicked Hope's pose, closed her eyes, and took a deep breath. "New leaves. Wildflowers. Moss. Water. Pine. Cottonwood. Piña colada."

"Piña colada?"

"My hand lotion. Are we racing home or touring?"

Hope climbed on her bike, the helmet Emmalyn's mother had sent her perched low over her eyes. "I want to ride so slow we can see the thin veins on the butterfly wings."

Emmalyn readjusted the strap on her matching helmet. "You're working on your poetry unit for English, aren't you?"

"How'd you guess?"

"Open book, Hope. You're an open book."

And just like that, the book closed. Emmalyn didn't know if her sudden descents into quietness were the normal fluctuations of an almost thirteen-year-old, or of a young girl who'd recently lost her mom, or solitary ponderings about getting her dad back in a few weeks, if all went well.

Emmalyn had her own pondering moments, most of them late at night. Life was about to change. Again. She and Max had conquered a few long-distance marriage maintenance techniques. They no longer wasted valuable phone time on trivial disagreements or discussions they couldn't complete. They consulted each other as they would have if separated by a hallway rather than a long stretch of highway. They filtered out the bad but never the truth.

How would they function as a couple in an 800-square-foot cottage with a built in pre-teen and a dog that was one-paw-in, one-paw-out?

She reached up to adjust her helmet. What would Max do for a living? Work at The Wild Iris? Take Pirate Joe's place when he left for Florida? Create a business he could manage online, since Emmalyn didn't plan to anymore? Become a stay-at-home dad?

Madeline Island had worked its way into her bones and sinews. What if Max didn't have the same reaction to this place? What if the maple tree on their property was just a tree to him? The elbow of road just a curve? The sandy/rocky shore any old beach? The water—clear and bitingly cold even now—a lake, not The Lake? What if his first decision as a live-in husband was, "Let's move. Let's start over somewhere else"?

She breathed harder as her legs worked the pedals. Hope ahead of her wasn't biking slowly enough to trace butterfly veins. Emmalyn strained to keep up.

She'd found love and fulfillment, healing, friendship, here in this unexpected place, in unexpected ways, among people and crises she wouldn't have chosen for herself. She'd watched the water carry the storm debris of her life far from shore.

How could she leave now? But what if staying kept Max from his heart's desire? He hadn't tasted the air of freedom in five years. How could she chain him to the cottage?

Emmalyn said, "The cottage needs a name, Hope. It still needs a name."

She turned her head and called over her shoulder, "You didn't like my last suggestion?"

"We're not naming it The Cottage."

"I had other ideas."

Emmalyn pulled her bike closer, leaving a safe enough margin between them. "Not going to do The *Tame* Iris. Not going to name it Used to Be Broken, although that does have metaphorical merit."

"Did you know that a duck's quack doesn't echo and no one knows why?"

"And this applies how?"

"In case you were thinking of naming the cottage Duck Echo Cottage. Because that would be impossible. But quirky."

"Hope?"

"Yes?"

"I love you."

"I know." Her young legs dug in and she shot forward, putting a good twenty feet between them.

Emmalyn shouted, "Slow down! I thought of a name!" It had come to her at three in the morning, like all good thoughts. Menopause insomnia, she assumed. Her doctor told her it wasn't uncommon. Just because her perimenopause was premature didn't mean she got to skip any of its *wonders*. She'd gotten up and sat in her bedroom chair for a while in the dark, listening to the waves and watching the stars attempting to outshine each other. Eventually she'd picked up her Bible and flicked on the small reading lamp. She turned the fragile pages randomly, enjoying the sound and texture as much as the hope she'd find something new to chew on.

She did. A verse in the book of Job she couldn't remember seeing before.

Hope pulled onto the wide, sandy shoulder at the edge of the property near the maple tree almost fully leafed out. She hopped off her bike and leaned it against the tree. Emmalyn followed.

"So," Hope said, "what name?" She started toward the beach.

They did their duck walk to get through the soft sand. "As Waters Gone By."

"Sounds Native American."

"Much older than that."

"What's it mean?" Hope stood near the water's edge looking back at the cottage as if ready to test the name on the building like a mother would gauge a name against the look of her newborn.

"Job 11:16 NIV. 'You will surely forget your trouble, recalling it only as waters gone by.'"

The waters that had called to her, comforted her, lullabied her many a sleepless night, impressed upon her heart a truth she could hold onto. She couldn't undo what had been done, couldn't call back the waters that had slipped past her while she watched.

But she could anticipate a day when her troubles would be a memory, like waters gone by. She could let the waves washing against the shore of her pain round the sharp edges of her disappointment. And Hope's loss. And Max's sentence. And their regrets.

Hope crossed her arms across her budding chest. "Hmm. I like it." Her voice disappeared like wisps of fog.

"I thought you might."

"I think Daddy will like it, too."

Like the cottage. Like the name. Like the concept. Like the life we've built here. Yes, please, Max. Like it all.

Bougie's winter/spring semester at UMD had ended. She returned to the helm of The Wild Iris as the tourist season ramped up.

Memorial Day weekend promised an influx of weekenders and the beginning of three nonstop months of customers. Their new menu stood at the ready. Emmalyn and Bougie worked well as a team. But Emmalyn thanked the Lord every day that Hope's studies let up for the summer when life at The Wild Iris got crazy. Crazier.

Max's release date, circled in red on every calendar on the island, neared. In four more days, Hope and Emmalyn would take the ferry across the water, pull onto that ribbon of endless highway, and make the trip to the correctional facility for the last time. No ice road to maneuver this time. No windsled trips before the ice road opened. No winter advisories. No threats of visitation cancellations. No gut-wrenching good-byes and tear-filled return trips back to the island and its winter isolation, the exile and refuge in one three-mile-by-fourteen-mile package. No more misery over a dropped phone call or empty mailbox. They'd bring him home.

How could something so freeing be so unnerving? Would he burn up on re-entry? Would he need counseling to adjust to freedom? She knew she was skirting around the real issue. They'd made it work long-distance. Could they make it work face-to-face?

She asked the questions to the bathroom mirror on this rare day off. It refused to tell her what she needed to know, so she headed downstairs to start breakfast. Hope deserved to sleep in. She'd been a trooper about getting up at four on the days Emmalyn opened the café.

Emmalyn made coffee and took the eggs out of the refrigerator so they could come to room temperature before she tried a new omelet recipe. She set them beside the exquisite flower arrangement delivered to The Wild Iris. With her name on it. From Max. How had he managed that? He couldn't buy and sell from prison. Bougie claimed she hadn't been involved. Hope pled the same. Cora, too.

It wasn't the first time he'd sent flowers during the past five months. A mystery each time. What had he gone through to show her such grace? Like other mysteries, it wouldn't be solved until she could see him face-to-face. She bent to the fragrant blossoms and filled her lungs with what they represented.

Braced and tenderized, Emmalyn took her cup of coffee to the porch, determined to tough out the morning chill for the sake of the early morning air.

She wasn't alone. A figure stood where the sand and water met, hands in his pockets, the back of his head and angle of his shoulders achingly familiar. How had he gotten there? What was he doing home early? That never happened, did it?

Emmalyn left her coffee on the porch and headed for the beach, uncertain if she should call out to him or surprise him or if the fact that he hadn't come to the cottage meant he wasn't sure he could. He must have heard her approaching through the sea grass and across the sand, but he didn't turn. He faced the water, the horizon, the future. She stood beside him and did the same.

She reached to draw his hand from his pocket and linked her pinky finger with his.

"This is your view every morning?" he said, his voice husky with emotion.

"No. It's different every morning. But it's the same setting every day."

"I wouldn't have recognized the place."

Emmalyn leaned her head against his shoulder. "A little paint and a new roof can do wonders."

"Not the building," he said. "This. My view of things is so different now that even this looks unfamiliar"—he turned to her—"in the best possible way."

She smiled, then retracted it, unsure where his thoughts were headed. Her heart thundered in her chest. If she listened closely, she could hear his thundering, too.

"I like the name you chose." He gestured toward the sign Hope and Emmalyn had hung on the porch railing. "'As Waters Gone By.' You got that from the book of Job, didn't you?"

"You *know* that verse?" She and Hope had kept that one secret—the cottage's name—to share when they could tell the whole story.

Max pulled a scrap of paper from his opposite pocket, not letting go of the pinky connection. He smoothed it on the thigh of his jeans and handed the paper to her.

Even through the tears forming, she could read the block-print words: "As waters gone by . . . "

"I had it taped to the underside of the bunk above me. It helped keep me sane."

Emmalyn's breathing grew more ragged. "Max, do you remember that scene in *Shawshank Redemption* when the character says all he wants when he's released is 'a warm place with no memory'? Remember?"

"I do."

"Welcome to a warm place with new memories."

Emmalyn wiggled three more fingers into their tentative grip as a voice behind them called, "Daddy!"

Group Discussion Guide

1. The main character—Emmalyn—appeared on the scene both devastated and taking bold steps. Does that make her unlike the people you know, or a reflection of people you know? In what way?

2. The Wild Iris owner, Boozie, exhibited both an eclectic style and an incomparable heart of compassion. What do you think might have changed in the story and in Emmalyn's outcome if she hadn't had a person like Boozie in her life at that critical point?

3. Emmalyn's relationship with her mother and sisters suffered several blows before the story opens, and more as the story developed. What signs in the story made you think there was hope for restoration for that family?

4. More than miles created distance in the lives of many of the *As Waters Gone By* characters. What actions contributed to lengthening emotional distance? What was required of the characters to shorten emotional distance?

5. Symbolism abounds in *As Waters Gone By*. What did the cottage represent? The dog? The young girl? The waves? What role did the ferry play? The shed behind the cottage? The maple tree?

6. In what ways did the Wild Iris Thanksgiving meal serve as a turning point?

7. Life didn't turn out as planned for Emmalyn. She's not alone on that count. If you were to write the story of the next five years of her live—beyond the final page of the book—what do you think it would hold? How would she cope? Would she still live at the cottage?

8. Emmalyn described the island as her place of exile, early in the story. How would you describe it? Why?

9. It's always remarkable to witness a scene when peace settles someone's heart even before their circumstances change. At what point in the story did you see the first stirrings that peace might lie on the horizon for Emmalyn?

10. We're given only hints of Boozie's background, the life events that formed who she was as a person, a friend, an encourager. In what ways did Emmalyn serve a role Boozie needed?

11. The tree, the L in the road, the stretch of beach and sea grasses are all very real places on Madeline Island. How strong was your desire to see the place for yourself when you finished the story? Why? (Author's Note: The cottage was a work of imagination. The land on which it rested in the story is private property in real life. The author visited the area twice in recent years and still can't shake the longing to purchase that little bit of land hemmed by water.)

12. Why do you think the author set the story primarily in late fall and early winter?

13. How would you describe Emmalyn's faith when she arrived on the island? How would you describe it at the end of the book?

14. What turned the hunting cottage into a home? What does that say about the hopes for Emmalyn's future?

Want to learn more about Cynthia Ruchti
and check out other great fiction from
Abingdon Press?

Check out our website at
www.AbingdonFiction.com
to read interviews with your favorite authors,
find tips for starting a reading group,
and stay posted on what new titles are on the horizon.

Be sure to visit Cynthia online!

http://www.cynthiaruchti.com/
https://www.facebook.com/CynthiaRuchtiReaderPage

We hope you enjoyed Cynthia Ruchti's *As Waters Gone By* and will want to continue reading works by this award-winning author. Here's a sample of her debut novel, the critically acclaimed *They Almost Always Come Home*.

1

From the window [she] looked out.
Through the window she watched for his return, saying,
"Why is his chariot so long in coming?
Why don't we hear the sound of chariot wheels?"

—Judges 5:28 NLT

Do dead people wear shoes? In the casket, I mean. Seems a waste. Then again, no outfit is complete without the shoes.

My thoughts pound up the stairs, down the hall, and into the master bedroom closet. Greg's gray suit is clean, I think. White shirt, although that won't allow much color contrast and won't do a thing for Greg's skin tones. His red tie with the silver threads? Good choice.

Shoes or no shoes? I should know this. I've stroked the porcelain-cold cheeks of several embalmed loved ones. My father and grandfather. Two grandmothers—one too young to die. One too old not to.

And Lacey.

The Baxter Street Mortuary will not touch my husband's body should the need arise. They got Lacey's hair and facial expression all wrong.

I rise from the couch and part the sheers on the front window one more time. Still quiet. No lights on the street. No Jeep pulling into our driveway. I'll give him one more hour, then I'm heading for bed. With or without him.

Shoes? Yes or no? I'm familiar with the casket protocol for children. But for adults?

Grandma Clarendon hadn't worn shoes for twelve years or more when she died. She preferred open-toed terrycloth slippers. Day and night. Home. Uptown. Church. Seems to me she took comfort to the extreme. Or maybe she figured God ought to be grateful she showed up in His house at all, given her distaste for His indiscriminate dispersal of the Death Angel among her friends and siblings.

"Ain't a lick of pride in outliving your brothers and sisters, Libby." She said it often enough that I can pull off a believable impression. Nobody at the local comedy club need fear me as competition, but the cousins get a kick out of it at family reunions.

Leaning on the tile and cast-iron coffee table, I crane everything in me to look at the wall clock in the entry. Almost four in the morning? I haven't even decided who will sing special music at Greg's memorial service. Don't most women plan their husband's funeral if he's more than a few minutes late?

In the past, before this hour, I'm mentally two weeks beyond the service, trying to decide whether to keep the house or move to a condo downtown.

He's never been this late before. And he's never been alone in the wilderness. A lightning bolt of something—*fear? anticipation? pain?*—ripples my skin and exits through the soles of my feet.

The funeral plans no longer seem a semimorbid way to occupy my mind while I wait for the lights of his Jeep. Not pointless imaginings but preparation.

That sounds like a thought I should command to flee in the name of Jesus or some other holy incantation. But it stares at me with narrowed eyes as if to say, "I dare you."

Greg will give me grief over this when he gets home. "You worry too much, Libby. So I was a little late." He'll pinch my love handles, which I won't find endearing. "Okay, a lot late. Sometimes the wind whips up the waves on the larger lakes. We *voyageurs* have two choices—risk swamping the canoe so we can get home to our precious wives or find a sheltered spot on an island and stay put until the wind dies down."

I never liked how he used the word *precious* in that context. I should tell him so. I should tell him a lot of things. And I will.

If he ever comes home.

∞

With sleep-deprived eyes, I trace the last ticks of the second hand. Seven o'clock. Too early to call Frank? Not likely.

I reach to punch the MEM 2 key sequence on the phone. Miss the first time. Try again.

One ring. Two. Three. If the answering machine kicks in—

"Frank's Franks. Frankly the best in all of Franklin County. Frank speaking. How can I help you?"

I bite back a retort. How does a retired grocery manager get away with that much *corny*? Consistently. One thing is still normal.

"Frank, it's Libby. I hate to call this early but—"

"Early?" he snorts. "Been up since four-thirty."

Figures. Spitting image of his son.

"Biked five miles," he says. "Had breakfast at the truck stop. Watered those blasted hostas of your mother-in-law's that just won't die. Believe me, I've done everything in my power to help them along toward that end."

I don't have the time or inclination to defend Pauline's hostas. "I called for a reason, Frank."

"Sorry. What's up?"

I'm breathing too rapidly. Little flashes of electricity hem my field of vision. "Have you heard from Greg?"

"He's back, right?"

"Not yet. I'm probably worried for nothing."

He expels a breath that I feel in the earpiece. "When did you expect him? Yesterday?"

"He planned to get back on Friday, but said Saturday at the latest. He hates to miss church now that he's into helping with the sound system."

"Might have had to take a wind day. Or two."

Why does it irritate me that he's playing the logic card? "I thought of that."

"Odd, though." His voice turns a corner.

"What do you mean?"

Through the receiver, I hear that grunt thing he does when he gets into or out of a chair. "I had one eye on the Weather Channel most of last week," he says.

What did you do with the other eye, Frank? The Weather Channel? Early retirement has turned him into a weather spectator. "And?"

"Says winds have been calm throughout the Quetico. It's a good thing too. Tinder-dry in Canada right now. One spark plus a stiff wind and you've got major forest fire potential. They've posted a ban on open campfires. Cook stoves only. Greg planned for that, didn't he?"

"How should I know?" Somewhere deep in my brain, I pop a blood vessel. Not my normal style—not with anyone but Greg. "Sorry, Frank. I'm . . . I'm overreacting. To everything. I'm sure he'll show up any minute. Or call."

From the background comes a sound like leather complaining. "Told my boy more than once he ought to invest in a satellite phone. The man's too cheap to throw away a bent nail."

"I know." I also know I would have thrown a newsworthy fit if he'd suggested spending that kind of money on a toy for his precious wilderness trips when I'm still waiting for the family budget to allow for new kitchen countertops. As it stands, they're not butcher block. They're butcher shop. And they've been that way since we moved in, since Greg first apologized for them and said we'd replace them "one of these first days."

How many "first days" pass in twenty-three years?

His *precious* wilderness trips? Is that what I said? Now *I'm* doing it.

Frank's voice urges me back to the scene of our conversation. "Hey, Libby, have him give me a call when he gets in, will you?" His emphasis of the word *when* rings artificial.

"He always does, Frank." My voice is a stream of air that over-powers the words.

"Still—"

"I'll have him call."

The phone's silent, as is the house. I never noticed before how loud is the absence of sound.

⟨⟩

It's official. Greg's missing. That's what the police report says: Missing Person.

I don't remember filing a police report before now. We've never had obnoxious neighbors or a break-in. Not even a stolen bike from the driveway. Yes, I know. A charmed life.

The desk sergeant is on the phone, debating with someone about who should talk to me. Is my case insignificant to them? Not worth the time? I take a step back from the scarred oak check-in desk to allow the sergeant a fraction more privacy.

With my husband gone, I have privacy to spare, I want to tell him. *You can have some of mine. You're welcome.*

I shift my purse to the other shoulder, as if that will help straighten my spine. Good posture seems irrelevant. Irreverent.

Everything I know about the inside of police stations I learned from Barney Fife, Barney Miller, and any number of *CSI*s. The perps lined up on benches along the wall, waiting to be pro-cessed, look more at ease than I feel.

The chair to which I've been directed near Officer Kentworth's desk boasts a mystery stain on the sitting-down part. Not a chair with my name on it. It's for women with viper tattoos and envelope-sized miniskirts. For guys named Vinnie who wake with horse heads in their beds. For pierced and bandanaed teens on their way to an illustrious petty-theft career.

"Please have a seat." The officer has said that line how many times before?

Officer Kentworth peers through the untidy fringe of his unibrow and takes my statement, helping fill in the blanks on the Missing Person form. All the blanks but one—Where is he? The officer notes Greg's vehicle model and license plate number and asks all kinds of questions I can't answer. Kentworth is a veteran of Canadian trips like the one from which Greg has not returned. He knows the right questions to ask.

Did he choose the Thunder Bay or International Falls crossing into Canada? What was your husband's intended destination in the Quetico Provincial Park? Where did he arrange to enter and exit the park? Did he have a guide service drop him off? Where did he plan to camp on his way out of the park? How many portages?

I should have sent Frank to file the report. He'd know. Greg probably rambled on to me about some of those things on his way out the door seventeen days ago. My brain saw no need to retain any of it. It interested him, not me.

Kentworth leans toward me, exhales tuna breath—which seems especially unique at this hour of the morning—and asks, "How've things been at home between the two of you?"

I know the answer to this question. Instead I say, "Fine. What's that got to do with—?"

"Had to ask, Mrs. Holden." He reaches across his desk and pats my hand. Rather, he patronizes my hand. "Many times, in these cases—"

Oh, just say it!

"—an unhappy husband takes advantage of an opportunity to walk away."

His smile ends at the border of his eyes. I resist the urge to smack him. I don't want to join the perps waiting to be processed.

I want to go home and plow through Greg's office, searching for answers I should have known.

Greg? Walk away?

Not only is he too annoyingly faithful for that, but if anyone has a right to walk away, it's me.

<hr />

I thought it would be a relief to get home again after the ordeal at the police station, which included a bizarre three-way conversation with the Canadian authorities asking me to tell them things I don't know. We won't even mention the trauma of the question, "And Mrs. Holden, just for the record, can you account for your own whereabouts since your husband left?"

Home? A relief? The answering machine light blinks like an ambulance. Mostly messages from neighbors, wondering if I've heard anything. A few friends and extended family—word is spreading—wondering if I've heard anything. Our pastor, wondering if I've heard anything.

I head for the bedroom to change clothes. The cotton sweater I wore to the station smells like tuna and handcuffs. Or is that my imagination?

Quick census. How many cells of my body don't ache? You'd think I'd find this king-sized bed and down comforter impossible to resist. But it's another symbol that something's missing. Something's wrong and has been for a long time. Moving from our old queen-sized mattress to this king represented distance rather than comfort. For me, anyway. I needed a few more inches between us. A few feet. I guess I got my wish.

I throw the sweater in the wicker hamper, which ironically does not reek of Greg's athletic socks today. On the way from the hamper to the closet, I clunk my shin on the corner of the bed frame. The bed takes up more of the room than it should. Old houses. Contractors in the 1950s couldn't envision couples in love needing that much elbow room. My shin throbs as it decides whether it wants to bruise. That corner's caught me more than once. I ought to know better. About a lot of things.

I pull open the bifold closet doors. Picking out something to wear shouldn't be this hard. But Greg's things are in here.

If he were planning to leave me, couldn't he have had the decency to tidy up after himself and clear out the closet? For the ever-popular "closure"? How long do I wait before packing up his suits and dress shirts?

One of his suit jackets is facing the wrong way on the hanger. Everyone knows buttons face left in the closet. Correcting it is life-or-death important to me at the moment. There. Order. As it should be. I smooth the collar of the jacket and stir up the scent of Aspen for Men. The boa constrictor around my throat flexes its muscles.

With its arms spread wide, the overstuffed chair in the corner mocks me. I bought it without clearing the expenditure with Greg. Mortal sin, right? He didn't holler. The man doesn't holler. He sighs and signs up for more overtime.

Maybe I'll find comfort in the kitchen. This bedroom creeps me out.

Greg has thrown us into an incident of international intrigue. Melodramatic wording, but true. We're dealing with the local authorities plus the Canadian police.

Staring out the kitchen window at the summer-rich backyard proves fruitless. It holds no answers for me. I'm alone in this. Almost.

Frank's my personal liaison with the Canadians—border patrol, Quetico Park rangers, and Ontario Provincial Police, the latter of which is blessed with an unfortunate acronym—OPP. Looks a lot like "Oops" on paper. I can't help but envision that adorable character from *Due North*, the Mountie transplanted into the heart and bowels of New York City. Sweetly naive as he was, he always got his man. Will these get mine?

Frank will be much better at pestering them for answers. My mother-in-law would be better still. Pestering. Pauline's gifted that way.

I'm no help. Big surprise. When I spoke with the north-of-the-border authorities, I either tripped over every word and expressed my regrets for bothering them or shouted into the phone, "Why aren't you doing something?"

They are, of course. They're trying. Analyzing tire tracks. Interviewing canoeists exiting the park. Looking for signs of a struggle. The search plane they promised is a nice touch. Under Frank's direction, they'll scan Greg's expected route to check for mayhem.

While I wait for yet another pot of coffee to brew, I brush toast crumbs—some forgotten breakfast—off the butcher shop counter into my hand. Now what? I can't think what to do with them.

The phone rings.

It's Greg's district manager again. He's the pasty-faced, chop-stick-thin undertaker hovering just offstage in a lame Western movie.

No, no word from Greg yet. Yes, I'll let you know as soon as I hear something. Yes, I understand what a difficult position this has put you in, Mr. Sensitive, I mean, Mr. Stenner. Can we request a temporary leave of absence for Greg or . . . ? Of course, I understand. Not fair to the company, sure. Only have so much patience, uh huh. God bless you too.

Right.

Oh, and thanks for caring that my life is falling apart and my husband is either muerto or just fine but not with me and either way he's a dead man.

I slam the phone into its base station, then apologize to it.

The sweat in my palm reconstituted the bread crumbs during the call. Wastebasket. That's what one does with crumbs.

How long will it take me to figure out what to do with the crumbs of my life?

And where will I find a basket large enough for the pieces?

CPSIA information can be obtained at www.ICGtesting.com
Printed in the USA
LVOW08*1145250515

439495LV00001B/1/P